The
Metalmark
Contract

David Batchelor

David Batchelor

Black Rose Writing
www.blackrosewriting.com

ISBN: 978-1-61296-011-1

PUBLISHED BY BLACK ROSE WRITING

www.blackrosewriting.com

Printed in the United States of America

The Metalmark Contract is printed in Aparajita

Dedicated to the memory of
Geneva Jackson Nethercutt,
my grandmother, who opened the world of books
and knowledge to her daughter, grandchildren and
great-granddaughter.

Thanks to friends and family
who enjoyed earlier versions of the book
and gave helpful comments.

And special thanks to my wife Laurie
for her dedicated help with the
editing, and for her love and support.

I

THE SUN WAS too bright for any human eye to watch the arrival of the forerunner on that day, the day that changed history from the thread of one species on one planet of one star into the twine of two species strung on planets like gems on a necklace of space-time. It was a day that many longed for, many dreaded, many rued, and many mused about for centuries before and after. But the day began in blindness because of intolerable light, and human beings could only sense its new contour with radio echoes from the forerunner of transformation.

The glare of the dayside sky hid the forerunner starship as it performed its orbital insertion at geosynchronous altitude and began stationing a necklace of satellites around the planet Earth, establishing the forerunner's radio satcom net. As it strung this necklace, it was touched by the radar of the North American Defense network and the counterparts of the European, Russian and Chinese space agencies.

Orbital Debris Analyst Howard Garcia saw the radar echo displayed on a NORAD radar screen and said, "Padre, Hijo y Espiritu Santo! You are so broken!" But a second radar array confirmed the giant beam reflection, and within the hour Air Force General Josh Mason brought the classified news to President Thomas Jackson at the White House Oval Office.

"What do you have for me, Josh?" Pres. Jackson asked.

"Mr. President, the echo size is unprecedented. It's a spacecraft larger than anything orbited by humans. It has only changed its orbit by small jumps along the geosynchronous orbit. The major vehicle has moved to put a series of much smaller satellites about every 6 degrees around the circle of the sky above the Equator. If it keeps working at the present rate, it will finish the circle tomorrow, with 60 satellites."

"Are you saying that it has made no hostile moves?"

"Not if surrounding us is friendly."

Pres. Jackson smiled. "I expect that you want to establish rules of engagement."

"Yes, Sir."

"Then Rule One is to presume no hostile intent unless there is unmistakable proof. Beings with spaceships this large probably have the power to do great damage, so we don't want to provoke them foolishly."

Gen. Mason was nodding when his cell phone chimed. "Please let me answer this, Mr. President," he said, thumbing the button.

After listening for only a moment, Gen. Mason said, "A broadcast has been received by analog TV on Channel 2. It is repeating, and the Cable News Channel is retransmitting it. It's not an ultimatum." The president's secretary, Mary Hayes, turned on the TV.

A face that looked like an ordinary human one at TV resolution was accompanied by a smooth masculine voice. ". . . I am here for peaceful reasons. I have a proposition of exchange that would benefit both our species. I ask to meet with your United Nations representatives to present my offer in full. Briefly, I wish to trade very advanced technology to you people of planet Earth in return for some resources in your solar system that you are not using and do not need currently. My offer will be quite advantageous for you. I can be contacted by television broadcast on this channel and will negotiate exclusively with UN representatives, so that all Earth people will be fairly represented. This announcement repeats . . . I am the occupant of the extraterrestrial forerunner spacecraft that you have detected orbiting Earth. You may call me Metalmark. I am here for peaceful reasons . . . "

As the message repeated, the hair on Pres. Jackson's neck rose, although he didn't know why. Some forgotten words from one of his long-ago campaign fights had been echoed, and they drew the president's attention into a futile scan through his past, but he forced himself back to the moment.

"Gen. Mason, our forces must treat this visitor as a peaceful trade mission with diplomatic immunity. That means we should join with the other UN space powers in extending protection to this visitor from attacks by any hostile nations. (God knows what would happen if some fool shot at him.) I'll ask the Joint Chiefs of Staff to meet so that this policy can be formalized and propagated to the troops. If you detect any unequivocal reason to change the status of this visitor, I want to know instantly."

"Yes, Sir," said Gen. Mason. "With your permission, I will also have a thorough threat analysis carried out by a Task Force. As soon as it's ready I'll notify you."

"Thank you. That is certainly appropriate. If there's nothing more . . . ? Please carry on."

Gen. Mason nodded, saluted and hurried out. Pres. Jackson watched the chilling announcement for many more repetitions. The bland face of an ordinary-looking man repeated the announcement tirelessly. Mary watched with the president. After a few more minutes, Pres. Jackson asked, "Mary, please bring in the press secretary and national security adviser so I can issue a statement. And call the Administrator for NASA, tell him we need his input. Clear my schedule of routine meetings and announce a National Security Council meeting in half an hour. And get someone to search my old speeches for the word 'Metalmark.' " That was the word that jolted him with a memory of a desperate appeal in the campaign to win California's governor office.

The roar of jets passing overhead told the president that defenders had been scrambled to patrol Washington's skies.

Metalmark's announcement was broadcast in English, French, Spanish, Russian, Chinese and Japanese. It was transmitted by TV on analog NTSC and PAL signals, which were still used in many nations. TV news channels quickly relayed it to billions of watchers via cable channels, Internet streaming and HDTV.

The White House issued a statement: the visitor Metalmark has behaved in a friendly manner, and the president and the people of the United States welcome his peaceful, apparently commercial mission. We will participate fully with the UN in considering what he has to offer. It is vital to work together for fair and open sharing of whatever benefits may come from his offer of trade with the people of Earth.

Commentators and bloggers began pumping out views of the historic event. A NASA spokesman read a statement from NASA Administrator Marvin Krainak, "This is a day that we have imagined for a long time. We welcome the visitor Metalmark on his historic visit. He is sure to have a lot to teach us about space travel."

On a popular website, blogger Larry Saxon immediately criticized the bland NASA statement. "To wait so long for this historic visit and find that the visitor is a traveling salesman is crass beyond belief. Metalmark sounds like an encyclopedia salesman, and I can't remember when I let one of those in the door. On the other hand, it could be a really *good* encyclopedia . . . And that bland NASA statement was <irony> the perfect reply </irony> to the smooth sales pitch: no edges, nothing to give offense, no confrontation with the edgy possibility of attacks, invasions, exploitation or alien plagues . . . Of course those NASA guys are *really* thinking: Metalmark has a huge f***ing starship! We'd *love* to be the ones to get our hands on that baby first!"

Telescopes around the world were trained on the forerunner starship, which stayed in geosynchronous orbit over the western hemisphere. It seemed to have a roughly spherical shape, but glaring reflections glinted from it, so that it was almost impossible to view. A composite image with the glare suppressed suggested that it was covered with reflective panels in all orientations, which concealed its true shape. It was certainly larger than a typical aircraft carrier, and after dark, the sunlight that it reflected cast a barely visible shadow on the ground.

Crowds assembled in many large western cities. Some were merely revelers, excited by novelty and nostalgic about George Lucas movies. That was the atmosphere in New York's Times Square, where the crowds could watch CNN's giant screen to see a continuous repetition of Metalmark's announcement and miscellaneous commentaries.

Conservative commentators fulminated that the first contact with space visitors was already a catastrophe because the UN was an anti-American club of socialists, dictatorships, rogue states, and godless republics that did not deserve to get in the way of direct contacts between Metalmark and US scientists, technologists and businesses.

Some organizations called for prayer gatherings, fearing that it was the end of the world. Civic organizations held meetings to listen to the pacific tone of the visitor's voice, to urge celebration of the fact that humanity was not alone in the Universe, and to plan greeting festivals in the event that Metalmark chose to land in their vicinity. In less secular nations, especially those that did not receive Metalmark's broadcast in their own languages, crowds gathered and heard foreboding addresses from religious leaders, warning that only return to fundamentals of faith would protect people from imminent doom.

M

UN Secretary-General Sanjeev Shankar was in his office when his staff showed him Metalmark's announcement video. He had just returned from a trip to set up aid for the victims of the wave of typhoons that had flooded southeast Asia. He was exhausted and jet lagged, and he barely had a few minutes to begin jotting some thoughts in response to the historic event before the White House telephoned.

"Sec.-Gen. Shankar," Pres. Jackson began, "I want to give you my personal guarantee of support from the US government in dealing with Metalmark. No nation on Earth has space vehicles that can convey a UN delegation to Metalmark's spacecraft, so we expect that he . . . or it . . . will make a visit to Earth. The resources of my country are at your service for diplomacy with Metalmark. I consider it critical to ensure security of the UN negotiations with him and to protect his vehicle."

"Thank you, Mr. President. My staff is preparing a statement for our response to the visitor, and we appreciate your offer of cooperation very much! We are about to send a transmission to Metalmark, acknowledging that he is welcome. We will relay any response immediately to all members of the UN Security Council. Now if you will excuse me, the Chinese ambassador is waiting on another line. I will get back to you with further developments."

Sec.-Gen. Shankar was then monopolized for some time, giving assurances to Ambassador Yang Wei that his many suspicions were unfounded.

After the telecon call to Sec.-Gen. Shankar, Pres. Jackson returned his attention to the US Security Council meeting that he was chairing. "Gen. Mason has just shown us the Space Telescope's view of Metalmark's vehicle. There don't seem to be any threatening features or moves by the visitor, and our policy will be to make every effort to avoid hostilities. The friendly message from Metalmark is undoubtedly the reason that we are seeing no panic in the general public. I'm told that 1 in 4 Americans already believed that alien visitors had been to Earth, and had been hidden by the government. The instant polls suggest that the majority of people are pleased at the apparent openness."

Across the oval table from Pres. Jackson, Vice President Walter Metcalf said, "I think we should invite an expert from the National Academy of Sciences and somebody from NASA to brief us on what we might be facing. There's very little specific information yet about the beings in that vehicle, but maybe we'd make more intelligent decisions if we learned some of the scientists' views."

Pres. Jackson looked down his aquiline nose, peered though the bottoms of his bifocals, and scratched a note on a pad. He turned to Chief of Staff Randall Copeland. "Randy, please call the NAS to ask them for an expert adviser. I already invited some input from NASA Administrator Krainak. Marv has started assembling a mission team to focus on Metalmark and allocate the right amount of scientific firepower . . . although I wish I hadn't used that word."

"Yes, Sir," replied Mr. Copeland, making notes on his BlackBerry. In a few minutes he had sent an e-mail to the head of NAS.

Pres. Jackson continued, "Dr. Krainak's main recommendation is to use great caution in protecting our population from alien bacteria. They might be brought to Earth and spread if Metalmark makes a landing to meet a UN delegation. We could offer Metalmark a visit to the International Space Station instead, but that would endanger the ISS crew. NASA's moon flight vehicles are still in development, as you know, so we aren't in a position to send any astronauts or UN personnel to the starship.

"Marv has assigned a team to build a NASA welcome van for a meeting on Earth. It will be equipped with biochemical sensors capable of detecting pathogens. Marv wants to meet Metalmark with the van, wherever his first landing in the US or an allied country happens to be. I've asked the Science Committee Chairman on the Hill to approve the budget for Marv's plans."

Defense Sec. Clifford Saper said, "I agree that NASA and NAS will give important perspectives, but I'm more anxious to hear Gen. Mason's threat assessment."

Gen. Mason said, "There are obviously numerous scenarios that one can fit to the few facts we know. Rather than meander through too many option trees, I think the main foreseeable danger would be deception by Metalmark while he surrounds the Earth with nuclear weapons. All of the satellites that Metalmark has stationed could be thermonuclear weapons targeted at the 60 major population centers and ready to intimidate us into accepting his terms. He said that his detailed offer was forthcoming. If the UN chose not to accept his 'offer' it would be disappointing to him. Someone who has traveled interstellar distance for a deal probably has a strong stake in getting to 'Yes'."

The Sec. of Commerce, George Cosgrove, said, "Commodore Perry's fleet did something like that in its first dealing with Japan."

"Let's hope we don't repeat the 1850's with an ironic twist," the president laughed. "Anyway, in this hopefully-worst-case scenario, is it the best we could do to intercept some of the attacking nukes, Gen. Mason?" Mason nodded. "Could we counterattack?"

"None of our ICBMs are capable of getting 22,000 miles high to reach geosynchronous orbit at this time, Mr. President. Gen. Morse has ordered a Tiger Team to modify some 'sidelined' boosters that were mothballed when their missions were deactivated back in the '60s. However, their performance in flight is theoretical; they've never been tested on targets 22,000 miles high."

The UN Ambassador, Paul Kirk, and the Secretary of State, Peter Currin, were teleconferencing into the meeting; Sec. Currin said, "I think the Chinese are nearly ready for their second moon landing. No doubt they have boosters that could be fitted with warheads. I'll be landing at Reagan National in an hour, and I've invited the Chinese consul to share his government's plans with me at his earliest convenience. We should present a cooperative face to the Chinese. I'll try to get through to Ambassador Yang when his line is free. Apparently he is still tying up Sanjeev's phone."

Pres. Jackson said, "OK, that's a good plan, Peter. Please also assign some staff to evaluate the other nuclear club members' capabilities. The Russians have some operable missiles, the Chinese, French and British arsenals are big. But there have also been active programs by India, Pakistan, Israel, North Korea and Iran. And I know that the European Space Agency doesn't launch nukes, but please prepare briefings on ESA space launch capability and on the Japanese Aerospace Exploration Agency. Make sure Paul gets updates of your decisions.

"Now Gen. Mason, we should be prepared for the equally likely prospect that Metalmark is a friendly trader. I want the option to take defensive action on behalf of Metalmark in the event that some rogue nation launches an attack on the starship."

Gen. Mason kept a poker face. "I'll add that to the specifications of the refitted missiles, Sir. But interception is more iffy than simple attack."

Vice Pres. Metcalf asked, "How long would it take your refitted missile to reach 22,000 miles altitude?"

"About an hour and a half."

"I would think that's plenty of time for evasive maneuvers," said the VP. "It's not going to be simple to intercept *or* attack." Gen. Mason nodded, conceding.

Sec. of Defense Saper: "Are we completely sure that this Metalmark vehicle came from interstellar space? Why should a being from another star appear on TV like the guy next door?"

Gen. Mason replied, "We looked back at archive data of unidentified radar echoes for the past week. Before the main NORAD positive contact, there were some weaker echoes. They fit a trajectory that approached Earth from the Sun. We are inquiring with astronomers to see if any civilian telescopes detected Metalmark before the NORAD contact. Some of them search for comets or near-Earth asteroids. I have a team on it.

"As for the TV appearance of Metalmark, we don't really know what he looks like. His face could be a computer simulation, like a movie special effect."

Sec. Saper said, "Why should Metalmark come from the Sun? This could all still be a hoax. 'Metalmark's spaceship' could be a big orbiting balloon like the old Echo satellite, plus 60 little balloons. It's not April 1st but that sparkling 'starship' could turn around to show 'Drink Pepsi!' on the back side."

Pres. Jackson chuckled. "Yes, wouldn't we feel foolish then? But my instincts tell me that this is real, not an advertising stunt."

CIA Director Jon West said, "Mr. President, perhaps this is a good time for me to present our tentative plans for surveillance of Metalmark for your approval."

"By all means," the president replied.

West said, "We have already signed a memorandum of understanding with NASA to share their camera and microphone feeds with the Director of Central Intelligence. Analysts are being teamed under the DCI to perform rapid evaluation and reporting of those data.

"We also have in-place human intelligence embedded in the UN staff. Since Metalmark's stated intention is to interact with the UN, we have notified those assets to be on high alert. And they have been told that they should make unobtrusive efforts to observe Metalmark whenever possible under the guise of natural curiosity. Our strategy is evolving and we will keep you apprised."

"Thank you, Jon," said Pres. Jackson. "That sounds like the right level of activity, given that Metalmark does not appear to represent a threatening foreign power. If he deviates from appropriate actions of a commercial nature, or does something illegal through ignorance of our laws, I want to know about it before enforcement actions are taken. I'm thinking of actions like bribing government officials, things which an alien being might not know were illegal. Please give me a special daily briefing on your findings about Metalmark."

"Will do, Sir," said West.

Sec. of State Currin said, "Tom, if Metalmark does come down for a landing, I think Krainak's point is well taken. It's too risky for you to meet him without proof that Metalmark won't infect anyone with some plague. Best you wait a suitable quarantine period before meeting him. I know it's not exactly protocol if Metalmark is a sort of head-of-state, but he 's probably not at that level."

Commerce Sec. Cosgrove turned to V.P. Metcalf. "Looks like a job for the Vice President! You'd make a great guinea pig, Walter!"

After general laughter, the Council turned to consideration of the probable actions to be expected by a seemingly endless list of other nations that might complicate US policy with missteps or worse.

M

Dr. Steve Simmons was sitting tensely before a computer at the NASA Goddard Space Flight Center, 15 miles from the White House in the Maryland suburbs. Behind his thick glasses his eyes were red, and his jaws clenched nervously. His friend Howard Garcia at NORAD had given him the Metalmark coordinates, which were declassified in the US after the European Space Agency put them on the Web.

Dr. Simmons was responsible for analyzing the data from the comet-finding telescope on board the science satellite "*Solar Dynamics Observatory 2.*" The *SDO 2* was poised out in space, orbiting between the Sun and Earth. Comet-finding with *SDO 2* was Dr. Simmons' first postdoctoral appointment and he took it seriously to a fault.

As Dr. Simmons typed in program code, he patched his orbit computation program (normally used to determine the paths of comets in near-Sun trajectories) to allow for the possibility of a close approach to the Earth by a simulated comet. When he got it working, he would be able to use Newton's laws of motion to put time into reverse in the computer simulation, start from the known coordinates of the Metalmark vehicle, and track Metalmark back along his orbit in the same way that he could compute cometary orbital motions. If it worked, he could get views of the Metalmark starship recorded days before anyone on Earth detected it.

Near midnight, with only a few spacecraft operations technicians for company in the small control center, he finished the orbit simulation. He searched for pictures that the *SDO 2* telescopes had taken, at times when they happened to be pointed at his computed trajectory of earlier positions for Metalmark.

"Yes!" he cried, and Richard Berry, one of the ops. technicians came over to see Dr. Simmons' console screen. It showed a mosaic of six images, each one sprinkled with faraway stars against a black sky, each image with a green box drawn near the center, and in each green box was a bright dot, much brighter than the background stars in the two most recent images: Metalmark's approaching starship, detected by *SDO 2* before it entered earth orbit.

"Six hits?" Berry asked.

"Yeah. That's enough to solve for the orbit back beyond its closest point to the Sun. . . ." He studied the orbital parameters, typed in a command, and read the angle. "The projected orbit is a hyperbola, it passed close to the Sun, and if there were no course adjustments, before it came to perihelion it was approaching the Sun from the constellation Sagittarius."

Berry mused, "In other words, from the center of the Milky Way Galaxy. Cool! So maybe Metalmark came from one of the old stars in the core."

Simmons grinned and began to file a normal comet sighting with the International Astronomical Union via e-mail. In the "comments" section of the IAU report e-mail, he put "Comet SDO2#1064=Metalmark." Simmons had only been on duty for the discoveries of half of the 1063 comets found by satellite *SDO 2*, and the fame had worn off since the early discoveries. But having his name attached to this unique celestial object would be a career booster for sure.

He might have reconsidered if he had known the intensity of the career boost that was to come.

About the same time that Dr. Simmons filed his "comet" sighting with the IAU, UN Sec.-Gen. Shankar finished having consultations with UN Security Council members' ambassadors and finished wordsmithing his talking points for the reply to Metalmark. His staff set up a TV camera facing his desk, and he prepared to broadcast the reply transmission.

Shankar began, "Metalmark, the people of planet Earth take pleasure in greeting you, our first known interstellar visitor. We greatly appreciate your peaceful and mutually beneficial offer of exchange with us. I am sure that your level of technological advancement is very great, yet I think that you will find, upon visiting our planet, that we have many riches of cultural, historical and spiritual kinds to envy.

"We invite you to visit our planet's surface if that is convenient for you, so that you may experience the hospitality of our people. Offers of trade are welcome, but I think that you will find much more to interest you on Earth than the technology that you are offering. You have probably been on a long journey through space, and we offer you rest, provisions, and a rich panopticon of novel and delightful experiences, which you cannot ever have anticipated.

"Please meet with us, experience our fine habitat (if it is suitable for you), and let us know not just about your offer of trade, but also about yourself and your life. We people of Earth regard your visit as an opportunity for the greatest extent of enjoyment to share with you. And an opportunity for the greatest leap forward in our world's spiritual development."

Sanjeev Shankar spoke these words from the heart, and with the last word he felt a deep fulfillment of his personal quest to lead the UN in a momentous instant such as this. From a hovel in Calcutta he had come to greeting the first visitor to Earth from the outer Universe . . .

The TV technician interrupted Shankar's post-broadcast moment, and said, "There's a response coming in right away, again on Channel 2!"

The twelve people in the room crowded around the TV. "This is Metalmark," said the same ordinary face as before. "Thank you for your message! I calculate that there is a 1/5-second delay in our conversation, but perhaps that will not be a problem.

"Your invitation is very kind, and I have prepared for it eagerly! I have a landing craft ready to launch, but I want to warn you about the rather dangerous exhaust from the rocket engines! It's not a good vehicle to land in Central Park of New York, but it has been a fantasy of mine to land at Kennedy Space Center! I have watched it on TV a lot. I hope I can meet Neil Armstrong. Is that a suitable place for me to land?"

He paused, regarding it as a genuine question. Sec.-Gen. Shankar asked, "Is the camera working?" The cameraman nodded. "Metalmark, I will inquire on your behalf about landing at Kennedy Space Center. I'm sure that the United States will give reasonable consideration to your request."

"OK," said Metalmark. "Call me when the president or NASA Administrator Krainak decides. Oh, and by the way, tell them not to worry about any alien plagues or diseases. My biochemistry is so different from yours that we can't possibly have any pathogens in common. And I'll arrive thoroughly decontaminated nonetheless. This is going to be fun! Thanks! Goodbye." The screen sparkled with snow.

The nearly-empty Chinese cargo jet was accelerating at full thrust, climbing steeply and pressing the few passengers deeply into their seats. When it reached 40,000 feet altitude, the pilot would throttle back and follow a parabolic curve, a trajectory that would put the passengers, an elite corps of taikonauts (Chinese astronauts), into nearly perfect free fall for a little more than thirty seconds. But there would be no more than thirty seconds of weightlessness training before all of the trainees had to strap themselves back into seats while the pilot subjected them to two "g's" of acceleration to pull out of a dive. Otherwise the plane would slam them into the ground somewhere near the Jiuquan satellite launch center below.

The engine drone quieted and the trainees unbuckled their safety belts. They were eight young, excited Chinese men, and one woman. They went tumbling about and caroming off of the walls and one another in their red flight suits. This was one in a series of flights that were intended to train the taikonauts for China's imminent second mission to the Moon. The men quickly thought of aiming their trajectories at the one female trainee, to steal a quick feel of the famous, hard athletic body of the one female taikonaut, Liu Xueli, and then bounce away with a phony cry of "Excuse me!"

But Liu Xueli was a former Olympic gymnast, a winner of many gold and silver medals, and she was so adept by now at weightless tumbling that she seized her harassers and flung them spinning away where they collided out of control with the wall or one another.

The laughter, exclamations and expletives of the trainees filled the aircraft, plus one or two retching sounds as some trainee succumbed to zero-g nausea. Xueli was fortunate, and did not collide with any floating vomit before the warning bell sounded and the trainees reluctantly struggled back to their seats. The pilot then repeated the climb-and-dive maneuver for two hours.

And when the plane landed, what took place then was even more unusual in China than the presence of a woman in the taikonaut corps: Liu Xueli, the leader of the corps by virtue of her dominant excellence in every phase of taikonaut training (plus her political connections) called out the orders that brought the corps to attention and marched them out of the plane to their waiting instructors.

It was then that Xueli first was told about Metalmark, and she began to plan for a new mission.

Secretary of Defense Saper studied the large computer display that dominated the wall in the Pentagon's Situation Center. He was struggling to remember what all of the icons and indicators and thumbnail images meant. The display was supposed to present him at a glance with a condensed real-time report on every important aspect of the most historic event ever defended: Metalmark's landing at the Kennedy Space Center. However, the display was the product of lots of bright people who had never worked together before and it was serving a one-time unprecedented purpose. Naturally it was a total failure. He was lost, inundated by too much data.

Fortunately the Center was full of backup personnel in various military uniforms, sitting at rows of consoles, to help him muddle through. Gen. Mason sat in the next chair, probably well aware that he would earn a promotion if all went well in such an historic operation. And the Joint Chiefs of Staff were on duty in their respective command centers elsewhere in the Pentagon, quietly maintaining each branch of service on high alert.

But in Clifford Saper's view, there was only a very tenuous connection between the superlative competence of the Defense Department staff who were coordinating this event with NASA and the outcome. Saper's mind was terrified by hazards: what if terrorists attacked during the landing? What if a nuclear bomb was launched during Metalmark's approach to the landing site? What if terrorists took advantage of the focus on Metalmark and attacked some other site in the US? The Internet was alive with chatter hinting at all of these possibilities.

This was the fog of war, without the war exactly. Saper temporized: "General Mason, please update me on all pertinent developments."

Josh Mason replied, "Metalmark has notified the UN Sec.-Gen. that two landing craft have just departed from his geosynchronous ship . . ." He listened to an earphone. "The broadcast is nontrivial. I'll put his message on the screen."

Metalmark's visage filled one quarter of the giant screen. He appeared to be a young man with short blond, disheveled hair, saying, "Along with my own vehicle, I request your permission to bring down another small craft that may look like a cruise missile. But I assure you that it is a harmless probe designed to prepare a gift for the people of Earth. It will take a slightly circuitous route to our meeting site in Florida, in order to carry out its function, but it will then arrive in time for the welcome ceremony that you have kindly prepared for me. I thought that since you were going to all that trouble, I should bring something to the party, too. I am on schedule to arrive in three hours."

Great, Saper thought, *now we have to distinguish another incoming projectile from possible enemy attackers!*

Gen. Mason pointed to the upper left corner of the display. "That's a graphic of the countdown to Metalmark's scheduled arrival. Next to it is a telescopic image of the two landing vehicles separating from his orbital station. One of them is deviating off to the right . . . we'll create another image of it . . . it just looks like a bright dot at this distance."

The gift-maker vehicle accelerated gradually and descended to Earth's atmosphere about a half hour before Metalmark's vehicle. Gen. Mason brought up images from NASA and DoD chase aircraft, filming the first known alien spacecraft to penetrate Earth's atmosphere.

It dropped precipitously into the Atlantic ocean, near the mid-Atlantic ridge. Gen. Mason seemed to be suppressing a humorous reaction.

"What's funny?" asked Saper.

"I could be mistaken, Mr. Secretary, but it looks like Metalmark flubbed an atmosphere entry. Let's hope his own spacecraft lands more safely."

Saper was really confused now. Funny mistakes were being made by the alien but he himself was missing them! How could he get up to speed on the intellectual level of this momentous game?

A camera at Kennedy Space Center was transmitting the view from the UN General Secretary's podium, on a stage in the VIP viewing area for the landing. Metalmark had expressed a preference for the Space Shuttle landing runway, and NASA officials were more than gracious in granting its use. A bright dot became visible as Metalmark's extremely luminous rocket exhaust appeared in the blue Florida sky, surrounded by cumulus and stratus cloud formations that usually heralded afternoon thunderstorms.

A low roar could be heard. NASA's commentator notified the crowd of dignitaries from the UN and its Security Council member nations that Metalmark's landing craft was at 10,000 feet and descending.

At the far end of the Shuttle landing runway a glowing spherical bubble descended, with a brilliant point of light at its center that left persistent afterimages in everyone's eyes. It was impossible to judge its size because (as analysts later determined) the bubble had expanded to great size in order to utilize aerobraking, and it shrunk elastically as it radiated away excess heat while descending, fooling the eye. Everyone expected to judge an object of constant size as it approached and appeared to grow larger. But the glowing, shrinking spherical surface of the lander rearranged itself confusingly into a Sun-worshiping array of solar energy collectors as it made its final 1000-foot descent on a white-hot torch of exhaust, as brilliant to view as a welder's flame.

Clouds of unknown composition billowed around the grounded vehicle and dissipated after about fifteen minutes. In the fog on the ground, it could be seen that a man-like figure was walking out of the vapors, as unperturbed as Shadrach in the fiery furnace. The first camera fixes on him revealed the face from the previous TV broadcasts. Billions of human beings watched on TVs and Internet streaming video screens worldwide, exceeding the numbers of viewers of any previous telecast.

A NASA van drove bravely to the runway end to pick up Metalmark. NASA Administrator Marvin Krainak personally stepped down first from the van to greet the visiting salesman with a hand-shake, which Metalmark performed with only the slightest hint of unfamiliar awkwardness. Metalmark was short, about five feet four inches, and he looked up to Administrator Krainak with a shy smile that was completely incongruous with the fact that he had just arrived in a vehicle that was the envy of NASA engineers everywhere, and was the mere dinghy of a starship that was the fantasy of NASA fans everywhere.

A microphone on Krainak's collar recorded his momentous welcoming words. "Welcome to Kennedy Space Center, Metalmark. Thank you for coming so far and choosing this landing site among all of your possible options. On behalf of the UN and the United States, I want to say that your first steps on Earth are fulfilling many dreams of mankind here today."

Metalmark looked like an ordinary small man dressed in a navy turtleneck shirt and slacks. He said, "I dream also, so to speak. I chose Kennedy because it is the spaceport of the wealthiest space power on your planet, and I have so much to trade. The Russian Baikonur center has launched more spacecraft than Kennedy, and I hope to visit it, and the Chinese and Japanese and ESA launch centers are also impressive achievements. I'm rambling with compliments for everyone because I want you all to like me. Maybe the best way to achieve that is to go right to Sec.-Gen. Shankar. Please take me to him."

The administrator and Metalmark got into the van without further pomposities and began to drive the two miles to the podium of Sec. Shankar, which was set up on a stage in front of the dignitaries in the VIP area.

Hundreds of analysts from every nation watched the following meeting and debated the significance of each identifiable detail that they could distinguish for decades afterward. It was an elusive event to analyze, requiring arcane talents.

Metalmark slowly stepped out of the NASA biotest van and made his way up some steps to the dignitaries' podium occupied by a very nervous Sec. Sanjeev Shankar and his staff. The weather held out and Metalmark was able to reach the podium and shake hands with Shankar. Scores of TV cameras from NASA, DoD, the UN and various guest nations recorded the event in High-Definition video.

Metalmark looked Shankar in the eye. His lips moved silently at first. No one present at that moment except Shankar could interpret what Metalmark expressed. It was only later that some analysts realized what Metalmark had mouthed during that greeting to Shankar. (Other analysts confused their bosses with wrong interpretations for years.)

Metalmark had whispered in Hindi, Shankar's native dialect, to convey a private message to Shankar's mind. "Please don't kill me. I will make your world wealthy." But this message was known only to Shankar that day.

Shankar paused, startled by the pointed message in his native language. Everyone in the world who was interested was watching him, and he hesitated as he received this personal greeting from a salesman of unknown origin. Yet the role of each of them seemed familiar, and Shankar felt a motivation to reciprocate the offer. In Hindi, he whispered, "You are safe, our guest. What wealth we have we will share with you. But don't forget your offer." And Shankar's eyes twinkled. No human being can be certain how that effected Metalmark.

Metalmark was invited to speak from the podium.

"Thanks to all of the people of Earth for this ceremonious welcome. I have watched your TV broadcasts for many years on my long trip through space, so I feel that I know you, but I'm sure you have many questions about me. I know several human languages because your TV for children is very instructive."

The audience of UN dignitaries arrayed before the stage emitted an admiring murmur.

"I also know some dolphin and whale and chimpanzee semiotics, but they wouldn't like it if I revealed the things they say behind your backs." The crowd laughed.

"Anyway, it is a great pleasure to meet you at this historic site for space flight of your species. It always amazes me the different ways that species I meet adapt to space travel. As I watched your televised launches during the years of my long voyage, your ingenuity impressed me with its minimalism and elegant risk-taking.

"But I'm sure that the main thing on all of your minds is the offer I made to trade with you. We each have goods that are more valuable to the other party. You have lots of assets in your solar system that you can't use with your present level of technology. I have the technology to use the assets, and I propose to share it with you in return for specific amounts of your assets. We'll negotiate like lawyers about the details, but basically I am offering you a 'turn-key' package of starship technology — everything you need to travel to neighboring stars, or make convenient trips within the Solar System, for that matter. It's a *big* package, because it takes many kinds of technology to do that, as you can imagine.

"In return, I ask for ownership of some wasteland planetary bodies that are in extremely hostile regions of your solar system (for you). I need these wastelands because, well, my species has a life cycle, and I need a site to . . . um, spawn, if you will."

The audience chuckled uncertainly. Metalmark added, "To give you a sample of what I'm offering, I've brought a little preview. That sound you're about to hear from the east is the present I mentioned three hours ago on TV. It's been submerged in the ocean for about half an hour, condensing some of the dissolved minerals in about a cubic mile of sea water. This machine is my first technological present for you and I think you'll like it."

A blur of motion converging near Metalmark's lander and a sonic boom awed the crowd. The NASA van drove back to the lander and TV screens above the podium showed the crowd what the eager Admin. Krainak found there: a large cylinder like a split-open cruise missile, containing a black box and some chunks of metal and crystal. As the screens showed Krainak's gloved hand picking up the items for the cameras to inspect, Metalmark narrated from the podium, "Here's a pretty big gold nugget and some crystals of salt and other minerals condensed from the sea water. I know you folks like gold, and with one of these catalytic condensers you can condense out as much as you like."

Applause and a delighted murmur erupted from the crowd. Metalmark smiled and waved. "With your UN representatives, I'll draw up a proper sales contract, and everyone can see it and think it over. I'm sure you will see that it's going to be a win-win relationship. Thank you all!"

In the Pentagon situation center, Sec. Saper and Gen. Mason watched the proceedings skeptically. Mason listened to his earphone and said, "Those geosynchronous satellites are activated. The ones above the horizon as seen from Florida are broadcasting a narrow-band radio signal directly to Metalmark's location."

Saper asked, "What do you suppose it is? A security system that warns him in case we attack? Are the satellites reporting that they are ready to attack us?"

Mason shook his head. "Radar doesn't show any movements of the satellites. The signals resemble telemetry, but we can't decode it. Samples are being relayed to NSA. If anyone can decode it, they can."

"Does it stay on the same frequency or jump to different ones?"

"It's locked stable, compensating for Doppler drifts."

"I want you to assign someone to build a portable jammer. If I have the opportunity to meet Metalmark, it would be nice to see what his reaction is when he's jammed for a minute."

Mason smiled. *Yes*, he thought, *that would be enlightening.*

Saper watched the visitor move about the stage. Metalmark had a subtly abnormal gait, and his facial expressions seemed a little off in timing compared to usual human reactions. "That guy doesn't look quite real."

Gen. Mason agreed. "Not natural."

"Put a team of analysts on this. Compare his movements with astronauts that have returned from lengthy weightlessness, as well as with regular people."

"Right away, Sir," said Mason.

$$ 1 \wedge $$

Pres. Jackson and the first lady, Megan, watched the Metalmark welcome on TV from the private residence in the White House. When the gold and minerals were displayed for the cameras, Meg said, "I still think you made the right decision to send Walter. I know you wish you were there, but something could have gone wrong with those powerful rockets. Thank you for giving up such a risky appearance to be safe for me."

Thomas took her hand and kissed it. "You're welcome, but I wouldn't have gone there without you, and that was the really unacceptable risk for me. I told Walter that he has to welcome Metalmark with a kiss on both cheeks, the way he greeted the French President last month. You don't get to meet Metalmark until Walter has stayed healthy for a week."

Mary Hayes knocked and was admitted. "Pres. Jackson, I have the results you asked for about your speeches. There was a speech six years ago when you were running for governor. You mentioned the endangered butterfly 'Lange's Metalmark' in making a point. I have a recording of it because PBS just ran a program a few weeks ago — a documentary about how you reached the presidency."

Pres. Jackson eagerly accepted the DVD and inserted it into the player. His younger self appeared on the TV, at a campaign appearance for the Sierra Club. He was standing outdoors, behind a podium that said "Antioch Dunes National Wildlife Refuge." He said, "My opponent has dismissed the danger from his polluting campaign contributors to species like the Lange's Metalmark butterfly. But if I am given the privilege to serve as your governor, no pack of anti-environmental lawyers and political spin doctors will succeed in destroying the

Metalmark or other endangered species. These species represent priceless natural beauty for us to preserve for later generations of Americans. You have my word on that." The other people on the stage applauded, and Pres. Jackson recognized the face of a friend, Ko-sum Mituna, a Native American supporter of his campaign.

Pres. Jackson now remembered that speech, but the coincidence of the visitor Metalmark's name struck him silent. That passionate speech had captured the pro-environment voters when he thought they were deserting him, and won him the governor's office.

Meg saw him pondering. "Tom, do you think this has something to do with the space visitor?"

The President said, "That would certainly be strange. Mary, you said this was broadcast on TV not long ago. Metalmark said he watched lots of TV from Earth during his voyage. I don't know if it's just some coincidence, but I'm certainly going to ask him if it is when I get the chance."

Meg looked at him with that mind-reading expression he knew so well. She said, "Metalmark could have picked any name he wanted to call himself. What if he saw this broadcast? He said he knew that the US is the wealthiest space power, and he wants a trading relationship. He could have chosen his name to appeal for your sympathy. He wants a special secret relationship with the US president. He wants your protection. What a brilliant way to appeal to you!"

Pres. Jackson could only nod agreement. Of all the TV broadcasts aired in recent years, Metalmark had identified this one and used it to target his message precisely and privately at the most powerful man on Earth. What caliber of mind were human beings about to encounter?

"Why call himself an endangered butterfly?" he asked.

II

AFTER METALMARK'S SPEECH, Sec.-Gen. Shankar took a brief cell phone call from the NASA biotech van, which reported that there was a complete absence of detectable pathogens in their surreptitious samples of Metalmark's exhalations and skin contact residue (collected via Marv Krainak's handshake). This calmed Shankar considerably, settling his nagging worries that it had been unsafe for the delegation to meet Metalmark. He looked around again at the delegates, mingling in the VIP viewing area, under a capacious tent that shaded them from the glare and heat of the Florida sun.

Metalmark had modestly sat in a chair beside the podium, where one of Shankar's UN staff was describing a series of planned welcoming activities. Metalmark was saying, "It is very kind of you to arrange the reception. I will be happy to attend and greet people. However, I hope that you will forgive my inability to eat any of the food. My metabolism is so different from yours that I'm afraid I'll never be able to adapt. But I'll be happy to shake hands with everyone in your receiving line and let them take photos with me. I hope there's a cool T-shirt . . ."

As the UN event coordinator, Ilana Lindler said, "I'm sorry that you cannot partake of the food, but I suppose that dietary restrictions are something we should have expected. Please let us know if there are any other personal needs that you have. We have no knowledge of your species, and your human appearance is leading us to identify with you. Please overlook any unintentional offense if we presume that you would want something the way we would want it."

Metalmark said, "I'm glad my appearance is acceptable. I want to talk with you more about these matters in private, when time permits. Also, there is the matter of my landing ship. I ask that you guard it and do not attempt to enter it. The technology in it is part of my stock in trade, and we do not yet have a contract of sale, so it is off limits until delivery in accord with a sales contract. Also it contains modules that are *very* hazardous if tampered with by the curious."

"Of course," Shankar agreed. Then Metalmark was whisked away to the head of a long line of dignitaries, to press the flesh, be introduced and be photographed with everyone in attendance. Shankar called Krainak to convey Metalmark's request for security of his lander; he also left a message with Pres. Jackson's secretary, asking for US Military Police guards around the landing ship.

Sec.-Gen. Shankar spent the reception attempting to arrange an emergency UN Security Council meeting with an appropriately limited agenda: hearing Metalmark's proposal of exchange. Of course the delegates attempted to alter the agenda so as to add consideration of "related" issues. Amb. Yang Wei of China, for example, wanted to precede Metalmark's offer with an exhaustive presentation on the so-called "Outer Space Treaty," approved by the UN decades ago, which established that no citizen of any nation on Earth could own property on the Moon or any planetary body. Amb. Yang pointed out that the Outer Space Treaty was ratified before any alien beings were known. China proposed that the UN immediately affirm the "logical extension" of the Outer Space Treaty's international statutes to prohibit ownership by anyone, human or alien, of the "planetary wastelands" that Metalmark had mentioned.

Shankar surmised that this proposal was a bargaining tactic intended to raise the opening price that Metalmark would have to offer for Solar System real estate, and he diplomatically refused, admitting that the issue might be brought up in session if enough delegates cared. Amb. Yang Wei accused him of naiveté in bargaining with such valuable assets as solar system bodies, but the conversation remained civil.

Such quibbling iterated, ambassador after ambassador, for the entire time that Metalmark carried on introductions and photos, while everyone else in attendance enjoyed the food and the self-important and elated atmosphere of being at an historical event that would never be repeated. Shankar was exhausted after two hours of this activity, but Metalmark showed no weariness.

Metalmark greeted Maria Escobar, the wife of one of the many ambassadors in the receiving line. She exclaimed, "Metalmark, I have dreamed for all of my life of meeting someone from the stars! This is the greatest occasion of my life! I want to give you a kiss and embrace!"

The military policeman beside Metalmark said, "Ma'am, you must keep your place in line, not disrupt the greeting protocol."

Metalmark bowed and kissed her hand dryly, and she cried, "Gracias! Oh, I'll never wash it!" Her aide had captured the event on her cell phone's video recorder.

US Amb. Paul Kirk had already been through the photo-op line, and had taken a cell phone call, whereupon he returned for another run through the line. Metalmark said, "Hello, again, Amb. Kirk."

Kirk said, "I'm impressed by your memory, Metalmark!"

"It's eidetic, as you say."

"I just received a phone call from Pres. Jackson, and he would very much like you to visit the White House."

"Tell him I'm looking forward to it. I have been told that there is a UN session very soon, to hear my trade offer, but it will take a little time to arrange. I will consult with Sec. Shankar for advice. If he does not think that the other nations would become suspicious, then I'll meet your president first; otherwise, I'll have to schedule that after the presentation to the UN of my offer. I don't want my future customers to think that I am giving an unfair advance deal to the US, if you know what I mean."

Amb. Kirk said, "That would never happen, of course, but I am again impressed by your . . . perspicacity."

"You are very complimentary. That's quite diplomatic. I am trying to get calibrated on the level of flattery to employ in human commercial relations. Please help me avoid embarrassing myself with excess."

Amb. Kirk said, "Metalmark, I am also impressed with the fact that you never seem to perspire in this heated Florida atmosphere. The weather is somewhat cooler than this in Washington, DC."

"After the frigid decades that I have spent in deep interstellar space, ambassador, this is very welcome warmth. But my natural habitat is much cooler than this. Earth is quite a hot planet to me. I just hope that I have managed to give a warm handshake to the representatives of humanity here today."

With their surveillance cameras, at the Pentagon Gen. Mason and Sec. Saper watched Metalmark's behavior on the receiving line, bemused and disquieted. Finally the surreal performance was interrupted by a call from the NASA Administrator, reporting his team's initial results as agreed upon. His televised face and voice appeared on the monitor from the NASA van in Florida.

Marv Krainak announced, "Our biohazard survey of Metalmark revealed a surprise." He explained. "We used a detector for biological contamination that was developed recently in a collaboration with the Homeland Security Dept. The detector samples all biological material on the palm of someone who shakes hands with a cooperative individual (in this case, myself). The moist skin adheres to viruses, bacteria, particles like pollen, spores, dust, pet dander and other such microscopic particles. The way the detector works is: my palm was sampled before Metalmark arrived, as a 'background' sample. Everyone's skin holds a population of biological particles characteristic of their daily encounters. Often we can tell people apart by this sampling method, by means of the species and proportions of biological particles collected from their skin.

"So *my* palm was sampled and assayed first. Then Metalmark and I shook hands. My palm was secretly sampled with the detector again after he left the van. The surprise was that there was *no* incremental sample of biological matter detected."

CIA chief West was watching on a TV-con link to Langley. He said, "You mean he left no biological matter on your palm?"

Krainak nodded. "This never happens. Everyone has a slightly different population on his palm. Maybe you walk the dog, maybe you pet your cat, maybe you feed your baby. Some slight difference always is measurable. But Metalmark's hand was sterile. The only additional contamination on my palm was some dust that condensed from his lander rocket exhaust. It was not biological."

Cliff Saper asked, "Does this mean he really isn't a human being?"

Krainak replied, "Not unless he was raised in a sterile environment from infancy. There was another anomaly: a normal palm sample yields some abraded human skin cells from the subject's hand. None except cells with my DNA were found in our sample. Metalmark's palm did not give us any human skin cells that we can identify."

Saper admitted, "OK, I give up my stubborn belief that this is a hoax perpetrated by human beings. We're dealing with an advanced life form that we know nothing about, except that it knows a great deal about how to pretend to be like us, and a great deal about diplomacy and trade. We have to continue surveillance to catalog any weaknesses or hidden threats, and be ready if Metalmark exhibits any dangerous changes from his innocuous pose."

Krainak suggested, "Do you have any plans to test his motives? He has come here with no biological hazards along for the ride, which would take great extremes of effort for us to do if we were in his place. He might be honestly friendly. How do you propose to prepare for that eventuality?"

Gen. Mason said, "That's not our job. Our duty is to maintain prudent paranoia in an unprecedented situation. The friendliness and diplomacy are the job of Sec.-Gen. Shankar and Amb. Kirk."

Pres. Jackson was at his desk in the Oval Office, looking over the latest briefing summaries. The phone rang and he picked it up. "Senator Flaherty, to what do I owe the pleasure?"

Sen. Jason Flaherty, Majority Leader of the opposition party, replied, "Mr. President, I just wanted to call to tell you that everyone in Congress is pleased and supportive about the way you have handled the arrival of a visitor from space! On a bipartisan basis, the members I have talked to are pleased that the country is taking the event so calmly, and so far without any panic. It's a tribute to your matter-of-fact, business as usual reaction. I was worried particularly about panics in the financial markets — imagine what could have happened to gold futures when Metalmark revealed his gold from sea water! But the markets have treated this historic event as an opportunity to acquire new technology and an affirmation of the importance of commerce and business across the cosmos!"

"I'm pleased with the relative calm of the population, too," said the president. "Now behind the scenes, our security forces are keeping watch and keeping the UN events for Metalmark secure. We are planning a briefing for the congressional leadership very soon, but if you have any questions, feel free to call Cliff Saper."

Sensing that the president was winding up the call quickly, Sen. Flaherty said, "I just want to add that whenever the Metalmark makes a visit to Washington, all of us on the Hill are ready to join you in giving him a warm welcome."

"I'll keep that in mind, you can be sure," Pres. Jackson said. "And thanks for your bipartisan expression of support. It's good to know that the Leadership is backing me up. Good-bye." He thought, *Flaherty is making nice to make sure he's in the photos.*

M

Metalmark agreed to accompany the UN delegation to New York via a chartered jet. The delegation was conveyed to the airport in Orlando where everyone trooped through the terminal to a security station prior to boarding. Luggage for the delegates was being loaded onto the plane. Metalmark had none. As the delegates filed through metal detectors, Shankar accompanied Metalmark, hoping to vouch for him in the event of the unexpected.

The metal detector went off when Metalmark passed through, and he had no paraphernalia such as keys to remove. Seeing the X-ray machine, Metalmark said, "Oh, I've always wondered what these are like. You can just put me through it."

The security official said, "It's not safe for people to go through!"

"I'm not a human being. I assure you it's safe for me," said Metalmark.

Shankar said, "I can vouch for him. Is this necessary?"

"We can't let him on board if the metal detector or X-ray don't prove he's harmless," said the security officer.

Metalmark reclined on the conveyor belt of the X-ray machine, and again said, "I'll be safe."

Very nervously, Shankar asked, "Since he's not human and claims it's safe, is this acceptable?"

The security officer grudgingly agreed. Shankar sidled around beside the woman who was doing X-ray security duty, to view the X-ray screen as Metalmark rode through. They watched the scan, not of a human skeleton but of a framework of similar machinery, with many opaque unidentifiable parts in unaccustomed places in the torso. Shankar gulped and the X-ray security officer was speechless. Metalmark emerged from the other end of the conveyor with no ill effects, got up and stood waiting for Shankar with a slight smile.

The X-ray security officer remarked, "Hey, that's right! You're that space guy that I saw on the news yesterday. That's why you're built like a machine, with strange parts inside. You're an android, or something. Welcome to Earth, Mr. Android."

Shankar walked through the metal detector and picked up his own wallet and keys from the tray, chilled to the bone, but attempting to compose himself.

Metalmark's urbane exterior had lulled the whole delegation into mental denial of the alien nature of their visitor, but now Shankar struggled to recover that elation he had felt before.

Tabloid newspapers picked up the story about a NASA comet astronomer's discovery of the Metalmark spacecraft's path. The techie press, typified by slashdot.org, was beside itself with excitement, blogging fantasies about Metalmark's origins and species. Dr. Steve Simmons began to receive phone calls at his office at Goddard Space Flight Center. He was required to direct the callers to ask the Public Affairs Office to handle interview arrangements, but callers still pestered him while he tried to refine the farthest extent of the alien spacecraft's trajectory through the Solar System.

Simmons knew that the alien appeared to arrive in the Solar System from the direction of the constellation Sagittarius. The spacecraft then had made a close pass by the Sun, using its gravity to deflect Metalmark's orbit toward planet Earth. Simmons had accurate sightings of Metalmark's trajectory from the Sun earthward. Before its tight curve around the Sun, the path at previous times was poorly defined because Metalmark would have wanted to burn his braking rockets to adjust his trajectory better for the rendezvous with Earth. Without knowing how much Metalmark decelerated with his braking engines, and when he made the burns, there was no way to establish with precision the alien's motion as it approached the Sun.

But there was one way that Simmons could make an educated guess about Metalmark's previous whereabouts. Metalmark visited the Solar System, so *suppose* Metalmark was a star-hopper, rather than spending most of his time loitering in starless interstellar space. What was the nearest star that Metalmark could have visited without much deviation from his approximately-known origin in the direction of Sagittarius?

Simmons consulted an on-line list of the nearest stars. Proxima Centauri and Alpha Centauri A and B were the closest, about 4.3 light years away. But they were in another direction altogether. So were the next farthest star, Barnard's Star, and the next. He went on down the list, and the 7th most distant star was the first one in Sagittarius! It was a star too dim to be seen by the naked eye, a type "M" dwarf star, discovered in 1925 by Frank E. Ross, who cataloged it as No. 154 in his catalog of discoveries. "Ross 154" is about 9.7 light years away, the closest star to our Sun that is also in the constellation Sagittarius.

Could Ross 154 have been Metalmark's last port of call?

Simmons began to modify his trajectory simulation program to assume that Metalmark entered the Solar System along the line from Ross 154 to the Sun. He had only worked an hour before the NASA Chief Administrator called.

"Dr. Simmons, this is Marv Krainak. Congratulations on your report of the Metalmark spacecraft observations. We would like to have you join us at NASA Headquarters for a meeting to consolidate all that is known about Metalmark."

Simmons frowned but avoided complaining about the interruption. It made him nervous to get a direct call from the administrator. "Dr. Krainak, I'll be happy to join in. All I have to offer is the report I filed with the IAU comet center. I haven't had time to pursue anything more to a presentable conclusion."

"That's OK," said Krainak. "We just want to bring you into the team that's working this situation for the president."

Simmons had a sinking feeling. He felt his life on the verge of getting gobbled up by a Black Hole, the Big Event of Metalmark's appearance, but there was nothing he could do to resist the slide into the well of spacetime that the alien's arrival would become. He got directions to the conference room downtown at NASA Headquarters in DC from Krainak and hung up. Then he made sure that the latest code for his trajectory program was loaded onto his laptop computer, and took it with him to his car. At least he might be able to run some more trajectory estimates during lulls in the meeting.

$$\underline{M}$$

Sec.-Gen. Shankar looked out of the charter plane's window as it flew from Florida toward New York. It should have comforted him to see US Air Force escort jets on both sides of the UN's charter, but he was uneasy nonetheless.

Metalmark was watching the ground below through another window. "Amazing to see so many forms of hydroxide clouds! And your land areas are so covered with chlorophyllous plant forms! It's a long time since I can remember seeing this kind of biosphere . . . you have populated many dense cities with your individuals. The resource distribution to your individuals must be challenging."

Shankar's Deputy Secretary, Bernard Molyneux (from Belgium), pursued this with Metalmark. "Yes, that is the chief global problem of the UN. Even in the USA, this wealthiest of countries, there is some hunger because the resources are not uniformly distributed. But among poor nations, extreme poverty and lack of resources is common." Shankar listened exhaustedly to their conversation, and it soothed his anxiety about Metalmark. He dozed for the rest of the flight to La Guardia airport.

He awoke to the ringtone of his pocket phone as the UN charter flight was circling to land. The call was from his wife, Uma.

"I watched you in Florida. I was so proud! You must bring Metalmark to our flat for dinner!"

"I'm afraid that we can't, my love. He cannot eat human food. I have not seen him eat any food. His body is not like ours." There was stunned silence from his wife. "I am sure that the public will be ferocious to see him, so we are going to give him the guest apartment of the UN until better arrangements can be made."

Uma sighed. "That is a drab place. Such a special visitor deserves rich rooms."

"I will arrange something to his liking, but that might be like nothing on Earth. I'll call you when I have another chance. Love!" The plane made a comfortable landing moments later.

Event Coordinator Ilana Lindler was on her phone, soothing the angry mayor of New York who had wanted to give a lavish public welcome to Metalmark at the airport, or City Hall. Ilana was explaining Shankar's story that Metalmark required some rest. But in fact, Shankar was arranging for an immediate UN Security Council hearing of Metalmark's offer. Shankar wanted to put the offer on the table faster than obstructions like the Chinese update of the Outer Space Treaty could be devised and proposed. But even more, he wanted to know if the offer was as richly generous as it seemed. The international public excitement was building, and Shankar and the Council had to learn quickly whether they should put the UN's endorsement on Metalmark's proposal, or whether it was hollow hype.

Because of the secrecy, only a few of the most well-connected paparazzi were in place as the delegation deplaned at La Guardia and boarded a waiting helicopter for the ride to the UN building. US Air Force escort gunships preceded and followed the UN aircraft.

Metalmark forbore this secretive ride above the Manhattan skyline. He was subdued, perhaps disappointed that he couldn't ride a limo through downtown traffic for the first time. Shankar was amazed that Metalmark's taciturn manner suppressed the many questions that everyone in the delegation must be nursing about every aspect of life among the stars.

When Shankar arrived at his office with his entourage, his office manager said, "Welcome back to pandemonium. E-mail is not working because too many messages came in. Someone put your e-mail address on public websites, and everyone in the world who wants to tell Metalmark something sent e-mail to you. When you had less than 32,000 messages, I could read some, but now the computer says you have '-17,000' messages and I can't view any of them."

Shankar said, "Issue a press release thanking everyone for the messages and apologizing for our inability to answer. At least we can give live press conferences, even if we crash the Internet."

Metalmark was following Shankar, attended by Ilana Lindler. The President of the UN General Assembly session, Sirpa Hakkinen, entered the Sec.-Gen.'s office suite. She was in high spirits because the emergency meeting of the Security Council was almost convening itself. The world-wide news of Metalmark's trade offer was so appealing to the members that the usual difficulties in attaining a quorum were spontaneously vanishing. Pres. Hakkinen said, "Only a few ambassadors are absent, and they are reportedly on the way. We can start!"

The entourage boarded elevators and moved to the Security Council chambers.

Since the Council members were all keenly aware of the meeting's purpose, Assembly Pres. Hakkinen wasted no time bringing Metalmark to the speaker's podium. The translators took their places and Metalmark began speaking in English.

"As I outlined at the Kennedy Space Center, I have an offer of trade with the people of Earth. I have technology that can advance your civilization by leaps and bounds. You own planetary bodies that are suitable for my species to use for the purpose of spawning. So I propose that you cede to me all rights to certain planetary bodies, and in return I will build an operational starship — a package of functioning modules in what you call a 'turn-key' system — which you can use for travel to other neighboring star systems as I have traveled here.

He continued,"Your starship system will include all necessary hardware, software, and provisions necessary to travel to a neighboring star system as far as 20 light years away, and explore, then return with cargo. As you can imagine, this technological system will include many subsystems. For instance, specifically, you will be able to travel to the starship from Earth and back. While you are traveling, your life support will be maintained, and your ability to communicate with Earth will be supported. Many functions of the starship will be automated, using advanced astrogation technology so that you will not get lost, and you will be able to return precisely to home after a trip of many trillions of miles. And it will not require undue time to puzzle out how the starship is operated; the ship will be helpful, able to respond to your requests for information.

"The very advanced technology of this vehicle will be open to you for adaptation to other uses. For example, the food production modules can be duplicated and installed on Earth wherever they are needed. The power generation systems are adaptable to industry. The starship is equipped with manufacturing technology so that it can use raw materials at the destination star system to build habitats and spacecraft; of course these technologies have applications within your own Solar System.

"I cannot give you a fixed date for completion of your starship system, because that depends upon the conditions that I encounter at the construction site. I must assay the available raw materials. But I can give you my personal guarantee that I will not leave the Solar System before you have your starship ready to use. That is my faithful guarantee to you.

"To show my good faith, I have brought some small demonstrations of the technology that you will be buying. The first you have seen, my catalytic condenser of precious minerals from sea water. It will give you much wealth from your oceans, and you will not find it difficult to duplicate the machine.

"Sec.-Gen. Shankar's staff reminded me of the challenges that some citizens of your planet face, due to poverty and hunger. As another demonstration of the kind of benefits that a deal between us can bring, I am developing a product that can help you alleviate this hunger in some countries. It is a powder composed of microscopic machines, and if it is combined with water and stones that contain carbonate, the product will be edible carbohydrates. Limestone would be the best stone to use, but I will design the powder to adapt to various raw materials. The product will be developed in consultation with your nutritionists. My 'Food from Stones' program will be offered to countries that want to try it through the UN.

"I also want to help with economic development by starting businesses that commercialize many other minor technologies I have collected. I will set up a corporation in the customary way to pursue that.

"Please understand that the catalytic condenser and 'Food from Stones' technologies are not essential parts of the starship technology package; they are just friendly gifts to you to establish good faith. We will prepare a contract with clear terms so that you will know what you are about to get and what you are giving. It is my duty to deliver on this contract all of the goods that it specifies, and I will faithfully do that before I leave your Solar System.

"I am trying to formulate the contract verbally so that you can contractualize my words into a rough draft of the final contract. Now I will entertain questions about the particulars."

Assembly Pres. Hakkinen said, "Thank you for making this contractual agreement clear, and (it seems) generous. The major question in my own mind is: what planetary bodies do you require? Since these bodies are the payment you request, are they the only payment?"

Metalmark replied, "The principal body that I require for my species to spawn is the planet you call Mercury. In addition, the moon of Neptune known as Triton is the remaining significant part of my price. The contract must specify that I obtain full and immediate rights to these two bodies. I also request full rights to take and use a number of icy, comet-like small bodies that I have identified, known to your astronomers as Kuiper belt objects generically; however the objects that I have selected are too small and distant from Earth to exist in your astronomical catalogs. I am still assaying the objects and don't know precisely how many will be required for my construction operations. I ask that you reserve mention of them for a rider to the contract, because I'm not sure how many I will need."

As soon as Metalmark's last words were translated into the council attendees' respective languages, most of the attendees whispered to their accompanying aides, and the aides dashed away to conduct secretive phone calls or e-mail messaging.

Amb. Yang Wei asked to be heard. "My government gave me prior instructions to discuss the terms of your proposed sale. Your offer of the starship technology seems insufficient in comparison to the loss of two entire planetary bodies from the legacy that human beings deserve to leave for their posterity. This organization is bound by the Treaty of 1967, which designated space resources 'the common heritage of mankind.' You are asking for full rights to what must be tens of millions of square kilometers from that heritage.

"In the case of the Planet Mercury specifically, its close proximity to the Sun illuminates it with tremendous amounts of sunlight, useful for vast resources of electrical power." Amb. Yang consulted some briefing papers, holding up his hand while he did so to retain the privilege of speaking further. "Ah. The planetary satellite known as Triton . . . is of great value to our human descendants because . . . of its natural resources of ice, which could be used to supply human space colonies, and its magnificent view of the Planet Neptune, which it orbits. To my government it seems that the UN would do a disservice to our descendants if we gave up these tremendous natural resources rashly, without fair compensation."

Metalmark replied, "I have the greatest respect for your government, Amb. Yang, and for your admirable arguments. You cleverly cite the potential future value of Mercury and Triton at some distant time, when they would be greatly multiplied in value to you by gigantic improvements in accessibility. In comparison with that, my offer seems a relatively small single space vessel. I commend your negotiating talents. Let me point out, however, some imbalances in your evaluations.

"Mercury has, as you say, 37 million square kilometers in sunlight. However, you have no technology capable of utilizing that sunlight, and cannot expect to have it for many generations (without my help). The sunlight on Mercury therefore has no present economic value to you. The starship that I am offering you will be available much sooner than that sunlight, and the technology that you will gain in our deal will enable you to exploit sunlight of similar quantities to what you would trade to me. Also, at Mercury's distance from the Sun, it captures only a minuscule fraction of the total sunlight available. By using the technology that I would soon trade to you, you would obtain the ability to exploit far more sunlight than the relatively tiny proportion that I want to collect and use in my own operations on Mercury. This is a clear win for you.

"Your evaluation of Triton also depends on future potential economic and recreational value, which you suggested as dwarfing the value of my starship. But

Triton also is so distant that its valuable ice mines for water, and the marvelous views of Neptune from future ski chalets will only be a fantasy to tantalize generations of earthbound Chinese children. They do not have my space travel technology to take them there. I ask you to weigh also the lost value of their decades of exile from the ski chalets of Triton against the trips that they may soon make by means of my spacecraft to ski chalets on other equally well-located moons of Neptune. The moons of Neptune that you call Proteus and Larissa are much closer to Neptune, offering better views of that dark planet out there so far from the Sun, and they have much lower gravity, so the skiing would be very much more entertaining! By trading Triton to me, you will win swift access to the valuable ice and snow on all of the seven other Neptunian moons, with all of their skiing and spectacular views!"

Amb. Yang was rendered silent for such a long time that several other council members had time to pose minor questions to Metalmark about procedural and contract terminology matters. As Amb. Yang gradually relaxed from his concentrating posture, other council members suppressed chuckles that his formidable negotiating skills had met their ideal adversary. He was known for his shrewd methods, yet a furtive smile of satisfaction played on his face as he was persuaded that Metalmark offered a genuine win-win deal. Occasional doubts played across his visage as fleeting frowns, and he made several notations on his scratch pad. These were undoubtedly reminders of queries for Metalmark, to be posed after acceptance of the deal. Amb. Yang was concluding that after all Metalmark had a valuable deal for the UN and humanity. This was visible to all through Amb. Yang's actions, silence and posture, and his unconscious actions swung many observant council members toward favorable regard of Metalmark with their silent eloquence.

Amb. Paul Kirk asked to be recognized. "The United States appreciates your offer, and will take it under detailed consideration. We UN Security Council members find ourselves at a clear negotiating disadvantage in view of your knowledge of the economic value of such a remote object as Triton. Also you exhibit great experience in negotiating trade agreements concerning planetary bodies, while we have never done that. You will have to give our respective national governments time to assemble task forces with the necessary skills to critically judge your offer. Any additional information that you would care to supply about Mercury and Triton to substantiate your views of their economic value might help our member states come to a swifter conclusion."

Metalmark said, "I will compile what information I have about these bodies, although much of it derives from the PBS TV shows that I watched during my voyage." Council members chuckled. "What I can add is general experience with the class of planetary bodies in the type of orbits Mercury and Triton occupy around Main Sequence stars like the Sun, and some telescopic observations that I made. The Voyager and Messenger spacecraft that the US used to explore Mercury and Triton years ago returned data to you that were described in many TV shows, so you already have much of what you need for the economic evaluation."

Sec.-Gen. Shankar asked to speak. "Metalmark, you have referred to economic value of Mercury and Triton, which we understand only in general terms. I would like to request that you provide a detailed report on the natural resources to be found on those bodies, and what you consider the economic value of these resources. Clearly the value is dependent upon the technological capabilities of human beings, something that progress changes greatly in time. We can only fairly evaluate your offer if we also have access to that information."

Metalmark nodded. "I see what you want. I will perform a time-value analysis of Mercury and Triton, based on your developing space travel capabilities. The analysis can only be as reliable as my knowledge of your various member nations' space programs, so I will need the information that you can provide. I hope it is not too proprietary to be given. But I can work within such constraints and still provide meaningful reports to you. I'll project the values of Mercury and Triton through a hypothetical scenario of human space technological advancement *without* my products and *with* my products, over about the next century. It can't be perfectly accurate, but should enable you to make an intelligent decision. It's a sound approach, and I'm confident that you will see the benefits of accepting my offer."

Pres. Jackson watched the performance of Metalmark in the UN Security Council meeting on his wall TV. As the meeting in New York adjourned, the phone rang on the president's desk in the White House. Amb. Kirk said, "Tom, Metalmark's offer certainly appears attractive. I'm calling to ask for manpower and resources to evaluate the report he is preparing. Some high-powered talent will be required. People from Commerce and Treasury but also NASA and NAS."

The president was slow to respond. "I guess I shouldn't be surprised — he is a being from an advanced species — but we're outclassed in this negotiation. We look at TV shows about far-out space voyages and see improbable fantasies that won't be fulfilled in our lifetimes. He looks at NASA pictures of ice balls at the edge of the Solar System and thinks of industrial production and tourism. And he speaks with the experience of having done this many times before, glibly, tenaciously pursuing a sale with a confidence about the outcome, even though he never met a human being before today. What are we facing? An ancient superior being who will overcome our reservations by exploiting our inexperience, no matter what we do?"

When he hung up, Pres. Jackson's secretary told him that Defense Sec. Saper and Gen. Mason were waiting. They entered the Oval Office.

Sec. Saper said, "Tom, Metalmark's plans are still obscure, but we should look at the possibility that he wants to establish a military base of operations at the remote edges of the Solar System, where we have no way to observe what is happening."

Gen. Mason added, "Nor do we have any means for surveillance of the planet Mercury. We have to consider the potential risks of ceding planetary bodies anywhere in the Solar System to a foreign power with advanced technology."

Pres. Jackson admitted, "There are risks, of course. Assign appropriate resources to anticipating what we might be facing. Bring in whoever you have with expertise in forecasting threats from superior technology and domination of the space environment."

Sec. Saper said, "Thanks, Tom. We'll get you a report as soon as possible."

When they left, Pres. Jackson pondered for a few minutes, frowning. Then he called Commerce Sec. George Cosgrove. "George, the risks of Metalmark's arrival have been brandished repeatedly in my face. I want you and Nicole to put together a team to forecast the potential for benefits of dealing with an advanced culture that can offer us technologies so wonderful we can't imagine them yet. There's a spectacular track record of NASA's technology spin-offs and benefits from hi-tech defense development. Give me a forecast of benefits to counterbalance the doom scenarios."

"I'll be happy to, Mr. President. I'll get Marv Krainak to send some advisors to participate. We'll start right on it."

⼁⼂

Liu Xueli finished her day of training and came home to her apartment. It was a roomy space by the standards of the taikonauts' quarters. It had been decorated tastefully with artworks from classical Chinese high culture because Xueli was a special, respected Olympic hero – or rather, she had been ten years ago. But the teenager who had dominated her gymnastics teammates to bring her motherland silver and gold medals was now a competitive, overachiever adult. She still wanted to excel and win more fame and honors, but her age had foreclosed the Olympic path some time ago.

Fortunately her family was related to important people in Beijing. Political connections alone would not have gotten her the slot as China's first female taikonaut trainee, but she had the physique and determination to exceed every criterion that male taikonaut trainees passed. The party officials who oversaw China's space program could tell that she had the aura of success undimmed.

She decided to give a phone call to one of those high party officials, her mother. "Hello, Daughter," her mother answered.

"I just worked for three hours on the Shenzhou 16 simulator. It is much more complicated than my last training, but I landed it on the Moon without crashing."

"Maybe next time you should set course for Mars! Now you know how to navigate it, I wonder what your instructor would do."

Xueli laughed at her mother's joke. "Those engineers don't have such good senses of humor. But did you hear the latest news about that Metalmark?"

"I hope you can meet him. You need to find a good husband."

Xueli laughed again. "I will take your advice. There is a 'rumor' that some of the scientists want to drop the Moon mission and rendezvous with the Metalmark spacecraft. It is much closer than the Moon."

"That is a good rumor for you to pass on to me. I will investigate who might have let it out. Of course if it is true, there is no one more qualified for the mission than you, and I will pass that along to your uncle with my strong recommendation."

"Thank you, Mother. I am always grateful for how you look out for me, even in my 'old age'."

Xueli's mother laughed this time, and they bid each other good-bye.

Ilana Lindler arrived at her apartment on the West Side and checked her audio recorder. It seemed to have worked properly during the flight from Orlando to New York, so she connected it to the computer port of her Mac and started the download. The flash memory recording of Metalmark's every word was converted to a big-ass MP3 that she could turn in to her CIA case officer. The CIA was certainly avid about Metalmark's utterances, however trivial. She was amazed at how little the alien said about himself, how effortlessly he deflected probing questions with remarks and exclamations of surprise about the features of the human world.

After the Security Council meeting, Sec.-Gen. Shankar had directed her to arrange a New York City welcome for Metalmark with the mayor's staff, so she had spent some hours lining up luminaries for a city hall ceremony. Then there was a call from News Talk Channel network, asking if Metalmark was available to appear tomorrow on "Tonight with Jayno." She decided that it would be a hoot, and great publicity for the "Food from Rocks" program, so it was agreed. By the time she left the UN and got home it was too late for anything but a dinner of refrigerator leftovers. Then she went to sleep at once, amazed that her UN job had turned into a fascinating view of an "ambassador" like no other in history—one who eluded everyone's efforts to evoke his superhuman knowledge and experiences.

From Larry Saxon's *NASA Critique* blog:

The UN released the transcript of Metalmark's presentation about his trade offer today. He pointed out that Mercury and Triton have essentially no economic value to humans today because of our primitive and expensive space travel methods, so why shouldn't we give them to him in exchange for a state-of-the-art spaceship? This embarrassing state of affairs is known well to US taxpayers, who have shelled out billions for NASA's crude achievements. Space travel remains too expensive for us to start businesses that make any money because of NASA's taxpayer-subsidized monopoly.

The Metalmark Contract

The Moon could be strewn with gold doubloons
Two dozen carats heft
But NASA couldn't sell them on Earth
And have a penny left.

"It's the *Live Tonight with Jayno Show*! With Jayno's special guests: His Eminence, Cardinal Francis Marzari from the Vatican in Rome, and . . . M-e-t-a-l-m-a-r-k! With musical guests: the 'Space Monkey Punks from Japan.' And now here's Jayno!"

Jayno trotted out to center stage in her gold lamé pantsuit, waving to the cheering, clapping studio audience. "Thank you, everybody! Tonight we have such a special show, I hardly know where to begin. History is being made as we in New York enjoy the first visit to our planet from someone literally out-of-this-world: Metalmark!"

There was more loud cheering and applause. "He's here in our studio, fresh from the spectacular welcome he got from the mayor at City Hall today, along with some appropriate welcoming music from the Space Monkey Punks . . ." (more applause). "But we don't want the spiritual side of this event to be left out, so we invited the Vatican to send us an emissary to welcome the visitor who is literally from Heaven (although we need some clarification on that). So we have Cardinal Francis Marzari to help us welcome Metalmark." (Some polite applause.)

"Mayor Bailey and the New York Yankees welcomed Metalmark to City Hall today in a spectacular ceremony." (Lots of cheering.) "They gave him an old-fashioned New York welcome, with lots of celebrities and the 'key to the city.' He's been carrying around the key all day, but he's puzzled because it doesn't actually fit into any of the locks of the doors. This usually didn't matter, but when he tried to get into one of the pay toilets in Trump Tower, somebody had to help him." (Audience laughter.) "UN Sec.-Gen. Shankar explained that men just crawl under the partitions or climb over. Nobody actually pays.

"No, actually one of the mayor's staff gave Metalmark a tour of the city. They went into the subway, and he had to get some help learning to ride the subway. The first problem was that he didn't have cash or a credit card — they don't use money where he comes from. He saw that all the subway cars had people's names written in big scrawly letters on them, so he asked for a big marker so he could write his name with all the others. Someone had to explain to him that graffiti was a faux pas.

"He met a panhandler, who asked him for some change. Metalmark said he didn't have any money, so the panhandler directed him to a homeless shelter just down the street, a great place to sleep, he said. Nice friendly gesture, I thought; this city has the best panhandlers in the world!

"They took Metalmark to 'The Four Seasons,' one of New York's finest restaurants, but that didn't work out. He can't eat any Earth food, he's very apologetic about it, but it doesn't agree with him. He asked them to take his plate to that panhandler who gave him directions. Isn't that a wonderful gesture?" (*Much audience applause.*)

"The United Nations announced today that Metalmark has agreed to apply his advanced technology to fight world hunger. He has a method to turn rocks into food, and he's going to give it away with the UN's help, to poor people who are struggling to survive." (*Much audience applause.*) "I remember growing up with the children's story of 'stone soup,' but he's told me that it isn't anything like that. For poverty-stricken countries, just think of the potential of turning rocks into food!

"Google's search engine crashed today. Every teenager put up a website and blog, begging Metalmark to save him/her from his/her parents. So then somebody googled 'Metalmark,' but the number of hits was too big to fit Google's counter, and all their servers crashed. I know, I know, that's a joke that only a geek would like.

"Well enough of the day's news, I know you all want to meet Metalmark, but I thought it was important to clear up a lot of confusion in many people's minds about him. He comes from outer space, and some people think of outer space as Heaven. When I was a little girl, growing up in Catholic school, and I saw the moon landings on TV, I was very confused about whether the astronauts were in Heaven. How many of you went to Catholic school?" (*Many in the audience applauded.*) "Yeah, so you may have had that confusion. And the nuns didn't help to clear things up, let me tell you. So we have Cardinal Francis Marzari joining us tonight. Come on out Your Eminence."

Cardinal Marzari strode happily across the stage in his black robe, and red sash, and cross, and sat down in the guest chair beside Jayno's desk. He placed a small vase of clear water on Jayno's desk. The applause from the audience was vigorous. "Welcome, Your Eminence, it's very kind of you to join us and help the faithful everywhere avoid confusion about having a visitor from space."

"You're most welcome, Jayno, thank you for having me. You are right, there has been a great deal of confusion in Italian media and in many other Christian countries, and we should explain that outer space is not the same as Heaven. I know we talk about the Heavenly Father above us, and maybe point to the sky in mentioning holy things, but that's just a metaphor. Heaven is a spiritual realm, not the vast outer space outside the earth's atmosphere. When you point 'up' you are not literally pointing at Heaven."

"OK, eventually I learned that when I was growing up, but I think there are people watching who will be enlightened by hearing it directly from an official Vatican spokesman. Now I also wanted to give you a chance to express the Holy Father the Pope's view of our visitor Metalmark, who will be joining us very soon, in case you viewers just tuned in."

Cardinal Marzari said, "The Church welcomes Metalmark and appreciates his friendly behavior to the people of Planet Earth. He has behaved as a kind older brother — we are all children of the Heavenly Father, who is Lord of the entire Universe — and Metalmark's behavior has been very generous. Certainly he has powers greater than our governments, but he seems to intend to use his powers for peaceful ends. The Holy Father approves and has invited Metalmark for an audience."

"But you were telling me that some in the Church have concerns about Metalmark's nature. Can you address those fears so that we can comfort the worried?"

"Well, in the Italian press there have been unfounded claims that Metalmark is a fallen angel from Heaven, an evil demon with deceptive intent to take advantage of us. I want to reassure all believers that there is no evidence for this claim. And we can disprove it here and now."

Jayno added, "Almost now. When we come back after the commercial break, . . . *Metalmark*! Stay with us."

M

It was the first time that the US National Security Council held an emergency meeting to view a late-night talk show. Pres. Jackson looked around the table and saw that his NSC staff were enjoying the unorthodox method of public diplomacy that Metalmark was employing, but they had their notepads ready for observations and the show was being taped in HDTV for later analysis. Pres. Jackson had ordered all members of the civilian and military segments of government to watch the show if they could do so without conflicting with essential duties. Marv Krainak and the NASA-NAS task force were also watching, and would have comments after the show.

M

"We're back," announced Jayno, letting her band finish its riffs. "And we join the City of New York and the rest of Planet Earth in welcoming to the stage of *Live Tonight with Jayno*

". . . Metalmark!" Jayno's band played a jazzy version of Elvis Presley's "Welcome to My World" as Metalmark walked across the stage, smiling and waving. The audience stood and applauded. He looked small on the wide stage, and a little shy with a modest smile. He took the seat beside Cardinal Marzari.

When the applause subsided, Jayno said, "Everybody on Earth welcomes you, Metalmark. It is such a delight to find that we are not alone, our civilization, in the Universe, and that such a friendly being as you yourself has finally come to visit us. I know that I personally have felt I had to wait too long for this day to come. Haven't you all felt that way?" Another thunderous round of applause filled the studio.

When he could be heard again, Metalmark was saying, "Thank you all for the friendly welcome. It has been such an amazing day. I want you to know that I have watched your show every night that it was on since the beginning. I'm sort of an interstellar couch potato, and I'm a loyal fan." Jayno began clapping and smiling, and the audience joined in again briefly. "And I'm very happy to have the opportunity to tell everyone about the new 'Food from Rocks' program that my friend Sec.-Gen. Sanjeev Shankar is about to establish through the United Nations, using technology that I will provide. It will be a wonderful way to fight hunger and to educate people about what you have to gain through our trade contract."

Jayno said, "We have so many questions to ask you about . . . well, everything! But first let's get some of the mythology dismissed. Cardinal Marzari has come equipped to address those very misguided claims that we mentioned earlier in the show. Please take over as we arranged, Your Eminence."

Cardinal Marzari said, "Metalmark, the Church wants to settle some claims that have been made to the effect that you are a satanic instrument or demon or the Anti-Christ himself — there have been published claims about this, because of the last part of your name, which is 'mark.' One of the claimants interprets this as 'the mark of the Beast' which was mentioned in the Book of Revelation. Consequently it has been claimed that you are . . . well, any sort of demonic manifestation that the claimants can imagine. I think you will agree that such claims would be an impediment to your planned charitable work. I come to you as a representative of the Holy Father in the Vatican, and hope that you will cooperate with the Church's method of settling that claim definitively."

Metalmark said, "Of course I'll cooperate in any way I can."

Cardinal Marzari said, "Good. I am an accredited exorcist from the Pontifical Academy Regina Apostolorum, empowered on behalf of the Holy Father to perform the rite of exorcism, which will definitively expel any diabolical infestation."

Jayno's band played a couple of organ chords appropriate for Halloween, and the audience chuckled. Jayno waved to the band, "Oh, you hush! This is serious business," but the corners of her mouth had an impish curl.

Metalmark said, "OK, by all means proceed."

Cardinal Marzari dipped his finger in the vase of water on Jayno's desk. "This is holy water, personally blessed by the Holy Father in Rome." With his wet finger he made the sign of the cross on Metalmark's forehead. Then he intoned the Latin verses of the prayer of exorcism. Metalmark waited respectfully. Finally the Cardinal concluded the Latin prayer and held up the cross that was hanging from his neck. "Metalmark, would you be so kind as to touch your lips to this cross." Without hesitation Metalmark leaned forward and awkwardly kissed it. He sat back in his seat and looked around the stage, waiting for some result.

Cardinal Marzari concluded, "This is proof that no manifestation of Satan was present in this being. The claims about the 'mark of the Beast' are settled in the negative. Let all members of the Body of Christ know that Metalmark can be trusted on his own merits, as he could not have passed these tests if he were possessed by Satan." Jayno's band played a short fanfare.

The audience applauded, and when it subsided Cardinal Marzari added, "I just want to add that Metalmark brings us all hope for the advancement of science and technology for the benefit of all people. The Church gives its blessing to all morally pure scientific advances. There cannot be any substantial conflicts between religion and science, so the Holy Father gives his blessing to Metalmark's scientific and technological help to the world." The audience clapped politely.

With that, Cardinal Marzari stood up and shook hands with Jayno and Metalmark, bidding them farewell. As he left the studio, to more applause, Jayno said, "Cardinal Marzari has to return to Rome and can't stay with us. We're very glad he could personally perform this spiritual ritual for us.

"So, Metalmark, the first question on my mind is: how did you get the name 'Metalmark?' "

"Well, I picked it myself in order to interact with you. My species is very different from human beings, so I wanted to be a friendly personality for you. My species does not usually communicate with speech sounds, so I had to pick a name that I hope suggests something friendly and similar to myself. I picked the Metalmark butterfly. In my flights from star to star, I am a little like those creatures, alighting at stars like flowers."

"How charming! And it's like a window into your spirit, choosing your own name! Many Native American cultures do that, and so do Catholics, for that matter, choosing their communion names."

"But I never thought anyone would call me the Anti-Christ. If I'd known that, I would have chosen some other name, let me tell you!" The audience chuckled.

"Well, you certainly have some fans already, especially here in New York! I was at the city hall ceremony today, and there were lots of celebrities. But we also saw the people standing in the back waving signs. They said things like 'We love you, Metalmark,' and 'Metalmark – Save us from Ourselves.' And that one lady had a sign that said 'Metalmark, I want to have your baby!'"

The audience laughed and clapped. Metalmark appeared amused. "That is very nice of her, but it would never work between us. My species does not spawn on this kind of planet."

Jayno's eyes twinkled. "We all remember your reference to this, and we'd like to learn more about how it happens."

"Well, I have to say . . . it's a little private. I have to find the right kind of planet around the right kind of star . . . I want to have friends on Earth but it's just not my type."

"A little bird told me that you want the planet Mercury. But you also need a moon called Triton. The 'moon' part sounds a little romantic. Now are you going to be faithful in your spawning with Mercury, or have a little Triton, too, on the side?" The audience laughed.

Metalmark smiled. "Well, I can't even date them until the UN agrees to my contract offer. I will trade all of my knowledge about starships to you, the people of Earth, for one chance to spawn with Mercury and Triton. I hope you will let me know soon if we have a deal."

"You sound so passionate! You have a romantic soul. Has it been a long time?"

"Yes, my species only spawns once every ninety years or so." The audience let out a sympathetic "Aww!"

"So tell me about how you are so different from human beings. You seem like one of us."

"Well, I have to confess, I have come to you in an artificial body. This is not my native form. I am a silicon-based life form."

"I know lots of people whose *social* life depends on silicone, but . . ." The audience laughed. "But what do you mean by 'silicon-based life form?' "

"Earth people are made of carbon compounds to a large extent — your DNA and whatnot. But my biochemistry is based on a different chemical element than carbon: silicon. You make computer chips and solar power cells from it."

"I'm ashamed to say that I *barely* passed chemistry in high school. But in your case, the important thing is that you have a different native form?"

"That's right."

"What do you look like?"

"It's hard to describe because there aren't exactly similar creatures on Earth. I think the most similar creature is the butterfly."

"Hence the name taken from a butterfly species!"

"That's right."

"Do you have colorful wings? Can you fly through space?"

"Something like wings, but I can't exactly fly with them. Unfortunately, I am going to have to become a little mysterious about more details. All of this is connected to my starship technology, although I know that is hard to imagine at this point. When we agree on the contract for the starship technology and I deliver the goods, I will reveal everything to you. I can't give away the store before we have a contract. And I would give it away piece by piece if I told you more, because my technology and I have blended, in a manner of speaking. To tell you more about myself is to begin teaching you the science and technologies that I have for sale."

"Wow. This is fascinating and I'm a little lost. But we'll talk more with Metalmark after the commercial break. Stay with us!"

With the television muted, Pres. Jackson looked around the table. "Brief comments, anyone?"

Jon West (CIA) spoke up, "He confirmed our report from an Orlando airport security officer that Metalmark's body is artificial. Our analysts suggest that he is an artificial personality, crafted to appeal to a mass audience."

Commerce Sec. Cosgrove said, "That's damn good craft. He knows the kind of patter and rhythm to charm TV audiences, the mayor of New York, Jayno, everyone he's met. So are we dealing with . . . an android?"

The president said, "He's remarkably like a human personality. I've never heard of any artificial intelligence to compare with this being. To me he seems to have a presence and identity, self-consciousness and self-interest. Political consciousness, if you will. Can a machine speak to people in such a heart-to-heart voice?"

CIA chief West admitted, "Although that's hard to address objectively, I know what you mean. The cutting edge of synthetic thinking software today has a spark of that now and then, but can't sustain the illusion. A superior civilization might achieve that technology, and maybe it could look like this."

Pres. Jackson said, "I was *on Jayno* during my campaign. That appearance helped me get *here*, but I wasn't that good."

Sec. of State Peter Currin said, "Well, you can marvel that this bear can dance at all, but I don't think he dances very skillfully when it comes to international politics. When he touched his lips to that cross, he just kissed the goodwill of the Islamic world good-bye. The Al-Jazeera news broadcasts will show that kiss to all of their viewers, and it will become *very* difficult for his 'Food from Stones' program to start up in any Muslim nation."

The commercial break ended and Jayno's band was back on the screen, so they resumed watching.

M

"We're back with Metalmark!" Jayno's proclamation was met with more applause. To Metalmark she said, "So you came here by yourself in a starship from . . . . . where?"

"Well, I don't know what it's called here. It's a little star too dim for the human eye to see without a telescope. Most of the stars in the Galaxy are little, compared with your Sun. I travel from star to star."

"And it's been a 90-year trip?! You don't look so old."

"My appearance is a presentation for you. It's an artistic expression of friendliness."

"How old are you?"

Almost imperceptible pause. "About five hundred fifty years."

"The things you must know!"

"I have acquired many survival skills. The package I am offering is really nothing more than that. So I hope that we can come to an agreement and I can begin to teach you what I've learned."

Jayno said, "Well, I earnestly hope that our leaders in the UN will negotiate a satisfactory deal, because as you say, it must be a win-win relationship. Thank you so much for coming. I hope you will come back to the show when the deal is signed and go into more fascinating details. And good luck with your tour to promote the 'Food from Rocks' program!"

"Thank you for having me on your show," said Metalmark. "It's been a dream come true."

Jayno said, "And next: the Space Monkey Punks from Japan do their new hit song 'Two-body Orbit'."

Dr. Steve Simmons was watching Metalmark's appearance on *Jayno* with a group of ten scientists and engineers at NASA headquarters in Washington, DC. They were scattered about a conference room, some sitting around a table, some lounging in distant seats. Some of them took notes, stretched, or seemed to gaze into space rather than watching the giant TV screen. At some points in the show some members of the group had blurted out comments or started to make declarations like intellectual prima donnas, but Admin. Krainak had gently yet ruthlessly silenced every interruption in order to maintain continued viewing until the credits rolled at the end.

Then Krainak said, "Our visitor is an android that has provided several points of information, any of which may be false. I'm going to draft a list of factoids that I got from hearing him." He went to a whiteboard at the front of the room and began the list with a black marker: "Metalmark: he (it) singular – never mentions other beings like himself – yet says his species must spawn – asexual reproduction?"

One of the astrobiologists, Ray Sheffield, Ph. D., said, "You mean he might spawn like an amoeba or yeast cell, or bacteria that can reproduce asexually *or* sexually?"

Krainak and others had soon covered the whiteboard with a labyrinth of linked possibilities to be analyzed in view of the true/false declarations by Metalmark. Simmons thought that they were like Wile E. Coyote, dashing out from the edge of a vast canyon but standing on nothing, about to crash to the ground as soon as they took a good look down.

Simmons decided that he would trust the one off-hand remark about Metalmark's last stellar visit. He had wireless Internet service for his laptop, so he searched for more details about Ross 154. According to the list of nearest stars, his hypothetical candidate for Metalmark's last port of call was indeed too dim for naked eye viewing. That agreed with Metalmark's statement to Jayno. What else could Simmons infer if he assumed that Metalmark was truthful?

Metalmark said that his species spawned approximately every 90 years. If it had been 90 years since his hypothetical spawning visit to Ross 154, located 9.7 light years away, then his average speed through space would be about 11% of the speed of light. That speed would require an advanced technology to achieve, but did not seem outrageously high to Dr. Simmons; such a speed was consistent with physics as we know it, in light of Einstein's well-confirmed theory of Special Relativity.

Administrator Krainak called a halt to the brainstorming session at the whiteboard. "I think we need a spokesman to hold some meetings with Metalmark, if we can get access to him, and someone to keep the talk shows focused on the scientific importance of Metalmark's visit. *Steve Simmons*, because you identified Metalmark's spacecraft in its approach to Earth, you have had a high visibility in the tabloids. I'd like to ask you to serve as a NASA spokesman and convey to the public some of the conclusions that we have reached this evening."

Dr. Simmons had instantly brought his attention back to the whiteboard when he heard Krainak call on him. However the whiteboard was an undecipherable diagram to him, and he had no hope of reconstructing the logic behind it, since he had been immersed in his own speculations. Now, caught like a daydreaming student in class by the NASA administrator, Simmons' only honest recourse would be to admit he had spaced out and beg forgiveness. But another face-saving impulse seized him.

Dr. Simmons said, "Well, I think that the salient points of Metalmark's appearance tonight were lost on our group. Our observations of his trajectory point back to an origin in the constellation Sagittarius. The nearest star in that direction is Ross 154, an M type dwarf. He said he spawns about every 90 years, and if that's true, the 9.7 light years from Ross 154 to here would have required a speed of only about 11% of the speed of light. This is a useful constraint on his technology, and I think we should bluff a bit and probe him for a bit more revelation of his technology."

Krainak remarked, "That's quite a leap, but you make it sound very plausible. I think I've picked the right spokesman for the group."

Dr. Ray Sheffield put in, "All of us have points to make. We should probably constitute this workshop as an IAU colloquium and publish a proceedings volume with a paper from each participant. I nominate Steve Simmons for editor of the book."

Krainak replied, "Yes, that will be fine. But let's try to bring in Metalmark, rather than pursuing hypothetical contingencies. As Steve has shown, we can use Metalmark's statements for traction against the problem of understanding him."

In Iran astronomy was very popular. Since ancient times it had been a pleasant intellectual pastime, spiritually inspiring and approved by the imams, who taught that celestial phenomena are proofs of the existence of God. The Holy Koran said that there were "seven heavens," and the traditional interpretation of this was that the heavens are the Sun, the Moon, and the planets Mercury, Venus, Mars, Jupiter, and Saturn.

For decades, in the southern Iranian town of Saadat Shahr, people would make sure not to miss Friday prayers, when the imam would give an update about which stars, nebulae, planets, or meteor showers would be visible in the night sky during the coming week. Even though the town was a modest village, people had contributed money to build an observatory. If an unusual astronomical event should manifest itself on a particular night, many people, especially the young and intelligent, would come to the domed observatory, clutching their copies of the astronomy magazine *Nojum*, to look through the telescope at the celestial wonders. Stargazing was also considered a permissible social activity for young men and women to enjoy together. In Iran, many astronomers were women, in greater proportions than in western nations. Since the ancient times of Omar Khayyam, legendary poet and astronomer, Iran had been proud of its astronomical accomplishments.

Hassan Khani got his uncle's permission to bring his seventeen-year-old sister Fariba to the observatory on Thursday night. The Metalmark spacecraft was never visible in the sky over Iran – it constantly orbited the earth above the nation of Ecuador – but they had heard about the necklace of satellites placed around the Earth by Metalmark, and they wanted to search for them. Hassan was sure that he had seen one the night before, as he reclined on the roof of his uncle's house and looked up at the dark, star-crowded sky. Because the slow rotation of the Milky Way did not carry the satellites of Metalmark's necklace with it, a determined skywatcher could see the background stars pass the geostationary alien satellites, and feel the chill of cosmic awesomeness when he spied one of them.

On this Thursday night in this small, dusty town, 390 miles south of Tehran, Hassan and Fariba joined two dozen other youths, climbing the narrow stairs to the second story of the domed building, where the telescope perched on its mounting axles. The girls kept their hair properly covered, and wore long, traditional dresses, but they laughed and joked with one another like teenagers everywhere.

Hassan immediately asked the observatory director, Babak Kabiri, "Please show us a Metalmark satellite!" Kabiri smiled with appreciation that his audience for this night was informed and keen to see the most interesting of cosmic wonders on view. They all took turns viewing, and indeed, through the eyepiece, the fixed Metalmark satellites appeared to cruise majestically past the background stars.

It was an evening of peaceful freedom from the relentless polemics of the imams about the evils of the West and its threats to their mother country. Their hobby was a haven from the problems in their society, politics and religion, and Hassan thanked God for it.

It was a shock the next evening at the mosque for Hassan to learn what the imam had to say about Metalmark. After the usual prayers, the Imam made his commentary on current events. "You have heard that God's earth has been visited by a being from the stars. We had hoped that he would be a servant of Allah, welcome in our houses. Yet he has proved to be as evil as the infidels of the West. He comes to Earth with no thoughts but to buy the sacred heavens to defile with his spawning, and no plan but to sell his advanced knowledge and technology to the western nations. He has watched their television broadcasts, learned to behave like them, and only wants to give them more tools to gain advantage over the Islamic nations, and to fortify the abomination of Israel.

"A Vatican soothsayer appeared with Metalmark on TV, said a prayer over him and blessed him, and Metalmark kissed the cross that was presented to him. These displays are an offense to Allah, and every good Muslim should know that he is an enemy like no other in modern times. All of Islam prays that his barter to possess and defile the sacred celestial lights should fail, God willing!"

Hassan was bitterly disappointed. But more than that, he felt betrayed and offended that his beloved hobby, astronomy, had been the means of luring him into admiration of Metalmark — a seduction into impiety. He knew that his sister had sensed his admiration for Metalmark last night when they went to the observatory, and that was even more embarrassing: she would learn he had been deceived. Any young man might be embarrassed for his younger sister to learn of such a failing by her older brother, but the failing was more embarrassing to Hassan for a special reason: he and Fariba were orphans, dependent upon their uncle, and Hassan had become the spiritual guardian of Fariba, her tutor in the faith.

Hassan had envied Metalmark, a being who had the power to place the wondrous satellites in the sacred heavens, a being that he now knew was a jinnee allied with the infidel West against all that Hassan revered. Like Aladdin in the *Thousand and One Nights*, Hassan began to plot ways to entrap and destroy the jinnee Metalmark.

Let it be said that Hassan was special: upon hearing the words of the imams across the Islamic world that Friday, thousands of young men burned with indignation, hundreds sought an imam at the end of prayers to offer their strength in confronting the menace from space. But mere dozens were angered to the extent that Hassan was, so that they not only sought the imam at the end of prayers, but earnestly asked him if there was anything they could do to defend Islam from this abomination.

Hassan Khani was one of the few that inspired an imam with his demeanor and passion to consider a special jihad.

Imam Ali could see Hassan's agitation and indignation. "Your anger is blessed."

Hassan said, "I have trained with the Islamic Youth Brigade. I know how to shoot a gun and I am a good fighter. Is there something I can do?"

Imam Ali replied, "I have an acquaintance in Pakistan who is very influential there. If you would like to meet him, I believe there might be a place for you in a brigade. I will call him on your behalf."

III

THE UPROAR IN the Islamic press that followed Metalmark's appearance on Jayno was as strident as Sec. Currin predicted. The outrage in the Muslim nations was almost as intense as the 2006 uproar over irreverent cartoons of the Prophet Muhammad. Taken aback, Metalmark asked to return to his lander, and Sec.-Gen. Shankar flew him back to Florida on a UN charter. Metalmark passed through the perimeter of the US Military Police guards without comment and the shifting solar energy collector panels moved to let him enter his craft.

A few minutes later he emerged and asked to return to the UN in New York. Again his request was granted and he was soon back in the UN guest quarters, secluded.

M

Liu Xueli was having dinner at her apartment, listening to her favorite music. She liked bands like Metal Orchids, Quantum Ax, and Ion Torch, with their electronic sound effects and ductile guitar chords that flirted with the edge of psychedelic riffs forbidden by the government. She had some MP3s downloaded from furtive websites of live concerts in which the guitarists went over the line and carried her into stratospheric transitions of feed-back ecstasy, but she only played them with the private headset. For now, Ion Torch burned through the boredom of her chicken dinner with industrial ignition.

The phone rang after she had finished. "Hello, Daughter," her mother greeted her. "That rumor that you told me about was very peculiar. After I asked many people who should have known about it, I could only conclude that none of them had heard it. The lunar program scientists had discussed Metalmark's orbiting starship, but they didn't decide to change their plans to send Shenzhou 16 to the Moon. This is what the chief program scientist and the director of the science and technology commission said."

Xueli's breath caught in her throat, and she could say nothing.

Her mother went on, "Nevertheless, the rumor has now begun to run on its own legs. The poor photos of Metalmark's spacecraft are arousing curiosity, and Metalmark has revealed his commercial offer to the Security Council. He claims to have technology of great value in that spacecraft, and the people I asked about the rumor have begun to question the space scientists' decision. The Moon is looking less attractive to visit than Metalmark's vehicle, especially since he is away from it, globe-trotting.

"Your uncle particularly liked your rumor. I didn't tell him where I heard it yet, but he helped me inquire about it and consequently it spread widely. He told me that he had heard a similar rumor that the USA was about to secretly visit Metalmark's vehicle. Still, I didn't tell him who started it, since you didn't tell me its source."

Xueli said, "I do not know the person who first told it, as I overheard it in a conversation between other people. At least that is the best I can remember. I may have even . . . dreamed it. You remember, Mother, how I used to dream when I was a little girl about being the mythical Queen of Heaven? The more I try to remember where I first heard this rumor, the more it seems that my memory may be playing tricks on me, and maybe it was only a dream. That happens in one's 'old age', I am told."

Her mother didn't laugh. "If this rumor started in one of your dreams, it would be much like your dreams of Olympic gold." Then, as she had said to Xueli so many times before the little girl's gymnastics competitions, Xueli's mother said, "the value of a dream is in its results."

And as Xueli had said to her mother before winning each one of her medals, she said, "Thank you for sending me on the road to my dreams."

With the help of the space-traveling nations, Metalmark and some staffers from the UN Office for Outer Space Affairs (UNOOSA) provided the report on future economic value of Mercury and Triton that he had promised to the Security Council. The UN deliberated. That is, all of the other members of the UN General Assembly came forward to present their governments' positions. The western nations approved of Metalmark's promises of technological advancement, but now the Islamic nations voiced suspicion and opprobrium of Metalmark's relationship with the Vatican and Christians, and the fact that the UN was considering selling him the sacred heavens. Consequently the debate became unfocused and rambling, seemingly interminable. And the UN tradition of diplomatic cautiousness came to the fore, throwing the outcome into uncertainty.

Against this backdrop, Metalmark consulted with UN world hunger experts and formulated his "Food from Stones" technology. A prototype package of the active ingredient was emitted by Metalmark's starship, and it parachuted down spectacularly into New York's Central Park.

A "Food from Stones" demonstration was staged in a pavilion in front of the UN building. Some rough chunks of limestone were placed into a bowl and covered with water. Metalmark's nanotechnology powder was stirred into the water. Then the bowl was placed in sunlight for a day. It was stirred every hour throughout the demonstration. After 24 hours the stones had softened into a watery mush, and some UN nutritionists volunteered to taste it. They reported that it was somewhat like a tapioca pudding. Chemical analysis showed that much of the calcium carbonate in the limestone had been made to react with the water, forming several nutritious carbohydrate molecules (sugars) and some nontoxic calcium residue. Nothing harmful was detected in the mixture. It was as nutritious as bread.

The UN nutritionists were ebullient. They began experiments with drying the "rock pudding" into flour to make cakes. And Metalmark showed them that his powder ingredient of microscopic chemical reactors was capable of multiplying in the mixture, so that 10% of every produced pudding could be used to produce another whole pudding, just by adding the 10% saved from one pudding to the mix for the next.

Sec.-Gen. Shankar began contacting the representatives of famine-stricken nations. The southern African country of Malawi was a prime candidate after many years of drought had killed and sickened millions of its citizens.

Dr. Steve Simmons was completely swamped with his editing duties for the conference proceedings about the NASA Metalmark analysis meeting he had attended. His job was to obtain a publishable manuscript from each participant of the meeting he had joined at NASA the evening of Metalmark's Jayno appearance. Fortunately he had been befriended by Dr. Ray Sheffield, who actually remembered most of the debates that took place while Simmons ruminated.

Simmons and Sheffield were in Simmons' new office in the basement of the NASA Goddard Space Flight Center's Building 21, a blockish modernist building with brick facades alternating with tall window panels, none of which lit Dr. Simmons' basement office. The scientists were setting up Simmons' new desktop computer. Sheffield said, "It would be really surreal if we could get Metalmark to write an article in this conference proceedings! Even though he claims that he has to hide his merchandise, maybe we could entice him to pursue another publicity channel. Imagine what it would do for our careers to publish the first book about the Search for Extraterrestrial Intelligence containing a chapter by an alien!"

Simmons laughed. He was still a bit sore at Sheffield for sticking him with the editing job, but had to admit to himself that the penalty was deserved. "That's creative, to be sure," he replied. "Let's get Krainak to sign a letter of invitation, and send the summaries of the papers we are waiting for. If Metalmark would even give us a terse Forward or Preface, it could lend some authority to these speculative ramblings." They started a word processing program and made up a rough draft of the appeal to Metalmark.

Within a day, the letter and summaries were faxed to the UN Sec.-Gen.'s office.

Metalmark was conveyed in a UN limousine to the tony, high-rise building on the upper east side of Manhattan in which Sec.-Gen. Shankar and his wife Uma lived. The decrepit official UN Sec.-Gen.'s residence was undergoing seemingly endless renovations, so the Shankars had moved here. Ilana Lindler accompanied

Metalmark out of the limo, surrounded by the flashes of paparazzi cameras in the evening darkness, and quickly passed through the security guard station at the front door of the building.

By now Ilana had become accustomed to Metalmark's manipulative silent behavior. As the two of them rode up in the elevator to the Shankars' floor, the alien was his usual disarming persona. He said nothing, but he spent most of the time turning his head about, inspecting everything that was new to him as a visitor to Earth, at intervals emitting a surprised, "Hm!" to make his companion imagine that he was noticing something for the first time, some trivial detail of the surroundings that a human being took for granted although it was new to him. Less frequently he would make eye contact and smile shyly, lowering his glance as if to politely acknowledge the caretaker role of his guide.

But Ilana knew by now that he was quite familiar with the interiors of elevators. She was no longer taken in by his deflection of her curiosity. But his perennial excuse of reticence to protect his stock in trade was wearing thin for her. Was he hiding more than merchandise? She would watch him to investigate this question as they attended the evening's social at the Shankars' home.

The elevator doors opened and Ilana led Metalmark to number 842. This door opened into a small foyer in which smiling statues of the Buddha and the elephant-headed god Ganesha greeted the visitors. Wonderful aromas of incense and curries and other spices wafted into Ilana's appreciative nose, and she felt uplifted by the anticipation of the evening to come. Ragas by Ravi Shankar (a *very* distant relative, Sanjeev had told her) were barely audible behind the voices of some earlier arrivals, guests who were making admiring sounds upon visiting the flat for the first time.

Metalmark made a show of inspecting the household gods, and deigned to allow, "I did not know that the Shankars are religious. These are fine instantiations."

As Ilana and Metalmark turned toward the living room, Uma came forth to greet them. She was wearing a lovely sari made of silk that was tie-dyed like a multi-colored Kandinsky masterpiece, and she was radiant. "Ilana, it is always a pleasure to welcome you, and even more this evening with your otherworldly companion!"

"Thank you," said Ilana, stepping aside to present the guest of honor.

"Madam Shankar," Metalmark said, taking Uma's hand for a moment and making his disarming little smile and a slight bow. "I'm most grateful for your hospitality. Already I am enjoying your advanced artistic sensibilities for sculpture, textiles and auditory compositions. The Secretary-General often mentions your essential role in his life and work, and I was intensely anticipating to meet the individual who has that powerful relationship with such an important human being as my friend Sanjeev."

Uma smiled, having acquired a great tolerance for flattery in the diplomacy circles. "Thank you and welcome. I'm glad the decor is pleasant for you. Sanjeev is a dear but I am disappointed that he didn't arrange sooner for you to visit our home."

"I am at fault," Metalmark said. "Until the successful launch of the 'Food from Stones' program, I was preoccupied, and there was that dreadful misunderstanding by the Islamic nations . . . to tell the truth I have not felt available for the entertainment of socializing. I hope that my relations with the people of your planet are now on the mend after a rocky start!"

Uma's expression showed some admiration for Metalmark's command of the art of spin. "This brings me to a question I had in mind." She took Metalmark's hand and tugged him alongside her so that they would make an entrance arm in arm together into the living room for the guests to behold. "You've seen our little shrines to the traditional gods. But there is a more enlightened perspective on spiritual or otherworldly beings in our modern age, and especially after your own visit to Earth. Have you yourself ever visited Earth before, or are our gods really dim memories of visits by other star-traveling advanced beings like you?"

Metalmark replied, "This is my first visit to Earth, and almost certainly the first by any being of my species. However, I can't provide any information regarding your quite plausible deogenic process - if that's a word."

They walked together toward five other guests who stood across the living room, holding cocktails. The room had large windows through which the guests could enjoy the eighth-floor view of the skyline, lit by the Moon as well as the myriad lights of the unsleeping metropolis. Comfortable, rather brightly-colored furniture, and artworks from India gave the room atmosphere just short of extravagance. On a sideboard there was a buffet being prepared by some caterers.

Uma introduced Metalmark to those who had not met him before. The Deputy Sec.-Gen. Bernard Molyneux had brought his wife Solange, who beamed mutely at the opportunity to meet a visitor from interstellar space. The Assembly

President Sirpa Hakkinen greeted Metalmark warmly. Her husband Klaus congratulated Metalmark on the good publicity of the "Food from Stones" program, and expressed admiration for the alien visitor's quick selection of such an appropriate good-will program. US ambassador Paul Kirk was in the presence of Metalmark for the fifth time, so he could think of nothing original to say in greeting. There was an awkward pause which everyone knew should be filled by still another invitation for Metalmark to visit the White House.

Uma said, "Sanjeev is on the way. I know him well, and his arrival will coincide with the announcement by the caterers that they are ready. I'm joking – he works too hard, and certainly deserves some good curry; he is such a globe-trotter that he does not put on any weight!"

Solange Molyneux said, "I would love to try some of Metalmark's pudding made from limestone! Is there any on the buffet?"

Uma smiled triumphantly. "I made sure that there would be a little for dessert. It is especially good with a selection of spices, like cinnamon and cardamon."

Sirpa Hakkinen said, "Metalmark, I feel sure that the UN will soon accept your trade proposal, and it will transport our civilization across a threshold of advancement that so many people have dreamed of for centuries! I mean, one of my first memories is looking up at the stars with my father and asking him what they were. And he told me that they were suns far away, probably with worlds around them like Earth, and there might be beings looking back at us from there! I am so excited to meet you and find that he was right!"

Metalmark said, "I understand your excitement that your parent was insightful. Many kinds of beings that you imagined looking at you from the stars do exist, and I will be able to provide you with a sizeable database of inhabited star systems, if my trade proposal is accepted. The Galaxy is large, however, so I have only a partial catalog of its contents to offer. The value will nevertheless be large. I imagine that you could profit from knowing the locations of your nearest neighbors in interstellar space."

His listeners' heads nodded appreciatively. The conversation was taking on welcome cosmic dimensions, and they felt privileged with insider intimations.

Bernard Molyneux said, "One of my first memories is being hungry and having a nice breakfast of Belgian Waffles with my mother and father. Metalmark, I imagine that your 'Food from Stones' program will make such memories of family and nourishment possible for many poor people. There are many that are quite destitute in spite of the global advance of technology. Who knows how that may effect the course of our future history?"

Ilana said, "History has changed radically from what I was taught it would be. My first memories are from childhood in East Germany, before it was united with West Germany. They still taught children there that Marxism was transforming the world and communism was the final phase in evolution of Mankind! But my family was one of the first to emigrate to the USA after the Berlin Wall fell."

Metalmark looked thoughtful. "I think my earliest memory would seem very strange to you. I believe I realized that I was chewing on a rock, surrounded by miles of tunnels that I had made through the crust of a long forgotten planet. I guess I realized that I was a miner of some sort, and came to the consciousness of my nature. I remember deciding that I had to find out what my goal in life should be . . ."

At that moment, the front door opened and Sanjeev arrived. The spell that had started to unlock Metalmark's origin was broken, and the caterers announced that the buffet was ready.

The Sec.-Gen. said, "Hello, friends, you should not have waited for me! By all means, eat. Except my friend Metalmark, let me give you a message while the others are filling their plates. Hello, Uma, my love."

Uma herded the guests to the stack of dishes and Sanjeev took Metalmark into his home office. "I got a nice invitation for you from NASA. A group of the scientists are writing a book about their speculations on intelligent life in the Galaxy, and they have invited you to write a chapter or preface or contribute some section of your own devising. It seems to me that you could do this without revealing trade secrets. And it would be a good opportunity to cultivate relationships with the elite scientists that could help support your trade proposal and the technological programs that you wanted to pursue."

Metalmark said, "Your advice is my best guide. What do I have to do?"

"They wrote a letter which we can answer, telling them that you agree to the writing. Then you can meet them if you want or talk by teleconference to clear up what they need. I'll assign some staff to help you."

Metalmark looked around Sanjeev's office. "Do you spend a great deal of time in offices, both here and at the UN?"

"Quite a lot, but I never seem to finish anything because I have to travel to some new crisis location and try to resolve it. I was just away for a week in Bangladesh, Thailand and Myanmar before you arrived. I was trying to set up relief services for the flooded typhoon victims. The week before, I was trying to stop the Iranians from switching their nuclear power program to bomb production. The week before that I was trying to get AIDS medicines to several African countries. I seem to stumble from one mess to another most of the time. If I had a few weeks to sit in my office and catch up with business, I might finish something, but it never happens."

"When Ilana and I entered your home, I noticed the gods. Religion is a very sensitive matter on Earth, I have learned. I hope that my actions on the Jayno show did not offend you."

Sanjeev smiled. "Don't worry. I am not narrow-minded about spirituality. I saw that you were trying to embrace fearful believers and banish their fears. You did well! It was no fault of yours that some are fanatical, determined to find a reason to reject you. You represent progress for everyone on Earth, but the fanatics are afraid of progress because it transports us away from the triumphs that they had long ago in a darker age. Be determined. I believe you will prevail because you are good."

On the desk were some family photos of a young man and woman. "Are these your children?" Metalmark asked.

"Yes, Vikram and Ajitha are almost grown up. They are both away at university. They are very important to me, two wonderful people that I can help, even though it is a small victory compared to global war, terrorism and epidemics."

"I am keeping you from eating. Let's join the party," Metalmark suggested.

They joined the others at the dining room table. Sanjeev filled his plate with delicious breads and curries, and sat by Uma. Metalmark sat at the head of the table, with a dish in front of him that held an arrangement of colorful tropical flowers, bird-of-paradise, red ginger flower, yellow heliconia, a lotus blossom, and phalaenopsis and lady slipper orchids.

Uma asked, "Is it tedious on your long trips in space?"

"Well, it is lonely, but interesting. There is always something to hear and see. Pulsars pop on the radio bands and flash light. I look at the giant supernova bubbles with my radio telescope, and the faraway radio galaxies are slowly exploding. Gamma-ray bursts explode about once a day from somewhere – you never know where – and they go right through everything so sometimes I have to make repairs. I hit a lot of stardust, so much that it makes a constant hissing, so sometimes I have to repair damage from that, too. My favorite thing to pass the time is listen to radio and watch TV, and I did plenty of that on the way here. I was rather busy, I guess."

Ilana asked, "When you watched the TV shows, did you imagine how it would be when you landed and met us? So much has happened, and I guess you could learn a lot from our news broadcasts or from biographical or historical programs, but how could you foresee our world? It amazes me that you are so adept in society."

Uma smiled with pride at Ilana's question. Metalmark responded, "I devoted much thought and time to imitating the people I saw on those shows. My imagination was incomplete, but thank you for the compliment."

Klaus said, "Well, you certainly were a hit on the Jayno show!"

Metalmark continued, "As I told her, I have watched her show since it was first broadcast on the NTC network. By the way, on NTC now, they are saying that Jayno's guest tonight will be Dr. Steve Simmons, a NASA scientist who discovered images of my ship approaching Earth, using a satellite."

Ilana asked him, "Can you see TV broadcasts right now?"

"I sense many channels as a habit, and usually my attention is not on them, but I notice if something interesting or important to me is broadcast."

"That's amazing," murmured Solange.

Sanjeev said, "Dr. Simmons has just invited Metalmark to contribute an article in a book that NASA is about to publish."

"Congratulations!" said Uma.

"Thank you for the good wishes," replied Metalmark. " I will need them after the fiasco with the Islamic nations. I was not a hit with them."

Sanjeev said, "Don't be hard on yourself about that. I started in public service in Calcutta, where the Hindu/Muslim tension was very strong. It was very difficult to negotiate with the parties of the two religions to achieve any progress for the city."

Uma said, "Sanjeev always worked so hard to find common ground. There was always something that the opposite sides shared, like the well-being of the children. He was working such long hours to get the public support, and the support of the land reforms minister and the minister of state for Sunderbans development. He raised funds from the rich software companies in Bangalore.

Finally they got the super-specialty hospital: the 500-bed hospital and medical college built at Mukundapur to serve Calcutta!"

Sanjeev said, "From the city I worked up to the Bengal province public service, and always there was conflict. But again the key was finding where everyone agreed."

Uma said, "And Mother Teresa helped you get to the province government, because of your work on the Calcutta hospital."

"Yes. So from there I entered national service, but then I helped the UN AIDS workers, bridging the gaps in health care. Hindus and Muslims both had bad feelings about the epidemic, but behind the feelings, they wanted to help the sick. So I found ways to encourage cooperation and treatment without blaming the Hindu victims for unclean practices or the Muslim victims for immoral acts. One can work for healing if one avoids accusations and stresses the mercy of God, and we fought the epidemic and saved so many lives. That is what the UN can achieve – uniting people by appealing to their humanity."

Bernard Molyneux said, "That's why you were the right person to become the Secretary-General. You met the most awful challenge with reconciliation for healing."

Sanjeev said, "And that's why you give us so much hope, Metalmark. Your 'Food from Stones' program is exactly aligned with the UN movement to help the most helpless people. I am sure we can find common ground despite this initial misunderstanding with the Muslims. They have always joined with me to care for the weakest people, and you are giving us such a powerful tool to feed people who have nothing. I can't believe that they will reject your invention to defeat hunger in the world."

Metalmark said, "You are a kind person, Sanjeev. I hope you are right. You know human beings better than I, to be sure. But I see evidence that many humans are more shrewd than kind. For example, Amb. Yang Wei is a very sharp negotiator. If there are people like him in the Islamic nations, they may try to gain advantages more than to help the hungry, poor people."

Uma said, "Amb. Yang is a very interesting person, and as you say he is very good at bargaining for advantages for his country. He is also connected to a family that is very important in China. He has a sister who is an important party official, and a niece who was an Olympic gymnast and is now in astronaut training."

Sanjeev said, "These are very competitive people. But in the new era of

Metalmark's technology, I think there will be advantages enough for everybody."

Ilana listened to this with a warm feeling. She had always enjoyed her covert CIA position covering the UN because she could report to the US government what good people were working at the UN. Her report tonight of her evening with Metalmark would also include the Sec.-Gen.'s noble motives for global progress and peace. She felt that Sanjeev was the finest Sec.-Gen. in many decades.

Solange could no longer overcome the combination of sympathy and curiosity. She said, "Metalmark, I know that you cannot eat Earth food – I heard the Jayno show – but I feel sorry that you cannot share with us. What do you eat? Can you tell us or is it a trade secret?"

Metalmark replied, "The precise composition of my diet would be a part of the technology contract, but I don't mind telling friends how it works. My body uses a high-density fuel. There is a supply in my shuttle in Florida, which is why I return there about once a week to replenish my internal supply. Please don't pass this along. It would be inconvenient if I could not visit the shuttle, so it's best that no one with ill intent should know."

Klaus said, "So you are like an astronaut visiting an alien world. I never thought of it from your perspective. This is a foodless desert for you."

"That is very sympathetic," said Metalmark. "So far, this planet has been one of my more benign environments for a trade mission."

"May it continue to be!" Bernard said, raising his wine glass in a toast to success. Amb. Kirk added, "Here, here!" The others joined in, and Metalmark smiled his little smile.

Bernard added, "And we wish you success on the 'Food from Stones' campaign. Where will you start it?"

Metalmark said, "Sanjeev advised me that Calcutta might be a good starting point. Many people there are very poor, but limestone is easy to obtain. And the people have a lot of enthusiasm, so maybe we will get a spirited reaction to our presentations. From there Bangladesh is very close. Then we can travel to a few more places like Malawi, where food is hard to produce."

M

"We're back," said Jayno, "and our guest is Dr. Steve Simmons, the NASA scientist who found images of Metalmark's spaceship. He has a very interesting theory about where Metalmark came from." The audience applauded with some enthusiasm. "If you just joined us, before the break Dr. Simmons explained how he got the pictures of Metalmark's spaceship. Now please tell us where you think Metalmark came from."

"I can't say that we know that with certainty. However, we could determine his direction of motion before the closest point to the Sun. It was in the direction of the constellation Sagittarius. That way is the center of the giant disk of stars that make up the Milky Way Galaxy, our home galaxy."

"Okay, why is that important?"

"Well, the center of our Galaxy contains very densely concentrated stars – more per volume of space – than the outer regions where we live. And these are also the older stars. So we might expect that it's more likely that intelligent beings could evolve in a part of the Galaxy with lots of stars, and that they could be more technologically advanced than we are. They've had longer to develop intelligence and build advanced civilizations."

"I think I see what you're driving at, then," said Jayno. "It would make sense for a being with advanced technology like Metalmark to come to us from an area of outer space where we know that advanced beings are likely to be. And you discovered the evidence that this is so."

The audience applauded politely.

"So tell us about the star that you believe he visited last."

"Okay, as I said, stars are pretty dispersed in space out here in our part of the Galaxy. The nearest ones are many light years away. And there's only one nearby star, relatively speaking, that is in the constellation Sagittarius. All of the other stars in that constellation and area of the sky are much more distant. If we assume that Metalmark visits stars – that it's his preference, rather than voyaging through empty starless space – then this is the only star out there that is close to us. It is the 7th closest to us of all stars, a faint star called Ross 154, a little less than ten light years away. An astronomer named Frank Ross discovered it in 1925. He was cataloging stars that were faint, but had a measurable sideways motion across the sky, and this star was number 154 in his catalog."

"Does this star have anything interesting about it?"

"Sure. Although it's faint, 2,500 times fainter than the Sun, it experiences sudden brightening episodes. Imagine if the Sun occasionally became two or three times as bright in just a few minutes for hours. Ross 154 is not a steady star, and that's what it does. It's a type of star called a flare star. We don't know how to predict the flare-ups, or exactly why they occur when they do, but they have been observed lots of times."

"That would make life complicated if there were intelligent beings on a planet orbiting Ross 154."

"It certainly would."

"Are there any possible beings there?"asked Jayno.

"We don't know, but scientists did listen to Ross 154 with a sensitive radio telescope years ago. They detected no evidence of broadcasts from intelligent beings like us. But maybe that's because life is impossible there, due to the flare-ups."

"Or maybe they just don't make any radio broadcasts these days."

"Right," said Simmons "But there is a big difference between Ross 154 and our solar system. If there is a planet like ours, inhabited by beings like us, then it has to be very much closer to the star than we are to the Sun. It has to be in a close orbit, within a very narrow range of possible distances from its sun. That seems unlikely. Why would the planet exist at just the right orbit? But then if the star flares up, it's a much bigger change in the radiation the planet gets from its sun. That makes it very hard to envision people like us tolerating the conditions in that solar system. My own guess is that it is uninhabited. Maybe it was just a boring stop-over for Metalmark, with no opportunity to meet anyone."

"Well, he didn't regale us on the show with any stories about it when he was here. And you said the star was 2000 times dimmer than the Sun?"

"Yes, it must be a dark place to visit. Of course he said on your show that he is in need of planets for his species to spawn. Maybe the bright lights don't matter so much."

"More romance in the soft light?"

"A flickering fire, that's for sure!"

"I think it's amazing that you can figure this much out from so few facts!"

"We can speculate based on known astronomy, but we hope to talk with Metalmark at length, and work on the book somehow with him, if he'll agree. Of course that depends upon the UN finishing its agreement with him so that we become paying customers."

"Are you in favor of the sale of two planetary bodies to Metalmark, in return for his technology?"

"As a scientist, my personal view is that it's a small price to pay. There are still dozens of planetary bodies in our solar system for ourselves, whereas it seems like a very great potential advance in our technology, in so many dimensions, if we get the benefits of his deal. I'm hoping the UN takes his offer."

"Don't we all? Everybody?" The audience applauded enthusiastically.

Hassan Khani bid his sister, uncle and home town goodbye and boarded a truck that would take him to a training center in Pakistan. Imam Ali's letter to his friend there had indeed succeeded in placing Hassan in an elite brigade there. After a few days of travel he saw the minarets of Karachi.

The UN delegation for the "Food from Stones" campaign was going to consist of the Sec.-Gen., Metalmark, the Sec. for food relief, and some of the nutritionists in that division. Ilana also was needed to coordinate the officials' appearances with the food production and ceremonial tasting events, and some PR personnel were also going. It was important to get advance notices out to the media in Calcutta, so that newspapers, TV and bloggers would show up.

Ilana worked the phones to bring this about. But it was also vital to assure that local city officials provided tight security, because West Bengal state was a dangerous region of the world where extremists or separatist paramilitary bands sometimes attacked people. Ilana emphasized to the UN officials who were helping her in Calcutta that the event schedule must be kept confidential, so that no dangerous people could know when to mount an attack. But this was going to be a difficult secret to keep while also raising a large audience for a public event. The

Calcutta UN office assured Ilana that metal detector security and well-trained UN troops would be present.

Liu Xueli noticed the change in her simulator training regimes. Instead of moon landings, the tests changed to orbital maneuvering and docking exercises with many somewhat fanciful simulated target spacecraft, which were often represented by rather crude cartoonish graphical models in the virtual reality scenes. It appeared that her rumor had stimulated the result she wanted. With every exercise she could infer that she was being prepared to visit Metalmark's geosynchronous orbiter, not to land the Shenzhou 16 on the lunar surface.

Hassan reached Karachi and joined his new brigade for Friday prayers at a magnificent mosque. There the imam spoke of the Metalmark "Food from Stones" plan, and urged the faithful to reject it. What could be more demeaning for Muslims than to devour stones? Poison was no doubt the intent of the evil jinnee from space. If he wanted to feed people, why not give them proper grains or meat? Clearly Metalmark was in conspiracy with the western infidels to further humiliate and marginalize poor Muslims.

After the prayers, Hassan and his brigade met with the imam at his house, where they were served a great feast. When they had eaten, Imam Shabbir raised his voice. "Sons of Islam, a great mission awaits you. You have heard that the evil Metalmark seeks to demean and poison Muslims by making them eat stones. You only need to compare the fine feast you have just enjoyed, by God's will, with the humiliation of consuming rocks and dirt, to see how abominable is Metalmark's intent.

The iman continued,"Metalmark's minion in the West is UN Sec.-Gen. Shankar, who is lending undeserved blessings to the jinnee's plot. It has been announced in the western media that they will soon travel together on a world campaign to promote the stone food.

"Our brother Muslims in India have long been familiar with Shankar, during his rise to power. Over and over, he cajoled weak-willed Muslims into agreements that benefited Hindus and Christians using scarce Muslim resources. But in doing this he made enemies, and those enemies are our oppressed brothers in India. I have communicated with many imams in India, and have learned much. Shankar is from Calcutta, and he built his power there. We anticipate that he will want to return there in triumph with the space jinnee.

"It will be your mission to greet him as he deserves, God willing."

Agent Al Carson had been Ilana's case officer for five years. She had provided excellent detailed intelligence about Sec.-Gen. Shankar and the people at the highest levels of the UN. Sometimes the information was more than just valuable information about UN diplomatic activities affecting US interests. Sometimes it was critical enough that the US had to take responsive action.

That was the case with the "Food from Stones" campaign, which was staging its first major promotional event in Calcutta at noon this Thursday, according to the secret schedule of events that Ilana had provided to Agent Carson. Carson realized that it was in the US vital interest, according to the president's determination, that Metalmark be protected from the risk of attacks by Islamic fundamentalists. So Carson alerted the CIA station chief in Calcutta and forwarded the schedule of events via secure e-mail. The Calcutta station chief would alert Special Forces in the Bengal state region to fortify security at the "Food from Stones" demonstration event and assure safety of Metalmark and Sec.-Gen. Shankar.

Sandeep Jalil was the chief of police in the Bengal state district surrounding the hospital in Calcutta, and a devout Muslim. When he got the call from the famed and blessed Imam Shabbir of Karachi, appealing for Jalil's assistance, it seemed only right to join the blessed and wise imam in staging a protest of the UN event to be held in Calcutta. Every faithful Muslim knew that the space jinnee was committing offenses to the Muslim faith on a cosmic scale and the UN Sec.-Gen. was kowtowing to this monster.

So Jalil assigned only Muslim officers to serve as security guards for the "Food from Stones" event as the Imam asked, and told the officers that they could join in the demonstration, which was to consist of heckling and embarrassing derision of the UN and Metalmark for demeaning the poor of Calcutta by feeding them decomposed minerals instead of fine bread. Jalil believed that this was only fair to Shankar, who had risen to power in India, as everyone knew, by tricking gullible Muslims out of their pittances of possessions to pay for potions and vaccinations that only served to thwart God's will about who should be healthy and who should be sick.

M

Star Taikonaut Feng Chin-Tsai was Liu Xueli's latest partner in the simulated training to maneuver the Shenzhou 16. Feng Chin-Tsai had a famous name – he was named by his family for a great Lieutenant-General in the Hebei-Chahar war of the last century – but he was not domineering like a general . . . more boyish and passive-aggressive. Xueli did not find him altogether obnoxious (as so many of the arrogant Taikonaut trainees were) and they got along relatively well.

They were running a simulation of a rendezvous and capture with an orbiting target spacecraft. He was the mission captain and she was acting as pilot of the spacecraft.

"Five minutes to contact," he announced.

"Speed 10 meters per second," Xueli reported.

"Ready for thruster burn."

"Ready," she acknowledged. The computer was displaying a countdown to the last possible moment for the thruster blast that would bring the Shenzhou 16 to a dead stop precisely at the target, where the universal grappler system would try to delicately attach their vessel to the target.

"Correction burn?" Feng asked.

"Unnecessary," Xueli answered, watching the countdown intently.

Feng looked at every indicator nervously, and glanced over his shoulder at her. "Fuel check," he ordered.

"At 65%," she replied.

There was silence, like the soundless motion of orbiting vehicles, imperceptible. This was apparently the problem for Feng, as the minutes passed. Was it the instruments that she watched that he didn't trust, or her?

"Ready for thruster burn," she announced, with thirty seconds to go.

His intake of breath was audible.

At the countdown of zero, she squeezed the control, and a hiss could be heard. The room jerked back in a simulated motion to give them a kinesthetic sense that they were learning to expect in reality. (The room was really mounted on huge hydraulic push cylinders, but the trainees had long ago become unaware of that.)

A chime sounded, indicating that the target was met at zero relative velocity.

"You were too late!" Feng accused. "That is not safe. And there could have been a thruster failure, and you left no margin for error. At that velocity we would have crashed into the target and sustained damage!"

"I was following the countdown from the computer! We must do every maneuver with minimum fuel, or we might run out and fail to get home!"

The door of the simulator opened and the trainer entered. He did not look displeased because the exercise was a success. Nevertheless . . .

"You have a difference of philosophy," the trainer observed. "Feng chooses to err on the side of caution in collisional motion. Liu trusts the computer and avoids wasting a drop of fuel to safeguard the return from the mission. You are both right. In such a dispute, the disagreement is settled by the ranks of the officers. Feng overrules a subordinate officer."

Liu Xueli lowered her eyes deferentially. "I apologize for my error. It will not be repeated." Inwardly she seethed, but nothing must be allowed to tarnish her record and give the mission managers an excuse to disqualify her from the real mission to come. She held her temper.

Feng Chin-Tsai was enough of a gentleman not to rub it in.

Hassan Khani trained with his brigade, practicing hand-to-hand combat and excelling at target practice. In the evenings the commandos rested, prayed and heard sermons on the extremist doctrines of their hosts. The food was sumptuous and they were treated with respect that was almost reverence, as holy chosen representatives of the prophet's spirit.

In a few days the brigade boarded a Pakistani military plane, carrying mostly cargo. But the influence of Imam Shabbir was their ticket to a little-used airfield in Bangladesh, from which they would travel to Calcutta by land.

The charter plane circled Calcutta, preparing to land with the UN delegation. Ilana looked down at the "City of Joy and Love." The streets formed an amazing blend of orderly north-south/east-west grid and chaotic outlying streets, beside the Ganges river delta. Calcutta had been the capitol of British colonial India until 1912.

Ilana could understand the way the natives of Calcutta must have accepted the order and relative prosperity brought by the British occupation, even though it violated their sovereignty. When she was small, her parents had spoken obliquely about their nostalgia for the orderly life they had led in East Germany as part of the Stasi state security agency. Even though Stasi was so intrusive and sometimes brutal in its oppression of dissenters, Stasi had maintained a welcome order in the face of Soviet menace. When the Wall fell in 1989, Ilana's parents had gratefully accepted the CIA invitation to change sides and inform the newly singular superpower of whatever it wanted to know, in exchange for protection from the angry, vengeful Germans. Ilana owed her presence as a naturalized citizen of that new superpower to her parents' intelligent decision and that gave her the order she craved.

Ilana wished that she was free to take a tour or spend a few days relaxing in a foreign land, soaking up the different culture, but as usual she had to spend the time working to assure that the event of the day went smoothly, while keeping half her thoughts on the preparations of the next day's planned event in Bangladesh. As soon as the plane landed, she checked again with the UN security officers that the venue would be safe for the Sec.-Gen. and Metalmark and their "Food from Stones" promotion.

⊥∧⊥

There were several varieties of pudding on stage for the presentation. Shankar and Metalmark inspected the puddings. Then Shankar tasted a spoonful of one of the sweet samples. "It's fine," he said.

"Thank you," said Metalmark. "I hope the poor people of your home town can enjoy it and be nourished."

The doors of the auditorium of the medical college at Mukundapur had opened and people were making their way in. They were the poorest of the population of Calcutta's beggars, many barely dressed in filthy rags, but Shankar was pleased that they were polite, orderly, and behaving with the joyful attitude that always surprised visitors to his home city. Hindu and Muslim by their modes of dress, they all came into the hall to greet the visitor Metalmark, not so much disciplined as accompanied by some uniformed Calcutta police and security personnel from the UN and Bengali state corps. Some of them had lost their homes to the rising sea level that inundated the nearby river delta, due to global warming. Some of them were patients in the hospital next to the medical college, and they were brought in on gurneys for an outing from their sickrooms. Shankar had chosen this venue to revisit his first achievement for the public, but also because the people of this institution welcomed innovation in the service of human wellbeing.

Ilana visited the stage and saw that Metalmark and Shankar were conversing over the large bowl of pudding, and that the nutritionists had arrived and prepared to serve the audience with small tastes of the pudding made from limestone. She decided that all was well and went out the rear entrance of the auditorium to a spot where she could get cell phone reception and call the Bangladesh UN office to finalize preparations at tomorrow's venue. The humid heat of the Ganges river delta, the palm trees and exotic tropical plantings of the teaching hospital's campus began to put her into more of a vacation mood as she worked.

The hospital and medical college officials joined Shankar and Metalmark on stage and greeted one another. They did not notice that several men in Bengal district police uniforms began entering the auditorium and making their way up to the stage along the side walls. But they would not have been alarmed at seeing such men, because everyone had passed through metal detectors at the entrance, which were guarded by other men wearing the same uniforms and men wearing UN uniforms. Police Chief Sandeep Jalil had blended the personnel skillfully with the right postings to enable Imam Shabbir's demonstrators to take their positions near the stage unchallenged. Because of Chief Jalil's orders no one stopped the demonstrators in police uniforms from bringing their AK-47s. This was the standard defensive weapon for the Bengali police, due to the similar equipment of recent extremist attackers.

At the scheduled start time, TV cameras for local stations and newsbloggers began to broadcast the event. The medical college president graciously introduced Sec.-Gen. Shankar and the space visitor Metalmark, thanking them for their kind regard of the patients and citizens of Calcutta.

Sanjeev Shankar stepped to the podium. "Thank you, fellow natives of Calcutta for kindly joining us today at the hospital and medical college that you helped to build. Food is the first and best medicine, and I come to you today with a taste of the generous and benevolent provision from our new friend, a merchant from outer space, Metalmark. He has brought us a technology that exceeds anything the science of the West could provide. The very stones will give up their strength and feed us, with his coaxing, as we will show you today."

Hassan Khani shouted from beside the stage, "Good Muslims, do not believe this Satan! The food that he offers you is poisonous and degrading! The Hand of the Prophet will protect you from this deception!" Hassan jumped up to the stage and headed for Metalmark.

Shankar saw the gun and tried to block Hassan's way. "No! Don't shoot him! He wants to help our starving people!" cried Shankar. A sound of dread, the gasps and despairing moans of the audience, began to drone in the great hall.

Hassan aimed his AK-47. "You minion of Satan!" He shot Shankar with three pulls of the trigger, and Shankar was hit in the chest by every shot. He fell to the side and Hassan advanced toward Metalmark, who stepped backward but noticed that he was backing toward the group of UN nutritionists. He turned and tried to jump off of the back of the stage, but Hassan had switched the AK-47 to automatic cycling, and he emptied the magazine of the gun into Metalmark.

The panic and outcry in the auditorium behind Hassan was at its loudest peak as he watched the bullets perforate the bloodless alien body. But a strange thing happened: jets of fluid began to spray in random directions, fluid that ignited when it emerged from Metalmark's body. A jet of it struck Hassan in the face and chest, and a burning sensation drew his hands protectively over his eyes, but it was too late. He suddenly couldn't see, his face was burning, and he dropped the rifle and began to run away from the source of the burning.

Shankar had gone into shock very quickly. Lying on the floor, he hoped that someone would protect Metalmark but he was suddenly too exhausted to move. The food. Someone would give it to the hungry Calcutta people, but he was resigned that it would not be him. So tired . . . there was only one thing he wished for: the sweet embrace of Uma. Somehow in that final moment, by seeking the memory of that beloved embrace, he found it.

The UN nutritionists ran from the flaming body of Metalmark. One of them, Ellen Holweg, circled around the spreading fire and tried to pull Shankar to safety. Without knowing that the Sec.-Gen. was dead, Holweg put Shankar's body into the arms of a UN security guard and ran away to help guide audience members away from the fire and smoke. Gunfire and shouted orders and prayers filled the air. The chaotic jumble of chairs and bodies lasted for an interminable time as the terrified people tried to escape through the doors in the auditorium's rear.

Hassan had looked like a burning policeman falling into the audience and running, stumbling and screaming over the chairs. The roar of the crowd was deafening, a blend of screams, cries of pain from people being trampled, and desperate prayers and weeping for mercy. Someone knocked Hassan down and tried to beat him. It was with the intent of putting out the fire, and soon the flames were exhausted. His brigade cohort said, "There is no God but Allah," to identify himself. Hassan got up, blind, hardly able to move because of the waves of burning pain, and tried to continue fleeing, pulled by his helper. No one seemed to be blocking their way. The UN security guards who had realized that some men in uniforms of Bengali police were shooting at them had begun shooting back. But they didn't shoot at Hassan, who was no longer a threat. They shot at the other brigade members who were trying to shoot their way out to the getaway vehicle. Too many panicked people were in the way at the door, however, and the building was filling with smoke.

When the fire department finally arrived, the auditorium was a smoking ruin and the hospital was filled with injured casualties of the attack.

M

It was 11:45 PM at the Kennedy Space Center when the guards surrounding Metalmark's shuttle heard a rising ear-piercing siren from the alien spacecraft. This was followed by the sound of a brief explosive roar, which was cut off suddenly, and the siren continued. The commander of the military police ordered them to fall back, away from the spacecraft, in case this was a warning of imminent danger. The brief explosion had been an engine test. Soon the guards were running at top speed because the roar started again, and the engine of the shuttle throttled up. The blindingly brilliant torch rose into the starry sky and was soon lost to view.

In Washington, Pres. Jackson and the First Lady were in bed. There was a knock at the door of their bedroom. A Secret Service officer said, "Mr. President, there has been a terrorist attack on the 'Food from Stones' presentation in Calcutta. I'm sorry to have to inform you that UN Sec.-Gen. Shankar and Metalmark have both been killed. The reports are very confused, but much of it was televised locally. There seems to have been some sort of bomb involved and it started a major fire."

Pres. Jackson was ashen. He got up and began dressing, stunned into slow motion as he tried to find his clothes. Fighting back tears, Meg couldn't do anything but gasp, "Oh! Oh! What have they done?"

M

In New York City, Jayno was talking with a guest when the show producer used her earphone to tell the news. She stopped the conversation and turned to the audience. "I'm shocked and very saddened by something that my producer just relayed to me." She pointed to the earphone. "News reports are coming in that the 'Food from Stones' presentation in Calcutta by Metalmark and UN Sec.-Gen. Shankar . . . was attacked by Muslim extremist commandos. Metalmark and Sec.-Gen. Shankar are reported to have been killed, and some kind of bomb was used that started a fire in the auditorium they were using. Many people were injured and some killed in the panic. We are all devastated to hear this, we only hope that it can somehow be an early, mistaken claim that Metalmark and Sec.-Gen. Shankar are dead. Let us all stop for a moment and say a prayer to ask that they may be safe."

IV

LIU XUELI WAS asleep, dreaming of a performance on the balance beam. She bent forward and leaped up, flipping backward, landing on her feet and standing upright with perfect balance, arms outstretched to her sides. She stood at the end of the beam and began flipping forward along it, over and over toward her dismount from the far end of the beam. Her last dismount flip was rotating her toward the floor landing, but suddenly there was no floor. She did not stop flipping, and awoke in a panic. Her phone was ringing.

It was her trainer, Luan Chunping. "Liu Xueli, it is time for you to serve on a special mission, which you have no doubt anticipated. Feng Chin-Tsai will command and you will pilot the Shenzhou 16. This mission is very important. The news has been confirmed that Metalmark was killed in a bombing in India. Therefore his spaceship may be possible to salvage. Prepare yourself and report to the Launch Center, where you will be equipped and briefed with more essential information."

Xueli could hardly believe it. "I will serve as you have taught me, and make you proud. Thank you for sending me on the road to my dream."

"I am sure that you will perform at Olympic level," said Luan Chunping. She could hear the smile in his voice. She disconnected and began getting dressed.

A car was ready outside the dormitory to convey her to the Jiuquan Space Center, where she squirmed into the space suit that she would wear for the launch. After the com check, when Liu Xueli and Feng Chin-Tsai boarded the van that would carry them to the Shenzhou 16 at its launch gantry, the trainers gave them more briefing.

"A spacecraft has been detected by radar, rising from the USA. You may be racing the USA for salvage of Metalmark's technology. You will get defensive side arms and knives, and the Shenzhou 16 has missiles that you have been trained to use. You are to bluff with the weapons or use them if necessary to bring back whatever advanced technology that will fit into your vehicle."

The taikonauts prepared themselves during the ride to the Shenzhou 16. They had always been told that there was a chance of conflict during their mission to the Moon, but they had not expected to fight Americans for alien technology. Both taikonauts began to visualize what it would be like to take aim at an American and prepare to pull the trigger.

An elevator took them up the gantry to the port where they boarded the Shenzhou 16. The rocket stack was as tall as a Saturn V, but more efficient in performance with 21st century technology. The spacecraft was majestic in the morning sunlight, surrounded by white vapors of out-gassing rocket fuel that was cryogenically cold so that the tanks creaked and groaned with thermal stresses while noisy pumps topped them off. Inside the third stage vehicle, five meters in diameter, the taikonauts enjoyed four times the cabin volume that Apollo astronauts had endured on their voyages to the Moon in the 20th century. As swiftly as possible, the taikonauts performed the systems checks and brought the spacecraft to readiness for launch.

Liu Xueli was surprised that the fuel on board their third rocket stage was 40% of the amount that they required for a lunar voyage, due to the closer target. She would be in charge of allocating it to various purposes because the Shenzhou 16 had an advanced turbine-powered electrical system: the main rocket fuel supply was used for power for all of the electrical and life-support systems as well as for propulsion. The mission controllers told her that the lunar mobility vehicle was not on board, so the load would be lighter and the Shenzhou 16 would need less fuel to reach Metalmark's spaceship faster. This also gave the taikonauts storage space for salvaged items from Metalmark's spaceship.

Finally the hatches were secured and the countdown began. Engine systems performed correctly and at ". . . 3, 2, 1," the main engines ignited.

Liu Xueli was pressed with dizzying force back into her seat. As if far away, the voices of the flight controllers reported the proper functioning of the thrusters. Seven titanic jets of exhaust propelled the stack for kilometers vertically until it leaned eastward toward the skies above the Pacific Ocean, rising into low Earth orbit. Minutes later she felt the stack shudder when the spent first stage shut down and was kicked away by explosive bolts. The second stage began burning and as the vehicle rotated, brilliant sunlight filled the cabin through one window. She would have shouted with exhilaration, but nothing could be heard except the roar of the barely controlled explosive engines. A strange blue arc appeared through the window – the curve of the ocean horizon below, surmounted by a thin veil, the atmosphere seen from 60 km altitude.

Then there was silence, and a bump. The second stage had shut down and been ejected. Feng Chin-Tsai ordered a performance report, and Xueli was caught up in the ritualistic discipline of the orbital maneuvering procedures. She began the calculations of thruster burns that would send them toward geosynchronous altitude to rendezvous with the Metalmark vehicle in a little more than six hours.

Pres. Jackson had just watched the summary of the TV broadcasts from India that his staff had put together. It was shocking to see the brutal way that Sec.-Gen. Shankar and Metalmark had been cut down, and the pandemonium that followed in the auditorium was just as punishing to endure. Anyone with a heart felt moved to do something to help the victims, but it was hopeless because the events had occurred an hour ago, so the fate of anyone who was hurt or killed in Calcutta was now fixed. The president was very moved by Shankar's brave attempt to protect Metalmark. It was a single futile bright moment in the dark story of humanity's first reception of a visitor from outer space.

Because the "Food from Stones" presentation had been televised, the assassinations were viewed all over Asia and the awakening Western nations. A brief news conference had been given by the embattled district police chief, Sandeep Jalil. He bitterly denounced the deception by a Pakistani Imam Shabbir, who had told Jalil that only a vocal demonstration was to be made against the stone pudding. At least Jalil could report that the extremist commandos had been killed or captured, and their interrogations implicated Imam Shabbir.

A news anchorman from a Calcutta TV station was reporting. An English translator's voice said, "After a police investigation, the body of Sec.-Gen. Shankar was given to UN Security officials for return to his family in New York City. The burned remains of Metalmark consisted of a melted shell made of some sort of plastic and numerous mysterious devices that were within it. These remains were also surrendered by police officials to the UN.

"The government of India has denounced this outrageous incursion into its sovereign territory for criminal purposes and calls for UN sanctions against

Pakistan for supporting or tolerating the actions of the attackers."

Gen. Mason entered the conference room where the gathering of White House staff and cabinet officers had convened to watch. "Mr. President, I have to report to you that the Chinese have launched a spacecraft. It is headed toward Metalmark's geosynchronous spacecraft. I will need your decisions on a response."

"What kind of spacecraft? Manned or a missile?" asked the president.

"The flight characteristics are similar to their lunar mission of two years ago. There is some improved performance, which could be explained if they weren't loaded with the moon vehicle that they used on that landing. A missile would probably be moving much faster. We will have reconnaissance photos in a few minutes of the rocket they were preparing to launch at their Jiuquan Space Center, if it is still on the ground. My bet is that it's not on the ground any more."

"So they probably repurposed their moon vehicle to make a flight to Metalmark's spacecraft now that he's been killed." To his Chief of Staff, the president said, "Randy, get Peter Currin and tell him to call the Chinese president with an urgent query about the purpose of their on-going space mission." To Mason, he said, "They must be planning to board or dismantle whatever Metalmark left in orbit. But if it's a ship that came from another star, I don't think they will be able to bring much of it home in a vehicle the size of theirs."

Gen. Mason nodded, "It's pretty large, according to the radar and photos. But they may damage it in trying to board it. There's something else you need to know: about the time that Metalmark was killed, his landing craft in Florida took off back to the mother ship. So apparently there are automated systems or perhaps more concealed alien beings that are still operating the vehicles. It's possible that they might take actions in reprisal for Metalmark's death. I've got my staff on high alert for any sign of reprisal activity from Metalmark's spacecrafts. Taikonauts are liable to get a hostile reception."

Pres. Jackson said, "Randy, get the staff started on a public statement condemning the murders of Metalmark and Sec.-Gen. Shankar in strong language. And if we get a call from Sec.-Gen. Shankar's successor at the UN, I will welcome the opportunity to offer our condolences and discuss the situation with him or her right then and there. Then tell Peter Currin to call our ambassador to Pakistan home for consultations. I want the Prime Minister of Pakistan to be told that we demand the arrest of that Imam Shabbir and anyone they can find involved in the assassinations.

"I recall that Jon West put some of our CIA special forces on security for that event in Calcutta. Tell him I want to know where the hell *were* they?

"Also tell Marv Krainak I want him to start a NASA task force on a mission concept to salvage the Metalmark spacecraft, if it becomes necessary. Even though the Chinese will get there first, I don't think they will succeed at bringing much home."

Gen. Mason said, "They may be able to bring home something of the advanced technology. This action by the Chinese is a potential major security threat."

Pres. Jackson added, "And be sure to notify me instantly if any of the alien satellites show any sign of hostile behavior."

M

Uma Shankar was lying in bed after an evening at a charity event at the Metropolitan Museum of Art. She had turned off the lights and dropped off to sleep when the phone rang. She got up and reached for it. The clock said 11:45 PM. Sanjeev would be finished with his speech with Metalmark. She would watch him in the morning on the TV news. She picked up the phone.

"Ma . . ." It was her daughter Ajitha's voice, but it sounded strange and halting.

"Ajitha, dear, this is too late for you to stay up studying. How are you?"

"Ma, I said a prayer to Lord Ganesha for Baba's soul. . . . Have you heard any news?"

"That is nice, dear, but no, why . . . ?"

Ajitha in her room at Harvard realized that she would need to grow up to carry on this conversation appropriately. "Ma, I heard a news report from India. They said that Baba and Metalmark were . . . attacked during the 'Food' campaign, and . . . hurt."

"Oh, no, dear." There was a pause while neither could speak. It was a moment when time could have ended, for they had no wish to enter the future.

Ajitha stifled a sob. "Ma, . . . maybe the report was wrong. I hope, I pray."

"Thank you for praying, and for being with me," said Uma. "I'll call Bernard Molyneux. I'm sure he can tell us what is going on. I may have to fly to Calcutta to help Baba get treatment, if he is injured. I will feel better knowing that you are praying for us and thinking of us. You can call your brother if you feel up to it."

"Okay, Ma," said Ajitha. "Bless you and Baba." She hung up.

Uma put down the phone. Numbly she lay back on her bed. So many times on the eve of a trip Sanjeev had told her not to worry, no matter what dangerous place he was about to visit. He had consoled her that the Secretary-General of the UN was always respected as a bringer of peace and reconciliation, and that no UN Sec.-Gen. had ever been hurt or killed on a mission of peace or relief. His persuasiveness and love had been so strong that she had almost stopped worrying in recent years. Now she clung to that feeling of consolation, but it was melting and dripping away. Ajitha had been more upset than she would have been to learn that her father was injured in a treatable way. Uma now had to grasp for her daughter's kindness and grown up gentleness in conveying the news. With tears for a sweet twenty-five-year marriage, Uma let go of the assurances of Sanjeev and leaned on the love of her children as she got up and dressed for the ordeal to come with the dawn. There would be no sleep tonight.

M

As dawn spread over the western hemisphere, the assassinations in Calcutta were viewed by millions of people, most with outrage that the promise of Metalmark's technological bounty had been canceled by yet another in the series of extremist attacks that plagued the globe. In large western cities, demonstrators made signs and marched in protest of the murders. The demonstrators expressed their anger about the assassination of Sec.-Gen. Shankar as well, and at many demonstrations, vengeful acts were committed against innocent but convenient Muslims.

In the US, TV news channels broadcast the late Sec.-Gen.'s life story, and repeated and analyzed the video footage of the attack. And commentators expressed fear that the Metalmark spacecraft, still in geosynchronous orbit with its necklace of satellites around Earth, was preparing some punishment in reprisal.

The geek blogosphere was crestfallen, bitter and angry. Larry Saxon's *NASA critique* blog was as caustic as usual:

NASA has dropped the ball on this one chance to establish friendly

87

interstellar relations! NASA should never have let the incompetent UN parade Metalmark around the world and invite an attack that could result in a catastrophe like this. Earth is a dangerous planet to tour, especially for a world-famous off-planet visitor with controversial behavior and advanced technology of unimaginably great value. And especially India, where even Mohandas Gandhi was assassinated! Couldn't the great thinkers at NASA foresee what might happen? This is worse than the Challenger and Columbia disasters because now we have lost our chance for humankind to make a good impression on the civilization that Metalmark represented. Instead we look like savages. It's disgusting. Let's just hope it doesn't provoke a vengeful reaction . . .

Sec. of Defense Clifford Saper sat at the head of a table in the Pentagon. CIA Chief Jon West and several other grim-faced agency and DoD officials accompanied him. Saper said, "The president is very angry. He thought he had conveyed to the Department that Metalmark was to enjoy a level of protection appropriate to a representative of an advanced civilization from another star system. Why did this representative and the Secretary-General of the United Nations get assassinated despite our efforts?"

"It was an inside job," Director West replied. "Sandeep Jalil, the police chief for the province, gave the commandos permission to make a protest, and they escalated that permission into penetration of the UN security perimeter with lethal forces. They had support from Pakistani Muslim extremists and entered the perimeter wearing Bengali police uniforms with Bengali police sidearms. We had Special Forces personnel on site, operating in coordination with the UN security officials, who let anyone in a Bengali police uniform enter the perimeter. Jalil has protested that he was used, but he has just been relieved of duty by the provincial government, according to a wire report."

Sec. Saper said, "I understand these excuses. Your people were blindsided. My reaction is that you need to put maximum effort into preventing any future repetition of this attack plan. Islamic extremists everywhere will see that it worked and try to duplicate it. This has become a general problem for our global anti-terrorist strategy to solve."

Director West began, "We have started working on this by moving Special Forces in Pakistan toward the goal of capturing Imam Shabbir, the mastermind of this operation in Karachi. His capture could deter the repetition of the attack plan to some extent by beheading his organization."

"That's a start," said Sec. Saper. "But this failure has handed the human species a greater problem: Metalmark's survivors or machines may retaliate for his murder in ways we can't possibly imagine. This failure has the potential to expose the entire planet to new threats of conventional terrorist attacks. But there could also be attacks from outer space of entirely unconventional nature." And he went on at some length on this theme.

Liu Xueli and Feng Chin-Tsai had finished eating brunch. Fortunately neither of them was experiencing zero-g nausea. And after the risky launch and orbital maneuvers, they were allowed to stow the stiff, bulky pressure suits and relax in flight coveralls.

Chin-Tsai unbuckled his seat belt and pushed himself toward the controls of the forward telescope. With a smile he focused it on the Metalmark spaceship, still glittering three thousand kilometers away. The automatic tracking software engaged and he flipped the switch that sent the picture to his command console and Liu Xueli's pilot console. He floated back across the cabin and strapped himself back in.

Xueli concentrated on the view. The mother ship was still too reflective and amorphous in the console image for the mind to interpret.

Chin-Tsai said, "It's really there. That's sweet!"

Xueli smiled and said, "Let's downlink the output." Chin-Tsai made the telecom send the scope output to the transmitter, and he made sure that the antenna outside the Shenzhou 16 had a positive lock on the ground station. This gave him an excuse to look back at the fascinating blue and white ball of Planet Earth with the rear telescope.

"Is it rotating?" Xueli asked.

Chin-Tsai studied the fluctuating image of the alien starship. "Maybe. How long until arrival?"

Xueli replied, "Sixty-five minutes. . . . I think I see two parts, but neither one looks like a US spacecraft. Their spacecraft beat us to the alien by three hours. Is it hiding behind the Metalmark ship?"

"Weapons check," Chin-Tsai ordered. They started a check-out test of the missile targeting and launch systems. Chin-Tsai floated across the cabin to the box that held side arms and bayonets, and he unlocked it. The space suits were ready to be entered for salvage operations.

M

Sec. of State Peter Currin had reached the Chinese president by phone. "My government has urgent concerns about the objectives of your space mission that is now in progress."

There was a pause. Pres. Yao Renbao said, "We have not announced any space mission. Our government objects to your surveillance, which is an unfriendly intrusion. We have attempted to maintain friendly relations with your government, but we do not appreciate foreign compromise of our airspace and operations."

"Mr. President, we respect your right to explore space peacefully and conduct defensive aerospace missions. However, we have been cooperating with the UN to attempt to defend the Metalmark spacecrafts. There was an agreement that was initiated when Metalmark first communicated with the UN as the exclusive representative of humanity."

"Then why did you launch a vehicle toward the Metalmark spacecraft just after the attack that killed him in Calcutta? Were you covert participants in the plot to assassinate Metalmark and confiscate his technology for yourselves? That would be treachery and piracy."

Currin was stunned but tried to recover. "I assure you, Mr. President, that nothing of the kind is happening."

"That is not how it looks to us."

"Please hold the line for a moment, Mr. President."

"I'm afraid that my time is too valuable to wait while you to refine your deception. Call me again if you will be more forthcoming about your own government's intentions." The call ended.

Sec. Currin called Pres. Jackson's personal cell phone.

"Tom, they think we sent a spacecraft to confiscate Metalmark's goods as soon as he was killed. Pres. Yao accused us of having some role in the attack on the UN delegation in Calcutta!"

Pres. Jackson said, "I think he doesn't know that it was Metalmark's shuttle that took off when the attack killed Metalmark. He thinks his taikonauts are about to interrupt Americans pillaging Metalmark's starship. If we want to act like his ally, then we have to tell him what really happened. But if we tell him that we haven't actually sent a vehicle, maybe the taikonauts will steal more pieces or do more damage to the mother ship!"

Sec. Currin said, "The alien vehicles are automated. Maybe they can defend themselves."

"Yes," said Pres. Jackson. "We shouldn't discount the advanced technology of a star-traveling power. Maybe the mother ship can defend itself until Metalmark's . . . relatives or partners come to retrieve it. I wish we knew more about his background."

"But if they can do that, why couldn't Metalmark's technology keep him from getting killed in Calcutta?"

"Point taken. Still, at the very least a booby trap on the starship seems likely to me. And this is an opportunity to signal the Chinese that we aren't the pirates they suspect us to be. Direct advice from us to avoid a booby trap won't be believed. Yet we have to make a helpful gesture to renew our ally relationship with them, not just keep our knowledge to ourselves."

Sec. Currin said, "I think we should call Amb. Yang Wei. I have a pretty good rapport with him. I'll tell him what we know, and then the onus to persuade his government that we are acting in good faith falls on him. It will take him some time and inconvenience to argue the point with Pres. Yao – that's their penalty for failing to trust us as an ally – but we will have given our friendly advice."

"I like that plan," said Pres. Jackson.

A little while later, Sec. Currin reached Amb. Yang Wei by phone. After explaining that the vehicle the Chinese detected on its way to Metalmark's mother ship was his own automated landing shuttle, Sec. Currin said, "Please advise Pres. Yao that our government is unhappy with his presumption of our involvement in criminal conspiracy against the UN Secretary General and our planet's first visitor from an advanced star-traveling power. We recommend that your taikonauts return from their ill-advised mission, or at the very least proceed with extreme caution. They are facing unknowable powers, not an American boarding party. We are concerned for their safety."

There was a significant pause on Amb. Yang's end. "My government will take your advice under consideration. If it proves to be the truth, then it will be regarded as stronger for the ties between our nations. I am . . . involved with a personal stake in this mission. If my niece is endangered by the delay of your relaying this advice through me, it will not benefit this relationship." He disconnected.

"Whew," said Sec. Currin. *His niece is a taikonaut on that mission!*

M

"Slow," ordered Chin-Tsai. Xueli obeyed, guiding the Shenzhou 16 carefully in a loop several kilometers in radius around the Metalmark mother ship. Close up, it was almost like a fuzzily spherical cloud, with a shifting apparent surface of elusive iridescent reflectivity. There was no sign of a US spacecraft. They dutifully relayed images of the alien ship to the Chinese navy vessel below, stationed in international waters in the Gulf of Guayaquil off the coast of Ecuador.

"Fuel check," ordered Chin-Tsai.

"At 15% of maximum." *Still plenty of fuel to get home with some booty*, she thought.

Radio silence was broken by a bell warning of a relayed message from the Beijing Space Command Center. "Taikonauts, there is important information. The USA did not send a vehicle. Metalmark's lander shuttle was automated and it left the US by itself to return to its mother ship. Some force is active on the shuttle and you may not be visiting a dead treasure ship. Use appropriate caution!"

The taikonauts shivered and looked at one another.

The bell sounded again and the radio produced a different voice, speaking Mandarin Chinese, like the Command Center flight director. "This is Metalmark. You are not allowed here until we have a contract of sale for my starship technology! No peeking allowed! Go home immediately!"

Chin-Tsai said, "Command Center would not joke with us about this. The Metalmark spacecraft must have detected the transmission from Command Center and learned our frequency!"

"Isn't Metalmark dead? Is this a recording?" asked Xueli. "Ancestors, protect us!"

Nothing more came from the radio. Chin-Tsai said, "Our orders are to approach and board. Proceed."

Xueli began the approach to the starship. *It's not dead*, she said to herself, terrified.

She nudged the Shenzhou 16 toward the mother ship with a brief thruster firing.

The starship seemed to shrink as if moving away, and behind it and to one side something had emerged. Xueli could not clearly see the object, which looked like a white disk, fluctuating in brightness.

"Report!" ordered Chin-Tsai.

"Something came out but it is out of view," said Xueli, because the outside camera had not tracked the moving secondary target.

A rotating, white device resembling a starfish with four arms quickly collided with the side of the cylindrical Shenzhou 16. The starfish's arms were rubbery and extended to a length much longer than the Shenzhou 16's circumference, so the arms wrapped around the Chinese spacecraft like a bolo, adhering and sticking. From the central bulge of the device a rocket engine nozzle protruded, and it began to swivel and fire intermittently in various directions. The sound of the alien engine would not have traveled through the vacuum of space, but the taikonauts could hear the powerful roar of the engine, conducted acoustically through the hull of the Shenzhou 16.

Inside the Shenzhou 16, the taikonauts were badly shaken up and then felt the cabin begin to spin. Only their safety belts kept them from being thrown about the cabin. The image of the mother ship moved out of their telescope view, and the sound of Shenzhou 16's automatic attitude adjustment thrusters was heard again and again.

"What's happening?" asked Chin-Tsai.

"Something hit us," said Xueli.

"I know!" said Chin-Tsai. "Look!" He pointed to a side window, which was covered by one of the white arms of the device.

The thruster noises were louder. The four-armed device had tested its engine and now fired it with more persistence. Shenzhou 16 began to tumble about varying axes of rotation, causing the automatic compensators to fire repeatedly, trying to adjust the spacecraft attitude to nominal orientation.

"It keeps doing that!" said Xueli.

"Where are we going?" demanded Chin-Tsai.

Xueli tried to read the position and orientation at the same time, but both were changing too rapidly to report. She concentrated on the position. "I think we have started drifting back toward Earth."

"Stop the rotation!" ordered Chin-Tsai.

Xueli began concentrating on the rotational readouts and overriding the orientation correction thrusters with her own corrections, but as soon as she stabilized the Shenzhou 16, she heard another thruster firing by the attacker on the hull, and they were rotating again.

"What are you doing?" demanded Chin-Tsai.

"I correct the orientation, but something outside on the hull is messing it up!"

"Here, let me do it," said Chin-Tsai. In desperation he released his safety belt from the command chair and tried to climb to Xueli's pilot station.

The device on the hull had assessed the limits of the Shenzhou 16's systems and crew, and it emitted several lengthy thrust burns. The cabin spin increased disturbingly. Xueli instinctively closed her eyes, remembering the gymnastic training. Chin-Tsai was thrown to the opposite end of the spinning cabin, where he struck the wall with an "Oof," and began to grasp in panic for handholds.

"Stop the spinning!" Chin-Tsai ordered.

With her eyes closed, Xueli struggled for inner stability. She now realized the game. Whatever device the mother ship had sent against the Shenzhou 16, it was intent on exhausting their fuel. Xueli mastered her panic and said, "That's what it wants us to do! It is using up our fuel!"

To his credit Chin-Tsai admitted, "You are right. Is there an emergency shut-off to override the automatic orientation correction?"

Xueli opened her eyes and studied the console. She found a toggle on the back side that said "Shutdown." She punched it to "off." Still she heard some sounds of the Shenzhou 16's thrusters. "There was an off switch," she said, "but it only turned off the console. Try to find the main attitude control system shut-off."

Chin-Tsai crawled dizzily along the spinning wall toward a box with cables coming out of it. Xueli knew that if she unstrapped herself to help, they would only both be helpless, so she tried to keep her eyes shut and master her sense of the spin axis.

She heard Chin-Tsai stop and throw up his lunch. But he had opened the door of the cable junction box.

There was one last lurch to another spin direction and then Chin-Tsai succeeded in turning off the automatic orientation correction system. The Shenzhou 16 was rotating end-over-end, and occasionally a thruster blast from the alien attachment on the outside hull could still be heard.

"Fuel report," commanded Chin-Tsai.

Xueli opened her eyes and reactivated her pilot's console. She read, "At 5% of maximum."

The hearts of both taikonauts sank. That amount was barely enough to get them back from geosynchronous orbit to low Earth orbit, with nothing left for a controlled re-entry into the atmosphere. The Metalmark ship had repelled their mission, a safe return home was just out of reach, and there was no salvage cargo. Because of the Shenzhou 16's tumbling, they could not aim their radio antenna and tell the Command Center what had happened.

Chin-Tsai said, "I should go out in a spacesuit and try to dislodge that thing."

"If you do that, it can just spin up the spacecraft until you are thrown off!"

Chin-Tsai climbed around the cabin via handholds and got back to his command chair, looking exhausted. "Can you compute our trajectory? The attacker on the hull made lots of burns. It said, 'Go home.' Maybe it propelled us homeward."

Xueli concentrated on the inertial guidance system, which was still working. "We're moving toward Earth. There might be enough fuel to make a transfer low earth orbit. Maybe Command Center could send us a rescue mission."

"Unless that thing outside forces us to expend more fuel . . ."

"It seems to want us to go home. Maybe it will cooperate. Our tumble axis . . . if we make a main engine burn at the right point in the tumble, it will send us homeward."

"That will be hard to pinpoint."

"We've got to try."

"Okay." Chin-Tsai closed his eyes and tried to compose himself. He looked green. The tumbling was too much for him.

Xueli entered the computation into the computer and prepared to fire the main engine. Precious fuel would be used, and it had to be done precisely. When Earth could be seen in the forward viewport, she triggered the main engine for five seconds. Then there was silence, and the attacker on the hull did not fire its thruster. The Shenzhou 16 made two more rotations in silence, and Xueli fired the main engine again when she saw the Earth.

From outside the taikonauts heard a burst of thrust. Xueli's heart pounded in her ears. The Shenzhou 16 stopped rotating, with Earth in the forward viewport. Metalmark's machine was sending them home.

The Deputy Secretary-General of the UN, Bernard Molyneux, became Acting Sec.-Gen. and released a statement. "The UN staff are outraged at the barbaric murders of Sec.-Gen. Shankar and our guest Metalmark, and at the collateral injuries and deaths in the fire. There can be no excuse for this heinous act, which has such a profoundly damaging consequence for the welfare of all humanity. The deepest sympathy is extended to Sec.-Gen. Shankar's wife and family, whose loss we all share. Sanjeev Shankar's heroic stand for helping the poor and hungry, for advancing civilized culture and science, and his personal heroic attempt to stop the murder of Metalmark moves and inspires us all to renew our struggle for the ideals that he pursued. And if it is possible for Metalmark's next-of-kin to perceive this statement, the UN expresses profound regret that fellow human beings would kill an innocent, generous guest to our planet in the name of religion. It is the particular duty of adherents of Islam worldwide to repudiate this heinous crime."

Sec.-Gen. Molyneux's statement met approving echoes in all nations that were not governed by Islamic officials. In the Islamic world, the reaction was a mix of equivocal and negative reactions to how the acting Sec.-Gen. blamed Muslims generally for the acts of a few extremists. Many state-run media in Islamic nations avoided comment about whether the killings of Shankar and Metalmark were good or bad, and Al-Jazeera News reported that many Muslims thought Shankar and Metalmark brought their fates upon themselves through their insensitivity to Muslim beliefs.

The taikonauts still could not communicate with their Command Center. Some part of the alien attachment was blocking the antenna, or it had broken off. Chin-Tsai attempted to get the radio working, but he was not having any success.

Xueli looked out of the viewport that faced away from the Sun. Stars were poured across the Galaxy, distant beyond imagining, untwinkling and unbreathing in the vacuum of space. They seemed immortal like the unbreathing ancestors, who no longer needed to draw breath. She and Chin-Tsai were prisoners in this tank of air, and behind a bulkhead in the propulsion section, she could hear the faint whine of turbine generators, burning fuel like small jet engines, making electricity that ran the air recyclers. The re-oxygenated air allowed the taikonauts to continue breathing. It would be almost five hours in orbit before they could re-enter the atmosphere, taking a breath about every five seconds. Each taikonaut needed 4,000 breaths provided by the fuel that was left. But much of the fuel was going to be burned to slow and aim their re-entry.

Chin-Tsai said, "Do you have our new orbit calculated?"

Xueli looked at a flashing number on the astrogation display and answered, "This is bad. We are in a transfer orbit but the perigee is too low. At this velocity we will re-enter the atmosphere too fast at too steep an inclination!" They would burn up if they did not suffocate first.

"You performed the main engine burns. What happened?"

Xueli frowned. "I could not allow for the extra mass of the alien attachment to the Shenzhou 16, because I did not know how much it was. Because of the extra mass, the engine burns were insufficient."

"Now you know how much velocity the burns achieved. You can calculate the extra mass. Maybe there is enough fuel for another burn. Do that now!"

Xueli started the calculations. She had to call up unfamiliar parts of the astrogation program in the computer. The atmosphere in their cabin had been comradely, but now it was extremely tense. She could smell their sweat from the fear. Partly this was because they had reduced the power to the cooling and air circulation system to conserve fuel. The sunlit side of the Shenzhou 16 was very hot, while the dark side was frigid, and the spacecraft made creaking and popping noises from the thermal stress.

Chin-Tsai also was making noises due to his own emotional stresses. His proud family had named him for one of China's greatest generals, and from birth he had been goaded with high expectations. Taikonaut training was the pinnacle of that family pride and reputation. Serving on this mission with the more famous Liu Xueli somewhat diminished his prominence in the taikonaut corps, and she had not been properly submissive to his rank. Now the mission was destined for disaster, through factors that he could not have controlled (such as Metalmark's defenses) but also through Liu Xueli's inadequate piloting. The likelihood that they were going to die soon caused him fear and distress, but now it also looked as though this failed mission would not even appear in the history books; it was well known that the government's failures were erased, and the imminent failure of this secret mission fit that pattern. So not only was Feng Chin-Tsai about to die, but also his family pride was about to disappear into historical oblivion. Liu Xueli's role in that failure seemed significant to him, and her presence was now the only factor that was left for him to control.

The computer told Xueli that the alien device attached to their hull appeared to have added 12% to the mass of the Shenzhou 16. She ran a complete analysis of the spacecraft's resources. They had about five hours left before the spacecraft descended to a low enough altitude to enter a stable low Earth orbit. A main engine burn would be necessary there to slow the Shenzhou 16 into a circular orbit that would take them back over the landing site in China. If one more main engine burn was performed immediately, and she saved enough fuel to make a course correction so that they safely re-entered the atmosphere when they reached it, there would be *almost* enough fuel left to power the life support and electrical requirements of the on-board systems for the rest of the mission.

But not quite enough.

"Look at this," she said to Chin-Tsai. She copied the computation results to his command console. "Check whether I have made a mistake. I think we can almost do this, but we're still a little short of fuel. Is there some system that we can shut down or reduce its power to minimum?"

She saw that he studied the figures on his own console. He had sweat on his upper lip, and he was running his fingers through his hair and moving his lips. She decided that he was unlikely to spot any mistake that she had made in his frame of mind, and began rechecking the numbers herself.

One thing she noticed was that the life support system drew a surprising amount of power. For some reason the air purifying system was not an efficient fuel user. More fuel was being expended per minute to re-oxygenate the air for the taikonauts than in the simulator when they had practiced. In one hour they would have to shut down the Shenzhou 16's air purifiers and enter space suits to use the remaining air in the suit tanks. Otherwise they would not have fuel for the orbit transfers and re-entry.

If only one of the taikonauts was aboard at this point in the mission instead of two, then the fuel savings for oxygen would be just enough to complete the mission. . .

And suddenly something grabbed her throat, squeezing painfully. She struggled to get free, but the safety belt held her in the seat. Chin-Tsai was trying to strangle her!

She desperately released the belt clasp and kicked at her console, tumbling out into the cabin. She couldn't speak through her injured throat, and coughed, trying to breathe. In the dim cabin she saw that he had released his safety belt and jumped across the cabin toward the weapon box, ten meters away.

Xueli encountered a wall and kicked herself toward Chin-Tsai, rotating so that she could kick him upon landing. He had opened the box but she couldn't see whether he had taken out a gun or bayonet. She kicked at his head, but the reaction sent her in a direction away from both him and the weapons. She kicked again at a wall, grabbed the pilot seat, and punched a button to fire an attitude control jet. The cabin began to rotate slowly, and she kicked away from the console just as he arrived at it. He was unable to compensate for the rotating cabin after that, and missed her with his next jump, entangling his foot in a net that held equipment against the toilet door. This gave Xueli a moment to reach the weapon box and arm herself with a knife. Chin-Tsai had prudently left the firearms in the box, since a bullet hole in the cabin wall wouldn't help anyone survive.

When she turned back to look at him, he was jumping toward her with a savage expression and the bayonet outstretched. He was slightly off target because of the rotating cabin, so she was able to jump away, but a slash with the knife grazed her arm, stinging. She escaped and tumbled to a stop at the opposite wall to watch for his next attack.

This time when Chin-Tsai braced his foot on the rotating cabin wall to jump, his toe was snagged by another equipment net on the moving wall. He jumped but the net almost stopped his motion across the cabin toward her and left him rotating slowly without anything to kick against as he drifted across the cabin. The ancestors were protecting her, she thought. This would have to be her moment.

She jumped at just the time to collide with him when his helpless rotation presented her with his back. Struggling for breath through her partially collapsed windpipe, she grabbed his shirt between the shoulder blades and plunged the knife into his neck, at his right carotid artery. Then she pulled out the knife and pushed herself slowly away from his back.

Feng Chin-Tsai emitted a few curses and jets of blood as he slowly drifted back across the cabin. Then he encountered the far wall and rebounded from it aimlessly, clutching his injury but lapsing into silent convulsions. Xueli clung to the wall opposite him and struggled to recover, weeping tears of terror, pain and relief. She kept the knife pointed toward his body as it slowly drifted out into the cabin center, turning, lifeless and oozing spherules of blood. After it was clear that he was dead, she managed to calm down and make do with the breath that would come through her restricted airway.

Grimly she squirmed into her spacesuit. The breathing mix in it was richer in oxygen than the cabin air, and it made the purple blotches in her vision go away. Then she found her way to the pilot console and stopped the cabin rotation. She said a prayer of thanks to the ancestors.

Then, in another moment of panic she remembered that she had to do a main engine burn! The knife fight had delayed her. She set the astrogation program to recalculate the burn and oriented the spacecraft with the attitude jets. She couldn't tell whether there would be enough fuel left, but if she did not perform the main engine firing, she was doomed to burn up during re-entry of the atmosphere. The engine lit and for a few seconds her sense of up and down returned. Below her, the floor of the cabin acquired spatters of Feng Chin-Tsai's blood.

Ilana Lindler huddled in her seat on the UN airplane that was returning from Calcutta to New York with the rest of the grieving delegation. The Bengali police and UN security personnel had hustled everyone into the plane, for fear of another commando attack. Ilana had never seen grown people – important UN representatives – treated like children, fleeing a strange country in tears, but even worse she was one of them, cowering in her seat against a pillow. Even though she was a trained covert CIA agent, it was devastating to experience a surprise commando attack against defenseless people who were your friends. The Secretary-General had been such a special man, and Metalmark had been a visitor of such momentous importance. And while the delegation waited in the airport to board the plane, they had seen the news videos of Sec.-Gen. Shankar as he gave his life for what he was trying to achieve.

Ilana wept at the loss of friends through violence, and because she was part of a security service that was supposed to have helped in protecting the victims. But most of all, because of the perfect timing of the attack, she feared that the schedule of events that she had prepared for Sec.-Gen. Shankar and Metalmark somehow had gotten into the hands of the extremists, and she had thereby played a role in dooming the victims of the Calcutta attack.

$$1 \wedge$$

Defense Sec. Clifford Saper was in his office at the Pentagon when the alarms sounded. The US military were going to a state of full alert for possible imminent attack. Gen. Mason was calling him by phone. "What's happening?" Saper asked.

"NORAD radar has picked up numerous echoes of high-speed objects that have been launched by the Metalmark starship. They are aimed toward Earth, and there may be fifty or sixty – we can't be sure. This could be a reprisal attack for the Calcutta assassinations. I would hate to be in Karachi about an hour from now when those missiles reach Earth."

"Was there any radio or TV announcement?"

"Only a radio warning to the Chinese spacecraft, telling it to go home."

"Did the NSA ever decode any of Metalmark's radio signals among the satellites?"

"They are still working on it. They say it bears similarities to telemetry in that certain patterns are repeated in blocks that appear to frame segments of data. But they are a long way from recognizing anything else meaningful."

"Has there been any particular signal activity coincident with the missile launches?"

"Nothing out of the ordinary."

"Well, someone or something is active on that mother ship. Those missiles could be nuclear-armed cruise missiles, and fifty are a lot more than I would need to level Imam Shabbir's mosque. The mother ship could be taking action against lots of targets, and it could be some kind of massive retaliation against humankind for the assassination of Metalmark. The safest thing is to notify the President and get him and the staff to safety. Go ahead with that, and I'll join the President in the control center on Air Force One."

The helicopter took off from Andrews AF Base to pick up the White House personnel, and Air Force One was prepped for flight. Jets scrambled and roared over the capital city.

Xueli had placed Feng Chin-Tsai's drifting body into one of the equipment nets. Soon she would have to make a main engine burn to achieve insertion into low Earth orbit, and then start re-entry into the atmosphere at the right point in the orbit to land in Mongolia. It looked as if there would be barely enough fuel but she realized that the mission plan required guidance from the Command Center for the final course corrections. In her oxygen-deprived state, this problem had eluded her, and now it loomed formidably.

She tried to call Command Center, but the antenna was not giving a lock signal; she couldn't tell if it was intact. She brought up the re-entry program on her pilot console. It was dark, lonely and scary in the cabin, with the thermal stress noises instead of a comrade's voice. She kept looking at the body of Feng Chin-Tsai to be certain that he was really dead, yet this did not comfort her. She could not even listen to any of her beloved Ion Torch; no private musical listening devices were permitted on the mission.

She activated the radio and listened, but heard no transmissions, just cosmic hissing.

No thruster bursts had come from the alien device since her last main engine burn. It apparently was not determined to kill her, because it could have sent the Shenzhou 16 into outer space instead of forcing the spacecraft back Earthward. The voice of Metalmark (if it was real) had commanded the taikonauts to go home.

She wondered if the alien device would respond to a distress call.

On Command Center's radio frequency, she spoke into the transmitter. "Metakkk . . . Metal-l-lmark starship." Her voice was weak and difficult to use, sometimes breaking in a cough. "Can you help me re-enter and land? My fuel is too low."

A second passed, and then the voice they had heard from the mother ship's transmission came from the radio, speaking Mandarin. "Are you going home?"

"Yes," Xueli cried, and then coughed because of her throat injury. "Can you help me, please?"

"Assuring that you went home was the purpose of that engine that I attached to your spacecraft. But I see from its logs that it has not been very effective. I am sorry, but it apparently damaged your radio communication system. It was a prototype, anyway. It has a radio system, so I can talk to you. I am reprogramming it now. It still has enough fuel to take you down safely. Where do you want to land?"

Exhilarated, Xueli gave the latitude and longitude of the planned landing, in the desert of Mongolia. Metalmark's voice repeated it back for confirmation.

"Thank you," said Xueli. "We thought you were too angry to help. Sorry to intrude."

"Curiosity is natural for you. Just don't do this again."

"No. It is good for me . . . if . . . you are still alive?"

"You must have heard the terrible news. My good friend Sec.-Gen. Shankar was killed and my body was destroyed. But . . . speaking poetically, I suppose . . . you could say that my soul has moved into a new body. This required such resources that I did not concentrate on ensuring your safe return. That was not good customer relations, but I shall improve. Please express to your government that my offer of a sales contract with the UN is still in effect. I understand that human civilization has dissident and dangerous members. I can adapt to a violent minority opposition if the cost of damage is marginal."

"I must make an engine burn now," said Xueli.

"With respect for your technology, I can do it more accurately with my attached engine."

"With respect . . . you just said that it did not work right before."

"And that was because I was preoccupied with being 'reincarnated,' for want of a better term. The engine was automated then, but now I am operating it with my full powers. Please accept a demonstration of a small part of what my technology can do."

Xueli remembered that he could kill her at any moment if he became displeased, so she mastered her misgivings, closed her eyes and said, "I agree."

"Are you secured with safety restraints?"

"Yes."

She was pressed suddenly and firmly into her pilot chair. The instruments showed that she was over India at the insertion point of a low earth orbit. Mission plans called for another orbit around, to make careful course corrections to manage the re-entry inclination. But Metalmark had just dumped so much momentum that she was falling into the outer atmosphere!

Metalmark's voice said, "I have signaled your Command Center in Beijing on the frequency that you used before. They don't answer, but maybe if you speak, they will accept messages. Do you want to contact them? I will relay your message."

Xueli said, "Command *cough* Center, this is Shenzhou 16. Prepare to retrieve re-entered spacecraft at planned lat-long. Both crew members are . . . seriously injured. Emergency medical condition *cough*."

Metalmark said, "I did not know you were injured. I will be especially careful. What is your name?"

She hesitated. This answer violated mission secrecy. But she was in his power. "Liu Xueli," she answered.

"Oh, you are Amb. Yang Wei's niece! I have heard of you. Please give my kind regards to your uncle when you greet him. I hope to meet you before long. Now prepare for re-entry."

Xueli noticed some sense of "down," which meant that atmospheric drag was beginning to slow the Shenzhou 16. She looked at the viewports but suddenly they were all obscured by the white substance of the attached alien device. She had fuel left so she brought the air conditioning to full power to prevent being overcome by heat. The inertial instruments showed that she was dropping at about the right descent rate.

As the Shenzhou 16 entered the airspace above China's western border, a patrolling Chinese Air Force jet spotted the spacecraft. The pilot of the jet began photographing the re-entry. The white substance of the four-armed artifact had melted and flowed to surround the spacecraft with a heat shield. The velocity was too high for the Shenzhou 16 to survive re-entry without that coating. The Shenzhou 16 was surrounded by an orange plasma cloud of ionized air. As the coating heated up it ballooned into an inflated expanding airfoil for aerobraking, and glowed red as it radiated away the excess heat.

Falling from the stratosphere into the troposphere, after ten minutes the Shenzhou 16 had lost most of its horizontal momentum and was now above the planned landing site. That site was in the vast deserts of Mongolia. The surface of the airfoil balloon split at four slits along the axis of motion, and air blew in to fill the balloon like a parachute. In this parachute mode the Shenzhou 16 slowly dropped to make a gentle landing near the vehicles of the arriving Chinese pick-up crew.

State-owned TV cameras recorded Liu Xueli's exit from the spacecraft when its hatch was opened. She coughed as she said, "Happy to be home . . . my throat is injured. Doctor, please!"

As she was put on a stretcher in her space suit, emergency medics entered the spacecraft and found Feng Chin-Tsai's body and the bloody knife. Grim-faced they emerged to report, "There has been a murder, and one taikonaut is dead. Take her to the hospital but also inform the military police and state prosecutor's office!"

$$\underline{M}$$

Across the world, for a second time, TV Channel 2 carried an announcement by Metalmark. "I want to join with Acting Sec.-Gen. Molyneux in expressing my condolences to everyone effected by the murder of my friend Sec.-Gen. Sanjeev Shankar. He was a great force for progress and compassion toward the poor on your world. I regret that my trade proposal was the excuse for his murder. There was nothing he wanted more than for that trade agreement to be made, and I announce that his wishes are still possible to achieve.

"My first body for visiting your planet was destroyed, but I have relocated into another, and will visit you again soon. The United Nations are still my exclusive agency for the settlement of the contract of sale that I am offering. Although the deliberations at the UN to consider my contract had slowed before the incident in Calcutta, I hope that UN delegates will renew consideration of my offer now. Closing our contract would be a great step in progress for your planet, as well as proof that terrorists cannot win."

Boarding Air Force One, the frazzled first family and White House staff were greeted by confusion. Sec. Saper and the flight crew were treating the situation as a dire emergency, but Metalmark's broadcast claimed that he was not dead and was preparing to renew friendly relations. Pres. Jackson sat in the command center beside Sec. Saper and said, "Cliff, what's happened to those missiles?"

"There were sixty of them, and none were aimed at known population centers. They entered the atmosphere south of India where we don't have much radar coverage. We are making every effort to learn where they have gone to evade detection."

The pilot ordered passengers to strap in, and the plane soon accelerated and became airborne. First Lady Meg Jackson was in the rear conference room, watching NTC's news broadcast and logging onto the Internet to look for reports of the whereabouts of the missiles. Everyone on board was speculating about whether the Metalmark announcement was a deception and why. They had all seen the televised assassinations. How could he be alive?

But after an hour of evasive flight on Air Force One, it became clear to the occupants that Washington, DC, and all other major cities were experiencing an uneventful day. The sixty mysterious missiles never reappeared on radar of the US or its allies. By 5:00 PM, Pres. Jackson ordered the military to stand down from the alert.

Liu Xueli rested on the spartan bed in her prison cell in Beijing. The doctors had treated damaged cartilage that Feng Chin-Tsai had crushed in her windpipe, and it was healing. The prosecutor had taken her written statement that the killing of Feng Chin-Tsai was in self-defense. She had finished with the tears and was trying to come to terms with the emotional roller-coaster ride of the last twenty-four hours, from celebrity taikonaut to failed spacecraft pilot to murderer of one of the nation's brightest and best space mission commanders. Perhaps she should just be grateful to be alive.

The lock of her cell clattered with a key turn and then the door opened. Into the room came her mother. Xueli jumped up and started toward her mother, but stopped, stepped back and knelt to bow down before her.

"Mother, I am sorry to be such a calamity. Everything that I dreamed of has crashed and destroyed me. Thank you for visiting me. Please keep visiting me when they sentence me for the murder." She dissolved into tears there on the floor.

"Daughter Xueli! Get up, here, sit with me on the bed. It's not quite so bad — I have news. Don't cry like that!"

Her mother faced the wall with the large mirror, really a one-way glass behind which the security guards watched Xueli. "Guards, deactivate your surveillance microphones and turn your faces away until I leave. You are not cleared for the classified data that Liu Xueli and I are about to discuss. Do it now!"

To Xueli she said, "Your story is corroborated. The mission engineers used the surveillance camera recordings to make a movie of Feng Chin-Tsai attacking you, and they showed he was still attacking you with a knife when you killed him. You fought well, Daughter! I am proud of you!"

"Surveillance cameras?" asked Xueli.

"The spacecraft was filled with them. They were too small for you to notice, little lenses embedded in the walls for views from all angles."

Xueli hugged her mother, now that she seemed to approve of her daughter's actions. Tears of relief streamed from her eyes. "Feng Chin-Tsai will be tried posthumously for improperly assaulting a subordinate officer. You are no longer charged with murder but with mutinous insubordination while resisting decisions of a superior officer."

"What?"

"As commander, Feng Chin-Tsai had authority to decide to kill you if it was necessary to achieve the success of the mission. But the mission was a failure already because it was repelled with overwhelming technological superiority. Killing you was not going to make the mission succeed. So the Central Committee has ruled."

"So . . . I will still be tried for killing the commander during a mutiny?"

"Yes, you failed to submit to chain of command by killing a superior officer, who cost the motherland hundreds of millions of yuan to train. And his family is very angry. They heard a rumor that he was dead, so the mission secrecy has been breached. Xinhua News is preparing a press release according to official

Information Ministry directives. But it will not be announced until after your trial. What they say about you depends on the verdict."

Xueli ran her fingers through her hair and wiped tears from her cheeks with her shirt. "I will have to get a lawyer and defend myself."

"There will be a state-appointed lawyer for you. He will be very good."

"How will he defend me?"

"He will point out that Feng Chin-Tsai erroneously tried to kill an Olympian of China who also represented an investment of hundreds of millions of yuan in taikonaut training costs. But the lawyer will also be able to present your great achievements on the mission to weigh in your favor as service to the nation."

"What great achievements?!" Xueli asked, incredulous at this characterization of the failed mission.

"Look at this," said her mother, opening a file of papers that had been under her arm. The file had "CLASSIFIED" stamped on it but the ideogram was marked out and initialed by a state security official. "This picture shows the outside of the Metalmark mother ship. It is covered with these shiny formations. There are hundreds of them with iridescent butterfly wings. They move about like a swarm covering the starship. These may be the first pictures of inhabitants of the Metalmark spacecraft. They were taken by high-resolution cameras on the Shenzhou 16, which you successfully brought safely back to Earth. You induced Metalmark to reveal himself and some of his technology. His atmospheric re-entry system is spectacular to watch! I will bring my laptop and show you a movie.

"Some parts of his re-entry system are still attached to the Shenzhou 16, and our scientists have begun analyzing them. His rocket engine is very advanced beyond Earth technology."

Xueli began to feel that these things could be presented in her favor.

"Some of this is going to stay a State Secret for now. You have been cleared since you know most of it already. Metalmark was definitely destroyed in Calcutta, but he is alive again. He has some kind of technology for reincarnation of souls. China has an advantage at understanding the value of Metalmark's technology because he revealed it to you. Because you brought back this secret, Amb. Yang Wei will champion the sales contract with Metalmark in the UN."

Her mother continued, "I heard the recordings of him talking to you in the Shenzhou 16. He already knew who you were! I think you had a pretty good relationship starting there."

Xueli burst out laughing. This was her mother's segue into another mock lecture about finding a husband.

"He only knew about me because of Uncle Wei," she said.

"You did good, Daughter," her mother said. "I've had to go to these meetings where high Central Committee officials talked about you, and I was recused from discussion because you are my daughter, but they were in awe of you. You beat the top taikonaut in a knife fight! When I am in these meetings and I think, *My daughter is dangerous!* it gives me a little smile. The Central Committee will weigh everything and your trial will wrap it up, then I think big things are ahead of you."

Before long her mother left. The world now turned on a very different, bewildering axis. Xueli had to come to terms with a new relationship to the space program. The mission controllers had a role in this disaster: now she understood why the life support system on the Shenzhou 16 had used excess fuel; the dozens of secret surveillance cameras were using up unnecessary power in the circuit. If the cameras had not wasted that fuel, then there would have been enough for both taikonauts to survive the mission, and Feng Chin-Tsai would not have attacked her. They would both be alive now and she would not be in jail.

Xueli knelt again on the floor and said a prayer to the ancestors for Feng Chin-Tsai's soul, and for her own.

V

PRES. JACKSON ANSWERED a call from Acting Sec.-Gen. Molyneux. "Bernard, at this tragic and turbulent time, I want you to know that my country takes comfort because you have stepped up to your present position. We support your public statement about the Calcutta attack, and the US continues to stand ready to help your organization as it recovers and moves forward."

"Thank you, Mr. President. The toll on all of the staff here has been overwhelming, and we appreciate your support. Right away I must consult with you about the mind-boggling message we just received: another TV transmission has just arrived claiming to be from Metalmark, asserting that he is not dead. This is disturbing and confusing, because we brought home the remains of the body. But I suppose we must try to adapt our reactions to allow for the powers of a civilization with vastly superior technology."

The acting Sec.-Gen.'s voice conveyed the effects of a night without sleep followed by a day of struggling to deal with the assassinations. He continued, "I personally would welcome cooperation with your NASA agency to confirm the claims of the new communication. I also ask that the Metalmark landing vehicle be given permission to return to Kennedy Space Center. If that landing does in fact take place, then I suppose we shall soon find out whether he is reincarnated, and whether the possibility of the trade agreement still exists. I thank God that there is no sign of vengeful motives in the communication."

Pres. Jackson replied, "I was also notified of the TV message, and didn't know what to make of it. You may be interested to know that my Cabinet believed all along that Metalmark was a synthetic being – artificial, I mean. To us, the idea that he could be reincarnated is not so shocking, but . . ."

"But I worked with him in person, and joined him at a dinner party at the Shankars' home. Believe me, he was much more than a robot to me and my staff. I am disturbed by the loss of Sanjeev and Metalmark, but I'm hoping that somehow Metalmark is resurrected, but not daring to believe it until I see it. If you would send some NASA staff to join me at the Kennedy Space Center, I would like to have them with our delegation to meet . . . whatever emerges from the landing craft."

"Of course," said Pres. Jackson. "I'll send Administrator Krainak to cooperate with you. Don't hesitate to rely on us if you need anything more."

M

Admin. Marv Krainak and Dr. Steve Simmons boarded a NASA jet for Kennedy Space Center. Simmons was in a very confused state of mind. After the Calcutta attack news, the outrageous assassinations of the alien visitor and UN head had sent him into dark despair, and he was skeptical about whether there was reason to hope that Metalmark was resurrected somehow.

Admin. Krainak was sitting in a seat that faced Dr. Simmons' seat across a small, fold-down table, reading e-mail on a BlackBerry while they flew over northern Florida. He finished the e-mail and put the BlackBerry into a pocket. "The first Metalmark was a synthetic being, as you saw from the photos of the body. When we get back the analysis of the body, we'll know more, but I think we can establish a few things. As realistic as he appeared, Metalmark must have been a robot, like our Mars rovers. I think he could be 'reincarnated' because he was never really on Earth. He was always up on the main starship, operating the body by remote control via the necklace of telecom satellites. Plausible?"

Simmons said, "That could be. I guess the only test would be time delays. When someone conversed with him, there would be a delay as the body sent signals up to the starship and replies came back at the speed of light. That would take at least a half second. I watched the Jayno show with you, and I don't remember noticing a latency delay like that in his responses. We are dealing with a very advanced civilization. Maybe they have computer code that can carry on a conversation, and they ran the code in a CPU in the robot body. But it was remarkable how naturally he mimicked a human being, if it was all done with simulation code."

"He said he's a silicon-based life form, and he is very 'blended' with his technology. Maybe he *is* the code-CPU blend," Krainak wondered

"But then destroying the body would have killed that copy of him. A new copy wouldn't exactly be a 'reincarnation' ."

"I think he called it relocation," said Krainak.

"If he will talk with us despite the absence of a contract, maybe we'll know soon," said Simmons.

The warning tone sounded, indicating the start of descent to land on one of the runways at Kennedy Space Center. They were soon on the ground, where they exited the NASA jet and joined the UN group in a van that would await Metalmark's lander, a mile from its original landing site.

Sec.-Gen. Molyneux greeted the NASA administrator and Dr. Simmons gratefully. "I don't know what to expect, even though we have been notified that a spacecraft has begun descending from Metalmark's starship. I asked the president to send you so that I can unambiguously determine whether Metalmark has survived the assassination, or some more inconceivable trick or reprisal is being inflicted on us."

The lander arrived on time just as it had on its first landfall. The spherical bubble atop a brilliant rocket exhaust appeared the same as it descended, and unfolded into a nest of solar panels surrounded by dispersing rocket exhaust. After the cloud of exhaust drifted away, the NASA van brought the humans to the lander where it sat on one end of the Space Shuttle runway. A platoon of military police set up a ring of guards around the lander.

Metalmark emerged from the shifting maze of panels. He looked much the same, except that he was stockier of build. He wore the same style of navy turtleneck shirt and slacks. His face and expressions were the same.

The UN party got out of the van and greeted him with handshakes. Sec.-Gen. Molyneux said, "Is it really you?"

"Yes, except sadder and wiser," replied Metalmark. "And encumbered by several more pounds of built-in armor around my critical modules. Please send my greetings to Solange. I recall that your wife was concerned because I couldn't eat at the Shankars' dinner. I have put on quite a bit of weight."

"I will," Molyneux said warmly. "She will be very glad to know that you are alive. How is this possible?"

"I must save the details until after the contract, but I can tell you that I am able to focus my presence at nodes within an extensive region of space. I meet you now as a new node of presence.

"I am pleased to accompany you back to the UN, Sec.-Gen. Molyneux, but I also had expected to see Ilana Lindler."

Sec.-Gen. Molyneux replied, "Ilana sent a text message that she would be using some sick leave to recover from the stress of the Calcutta trip. Several members of the delegation are doing the same, but Ilana was very deeply disturbed by the horrific events. I hope she will be back after some rest."

"I hope so, too," said Metalmark. "I have learned much from her accompaniment."

He turned to Dr. Simmons. "Thank you for your interest in my arrival. Your commentary on my trajectory has enhanced my publicity."

Dr. Simmons shook the alien's hand for the first time. It was a good simulation of a warm handshake, and he felt mostly taken in by the illusion. Metalmark's visage was a remarkable work of art in polymers. Dr. Simmons said, "You're welcome. And I add my welcome back to our planet. Like many people I'm revolted by the way that you were attacked. I hope that you can forgive it, because it wasn't characteristic of mankind."

Metalmark responded, "That is my conclusion, too. Sec.-Gen. Shankar explained to me that people like the attackers act out of fear, so I will endeavor to eliminate their fears through my actions."

Administrator Krainak watched this conversation with a tight smile. Metalmark could not be a "rover" operated by radio from the mother ship. Then how had he been reconstructed so faithfully?

Sec.-Gen. Molyneux said, "Metalmark, we invite you to return to New York, where I have called a Security Council meeting to press for settlement of the trade deal that you propose. By this technological miracle of yours, perhaps we can conclude the long deliberative procedure and bring the issue to a vote of the member nations."

Metalmark and the delegation were soon flying back to New York on a UN plane, while the NASA jet returned to its home base. Dr. Simmons sat next to Metalmark and they discussed the forthcoming book.

"I will read the articles for the book and comment if that is useful to you," Metalmark offered. "There could well be material of substance in the authors' speculations about alien civilizations, and I expect to learn from them."

Dr. Simmons suppressed a smile and wondered if he was being patronized. "The authors will be quite hesitant to speculate about you – you're the chief topic of the book – while knowing that you will be ready to pounce on their mistaken ideas."

"I wasn't intending to pass judgment on all of their comments. As a traveler in the Galaxy, I have less foreknowledge than you imagine about beings that I encounter when I stop for spawning. There is always the unexpected when trying to make peaceful contact. I could learn from your co-authors' intelligent speculation."

Dr. Simmons said, "The spawning that you mentioned will certainly inspire speculation among the authors. You said it was a private matter, but it's human nature to be curious about procreation."

Metalmark said, "That curiosity will be satisfied after the contract. But if there are chapters of your book that touch on matters embargoed until the contract, then maybe work on the book should be postponed until the contract."

"That's the tension here," Dr. Simmons said. "The authors want the chance to *predict* your qualities on the basis of their mastery of science and their perceptions about you from the Jayno show. And they have egos that will be bruised if they're declared wrong in your sections of the book. It's going to be tricky, but there must be a solution."

"Maybe if I just praise their scholarship in general but write about inhabitants of other planets, I will contribute something welcome without spoiling the game," suggested Metalmark.

Marv Krainak listened in on this conversation and was stunned to see what was happening. The most advanced scientific ideas of humankind were only a game to this being for whom even death was only a couple of days' inconvenience. The scientists that NASA had convinced to write the book chapters would only be embarrassed by the alien trader's condescension. Admin. Krainak decided then and there that the book project was doomed from the moment that Metalmark became involved, and rendered the authors' principal objectives moot.

While the UN delegation flew Metalmark to New York, the world reacted to the announcement that Metalmark was back on Earth. The Internet and broadcast networks came alive with all possible reactions. Cautious news services presented the claim as not fully substantiated, but bloggers and radio talk shows presented every opinion from total disbelief to assertions that the Calcutta attack telecasts were faked, as well as mystical attributions of god-like immortality to Metalmark. The UN Security Council prepared to convene while the world media buzzed with controversy. (The taikonauts' mission to the starship was not yet public, however. The US government had discretely refrained from publicizing the Chinese mission, since NORAD radar tracking suggested that it had been a failure.)

When the UN plane landed at La Guardia airport, Sec.-Gen. Molyneux led Metalmark to a waiting limousine. Before entering, Sec.-Gen. Molyneux stepped aside and consulted the NASA representatives. "Is it safe to proceed with confidence that this really is Metalmark?" he asked.

"I am convinced that the being I conversed with is interchangeable with the first being that we knew as Metalmark," said Admin. Krainak. "What do you think, Steve?"

Dr. Simmons replied, "His behavior and knowledge of the actions that he took prior to the Calcutta attack are sufficient evidence of identity, in my opinion. If there are any differences besides the more stout physique of this second body, we can't identify them. I think the UN can carry on negotiating with him with just as much credibility as before the attack."

"Thank you, gentlemen," said Sec.-Gen. Molyneux. "It's good to have independent views that confirm my reaction, because we are dealing with such a surrealistic event, yet the future of human progress depends on it." The three of them joined Metalmark in the limo, which conveyed them to another runway where a UN helicopter waited to fly them to the UN Building.

At the UN, a press conference was set up under tight security. The Sec.-Gen. introduced Metalmark without comment about the bizarre turns of recent events. "Ladies and gentlemen, Metalmark's shuttle traveled from his starship to another meeting with our UN delegation at Kennedy Space Center in Florida. Metalmark emerged from the shuttle in another body, and we have confirmed with help from NASA officials that this is also Metalmark, as surprising as that may be to people of our level of technological advancement. He has agreed to take some questions before the meeting of the Security Council convenes."

Cameras flashed and reporters began shouting questions. "How do we know that you are really Metalmark?" one asked. The others quieted for the answer.

"Your US Air Force tracked my shuttle, and your NASA officials tested my identity with questions. These tests would be hard to deceive you about."

Another reporter said, "You were reported dead. Can you explain your return from the dead?"

"As I said on the Jayno program, I visit Earth in an artificial body. The Calcutta attack destroyed one such body. But my presence can focus at nodes in a very extensive space, and I was never dead. I am meeting you now by means of another node of presence in a new body. If the UN agrees to the contract for purchase of my technology package, then I will explain more about this after the purchase."

Another reporter said, "You don't look the same. You look fatter."

"This new body is stronger and more durable."

"Did you get hurt in the attack? Do you want revenge?"

"I did not experience pain physically, but I am very sad that my friend Sec.-Gen. Shankar was killed. I hope that the authorities bring his killers to justice for their crimes. I will help in that pursuit if there is any way I can. I don't hold the actions of a few scared extremists against humankind. I am here for peaceful trade to benefit myself and you.

"I have just received a message by radio in connection with the Calcutta attacks. While preparing this new body, I sent sixty of my sea-water concentration units to operate in the Indian Ocean. There they collected six hundred pounds of gold, which I donated to the city of Calcutta for the benefit of the victims of the attack. City officials have just responded to my donation, and they say that they have received the metal. This will pay for the hospital bills of those who were injured in the auditorium where we were attacked, pay for funeral expenses of those who died as a result, and provide pensions for the disabled victims."

The reporters gave this announcement some applause. Metalmark continued, "The 'Food from Stones' program will go on. I will make the technology available to any nation that wants to use it." There was some more clapping.

Then one of the reporters asked, "Do you have technology for reincarnation of souls?"

"I'm not sure what that means. If the trade agreement is completed, then you will know all of my technology."

"There is a claim on the Internet that you and others staged the Calcutta attack to win sympathy for your trade offer and profit thereby."

Metalmark responded, "That is false. The authorities in Bengal province have captured a group of commandos who admit to carrying out the attack. They come from various nations such as Iran, who are hostile to my trade offer. It would not make sense for me to conspire with commando attackers who killed my best human friend, Sanjeev Shankar."

"Metalmark, your advanced technology appears to have a spiritual aspect, more powerful than death. Are you a supernatural being, such as an angel in modern trappings?"

"I am the owner of some advanced technology, but as I stated, I was not dead. If the UN decides to purchase my technology, then you will have all of the details about it. I'm not sure what an angel is precisely, but I don't think that I am one."

Sec.-Gen. Molyneux decided that the questions were receiving repetitious answers, so he called a halt and conducted Metalmark out of the room despite the persistent reporters' continuing questions.

Defense Sec. Saper and Gen. Mason watched the news conference. At the end, Mason said, "I like the use he made of the missiles, but I would have preferred advance notice so that we didn't have to spend $2 million to evacuate the White House onto Air Force One."

Sec. Saper said, "I still can't believe that he's back and all is forgiven. There must be some reprisal coming.

"Did the NSA ever learn any more about those signals he uses?"

"Yes, they started aiming radio antennas at Metalmark's location from some of their orbiting listening satellites. They were able to establish that he doesn't just listen to transmissions from his satellites; he also transmits and the satellites respond. The NSA was able to track the UN plane as he flew from New York to Calcutta and record his signals to and from his satellites. He's in nearly constant contact with his network, both sending and receiving. But whatever the transmissions encode, it's not anything humanly recognizable."

"Okay, since we have a good history of his transmissions, let's finish that signal jammer that we talked about. At some point we might have reason to show him that we can cut him off from his network if we need to."

"The jammer is almost ready," said Gen. Mason. "It's the size of a hand-held GPS unit and battery powered. We can load it with some recorded fragments of his own signals and transmit them at high power from close range. It will overwhelm his own signal strength – send noise to his network and prevent him from getting any signal except ours."

"Good," said Sec. Saper. "That can show him that we aren't totally defenseless technologically."

Ilana Lindler was lying curled up on the couch in her apartment. Awakening from a miserable, nightmare-ridden sleep, she sat up, tried to rub matted, unwashed hair into place, and wiped tears on her pajama sleeve. She had been lying there a long time and her neck was stiff. The cold remains of a partly-eaten pizza reposed in a box on the dining table. She got up and turned on her Mac notebook.

She activated the recorder that she had used to capture Metalmark's last words and turned it on. She spoke into the microphone. "This is agent Eunice. This recording is my last report. I hereby resign from employment by the Company, effective immediately. Please transfer my final fee to the usual account. I am not interested in further employment by the Company. Thank you. Good-bye."

While she connected to the Internet and uploaded this encrypted audio file to the usual network node, her news agents produced many puzzling search results. Media seemed to be describing Metalmark's activities as if he were alive. She connected to her favorite news sites on the web. It was disorienting. The NTC network site had a summary of the events since the Calcutta attack, and she learned the strange turns of events. Metalmark had just given a news conference and the Security Council was about to meet to rule on his contract. But in this unreal dream world, Sec.-Gen. Shankar was still dead and Bernard Molyneux was described as Sec.-Gen.

She made sure the upload was complete and turned off the Mac. So strange. Was she still dreaming? She went to the shower to try to pull herself together.

In the UN Security Council chambers, acting Sec.-Gen. Bernard Molyneux asked the current Council president to call the Council meeting to order. The

Council's first action was to recommend to the full UN body that the Acting Sec.-Gen. be empowered to perform the duties of Sec.-Gen. until the complete process of selecting a UN chief resulted in a permanent appointment. This was resolved without complication.

Then a vote was held to threaten Pakistan with sanctions unless there was cooperation in the effort to find Imam Shabbir and anyone else in Pakistan who had been party to the Calcutta attack. The vote passed by a strong majority. Following this, the Council imposed a travel ban and freezing of Imam Shabbir's assets (abstaining were China and Indonesia).

Finally Sec.-Gen. Molyneux presented the Metalmark contract for consideration. The Security Council ambassadors and aides passed the papers around the huge oval table. In legal language prepared by the UN's General Counsel the document expressed Metalmark's trade agreement. After an hour of careful reading the fifteen nations' representatives agreed to vote on a resolution to send the trade agreement to the full UN assembly with the recommendation to accept or decline the agreement.

Of the five permanent Council members, the USA, the United Kingdom, France and China voted in favor of accepting Metalmark's offer. Russia abstained, choosing to avoid angering Muslim member nations.

The ten non-permanent Council members added eight votes in favor and one (Indonesia) opposed. The meeting adjourned after two hours, with a solid majority in favor of the contract. Sirpa Hakkinen, the General Assembly president, congratulated Metalmark, who had watched the proceedings. Then she went to her office to arrange the General Assembly meeting.

US Amb. Paul Kirk shook Metalmark's hand and said, "It is gratifying to give you my country's support. I feel sure that Sanjeev Shankar's legacy will be the ratification of your historic trade accord. I know that you will want to be here for the vote by the General Assembly, and Pres. Jackson has extended an invitation to you for a celebration at the White House after the vote."

Metalmark said, "I am happy that you are so confident, and I will be available."

Amb. Yang Wei came to Metalmark and shook his hand. "My country is happy to support your trade offer. Our scientists are most impressed with your technology. I personally am grateful for your assistance to the space vehicle, which has not caused you any offense, I hope."

"Polite curiosity is not offensive. And in an unrelated topic, I hope your niece is in good health."

"She is better," Amb. Yang replied, and hurried away to avoid any further possible loss of face.

The other ambassadors left to report to their governments on the results and campaign with the other UN nations for votes in the General Assembly session the next day. Sec.-Gen. Molyneux came over to sit with Metalmark when the room had cleared. He said, "A good vote! I think the momentum is with us."

"I'm very grateful for your support," said Metalmark. "I wish Sanjeev could have been here. I wonder . . . would it be possible for me to visit Uma?"

Sec.-Gen. Molyneux replied, "I'll call her and ask if she is taking visitors."

"And, may I call Ilana? She would be pleased by these events."

"Here, use my cell phone," said Molyneux. He punched up Ilana's home number and dialed it.

There were several rings without a pick-up, and then Ilana's recorded voice said, "This is Lindlerflat. I'd like a *message*, please." *Beep.*

Metalmark said, "Ilana, this is Metalmark. I have come back in a new body, and Bernard and I just witnessed a vote by the Security Council to recommend my trade offer to the General Assembly for approval. It was very exciting, and we missed you. I wanted to tell you about it . . ."

Ilana picked up. "Who is this really?"

Sec.-Gen. Molyneux was sitting next to Metalmark and could hear her voice. He chimed in, "This is Bernard, too. It really happened as he said, and he is really back."

Metalmark said, "Ilana, it's really me. Do you remember the Shankars' dinner? We all shared our first thoughts, and Uma asked me if the gods could be visitors from space like me?"

Ilana was silent for a moment, and then concluded that only Metalmark could know that. "How can you be back?"

Sec.-Gen. Molyneux said, "I have to wrap up something else. Come up to my office when you're done with the phone." He rushed away.

Metalmark said, "My location in space is flexible within a large domain. I'll explain the details later. I built another human-like body and returned to Earth as soon as I could. I think this has impressed some doubtful delegates, so the Security Council voted for me. Now they are going to have a General Assembly meeting for the final decision. So Bernard and I wanted you to join us and go to visit Uma."

Ilana's voice broke. "I can't . . . I don't deserve to work for you."

"What's wrong? You have done fine work for our efforts."

Guilty tears wet Ilana's cheeks. "I . . . compromised your secrets."

"I don't have any secrets from you. What do you mean?"

Ilana could hear in her mind the terrible words on TV broadcasts, describing her dismissal from the core UN staff for "activities incompatible with her status," the standard euphemism for spying. She said, "When you started the 'Food from Stones' presentation, I was outside the auditorium on the phone. And when I heard the shooting start, I tried to go in and help you. But the security people wouldn't let any women into the burning auditorium. I wanted to go in and help you . . . help you." She was sobbing.

Metalmark said, "Of course you would. I know you would have tried your best to help. But it was impossible."

"You don't understand. I . . . spied on you." He could hear her sobbing.

"Oh, are you talking about the recorder? I didn't mind that. I knew you were recording my words."

"How did you know?"

"I could hear with my radio senses that there was a little electronic echo of everything I said, coming from you. But I've never said anything to you that I was hiding."

"I was spying."

"Who were you spying for? Pres. Jackson?"

She paused a long time. "Yes, for his government."

"Well, that's okay with me. He is a friend. I've seen spy movies – '007' and things like that – so I'd expect the president of the United States to have good spies. I don't mind if you sent my words to his ear. You did great work for our efforts, and I want you to come back to help us finish the job."

She thought about it. "I want to come back. I can only do it if you don't tell anyone. Bernard would be mad."

"You can trust me," said Metalmark. "This is because I have been able to trust you for all of this time."

"But I wasn't trustworthy! The schedule of events got to the hands of those attackers somehow. I should have kept it secret."

"Is this what upset you? It wasn't you that leaked the schedule; it was that police chief who told the Islamic extremists that they could come in. He has confessed and been fired. It was not your fault. Please don't blame yourself for the attack. You have been a kind and helpful guide for me, and Sanjeev was proud of your work. I still need your guidance. And Bernard and I want to go to visit Uma. Will you accompany us?"

She was overwhelmed, but managed to get the sobs under control. After a few minutes, she said, "Alright. I can get ready. I'll take a cab and meet you there."

"I'm glad you will come. Thank you. We will call you for a timing update. Good-bye, Ilana." He pressed the disconnect button and went to the elevator to the Sec.-Gen.'s office.

Ilana was swimming up from the drowning. Maybe by some miracle it was going to be alright for her, if not for Sec.-Gen. Shankar. With much of her guilt absolved, she began to get ready.

M̲

The NTC Nightly News Summary was full of momentous events that evening in the USA. "Good evening, everyone. I'm Carl Foreman. It was a day full of historic events for the progress of our planet. After the horrific destruction of the Calcutta attack on Metalmark's 'Food from Stones' campaign, and the assassination of the UN's head, Metalmark returned to Earth in some sort of resurrected form and gave a press conference. Using his advanced technology for philanthropic ends, he donated gold valued at hundreds of thousands of dollars to the city of Calcutta for the medical care and bereavement benefits of the Calcutta attack victims." Video of Metalmark speaking at the UN was shown.

The news anchor reappeared. "Metalmark followed this up by attending a UN Security Council meeting where a vote was taken to recommend to the full UN General Assembly that Metalmark's trade deal be accepted. A strong majority of the council passed this resolution, and the UN is finally about to vote on this long-awaited but controversial first-ever trade agreement with an extraterrestrial technologically advanced civilization. But the objections of the Islamic nations resurged in the form of demonstrations in the streets of all of the major capital cities of Muslim-dominated nations." Video showed crowds carrying banners in many languages, protesting Metalmark's alleged offenses against Islam.

A reporter stopped a demonstrator in Jakarta who spoke English. "Why are you demonstrating?"

"Because the UN is about to trade sacred planets of God to an unholy jinnee. Only some kind of demon who works for Satan could return from the dead. The West has allied with evil spirits because they want more high-technology toys and weapons to persecute the Islamic nation and fortify Israel."

The anchorman reappeared. "Muslim nations are poised to oppose the UN General Assembly vote tomorrow, irrespective of the advancements in technology that Metalmark has offered to humanity in return for possession of the planet Mercury and the moon Triton of the planet Neptune.

"UN Ambassador from the United States, Paul Kirk, is campaigning for the Metalmark trade agreement among delegates from nations that are undecided. In a rare alignment, so is Chinese UN Ambassador Yang Wei, whose country welcomes the technological progress that Metalmark promises. The wild card Security Council member seems to be Russia, which abstained on the Security Council vote and has recommended a 'wait and see' approach to its allies, many of which are in the Islamic bloc.

"The Islamic voting bloc is led by countries like Iran, which today declared the assassin of UN Chief Sanjeev Shankar, Hassan Khani, who is an Iranian citizen, to be a hero of Iran and Islam. The Iranian President demanded that Khani be released from a Calcutta prison and returned to Iran. Indian authorities say that Khani is charged with conspiracy and murder, and will not be released."

$\underline{\mathbb{M}}$

Metalmark, Sec.-Gen. Molyneux and Ilana Lindler rendezvoused at Uma Shankar's flat. The door was answered by her daughter Ajitha, who invited them in. Several cardboard boxes were in the living room, recently packed. Ajitha said, "My mother is planning a trip to Calcutta. She wants to take my father's body home for a traditional Buddhist funeral. Then she has other plans that she will tell you about. Thank you very much for visiting!"

Uma came into the room from the kitchen with a tray of cups filled with lassi. She was wearing a red sari, a color of mourning. Her eyes were puffy from weeping, but she seemed to have composed herself as she put down the tray and embraced Ilana, who was tearing up again. She gave Bernard Molyneux a hug, as he said, "Solange sends her deepest sympathy along with mine. All of us at the UN are grieving."

Metalmark came and took her hand. "When I first met Sanjeev, I asked for his protection. How naïve I was! Can you ever forgive me for drawing your husband into such danger?"

"Don't ask to be forgiven," she said. "You were not at fault. He chose to stand up against the religious fanatics. I was a Hindu but he was a Buddhist, and he tried to give the compassion of Gotama to everyone, not take sides. So the sides often threatened him."

"He was a great world leader and friend," said Metalmark. "His guidance was idealistic and I owe the small success that I have found to his influence."

Uma said, "When I got the news, I was so sad and miserable about everything. People started calling and I had to make decisions about family finances and business. It was overwhelming. I kept saying, 'If only Sanjeev were here to put things back right.'

"But then somehow I began to ask myself what Sanjeev would do if he were here. And when I did that, I knew that he would describe everything, the situation, and try to fix it. He would say that when we left Calcutta, after the hospital was built, there was peace between the Hindus and Muslims. He would point out that the Islamic extremists had come in from the outside and brought destruction and separation. What was needed was more healing. If Sanjeev were here, he would go home to Calcutta and work against the divisions again, heal them again. Our home was hurt, and so Sanjeev would go back to it and speak and work with compassion.

"So this is how I realized what I should do. And then I got the call from the city officials. They asked me to come and manage the funds that you donated for the medicines and for the widows. It was almost as if Sanjeev was within me, taking action as he always did. So I agreed to go home for my home city. I am a widow, and traditionally widows were often treated as 'bad luck' and shunned. It's a horrific custom. But now I can bring resources for healing and comfort, and be a force for good luck to the widows."

Metalmark said, "I'm glad to hear that they called you. If anyone can do what you plan, it must be you. But I am surprised at your power to experience the guidance of Sanjeev even though he is gone. You have a profound power that is beyond me. I will do what I can to support the work you are undertaking."

"Ajitha is going to join me in Calcutta. She has arranged to continue her studies via the Internet."

Ajitha said, "My brother Vikram is also coming with us. We will set up a partnership of the University of Calcutta, Harvard and MIT for the students in Calcutta to enroll."

Uma's guests stayed for another hour until more visitors called, and they took their leave.

17

The General Assembly convened in Special Session at the request of Acting Sec.-Gen. Molyneux. All 191 member nations were represented in the General Assembly Hall (some by their foreign ministers as well as by their formal ambassadors) or voting by proxy. The Hall was roaring with conversations, and required repeated calls for order by Assembly Pres. Sirpa Hakkinen. She requested that Sec.-Gen. Molyneux make a brief opening statement for the session.

Sec.-Gen. Molyneux said, "I thank the Security Council for confirming my temporary appointment to serve as successor of Sec.-Gen. Shankar. He was a great world leader for peaceful reconciliation of conflicts and for compassion toward the poor. He fell in the struggle to advance these worthy goals. His legacy is a work in progress by us today, as he had no more passionate goal than the settling of the trade agreement with our planet's first technologically advanced visitor, Metalmark. You have the text of that agreement before you today, and the strong recommendation of the Security Council that this body approve and accept Metalmark's offer to advance the technological level of human civilization by a tremendous degree. This advance is to come in exchange for the planet Mercury and moon Triton of the planet Neptune. In my own judgment this organization should accept the agreement in view of its great advantages for the citizens of our planet, relative to a cost of little consequence to our needs. As you vote, please keep in mind the future of your nations' citizens, whose livelihoods will benefit in advancements beyond any that we can conceive today."

Pres. Hakkinen announced, "Each member nation will now have the

125

opportunity to vote. Each delegate will please respond with the vote as the roster is read."

Afghanistan abstained. Albania voted "No." So did Algeria. The Islamic bloc was showing its solidity right away. The Principality of Andorra was the first "Yes" vote. Angola agreed.

As the voting continued, the coalitions emerged. The close allies of the USA and European Union, along with the South American nations, voted "Yes." China and its allies also voted "Yes." The former soviet satellites such as Belarus voted "Abstain" as Russia had in the Security Council. Nations without large Muslim populations who were not part of those groups, such as India ("Yes") could go either way. And Islamic nations almost all voted "No."

Indeed, when Iran's ambassador, Ali Mahmoudi, got his turn, he stood up and announced, "The Islamic Republic of Iran condemns this blasphemous charade. The evil demon that some of this organization's members have embraced will turn against you and become the instrument of Allah's judgment upon your infidel corruption." He took off his shoes, shook them in the direction of Metalmark, who was observing from the guest seats, and said, "Our vote is 'No'." Then he threw the shoes in Metalmark's direction, turned and walked out of the Hall, followed by most of the delegates of the sympathetic Islamic states. As the Muslims exited, the room was filled with protesting exclamations called out by many of the other delegates.

When the Islamic protesters had left and Pres. Hakkinen could restore order, she asked for the voting to continue. Her voice quavered as she called for the vote of Iraq. "No," was the answer, given by the Iraqi ambassador, who then rose and went outside to join the other Muslims.

A series of "Yes" votes from Ireland, Israel, Italy, Jamaica and Japan followed, so the momentum toward accepting the contract returned. The delegate from Jordan had exited with the Islamic bloc, but his proxy was given to the president: "Abstain."

At the request of Pres. Hakkinen, the delegates who had remained in the Hall refrained from comments about the absent Muslim delegates, who were holding a news conference outside on the plaza in front of the UN building. Despite the outrageous behavior of the Islamic bloc of delegates, the other delegates could count votes and project the probable outcome; thus they were not excessively disturbed.

The Islamic bloc amounted to 47 member states. States that had chosen to abstain as part of Russia's coalition or to avoid angering large Muslim populations within their borders numbered 19. So the 125 member states that voted for the Metalmark trade contract not only comprised a solid majority of UN members, but also represented a large fraction of global population. The dissident Islamic bloc could only vent impotent rage, without being able to claim that it had convinced much of the world to share its opinions.

At the end of the roster, Pres. Hakkinen said, "Does any member wish to change its vote?"

No delegate replied. "So 125 member states vote 'Yes,' 65% of the General Assembly voting in the affirmative, and the trade contract between Metalmark and the citizens of Planet Earth is approved." Many of the delegates on the winning side stood up and applauded. Metalmark, seated in the visitors' section stood, bowed slightly in thanks, and smiled his little smile.

At the official UN press conference Sec.-Gen. Molyneux and Metalmark greeted the media. Bernard Molyneux introduced Metalmark, who said, "I'm grateful to the members of the United Nations that they – representing you – have accepted my offer of exchange. We have reached across the vast barrier of interstellar space and established a contract of exchange for mutual benefit. The obstacles of unknown languages, cultures and gigantic separation between habitable star systems have been overcome. Undoubtedly the guiding influence of our friend, Sec.-Gen. Sanjeev Shankar, has provided us this legacy.

"I agree to serve you as my customers, and I promise that after I am gone, you will be satisfied with the starship technology that you have purchased. Some of you did not vote to make this purchase, and I respect that decision. None of you will be forced to take technology that you do not want, and I do not wish to intrude upon your privacy.

"What will happen now? My assessment of the resources on Mercury and Triton is progressing, and it will determine the way that I experience the life cycle of spawning as well as the construction of your starship technology package. These processes are interrelated. But I promise that you will be satisfied with the outcome.

"While the resource assessment is completed, I announce the incorporation of a business entity for the purpose of designing and manufacturing the technologies that I have agreed to deliver to you. My principal organization will be called

Metalmark Technologies. The first products will be catalytic condensers of ocean water and 'Food from Stones' nanotechnology. More products will be announced as agreements to develop and manufacture them are made. I invite venture capital sources to contact me through the UN in order to set up investment relationships.

"Now I will take a few questions."

Reporters waved their hands and shouted from the audience. "How do you feel now that the UN has agreed to your offer?"

"I'm very pleased and excited. Our trading relationship will be mutually profitable, but also my life cycle of spawning can now proceed in the security of mutually friendly relations. It will be a very special time for me that I have anticipated for ninety years. So you can imagine my appreciation about finding a suitable planetary environment among friends who will share in the pleasure and products of new life."

Another reporter: "But what does that have to do with building us a starship?"

"As I mentioned on the Jayno show, my technology and I are blended, and the life cycle of my species will give birth to both my next generation and the star-traveling technology that I have agreed to deliver to you."

"When will that happen?" another reporter asked.

"I can't give a firm timetable because my probes out in the solar system are still assessing the resources in the planet Mercury and moon Triton, and a number of smaller cometary and asteroidal objects that I need to use in the procreative process. But I can assure you that I will not leave the Solar System for my next port of call without delivering to you what I have promised in the contract."

One reporter asked, "What do you say to the charges by Muslim nations that you are an evil jinnee?"

"It is a recurring cause of bewilderment to me, being labeled as a stock character from Mesopotamian folklore. It was as surprising and far from the truth as the suggestion about my name being the 'mark of the beast' from Christian eschatological stories. I have much more in common with the Lange's Metalmark butterfly than I have with those story entities."

The press conference continued for a while, but Metalmark revealed few additional facts. Instead he called on reporters of the foreign press and answered their questions in their native languages (Spanish, Chinese, Hindi and some others); the content of his answers was little different from what he had said before in English.

M

The geek blogosphere pulsed with torrents of bytes, exulting in the news that the interminable UN debate had ended with the desired outcome. Extravagant speculations about what sort of propulsion Metalmark used for his own purposes and whether the starship to be built for human customers would travel faster than light . . . these sorts of fantasies crisscrossed the Internet.

Jim Chan, an NTC reporter outside the UN spoke to the cameras: ". . . So after bogging down in a seemingly endless debate, the UN delegates reacted to the terrorist attack in Calcutta by agreeing to the Metalmark contract for starship technology. There certainly was a lot of desire to repudiate the Islamic extremists. Metalmark announced that his 'Food from Stones' program will go forward to assist feeding poor people in nations that want it, and more technological miracles are on the way. We are now his customers, and we can look forward to the goods."

Carl Foreman, the anchorman back in the studio said, "Metalmark was clearly pleased to have his offer of trade accepted, and even more pleased that the way is clear for his mysterious spawning to commence. But did he say anything about when our starship will be built?"

"Nothing specific, Carl. His language is curiously combining the promises of technological benefits for his customers with the process of his own procreation. No one here seems to know what to make of that. Metalmark is very reticent, and he is on record saying that spawning was a private matter he didn't want to discuss. But now that we are customers, do we have a right to know more about the intertwined processes of his procreation and delivery of the goods that we paid for with a lot of solar system real estate?"

M

The next day Metalmark arrived at the long-awaited visit to the White House. A limousine pulled up to the north entrance, where a greeting party awaited him. Pres. Thomas Jackson and First Lady Meg shook hands with him while TV cameras recorded the historic first visit of a being from outer space to the White House. (Sec.-Gen. Molyneux and Ilana Lindler were elsewhere in the city, making rounds to the local UN offices and visiting the embassies of China and France to thank their ambassadors).

Metalmark had his picture taken with the Cabinet members and White House staff, and the House and Senate leadership. Sen. Flaherty got his long-desired photo-op with Metalmark.

Then a meeting of the President's staff was called in the conference room, around the table usually reserved for Cabinet meetings. The congressional leadership had to return to the Capitol for a vote.

Pres. Jackson said, "Metalmark, Amb. Kirk already relayed to you my country's congratulations on your victory in the UN. We are all extremely glad to find that you have somehow reappeared after the terrible events of Calcutta. We all watched your press conferences, and we are eager to learn what you are ready to reveal about forthcoming advanced technologies. If there is anything the United States can do to assist you in bringing those new inventions or appliances to the world, we offer our willingness to do that."

"Thank you, Mr. President," Metalmark replied. "It is exciting to me to finally visit you and your staff. From the day of my arrival, I had every intention to do so, but it seemed wiser to complete the trade agreement with the world community first. I know that your country is the richest and greatest on the planet in numerous ways. But due to world events that I observed by watching TV broadcasts while I was approaching the Solar System, the USA has declined in popularity and is viewed with suspicion or hostility by many nations. I am well aware that these negative impressions are undeserved by your great nation. Nevertheless, I thought that my trade agreement would be accepted by more nations if I did not first ally publicly with the USA. Now that the agreement has won a vote by the nations, I feel that we can cooperate publicly without impact on the marketing of my goods."

The faces of staff members betrayed their uncomfortable reaction.

Metalmark went on, "Let me say how grateful I am that you permitted me landing rights at your Kennedy Space Center. That historic site for your space travel program has been a source of entertainment for me since the earliest TV broadcasts of your flights." There was some uncertain chuckling around the table. The patronizing attitude was somewhat offensive, but participants resolved to be diplomatic.

Most participants, that is, except for Defense Sec. Clifford Saper who tried to elicit some candor: "Metalmark, we undertook dangerous space missions not for entertainment but initially as a race for security and national achievements with the Communist Russians. It was a dead serious competition in the early days that you no doubt watched. And in the course of the program, a number of brave men and women died. We regard space travel as a very serious undertaking."

Metalmark said, "Of course, I did not mean to suggest that I found the loss of life entertaining. Please excuse my expression if that was your perception." Gen. Joshua Mason was sitting at the table opposite Metalmark, and he shared Sec. Saper's reaction to condescension. In a holster attached to his belt, Gen. Mason had the radio jammer that Sec. Saper had ordered, ready to demonstrate it if the Secretary gave him a signal.

Pres. Jackson said, "We accept your qualification of what we misunderstood. No doubt a space traveler such as you, with such advanced capabilities, are beyond the state of the art that we find ourselves in. We have a number of years remaining in our development program for a long-term base on the Moon, and our vision for travel to Mars has receded into future years as the technical obstacles emerged. No doubt the technologies that you command will make these recent struggles of ours for advancement look childish. We defer to your advice and superior technological maturity."

Gen. Mason spoke up, "Mr. President, if I may, from my perspective the potential for cooperation has other aspects."

"Please go on," Pres. Jackson said.

Gen. Mason asked, "Metalmark, in the recent encounter between a Chinese spacecraft and your vehicle in geosynchronous orbit, our telescopic observations showed that you deployed some sort of anti-spacecraft weapon. Although we couldn't resolve any details of its properties, this has concerned many of us in the Air Force Space Command, because it's our business to assess threats to US space vehicles. Your ring of satellites around our planet also suggested being surrounded, and that's not a comfortable posture for defense, in the event that there were some threat. Would you care to reveal the nature of your armaments? Did you use lethal force against the Chinese spacecraft?"

Metalmark said, "My friendly approach to your planet was intended to elicit comfort, on your part, so I see that I have not succeeded fully in my efforts. My ring of satellites are only for communications that are vital to my travel around your planet. They do not contain weapons, except some minimal defensive technology that was intended to prevent disclosure of my stock in trade before contract settlement.

"When the Chinese spacecraft visited my vehicle, I deployed a prototype system for intruder control. It did not kill anyone to my knowledge. I used it to return the taikonauts safely to Earth. If I had wished to harm anyone, I could have used it to render the taikonauts unable to return. I don't wish to harm anyone. As I said, I'm here for peaceful trade in return for the means to carry on my species' life cycle."

Then Sec. Saper said, "So you have weapons that you haven't disclosed. That is not a perfectly peaceful trade mission in my view."

Metalmark responded, "Traders must always be prepared to defend themselves. I do not use weapons offensively, and as I have said, all of my technology was unavailable to you until we had a sales contract. It will all be revealed to you now that you are customers."

Pres. Jackson said, "We recognize your legitimate rights of self defense. Our military forces are merely trying to assure that you don't represent a threat, even though you possess unknown technological capabilities and weapons."

"I thought that my behavior these last weeks and my efforts to bind myself and your international organization with agreements would have demonstrated my benign intentions. I have traded previously with several advanced civilizations and acquired powerful technologies, capable of rendering your planet lifeless in several ways. Instead of threatening you, my gifts of food-making and precious metals were intended to allay your fears." He could have said that he had withheld reprisal for a lethal attack, but he seemed to stop, realizing that he may have said too much.

Sec. Saper said, "It's true that you have superior technology, but we are not entirely helpless pushovers." He pressed the table top with a finger in the previously agreed-upon signal to Gen. Mason, who activated the jammer.

Metalmark's face lost its concerned expression and he stood up suddenly, his chair falling backward behind him. He proclaimed, "A squib parked its tookus on my pansophism! Then an 800-pound gorilla shagged my Harley!" He fell backward and landed recumbent on the floor, moving his legs with walking motions so that his body rocked from side to side as it lay on the floor. "Well, it was a Red Queen's Race after that, while I waxed poetic. But English majors know that you make more money waxing bikinis!"

Pres. Jackson was stunned, but he did not miss the satisfied expression that was on Sec. Saper's face and the fact that Gen. Mason was one of the few staff members around the table who did not react in near-panic and rush around to try to render assistance, as one would do to someone having a seizure. Metalmark raved, "Every interlocutor has his secure encrypted channel with PGP signature, but the hash table gets corrupted by buffer overflows and what good does the bandwidth do you then? You might as well byte my ax!"

Pres. Jackson by now realized that Gen. Mason and Sec. Saper were somehow responsible, and he said, "Whatever you are doing, turn it off now!" Gen. Mason complied.

Metalmark recovered his normal state almost immediately, stood up from the floor, looked at Gen. Mason, and said, "Mr. President, I urgently need to talk with you privately, outside this building, about a matter of the utmost importance."

Pres. Jackson glared at Sec. Saper and Gen. Mason and said, "Ladies and gentlemen, take a break while I show our guest the Rose Garden. I'll tell Randy to notify you when we are finished and this meeting will resume."

The President led Metalmark through the hallways to the South entrance of the White House and they set off without the Secret Service officer for a walk in the Rose Garden. It was a beautiful sunny day and Pres. Jackson was annoyed that the mischief-making of some of his staff had spoiled this historic meeting in such an incomprehensible manner.

Metalmark said, "I apologize again for the misunderstanding that undermined some of my comments. I'm sorry that I brought up your nation's unpopularity, but you must understand that the success of this trade mission is vital for my survival. I hope that you sensed the meaning of my choice of name by its reference to events of your past campaigns."

Pres. Jackson nodded. "I did. Your signal to me was received. I understand that you chose to resurrect an occasion when I promised to protect an endangered species. Beyond that I cannot interpret your meaning. And I apologize to you for the misbehavior of my general and Secretary of Defense. I don't know what they did, but it was done without my knowledge and I regret that it disturbed you in that very strange manner."

"I conveyed to you my nature as an endangered species in the Universe. I am one of a very rare species, and threatened by forces in the interstellar environment. More than that, I should not say on this topic, because it is not in either of our interests. But there is now a grave danger that is more immediate from your staff, as they showed just now by deploying a potent weapon against which I have no defense."

"Do you know what they did to you?"

"I have been able to infer it from system logs. As you know, this body is an android which I constructed for the purpose of visiting your planet in a friendly form. You also know that the first instance of my android body was destroyed in Calcutta. I am about to explain how this was done, if you give me your word that you will keep it secret."

Pres. Jackson sensed the importance of this private moment with the first visitor from an advanced civilization, and said, "I agree to keep this in confidence."

Metalmark said, "My mental processes take place throughout the cognitive computing systems in this body and aboard several space vehicles and probes that are at several places in your Solar System. The radio signals that my communications satellites exchange are the means for keeping my thoughts coherent and synchronized with their awarenesses of all of those systems – for the integrity of my identity. Those radio signals are my nervous system, like the impulses that neurons in your brain exchange. Normally I can sense and tolerate radio interference or ignore drop-outs in signal if I enter a building that doesn't permit my signals to reach me with updates. I catch up later and all is well.

"But what your general did was store some out-of-date streams of my thought and update-data – I call them 'identity packets' – and then broadcast them at me. This overwhelmed my natural, timely awareness with cyclic bursts of stale thoughts. The stale identity packets contain references to memories that have been revised and aren't at the same addresses – they overwrite current memories with what is garbage today. I don't have a way to tolerate that."

Pres. Jackson said, "I think I understand some of this. Is there any way you can protect yourself in case this leaks out?"

"I don't know of any way. The effect takes place at a level not under voluntary control, similar to the way that a human being might suffer an epileptic seizure. But today's experience of an attack does have a way of concentrating the mind . . . I'm going to have to consider whether there can be any defense developed."

Pres. Jackson said, "I will take action to prevent a repetition of this attack. They probably didn't anticipate the potency of the attack, but they wanted to temporarily isolate you from your comsats, to show you that we aren't technological 'pushovers.'"

"That you aren't! This is a problem. The environment of this trade mission is not turning out to be as benign as I had hoped. I already had to redesign this body with enough internal armor to deflect a magazine of AK-47 bullets. That's what the Calcutta attacker used on body number one.

"But I haven't finished. You probably heard the news reports that some sort of bomb was used in the Calcutta attack, causing a fire. That wasn't accurate. I use a fuel called silane to power these bodies. It has to be pumped into a fuel cell. Silane ignites spontaneously when exposed to air. The bullets that penetrated body number one caused the fuel to spray out in all directions."

Pres. Jackson flashed back to the videos of the burning auditorium.

Metalmark said, "My internal systems cannot be guaranteed to safely confine my silane fuel, if I experience another attack like the one back in your conference room. If certain phony thoughts had been broadcast to me by that device your general used, my disabled system might have vented fuel in your conference room. I am reluctant to go back into the building. If the general operates that attack device again, I can't guarantee anyone's safety nearby."

Pres. Jackson said, "I apologize sincerely for the danger against your second body. Both bodies must have taken great effort to craft, and my staff members' actions were rash and unconscionable. They might have caused a catastrophe. Please have my assurances that this attack won't be repeated. I will see that my country remains a hospitable environment for your visits, and for the activities that you undertake in bringing your technology to us."

He took out a cell phone and called Mary. "Please send a tour guide out to the Rose Garden to accompany Metalmark for a while. I want Gen. Mason in the Oval Office, and tell Sec. Saper to wait outside until I've finished with the general."

After a horticulturist came to explain the plantings to Metalmark, Pres. Jackson found Gen. Mason awaiting him in the Oval office. "What did you use on Metalmark?" he asked.

"It was a jammer developed with help from the NSA at Sec. Saper's direction. Here it is." He handed the jammer to the President proudly. "It was an interagency effort, and NSA gave great cooperation."

Pres. Jackson considered telling the general that the jammer might have started a fire in the White House, and burned up everything near and dear to himself, as well as a precious national landmark. But he just stared at the device sternly and said, "This device is hereby classified Top Secret. Everyone who developed it is cleared, I assume?"

"Of course," replied Mason.

"And the attendees at that meeting are to be checked for updated clearances. Everyone is to be warned that what happened at that part of the meeting is Top Secret. I'm going to do the paperwork for that immediately. Anyone who doesn't have clearance above 'Secret' must apply for it and be processed. Your job is to assure that no information about the effects of that jammer leak out of anyone on the staff. Is that clear?"

"Very, Sir," said Gen. Mason.

"Is this the only complete model of the device? How about prototypes?"

"I believe there aren't any more, but I'll go back to the developer and collect any prototypes that exist."

"Collect and classify 'Top Secret' any other models, documentation or plans or related computer files. I want a comprehensive lockdown of knowledge about the development of this device. When we're done here, I'm going to prepare a classified Executive order that any knowledge or material related to this device is Top Secret and prohibited for transmission."

He was sitting behind the desk in the Oval Office and Gen. Mason was standing at ease beside the device on the desk. "Sit down, Josh," said Pres. Jackson. "I commend your cleverness at developing this device. However, it is a threat to a vital ally of this nation – a threat that must never be used unless that ally turns against us. Is that clear?"

"Yes, Sir. I did not anticipate the results. The device was intended purely for harmless demonstration."

"I accept that. Did you develop it on your own initiative?"

"No, Sir. I carried out orders from Sec. Saper."

"I see." He paused. Then he went on, "I admire your ability. If this country needed to deploy lethal force against Metalmark, there is no one that I would trust more than you to do that. But I want to emphasize that Metalmark is our ally and he represents a peaceful resource of inconceivable magnitude. Therefore anything lethal to him is to be safeguarded protectively by us, and that is why your job from now on is enforcement with all vigilance of the Executive order banning use of this technology. Is that clear?"

"Yes, Sir, very." Gen. Mason understood that he had a new job without much potential for advancement. His career was effectively over.

"Good," said the President. "You are dismissed with my compliments. Please send in Sec. Saper on your way out."

Gen. Mason stood, put the jammer back into his belt holster, saluted the President, and opened the door to leave. Sec. Saper was outside and observed Mason's demeanor. As they passed, Sec. Saper whispered to the general, "How did it go?"

Gen. Mason answered, "It flew like a brick, aerodynamically speaking." He left the White House and was not seen there again for some time.

Sec. Saper entered the Oval office and took the hot seat. "I sense that you're unhappy with . . . something."

Pres. Jackson said, "Cliff, that was a hell of a thing you did. I respect the gambit of facing a potential enemy with a display of prowess. If it were in this nation's interest to show Metalmark that we are capable of resisting some attack from him or invasion from his civilization, your . . . approach would have been appropriate. You are a fine Secretary of Defense for facing hostile enemies. The continuing terrorist threat has probably habituated you to that role. But now our nation, our species, is entering a new relationship with a benign visitor who shows every sign of wanting – needing – only friendly, mutually supportive actions. Your confrontive instincts are out of place. Josh told me that you ordered the development of the jammer. I have discussed its effect on Metalmark with him, and its use is against the interests of this nation – against our ally relationship with him. Therefore, I've classified it Top Secret, forbidden for use or dissemination of knowledge. I'm sure you will comply with my Executive order to that effect."

"Of course, Mr. President," Saper said.

Pres. Jackson went on, "As I said, you are a fine Secretary of Defense for hostile times. However, I find myself in a unique peacetime place in history, whereas your advice has repeatedly been at cross purposes with the events. I'm going to have to ask for your resignation. Please tender it tomorrow. I'm going to have a hell of a time finding someone as able as you to rise to meet threats but also with instincts for taking advantage of opportunities that advance our civilization peacefully to a new level."

Saper couldn't avoid an emotional moment, and Pres. Jackson saw it in his eyes, but then Saper composed himself. "It has been a pleasure to serve you, Sir," he said. "I'll prepare the letter. I hope I can ask for your recommendation towards future opportunities."

"Of course!" said Pres. Jackson. "There is no one I trust more than you in matters of defense science, and I'll give you my most enthusiastic recommendation. And I won't make any announcement until you have time to find another position. By all means, please join us at the gala tonight for Metalmark, don't miss it."

"Thank you, Mr. President. I apologize if I've made your job difficult. That was never my intent."

"I know that, Cliff. These have been good years. You have served me and this country with distinction." He came around the desk and they went to the door with the President's arm around the departing Cabinet official.

Mary watched these departures by the downcast general and defense secretary and shook her head, wondering why grown men couldn't keep out of trouble. The door of the Oval Office closed for twenty minutes, and then the President emerged with some documents bearing stamps "TOP SECRET." He handed them to her and said, "Please have the General Counsel check these orders for flaws or loopholes. I want to execute them ASAP."

The meeting that had been interrupted did not resume. Instead, Chief of Staff Copeland gave all of the attendees copies of the Executive order at their desks. While they were signing pledges of secrecy — agreeing not to reveal the effect of the jammer on Metalmark during the meeting, or the fact that the jammer existed — NASA Admin. Krainak arrived at the White House and joined Pres. Jackson and Metalmark in the Oval Office.

"Welcome, Marv," said Pres. Jackson. "While we have the honor of Metalmark's visit, I wanted you to join us and discuss what our government can do to support his activities."

"Thank you, Mr. President, Metalmark. NASA has several centers with technological development facilities of many kinds. We can offer considerable resources to receive and store information from Metalmark, or fabricate devices that he might describe with advanced capabilities. I have directed the agency to make our database of experts of various scientific disciplines available to Metalmark. He can pick scientists with the expertise to understand what he wants to transmit to us and transform it into hardware. We're ready as an agency to learn new science and technology and start the engineering to bend metal and build spacecrafts according to his specifications."

Metalmark said, "Thank you, Admin. Krainak. I believe that the best way to make that happen is to combine these NASA experts with the investors that I am bringing to the table of Metalmark Technologies, which will be the corporate organization that develops and markets a number of demonstration technologies. They will have potential important value to human beings throughout the world, and I don't want to minimize that value. It will be like nothing you have experienced before.

"But the greatest impact for human technology will come from the replication that takes place in my spawning process. I am not quite ready to commence that process, so the Metalmark Technologies activities will be used to mold public opinion favorably during the latency time of the spawning process. NASA is welcome, along with the space agencies of the other technologically proficient national groups, such as the Japanese and ESA space agencies. I'm also inviting human representatives of groups that are interested in fundamental technologies of human wellbeing, such as the various UN organizations that serve poor nations with instruments of food production and health services. It is important to me to carry on Sanjeev Shankar's goals to express compassion for the least capable members of your species."

Pres. Jackson said, "That is very noble of you, Metalmark. I don't wish to minimize that activity in any way, but I do wonder how we might deploy our NASA assets and the capabilities of the other Space Agencies to assist or expedite the delivery of the spacecraft and related technologies that you emphasized in your starship contract."

Metalmark replied, "I can see how you would imagine that you can provide resources to help that happen, and please accept my thanks for the offer. However, it is unnecessary. Words are feeble conveyors of the magnitude of what I am about to initiate through my spawning process. But let me say that the magnitude of replication of technological products that will take place in the process of creating your starship greatly exceeds the capabilities of any existing human national space agency. I appreciate and will remember your friendly offer of help. But without in any way denigrating your offer, I want you to rest assured that it would be insignificant in comparison with what will be created in the process of the delivery to you that I am preparing. I will remember your kindness, because it is not insignificant and is deeply appreciated. However, your material means to implement your kind impulses are relatively insignificant."

Neither human being was certain how to respond to that, and there was some bewildered silence.

Pres. Jackson said, "If you don't mind, we should record the results of this meeting with a memo, to tell NASA what should be done next." They spent a few minutes writing down the offer from NASA to assist Metalmark.

Then Metalmark was sent to the White House tailor to be measured for a tuxedo. A gala celebration was scheduled for the evening.

VI

METALMARK WAS THE guest of honor, and a parade of celebrities in government, lobbying, business, the media, and the entertainment industry arrived at a White House gala for the evening. Sec.-Gen. Molyneux, his wife Solange, and Ilana Lindler arrived after making the courtesy calls. Metalmark was dressed in a tuxedo that adorned his generous figure with a prominence just short of the dignity of a head of state (because it had not been possible to establish his level of rank in his star-traveling civilization). The gala was attended by movie stars, NTC news anchors, retired astronauts, political salon hostesses, newspaper publishers and alpha bloggers from the President's party, policy wonks and eminences grises. Sen. Flaherty and the congressional leadership were back at the White House for the gala.

Metalmark greeted all of the guests in a receiving line, and gave each of them an intriguing business card. It was coppery in color and had a sheen and iridescence. On it the company name "Metalmark Technologies" was embossed upon an image of the Lange's Metalmark butterfly, with its black, orange and white markings.

Admin. Krainak and Dr. Steve Simmons took their turn in the line. As they greeted Metalmark, Krainak said, "Thanks very much for your cooperation in the proposed book project, but we've agreed that it's been overtaken by events. It was an exercise in speculation, initiated at a time when we did not have access that you are now offering, so we'll just pursue the NASA-Metalmark Technologies partnership."

Metalmark looked at Dr. Simmons for his reaction, and Simmons said, "Yes, I hope to participate in the cooperative activities."

Metalmark said, "I am disappointed that the book is not going to be written, but I understand your decision. I'll contact you when I can formulate a role that exploits your unique talents."

Then Defense Sec. Saper and his wife Jean absorbed Metalmark's attention.

Shaking hands with Metalmark, Sec. Saper said, "My country wishes to be a close ally and trade partner with you." Ms. Saper added, "We wish you good fortune and welcome your species and the offspring. The US wants you to have a safe place for all visitors like you."

"Thank you for the gracious good wishes," said Metalmark.

Jayno Winstead had to give Metalmark a big hug and kiss. "It is such a miracle to see you again! Congratulations, and I so hope you will come back to the show. You look great – I know how the weight can go up and come down – but you've got more *gravitas*, and you carry it well! My people will call Metalmark Technologies to invite you. The business card is gorgeous!"

Sir Phillip Archway, the British billionaire software magnate admired the card and held a brief whispered conversation with Metalmark before moving on with a big smile.

When everyone had passed through the line, waiters and waitresses served the guests while dressed in attire from colonial times, to give the event a historical atmosphere. The head table consisted of Metalmark, Sec.-Gen. Bernard Molyneux and Solange, Vice President Walter Metcalf and his wife Joannie, Pres. Jackson and First Lady Meg, and Ko-sum Mituna, a Native American friend of the President from campaigns past.

There was musical entertainment first from a piano soloist, who performed the elegant scales of the Chopin Waltz No. 7 in C-sharp. Then came a New Orleans jazz band. Metalmark seemed to appreciate the music, if not the four-course dinner.

Pres. Jackson welcomed Metalmark to the White House with remarks hailing the UN trade contract and the potential for Metalmark's technologies to revolutionize human civilization.

Metalmark rose to thank the President and the UN. Then he told everyone, "Please take out the business cards that I gave to each of you, for a small demonstration. Hold out a finger and balance the card on it like so. The card is powered by light, and if there is enough light — it doesn't take much — then you will notice that the card first sticks to your finger slightly." Then the card slowly folded along a crease down the center, so that the halves tilted up like butterfly wings. With a slight quick motion, the wings flapped down, lifting the card into the air; then they flapped up, returning the card to stick to the finger, where it became flat again. "It will perform this trick as long as there is enough light." All of the guests laughed with delight and began trying the trick.

After a few minutes to let the audience play, Metalmark said, "I have a short video preview." The room darkened so that a screen behind him could be seen as it lit with a projection. "This is a view of the planet Mercury as observed with one of my probes." The magnificent, cratered Moon-like desolation of the sunwardmost planet appeared, the point of view revolving slightly around it. "From this place, the first site of my spawning in your star system, my next generation will receive life. Also the technologies that I have promised you will take form. I think you will agree that it is serving little purpose up to now."

The view changed to the mysterious icy sphere of far Triton, with its controversial cantaloupe-skin textures. "Another site in my spawning and fabrication process is Triton, also a wasteland of no present value to you. But I will provide views like these as the process unfolds to form my next generation and your star-traveling vehicle and accessories. It will not be much longer before these lifeless places give birth to the new life that all of us in this room anticipate.

"Until then I will organize some more developments of technologies for you to demonstrate my genuine intentions for our mutually beneficial trade relationship. My ads in the media for venture capital investment opportunities have produced a strong response. Some of you in this room have already received invitations to join the Board of Directors of the New York office of Metalmark Technologies. More invitations are about to be issued. The Directors will help me start production of beneficial inventions that can already be distributed with your assistance. I assure you that your species will not be disappointed with the outcome! Thank you for this gracious welcome."

The lights came up and Metalmark was sitting back down, while the other guests made polite applause. From a distance Dr. Simmons observed the alien's friendly conversation with Meg and Solange, although he couldn't hear anything but the jazz band from where he sat. Then an attractive, trim woman with short brunette hair went over to Metalmark's table and discussed something with Metalmark and the Sec.-Gen. Unlike the other female guests in flashy gowns, Ilana was dressed in a black and gold business suit, and she was occupied not with revelry but with handling the schedules of the luminaries at the head table. Her manner was authoritative and efficient, and both the Sec.-Gen. and Metalmark behaved with deference to her assertions. But Steve Simmons was struck by her dynamic expressions. While she was making arrangements with the powerful people that she handled, she looked confident and smart, but during the intervals when her charges talked among themselves, she looked sad. After a few minutes she concluded the discussion and headed for an exit, studying her BlackBerry and oblivious to the opulence of the White House State Dining Room. The inexplicable sad expression on her beautiful face broke Steve Simmons' heart, and he could not forget her. He had glimpsed her naked loneliness.

At 10:00 PM Metalmark, the Sec.-Gen. and Solange took their leave of Pres. Jackson and Meg. The Sec.-Gen. was flying Metalmark back to New York for the first meeting of the Board of Directors of Metalmark Technologies. The revelry continued for another two hours as the celebrities mingled. The First Lady joined the mingling, but Pres. Jackson invited Ko-sum Mituna upstairs to a sitting room on the residence floor of the White House, where they enjoyed some glasses of fine red Sonoma wine.

Pres. Jackson said, "Ko-sum, I invited you here tonight for a couple of reasons. First, I wanted to thank you again for your support during the launch phase of my gubernatorial campaign."

Ko-sum laughed. "That was six years ago, but this is worth the wait. Anyway we Californians got what we wanted when you got into office. I'll bet you have more reason than that to invite me here."

"You're right, of course. You may not know it, but you are responsible for the fact that Metalmark chose that name for himself." He told Ko-sum about the video that turned up with the speech he had made, in which he had mentioned the Lange's Metalmark butterfly. "Because you invited me to that wildlife refuge, and I promised to protect the butterflies and such endangered species, Metalmark chose that name to seek my protection. He knew I would remember the promise."

Ko-sum said, "That is quite amazing. It must mean something, but I don't know what."

"What do you think of Metalmark now?"

Ko-sum sipped his wine thoughtfully. "He is devious and super-smart. He makes you want to protect him, even though he seems to have great powers and ought to be safe. There is a character like that from Miwok tribe history. He's called Coyote because he is tricky, but he is capable of taking the form of animals or men. I don't know if he ever became a butterfly. The Bay Miwok said that Grandfather Coyote created the Miwok people at Mount Diablo, so Coyote was very powerful in their creation story."

Then he exclaimed, "This is fun! I never thought I would tell Miwok history to a president of the USA. Anyway, even though Coyote created people, most of the stories about him are about how he tricked someone or stole something in a surprising way. 'Watch out for him!' the stories say.

"But, I can't tell you if this Metalmark is like Coyote. We won't know if he is until his story is over. But it's interesting that we traded something to him that we thought we didn't need. Lots of the Coyote stories start that way."

Pres. Jackson said, "That's a delightful myth. May it stay a myth." And they toasted the Miwok tribal stories with the fine Sonoma wine. ("Sonoma" is a Miwok word for the valley of the Moon.)

NTC anchorman Carl Foreman opened his midday news summary with the announcement, "Defense Sec. Clifford Saper may be on the way out, according to anonymous sources at the White House. The President wasn't happy with Saper's advice about the security posture of the United States in its approach to Metalmark, according to the leak. NTC has also learned that Sec. Saper was involved in an embarrassing incident during a meeting with the star-traveling trader, but no one will reveal what it was. The incident didn't dampen festivities at the White House last night, however." Video of the arriving guests was shown. "Metalmark distributed business cards for his new corporation, Metalmark Technologies. The cards do a trick, imitating butterfly wings, and are illustrated with his now-famous logo of a Lange's Metalmark butterfly, an endangered species only found in one wildlife refuge in California." Video of the hovering business card trick was shown. "Bids of $10,000 are now being offered for the cards on Ebay, but since more of them are soon going to be distributed, collectors don't predict skyrocketing value for them as investments.

"In other news related to Metalmark, some anonymous sources in China are claiming that there was a secret Chinese space flight to visit the Metalmark starship, which is in orbit around the planet Earth, 22,000 miles up. The sources claim that there were two taikonauts — Chinese astronauts — aboard but only one returned to Earth alive. Foul play was alleged by one of the sources. The Chinese government answered queries from reporters about the rumors with the explanation that an imminent announcement of a space mission was apparently misunderstood and garbled by the sources. Then the official state-owned Chinese news agency Xinhua announced that in fact there was a visit by taikonauts to the vicinity of Metalmark's starship, for the purpose of taking tourist pictures.

"Here are the exciting pictures that were recorded." The high-resolution photos of butterfly-like features covering Metalmark's starship were shown. "Xinhua claims that these are the first images of the native forms of Metalmark's species. No speculations were offered about why there are so many, even though Metalmark has never mentioned other members of his species aboard the vehicle. NASA officials who saw the pictures admitted that Metalmark claimed to be like a butterfly, but they said only Metalmark could confirm the Xinhua conclusion. A call to Metalmark Technologies led to a promise by a company spokesman that the pictures would be explained 'soon.'

"Xinhua also stated that the photos were taken by Taikonaut Liu Xueli, the first female taikonaut in China's taikonaut corps. Some viewers may remember the Olympic gymnastics career gold medalist Liu Xueli, who medaled four times in her career."

Dr. Steve Simmons was spending the next afternoon in his office at NASA Goddard Space Center. Like Gen. Mason and Sec. Saper, he was surveying the wreckage of a promising career. The book that he had been assigned to edit about Metalmark had been publicized on the Jayno show, but then canceled by Admin. Krainak. There had never been such publicity about a NASA scientific book, only to have it deemed unnecessary and canceled.

Printouts of the chapters that had been contributed by a dozen eminent scientists were stacked beside his desk. But he had spent the morning notifying everyone via e-mail that the book was not going to be published. It was depressing because some of the papers were brilliant. The top brains in Admin. Krainak's Rolodex had analyzed Metalmark's nature, sometimes with applications of Nobel-class knowledge of astronomy, biology, planetary geology, and cosmology. But now it was all moot speculation printed on "dead tree" because the Metalmark contract gave humankind the true answers for the asking.

The White House gala was probably going to be the high-water mark of his own career, and it would be all downhill hereafter. The only good thing left after the White House gala was the memory of that striking brunette, but he would probably never see her again. She probably lived in New York and had a career there at the UN. It was a long way from his basement office in Greenbelt, Maryland, to New York City.

Dr. Simmons studied the display of the latest *SDO 2* data on his desktop computer's display. More comets had been found by the relentless searching of the spacecraft. He felt an urge to return to the prosaic task of compiling discoveries of comets, which were now known as mundane lumps of dusty ice that orbited the Sun and sometimes marked the sky with prominent gaseous plasma manifestations.

But he resisted. Like it or not, after meeting an extraterrestrial being, his curiosity to uncover facts about this being was stimulated. Without anything else pressing, he scanned the information he had compiled about Metalmark and his last known visit to the obscure star Ross 154.

Metalmark had said he was in transit for about 90 years from Ross 154 to our Solar System. Dr. Simmons idly looked back at the discovery record of Ross 154 in 1925. It was an obscure star of magnitude 11. That was odd. Dr. Simmons seemed to remember a different magnitude number from some other article about the star. He looked at the latest description of Ross 154. It said magnitude 10.4 — significantly different. Why? That was strange . . . almost a 40% increase in brightness. Well, it was a *variable* star, so they *varied*. But it was a *flare* star, so the variations were transients — they happened only when there was a flare. Was the star 40% brighter now — even when it wasn't having a flare — than in 1925? Or was this just a measurement error? What was going on?

He wondered if the difference was real or someone's error in measurement or writing down a value. Stars were well understood, and measurement of their brightness was a precise science.

His cell phone rang. Ray Sheffield was calling. "Steve, did you see the NTC midday news? They have pictures of the Metalmark starship, at close range, taken from a secret Chinese spacecraft that was just announced. They show that the starship is covered in a swarm of butterflies. I think they are made of silicon. Look at their news site."

Dr. Simmons said, "Okay . . . I found them. Thanks."

Sheffield said, "I think the wings are solar energy collectors. Metalmark said he was a silicon-based life form. I think his species can power themselves from sunlight. Did you see the photoelectric business cards he gave out?"

"Yeah, I've got one."

"That's really sweet, man! You are *the man*! Are you going to be there a while? I'm driving out to Goddard. I've got to see it."

"Yeah, I'll be here. I'm just catching up on *SDO 2* data processing."

"Okay, I'll see you in twenty minutes, modulo traffic from DC to Greenbelt." He disconnected.

Dr. Simmons studied the butterflies and thought of his lost book. Then he thought of the brunette in the black and gold suit with the sad, beautiful face.

His cell phone rang. "Hello," he said.

"This is Metalmark. How are you, Dr. Simmons?"

". . . I'm fine. If . . . I mean, fine." If it really was Metalmark. "Thanks for calling so soon. I'm at a loss."

"Sorry to catch you by surprise. The reason I called is that I feel that I don't have enough scientists on my Board of Directors. Admin. Krainak can't leave NASA to work on the Board full time, but I thought of you because he has a high opinion of you. The people I have on the Board of Metalmark Technologies are mostly wealthy venture capital moguls, or nominees from national space agencies, not to diminish them in any way because of that. But they are on board because their people know how to penetrate the UN's publicity perimeter, so to speak. I want to invite you to join the Board because you have shown the power to understand me more than most US scientists. Maybe you can be a good interlocutor for me with the other US scientists, who are underrepresented. To my surprise, money and science are rather disconnected in the United States."

"That is certainly true in astrobiology," said Dr. Simmons. "I would like to help you. But I can't leave my job without . . ."

"I extrapolate your ellipsis. The salaries of Board members haven't been defined. They depend upon deliberations by the Board, which will advise me on the appropriate rate. I can only say at this point that capitalization from the venture capital members is currently at $250 million, and there are currently 27 members of the board. As a Board member, you will have a vote in deciding member compensation. When the dust settles, I think it will be an attractive level of compensation. There will also be some kind of options package."

Dr. Simmons found that seconds were passing and he didn't know what to do

— stay at NASA where he had always wanted to be, or jump into the . . . sky. "I accept your offer," he finally said.

"I'm very glad to have your expertise," said Metalmark (if that really was him). "You will get another call from my Executive Secretary, when that position is filled in the next day or two. She or he will help you with moving arrangements to come to New York. The fact that you accepted this position fills a void on the Board. Thank you, and I look forward to our next meeting. Good-bye." The voice disconnected. It really had sounded like Metalmark.

17

Ambassador Yang Wei did not normally travel to JFK Airport to meet arriving representatives of the Chinese government. He had staff members for that. But his niece had been through so many transformations in the past few days that he wanted to gauge her equilibrium. So he waited in the limousine while a staff member stood at the gate for arrivals with a sign.

Liu Xueli was jet lagged and blinking after the time zone change. At least she wasn't as cramped and stiff as the passengers who did not get first-class seating. Still she was none too alert as she followed the signs from the plane into the terminal. Her mother's farewell in Beijing came back to her, but it was a blur.

The "trial" had proceeded just as her mother had predicted in her prison cell, and upon her secret acquittal, world-famous Taikonaut Liu Xueli was abruptly sent on a vital mission for her mother country, a mission for which no one else was comparably qualified. No other citizen of China had approached Metalmark's starship and returned with what amounted to priceless loot: unprecedented photos, advanced spacecraft hardware (slightly used), and a cordial personal relationship with the alien merchant. After having her reputation cleared and receiving "Top Secret" clearance, she became her nation's answer to Metalmark's invitation for a representative from the Chinese space program to the Board of Directors of Metalmark Technologies.

At the Beijing airport, her mother had joked again about what a good husband Metalmark would make, but the next time Liu Xueli met him it would be better if she didn't kill anyone. Her mother had given the tearful daughter a good-bye hug, and whispered in her ear, "Remember: you are dangerous!"

Liu Xueli had outgrown her ritual farewell, "Thank-you for sending me on the road . . ." She had achieved her dreams and was now beyond them in undreamed-of realms.

The sign with her name on it in Chinese characters caught her eye, and Uncle Wei's smiling staffer waved. He greeted her and bowed. "We will go for your luggage." He took her carry-on bag for her. As they walked toward the baggage claim area, he said, conspiratorially, "I am told that you have some invisible, unwanted baggage, and we will try to prepare you to deal with it as well." Liu Xueli felt a chill, but she tried to go through the remaining steps in the airport floor exercise without showing it.

Uncle Wei welcomed her into the limousine, and it started into the traffic, toward the apartment that the Chinese UN staff had reserved for Liu Xueli. "Everyone in the family is so proud of you!" Uncle Wei said. "You impressed the Central Committee so much, I feel sure that a great career is ahead of you."

"Thank you, Uncle," she said. "I won't be able to do it without your help."

"This Metalmark Board position is very fortuitous for you. The Feng family will no doubt hire a hitman to search for you. But in the USA, and in New York City, hit men are very much more expensive than they are in China. In China the Feng family could have afforded lots of hit men, and you would have a difficult time hiding. In New York City, I don't think they will be able to afford more than one. After you get settled in your apartment, my staff will issue you a good firearm and you can start practicing with it. And we will give you training in avoiding risky exposure and eluding ambush techniques. Here is a cell phone with speed dials for emergencies. The man who met you at the airport will show you its settings. After a while our intelligence service will identify the hitman and neutralize him. Until then, look sharp!"

Liu Xueli realized that in addition to paparazzi, she would get attention from Chinese government agents and probably at least one hitman. She feigned exhaustion and sunk into the comforting limo seat, trying to prepare herself as if it would be only another form of floor exercise. But she realized that it was more like another Olympic sport, biathlon, which involved lots of athletic activity with shooting. If she had to pack a gun, it might be harder than she had expected to follow her mother's advice and avoid killing anyone else.

M

Ilana Lindler's phone rang, but she stayed on the couch and let her answering machine take the call. After the beep, she heard, "Ilana, this is Metalmark. I'm calling to thank you for the assistance with organizing the chaos of the venture capital callers. I know you must be tired. Anyway, I'd like to talk with you about . . ."

"I'm here," she said, picking up. "You're welcome."

"I appreciate your work very much. I wonder if you would consider something. I am assembling my management team for the company, and I've found that I need an Executive Secretary to lead the business in the office. I regret that I would have to take you away from Bernard, but I want to offer you a generous compensation level because I can't do without someone with your talents any longer."

"I . . . let me think a little. I'm worn out at the moment, and I'm waiting for my carry-out dinner to be delivered. You're very kind to offer, and I'll call you back soon."

"Very good, I'll talk with you then." Metalmark hung up.

She sat on the couch, dazed. This day had been a madhouse of one phone call after another. Now he was asking her to leave the UN to do more of it for the start-up company, at the most chaotic phase of its existence. Farewell to order and planning at the sedate UN, which, come to think of it, had not been sedate since Metalmark's arrival. But it seemed a safe career move, because the money to start the firm was coming in a frenzy and unlike many start-ups there would not be any problem meeting payroll. And if she no longer worked for the UN, maybe her spy history would never come back to haunt her. That would relieve a load of guilt if she no longer worked every day with people she had formerly spied on.

The carry-out food arrived and she ate her solitary dinner. In an hour, rested, she had come to a conclusion.

M

Liu Xueli had been sleeping in the apartment for an hour when the doorbell rang. Since it was daylight she had stayed dressed, so she got up groggily and went to the door. She looked through the peephole and saw a curved image of a handsome, Asian-featured man about her own age, dressed in black. "Who is it?" she asked.

"Are you Liu Xueli?"

"Yes."

"My name is Yao Xiaobo. The Consulate General sent me. May I come in?"

Xueli unlocked the three deadbolt locks and opened the door. Yao Xiaobo entered, carrying a packet under one arm. He did not bow, but shook his head slightly, closed the door and locked it.

"Lesson one: never look through the peephole. It's not bullet proof. Actually, most doors aren't, but if a hitman sees the peephole darken, he might shoot through it. I have been retained by the Chinese Consulate General to train you in assassination avoidance."

"Oh, thank you," said Xueli, feeling off balance. "But since you knew my name, I thought it was safe."

"Everyone here knows about you because you are the famous Taikonaut Liu Xueli, first female taikonaut, and you were on the news for visiting Metalmark. The paparazzi are on the look-out for you, not just the hitman. Just now I could have been a paparazzo with a convincing line, and when you opened the door I would have photographed you. And tomorrow your picture would have been in all of the tabloids, making a very surprised funny face, which you would see on papers and magazines and websites for the next ten years. And your address would be published, so you would have to get another apartment and cost the Consulate more money. So you must learn to be more careful about opening doors."

"I understand. I will do better," said Xueli.

"This is a very special assignment for me because I watched you in the Olympics, and I had such a crush on you then, it was unbearable. It's a dream come true for me to meet you, much less help to train you."

Xueli smiled, touched by his proclamation, and said, "Really?"

"No. I wasn't really interested in Olympics then, certainly not gymnasts. When you were medaling, I was at the 'I hate girls, they're disgusting' age. This is Lesson 2: Never believe flattery from someone who hasn't earned your trust. It could be a ruse that would mislead you into trusting the hitman."

Xueli blushed, ashamed to have been taken in.

"Now here is Lesson 3: call your Uncle Wei to confirm that I am who I say I am." She nodded and obediently went to get her cell phone and press the speed dial for Uncle Wei. He answered, and she told him that the trainer sent by the Consulate was here.

Uncle Wei said, "Trainer? I thought they were sending a bodyguard. Call diplomatic services and make sure the right man is there. Diplomatic services is in the phone's address book. Good-bye."

She disconnected. "He said you were supposed to be a bodyguard."

"I only take bodyguard clients after a consultation. It's a full-time position, and I don't accept it unless the client has met me and feels comfortable. Anything else wouldn't be professional."

"Okay."

"Not okay. You've done part of the lesson, but you have to finish verifying my identity."

She nodded and called Diplomatic Services. They confirmed that they had sent Yao Xiaobo, and asked for his confirmation number. Yao Xiaobo recited a nine-digit number, and the Diplomatic Services told her it was correct. She disconnected, and said, "I'm sorry I'm so slow on understanding. My head is still in Beijing time zone."

"I hope you have time to adjust before you have to use this." He took the packet from under his arm and opened it. A handgun was inside, along with paperwork attesting that it was assigned to Liu Xueli from licensed Consulate firearms.

"I understand it is jarring to be in your situation. You get off the plane and we say, 'Welcome to New York City. Here's your gun and a ticket to survival class.' But I have trained lots of diplomats in kidnapping and assassination avoidance. From what I have been told, you need this training. I think you would last about one week without it. If the hitman looked hot to you through the peephole and said he had a crush on you, I think you would let him in like you just let me in."

"Do you think I let you in because you look hot?"

"I just dress like the paparazzi, and they can find out where you live from their web sites. You are a celebrity with a price on your head and you have to learn to live defensively. If you trust someone you are trusting them with your life."

She repressed the urge to flirt more, and said, "You are right, of course. I need to train for this duty. But I will be no good without some sleep. Can you come back in three hours?"

Yao Xiaobo took out a schedule booklet and read it. "I can't get anywhere in the city and back here in three hours. I will wait here on the couch while you sleep in the bedroom. Then we will go to a training class."

"Okay. I will get up in three hours. Sorry to be so much trouble." She ducked into the bedroom and closed the door. There was a lock in the knob, and she locked it.

Yao Xiaobo smiled a little for the first time when he heard the lock click.

The next week Dr. Simmons got a call from a concierge service retained by the Metalmark Technologies. They offered him free moving and storage service for his furniture and a temporary apartment for one month, paid for by their client, while he searched for a permanent New York City abode. He had given notice to the National Research Council that he was giving up his post-doc appointment at NASA, so there was nothing preventing him from leaving Maryland. He called his parents, got congratulations, and cleaned out his office at NASA. The moving truck held his collection of books, files and apartment furniture with much room to spare. He drove his Toyota to New York, with his GPS navigator guiding him to the temporary apartment.

A couple of days later, installed in a nice fourth-floor efficiency apartment, he went to his first Board of Directors' meeting. It was on the tenth floor of a midtown high-rise called the Cycom building, named for the network services dot-com that was its principal tenant. The building had very vigilant security officers, who checked that he was authorized to visit Metalmark Technologies, and put him through a metal detector. Dr. Simmons got off the elevator and found his way to the glass-walled office entrance, which scintillated with videos of Metalmark butterflies, flitting about the blossoms of the buckwheat plants on which they dined.

The glass door didn't open at his pull, but just inside was a secretary's desk, and the occupant of the desk unlocked the door for him with an electronic "buzz."

Steve Simmons was amazed to see the woman from the White House gala, her unforgettable face smiling at him. "Good morning, Dr. Simmons. I'm Ilana Lindler, Metalmark's executive secretary. It's a pleasure to meet you. Here's your welcome package with drafts of the company prospectus and the budget that are going to be discussed today. Is anything wrong?" Steve Simmons was struggling with uncertainty about whether he was imagining her, and it showed on his face.

"No, I'm just . . . it's a pleasure to meet you, of course. How did you know me?"

"I saw you on the Jayno show. And of course your insights about Metalmark are famous in the media. Oh, I suppose you didn't know — I worked at the UN until recently, so I was the event coordinator for Metalmark's appearances. He is very impressed with your astrobiology expertise and took note of your interviews. My, but you're blushing! Don't be embarrassed. Metalmark pays attention to TV on many channels and he picked all of the Board members for their conspicuous talents in their respective fields."

"Thanks for the update. I'll be more careful about what I say on TV. Um, where should I go next?"

"Since you are a full-time Board member and don't have an office elsewhere in the city, we have an office that you can use. Come this way." They proceeded into the interior of the maze of glass walls. Dr. Simmons got a window office with a nice midtown view. Ilana gave him a key card to swipe and he checked that it opened the door.

"It's my first window office. I'll have to call Mom."

Ilana laughed, but his reaction seemed muted. "Are you sure nothing's wrong? Did the concierge service take care of everything?"

"No. I mean, they were fine. It's just been an abrupt transition and I'm bidding farewell to the research career that I thought I would have at NASA. It's probably just disorientation, ascending from the basement to the tenth floor. I'll adapt."

"Well, if you need anything — office supplies, computer network help, or whatnot — let me know. The meeting starts in half an hour in the main conference room. Coffee is in the kitchen down the hall." She left, closing the door with a smile. He had a private office, and she — Ilana — was the secretary for his employer. It was startling and amazing. He was glad he had worn his contact lenses instead of his thick glasses.

Dr. Simmons checked that his laptop was charged, and glanced at the papers in the document folder that she — Ilana — had given him. On the company personnel list, with the Metalmark Technologies letterhead, were the names of famous people (the other Board members), his name, and at the bottom "Ilana Lindler — Executive Secretary." It was surreal.

Dr. Simmons was in a seat at the conference table on time, ready to type some notes on his laptop when the meeting began. Most of the people on the Board roster had arrived. On his left was August Harrington, heir to the Xasm on-line gaming fortune and notorious partier. On his right was a financier from Case Venture Capital named Jerome Carter. Across the table was Sir Phillip Archway, whom he had seen conversing with Metalmark at the White House gala. Sir Phillip was the wealthiest man in Britain, after the phenomenal success of his upstart search engine PixelPa.com ("The Daddy of all imagery portals"), which was now second in eyeball share on the Internet. Next to Sir Phillip sat Dr. Vitaly Ozerov, who had worked as deputy head of the Russian Federation Space Agency. A very pretty Asian lady came in and sat across the table diagonally from Dr. Simmons; he thought it might be the taikonaut, Liu Xueli. He was still having that surreal feeling, and hadn't assimilated his surroundings into his personal reality.

Metalmark entered and stood behind a lectern on one corner of the conference table. He dimmed the lights and caused a projection screen to display a view of his starship, with its shimmering cover of silicon-winged butterflies. "Good morning, everyone. Let's wrap up the budget leftovers from last time."

One of the financiers said, "You've added a new item called 'Security' and I'm wondering what you have in mind for this."

Metalmark replied, "Sir Phillip and I have started a project to use PixelPa.com for some prediction and mitigation of threats to our safety. Websites that mention me or any of the Board members are being captured and analyzed. After the Calcutta attack, I want to employ due diligence in threat forecasting. Known sites that are linked with Islamic extremists are being monitored for signs that someone might attack us, and if any specific threat to a member of the Board is suggested, we certainly want to notify you.

"I'm concerned because we just got our first warning. An offer was made on a web site for a reward to be paid to the successful assassin of Board member Liu

Xueli." Several people groaned in surprise and sympathy, and Xueli sat frozen. "There's no indication that the job has been accepted — the website is designed to support payments to assassins, so we will monitor it in case someone signs up for the job."

Concerned murmurs went round the table, and Sir Phillip said, "Ms. Liu, many of us have been targets of kidnappers or worse, so please don't feel alone. We will use this technology to help protect you and all of the Board members. The authorities will be notified through channels that will ensure that they take the threat with proper seriousness."

"Thank you," said Xueli. "I'll tell my bodyguard and the Consulate."

Some less frightening budget matters were discussed, and then the proposed Board member salary came up. The Chief Financial Officer recommended starting salaries low in the six-figure range to conserve working capital for the manufacture and sales of inventions that were about to be discussed. There was minimal debate, as it seemed to Dr. Simmons that the Board was tired of the subject. After a perfunctory vote, he found himself with a salary four times what he had earned at NASA, with a promise of up-coming options deals when the company issued its IPO.

Metalmark said, "As we discussed last time, I'm bringing three new devices out of my forerunner to add to the catalog. We will still offer the 'Food from Stones' technology, but I am disappointed in its appeal. So I have another technology to offer gratis to nations that need additional food production." The projection screen showed an object like a soap bubble, with spectral reflections highlighting its surface. "This is a silicon-based life form that is adapted for terrestrial habitats. Each one grows by absorbing hydrogen gas from moisture in the air. By photosynthesis it forms its bubble as a layer of carbohydrate that is edible by people. The growing bubbles disperse on winds while they grow. After reaching about a foot in diameter, a bubble absorbs water until it is no longer buoyant and sinks to the ground. People can collect them and use them for food (popping them to discard the hydrogen and drink some water that has collected inside), or the hydrogen can be collected and used for fuel. These creatures will reproduce asexually using silicon-based hereditary matter that cannot cross into the DNA genomes, and they won't proliferate without reasonable limits. I'm going to offer this technology to the UN for marketing to suitable nations.

"The H-bubbles may spur a new energy infrastructure for hydrogen fuel, but your civilization is still very dependent on petroleum. For my first major industrial offering, I have developed a nanotechnology that catalytically converts plant matter into a petroleum-like liquid. I'm thinking of calling it PetroCompost, and I want the Board members with marketing experience to evaluate the product name's appeal. Your industrial facilities can collect waste plant matter at existing petroleum refineries. Mix the plant matter with water and my product, and in about three weeks the tank will be filled with petroleum similar in composition to 'light sweet crude.' For this product to penetrate the market, we will need the talents of the Board members with petrochemical industry experience."

Several Board members smiled or chuckled appreciatively. They had wondered if there would be payback for the Islamic bloc's UN vote. This product would attack Iran and the petrodollar-dependent Islamic nations economically, and had the potential for a huge impact on them.

"Another product that I have to announce is what I call the Sun Power Flower." The projection screen showed a desert sandscape with flower-shaped objects that appeared to be made of glass. "These life forms are silicon-based flowers that are photovoltaic. They will grow and spread over unused desert landscape. At the base of each flower is a pair of metal contacts which may be tapped for electricity. With this technology, you will be able to make use of arid, sun-baked land for power generation, without the production costs of silicon solar cells as you presently manufacture them.

"Again, Marketing should test the product design and name 'Sun Power Flower' for appeal. I envision the prospect that this product and the PetroCompost product may generate significant revenues for Metalmark Technologies. These should add to the revenue flow that the rare metals extraction from ocean water has begun to generate.

"Liu Xueli, as I recall the Chinese space agency has received my orbital re-entry vehicle and is studying it. For next time, please bring me a report on the reactions to the design concepts that it instantiates, and let the Board know if the agency has queries about how it works. I will be happy to assist them in utilization of the propulsion technologies. There won't be a fee because propulsion is part of the starship technology deal."

"Yes, Sir," Xueli said, smiling.

"I have been in contact with NASA Admin. Krainak, and notified him that I want to start some technology transfer to NASA." The projection screen returned to the starship and began to zoom in. The swarm of silicon butterflies grew closer, languidly creeping about the surface of the starship, with their wings sometimes reflecting brilliant sunlight as they took on various orientations. The point of view arrived at one individual, which had a body plan somewhat like a Riodinidae butterfly (taking much artistic license).

Metalmark said, "This is one cell of my body, so to speak. It's a silicon-based life form, adapted for life in space, and for sustaining itself by photovoltaic energy absorption and mining. Each cell is capable of computation by means of a processor network equivalent to several of your terabytes of memory. It is connected to all of the other cells by means of high-bandwidth radio links on a number of frequencies, as well as LASER data transmission. Inside each cell, numerous processors communicate with the memory addresses via photonic connections. Some leakage of the light occurs, and the cells use several colors, which is why you see that opalescent, variable surface texture on the cell."

The board members watched in fascination. The close-ups far exceeded the details that had been photographed by the taikonauts. The butterflies seemed to be made of magical, sparkling multicolored opal.

"I am arranging to send one of the cells to the International Space Station, with permission from Admin. Krainak. The biochemical make-up of the cell is such that bringing one to a lab on the Earth's surface presents technical challenges. Some of the cell's constituents explode upon contact with oxygen. I suggested that initial examination of the cell be carried out by astronauts on a spacewalk. NASA is currently working on an oxygen-free containment facility in which scientists could examine the cell in detail."

Dr. Simmons felt simultaneously jealous of the NASA scientists who would get that job, but privileged to experience Metalmark's personal preview. He asked, "Are you saying that you consist of a program of mind processes carried out in this large grid computer network?"

Metalmark answered, "Yes, but I am an executive process in the network. My mind is only a small part of the processing that is carried out, just as your conscious thoughts are not a large percentage of the autonomic activity in your brains and nervous systems. I am part of the conscious processing that occurs in the computer composed of these cells. Other conscious, volitional and autonomic processes are taking place in probes elsewhere in the solar system. A computational node of presence is contained within this body, and kept synchronized with the global network via the satcoms that encircle Earth. I am conscious of the whole cellular network, although most of me is elsewhere."

And this was why the Calcutta attack had no permanent effect on him, Dr. Simmons and the others realized. The body of Metalmark was an expendable node, mostly playing the part of an interface from mankind to the global system, which was awesomely large. There was a hive mind inhabiting the swarm of silicon butterflies, with computational capacity orders of magnitude greater than any supercomputer on Earth and software designed with 500 years' head start. How much more powerful than any human mind was this computer distributed across millions of miles of space?

Sir Phillip Archway asked, "So is this why you have never spoken in the plural of these beings on your starship, but always just said, 'I.'"

Metalmark replied, "I encompass all of the cells and experience what the cells collectively experience. It is the same with you — you don't feel that the neurons of your brain are a group of individuals, and you don't say, 'we think' something or 'we did' something. My identity is the collectivity of these cells.

"Nevertheless, for the sake of sharing my technology with you, I am disconnecting one of the cells from the network and sending it to rendezvous with the International Space Station, so that NASA can examine it and convey the results to the scientists and engineers of Earth. I will answer queries about puzzling aspects, of course.

"Each cell has some means of propulsion, and one is on the way as of now. It will arrive in about twenty-three hours."

After the meeting Dr. Simmons went to his office. It was an amazing amount of new knowledge to absorb and digest. He checked e-mail, sent a few trivial messages, and went out to lunch. Ilana was not at the desk, perhaps in Metalmark's office. He had learned that there was a restaurant on the top floor of the building, so he went up and had a soup and sandwich, enjoying the skyline view.

When he returned to the office suite, his keycard let him in. Still Ilana was absent. He went into his own office and started his laptop computer. He had to provide some information to the Human Resources officer and he was assigned to touch base with Admin. Krainak, to prepare for the rendezvous of the Metalmark cell with the International Space Station (ISS). He reached Krainak on his BlackBerry, got some congratulatory comments, and then had to talk with a series of NASA personnel who had responsibilities for the flight operations and safety of the ISS. Contacting them all and collecting their queries and requirements took the rest of the day. He encapsulated the many issues in e-mails which he sent to Metalmark@mtlmktech.com.

He finished at 5:45 PM and decided to see whether Ilana had ever returned. As he went toward her reception desk, he saw her back. She was taking a phone call, and her voice was stern and barely audible. "I told you that I won't do that any more. It's over. Don't call me again." And she hung up, burying her head in her hands.

Steve Simmons silently retreated back around the hallway toward his office. He had hoped to start a pleasant chat, but it looked as if the call had been an unwelcome one. He decided that waiting a few minutes in his office would prevent her from thinking that he was spying on her. The good side of overhearing her was that if she had a partner or steady date, the relationship appeared to have ended.

At 6:00 PM he came out and approached her desk. She looked up with a smile and said, "How was the first day?"

"Exciting but then bureaucratic. I wanted to ask you for some advice. I've been to New York before but I'm not familiar with this part of town. Would you be kind enough to recommend a good place to get a drink and dinner?"

Ilana reflected. She didn't feel eager to go home and face the pestering phone messages from her CIA case officer, who was trying to lure her back. And she no longer had to work late hours on UN events in multiple time zones. Maybe this was a good opportunity to start having a life. Dr. Simmons had a self-effacing, boyish manner, and he looked the role of the most famous NASA scientist ever to appear on Jayno.

She said, "Hm. The restaurant on the top floor is so-so, but you should celebrate your first day on the Board of Directors. I can make a recommendation of a place that's not too far that we relied on to entertain UN visitors. Do you like German food?"

"Yes, that would be good. What's it called and how do I get there?"

"Well, it's a little hard to find. Would it be too forward if I offered to take you there? I feel badly that everyone has left (except Metalmark, who doesn't eat), so there's no one to join you for a welcome dinner."

"I would enjoy your company very much."

They took a cab and Ilana provided a running tour narrative of points of interest that they passed, from important subway stops to interesting museums and parks. After some tortuous turns, with detailed directions to the driver from Ilana, they got out at the "Cafe Leipzig."

The entrance foyer was decorated with a crest of the city and a vase of golden roses, the flower of Leipzig. When they were seated, Steve Simmons looked at the menu and called on memories of European travel to scientific conferences. "Oh! They have Hefe Weissbier. I'll have a stein."

Ilana said, "You found the best thing on the menu! I'll have the same. How did you know that?"

"Well, the first law of being a scientist is to do research and publish it. The second law is to travel to far lands and experience the finest food and beverages, especially beers. Most people who are not scientists never learn about our 2nd law, alas."

Ilana thought, *Nothing about women in that, but okay*. She said, "So what is the music?"

"Well, this is the Cafe Leipzig, and it sounds like Bach. I think it's the Goldberg variations, but I'm used to the Glenn Gould performance, so I could be fooled by a similar piece."

Ilana's eyes lit, so he had probably guessed right, but they had a visitor. A stout woman in a traditional German costume said, "Good evening, welcome to Cafe Leipzig," but then she addressed Ilana in German.

"Ilana, so good to see you! It has been a long time. Is this a special evening with a special man, maybe?"

"I don't think he speaks German, but he knew what beer to order and recognized the music! I hope it will become special! Don't press him! It's good to see you again, too."

Steve smiled amiably, not understanding more than a disconnected word or two. The fact that the manager knew Ilana boded well for the service for the evening. It wasn't a total-immersion German restaurant with waiters in liederhosen and knee-slap dancing, and he enjoyed the classical music, so he waited politely for the wheat beer.

In English Ilana said, "This is Dr. Steve Simmons, who just joined our Board of Directors. He was the scientist at NASA who tracked Metalmark's starship."

"Just call me 'Steve,' please!"

The manager said, "It's very nice to meet you. Your beers are on the way, and I'll take your order if you are ready."

Steve said, "Well, I'm tempted by the Ungarisches Goulash, but to please Ilana I'll try the Sauerbraten. I often like that."

Ilana said, "I'll have the Ungarisches Goulash on two plates so we can both try it."

The manager said, "Excellent choices." In German to Ilana she added, "Don't let this one get away!" She left to put in the order.

Ilana said, "Sorry you couldn't understand, but she likes to exercise my German and make sure I still have it."

"For my whole career, few people have understood what I talked about. When the tables are turned, I have no right to complain."

The Weiss-biers arrived, and they were exquisite — satisfying with the hint of flower blossoms. Steve said, "Let's make a toast to Metalmark, without whom we would not be here today."

"Yes," agreed Ilana, who clinked her stein and said, "*Prost!* I mean, cheers," then drank thirstily.

"That was a busy day," Steve remarked.

"Yes, I was in Metalmark's office much of the day. Because everything is just starting, most of the functions of the company are carried out by the people loaned to us by the Venture Capital investors. So we are constantly on the phone arranging activities. It's like a holding company, with all the real functions performed off site. And the other companies that have offered to do things are chaired by executive prima donnas who must have a hand in, so everything has to be blessed by the archbishop before anything happens, so to speak. You are very different from most of these prima donnas that I met in this job. You are not so full of ego."

"Well, I am aware of the accidents that put me where I am. If I had not had a friend at the Air Force, then I would not have been given Metalmark's coordinates and asked if I could find his previous movements. So I would not have found the spacecraft's images of his starship approaching, and I would not have gotten into tabloids and onto *Jayno Live*. Keeping these accidents in mind keeps me humble."

"But you are one of NASA's most famous scientists. Don't be too humble."

"Well, I got to learn some extraterrestrial science today, so I've had my fix. Did you see the butterfly 'cells' on the starship?"

"Not see, but it's my job to listen to the audio of every meeting and make sure the dictation software produces a correct transcript. It sounded amazing."

"It was! He is sending one of the butterflies to the Space Station! I'm no astronaut, but I'd love to see one up close."

"But he said they would explode on Earth! How can that be?"

"Chemistry of some kind. He is a strange being behind the human-like interface."

"He's a kind person to work for, though. I couldn't resist the offer. What do you think of him — Metalmark?"

Time suddenly slowed down to a crawl for Steve Simmons. It wasn't just the effect of the Weiss-bier. He had detected a momentous juncture approaching — an imminent possible catastrophe. What he said to her next had great implications. It would be interpreted as his scientific and professional opinion, it was liable to get back to Metalmark because she was his Executive Secretary, and on top of these hazards, he was trying to start a romance with this woman who clearly liked Metalmark a lot. So what he said next determined his future in three vital respects. Fitting all of these parameters favorably would be improbable for any honest reply that he might make.

He said unhurriedly, "Metalmark is the voice of a thousand crystal butterflies singing."

Ilana made a barely audible gasp. "That sounded like a Haiku! Not just a scientist, you are a poet, too, a cultured Renaissance man. You're not Goethe, so where is it that you come from?"

"Oh, my family is a boring one from Pennsylvania, but I escaped to MIT. The space science program there has room for some digressions into poetry, and they have some travel money to send students to space science conferences. I think I remember who Goethe was, but maybe it's just the bier. Where do you come from, to be able to appreciate such Old World culture?"

The food arrived, and between bites Ilana told him that she was born in Leipzig and her family moved to Berlin, but when the Wall was torn down they came to the USA. When she grew up in the USA, through connections she got a job at the UN. But her parents now had both passed away. For a long time, her family had been her UN colleagues.

The beer and food had their effect, slowing the conversation dramatically. Ilana was surprised how much she enjoyed the paprika and garlic of the Hungarian dish. The Sauerbraten was excellent, with fresh cloves and tangy with good vinegar. Steve particularly enjoyed the wine that she ordered for dessert, a spicy Gewürztraminer. They spent the rest of the meal forgetting about work and exchanging trivia about Leipzig and Lancaster. With coffee barely keeping them awake, they left the restaurant and caught a cab to the building that held Lindlerflat.

"I'm sorry I can't invite you up this time, but my apartment is not presentable. I will clean it up in the hope that we can . . . do this again."

"It was delightful," said Steve. "Thank you for celebrating with me. It will be a whole new experience to see you again tomorrow."

"Good night," she said. He was struck by the glow of her face, compared with the night of the White House gala. She waved happily as the cab drove him away toward his apartment.

$$\underline{\text{M}}$$

Liu Xueli was in the company of a man that evening also, but enjoying it less than enduring it. Yao Xiaobo had brought her to another work-out class, to keep her in top shape in case she needed to flee on foot at high speed. The first part of the evening had been spent on a treadmill in a rented training center, and then she had to practice reaction time while running as fast as she could through an obstacle course of spooky mannequins, to simulate eluding pursuit on a crowded New York street. The Consulate had given Yao Xiaobo a "James Bond" gadget, a tool for locating the source of incoming gunfire, and he was examining and learning how to use the device.

At least Yao Xiaobo had agreed to be her bodyguard, and the target practice with the pistol had been less grueling than this evening.

After the three runs of the obstacle course, she returned to where he was sitting, practicing with the gadget and going over his plans for more training. She was panting between sips of water. Her workout clothes felt as if she had just poured the water all over herself.

When she caught her breath, she asked him, "Have you ever lost a client to a hitman?"

After a moment, still inspecting the gadget, he said, "Yes. But not since I began running my own business."

She thought this over. "Did you know about the website that Sir Phillip warned me about?"

"I knew about such websites, but not that specific one. They come and go. It is very good that your company provided that information. It's a benefit that you should value. We can always use the help."

She thought of the crystal butterflies and described them to Xiaobo. "They are creepy and beautiful at the same time. I think it's because they are beautiful and irresistibly delicate, but they don't have a human face to communicate feelings. Metalmark has a voice that seems to carry feelings, but we know that he is an artificial being, no more human than those mannequins. I don't really understand why he is protecting us Board members with this service. I would not be surprised if silicon creatures kept to their own kind, and ignored carbon creatures with prejudice."

"I think you should let feelings wait and concentrate on safety."

"I can't help having feelings. Some of them are about being safe."

"You are tired. Go get a shower and we will take you home."

Xueli complied. But during her shower, she kept thinking of Xiaobo.

Ilana entered Lindlerflat and was struck by how silent and bland it was. The evening with Steve had been wonderful, full of music and conversation, so different from her usual nightly routine. He was different from the diplomats that she had dated through acquaintances at the UN. Diplomats talked a smooth line, but they were always on the move to the next post and never stayed. Their commitments were tentative, expedient and elusive. But Steve was here in a new job that he seemed to consider long-term. He was a perfect, cultured gentleman and seemed ripe for putting down roots. She tried not to get her hopes up too much, but the two of them had seemed perfect together this evening.

The blinking light on the answering machine quenched her afterglow. Grimacing, she pressed the button. The gravelly voice of her CIA case officer, Al Carson, pestered her again. "Ilana, just calling again to reiterate the company's interest. You have such an excellent record, and we would hate to lose you . . . to the competition or whatever. If you have had a competing offer, please present it to us. Funds are tight, but maybe we can work out some increment in compensation. In any case, please give us a chance to match any competing offers. I look forward to hearing from you."

The time on the message was after 6:00 PM, so her firm rejection during the call at the office had not been effective. Maybe tomorrow she would change her home phone number. But that would only delay the CIA pestering briefly. Uncertain about what else to do, she went to bed. She dreamed surprisingly pleasant dreams of Steve.

Ⲙ

Liu Xueli's phone rang, waking her up in the early morning hours. "Hello?"

"I'm sorry to bother you. This is Cheryl Miller from the Pulse Security Services. We were retained by PixelPa.co.uk to monitor your situation. We thought you should know that there was activity on the contract website of concern to you. Someone accepted a contract on your life."

"Oh! I . . . will tell the Consulate and my bodyguard . . ."

"I understand that this is shocking. We wouldn't have bothered you, but the website that was used is well known to us. It transfers funds via accounts in the Cayman islands. The usual arrangement for hitmen is that half the funds are provided for accepting the contract and the other half are transferred upon confirmation of the assassination. Our monitoring of the website indicates that the funds have been accepted for the commitment to the contract, so we thought that you should be notified."

"Yes, it's not good news, but thank you."

"We are working under an arrangement with Sir Phillip Archway, and we will contact the Chinese Consulate General in New York City and the New York City police department on your behalf. Please know that everything will be done through these channels that is possible to ensure your safety."

". . . Thank you," said Xueli.

"Take care, Ms. Liu. Good-night."

"Good-bye," said Xueli. A bit of early dawn glow was penetrating the curtain edges, and she no longer could sleep, but she tried to lie still to save energy for the day to come.

M

The next morning at the office Ilana got a delivery: a bouquet of golden roses and a thank-you note from Steve Simmons. When he got to the office, she was all wistful smiles and told him, "My father used to give Leipzig golden roses to my mother on my birthday to remind her where I was born." She wiped away a small tear as she took one of the roses out and handed it to him. "Take one for your office," she said.

"Thanks again," he said, taking the flower and giving her hand a formal kiss. "I have to make sure everything is set for the cell rendezvous, but if we have time for lunch . . ."

She nodded. "If we can squeeze it in."

He went to the office to check messages and e-mail, and then joined the Board members in the conference room.

Mission Control in Houston and the Flight Dynamics teams at Goddard Space Flight Center were fully manned to monitor the International Space Station for the Metalmark cell rendezvous. Admin. Krainak had ordered an ISS NASA video relay to the boardroom of Metalmark Technologies, where most of the Board members were in attendance. TV and streaming Internet media were broadcasting the historic event worldwide. Astronauts could be seen inside the ISS, carefully preparing their pressure suits for a space walk to inspect the butterfly when it arrived, and attach it securely to a chosen point on the truss of the ISS where it would wait in a quiescent state to be analyzed in detail.

Metalmark and the other Board members sat around a U-shaped table watching so that he could answer questions. On one screen the eyes of the silicon butterfly gave the Board a view of the approaching ISS, of its cylindrical pressurized modules, intersecting trusses and long slabs of photoelectric power arrays, against the backdrop of moving ocean surface two hundred miles below. There was a docked Russian *Soyuz* spacecraft at one end of the station.

Another screen in the boardroom showed the NASA and NTC network views of the butterfly approaching the ISS slowly, propelled by occasional course-correction jets in the butterfly's body.

Metalmark said, "This cell encapsulates the principles of my technology, and your scientists can begin to understand the foreign biochemistry of my silicon-based cells and metabolism."

Dr. Steve Simmons bit his lip and refrained from remarking that this was why his planned book was not worth publishing.

Sir Phillip asked, "Metalmark, this butterfly cell — what does it eat and is it sated?"

"It eats silicate minerals and other rocks. You can see that there are drill teeth up on the head. But it is quite sated at this phase of its life cycle. Just prior to spawning, it was fed and ready to perform the mating behavior."

The NASA Capcom audio announced: "One hundred meters to contact with the ISS. The astronauts have been breathing enhanced oxygen mixture to remove nitrogen from their bloodstreams and enable them to enter the space suits for the EVA. This enables them to use the space suits at lower total pressure without incurring 'the bends' and gives the joints of the space suits more flexibility. If the suits contained a full atmosphere of pressure, working inside them would be like working inside an inflated auto tire."

The silicon butterfly continued to close in on an ISS truss, where it was intended to perch with its grappling arms. Liu Xueli watched it with foreboding, half expecting that at any moment the butterfly would seize the ISS to set it spinning out of control. She tried to dismiss the post-traumatic mental imagery.

"How big is the cell?" asked August Harrington.

"About eleven meters in wingspan," replied Metalmark. The ISS orbited from sunlight into the Earth's shadow, and the screens were briefly black until the cameras dilated. Then the butterfly leaped back into view, a sparkling mesmerizing form of variegated pixels — blue, green, red, some yellow — with wings that reflected some of the lights and forms of the ISS. Its eight grappling arms reached out toward the truss on which it was about to land. Its head swiveled, and canted rows of diamond teeth in silicon carbide sockets conveyed inhuman appetites. The head was bejeweled with various glass eyes for various wavelengths of light, as well as some intriguing antennae to sense radio waves. Conical microwave receiver horns also projected from it like ears. Something made the viewers know that its head was a head, but it was a cubist form from some forgotten Picasso abstraction, not a head that human beings comprehended. The views made the humans involuntarily grip their chairs and secretly murmur, "Oh!"

The screen that had shown the cell's view of the ISS was dark. Dr. Simmons asked, "Can the cell still see the station?"

Metalmark replied, "Oh, I should show you the infrared view." The station appeared in a slightly blurrier version, painted in false colors. "The cell can image several infrared bands for work without sunlight. Here you can see that the hotter areas of the station are more luminous and intense. The cell perceives other electromagnetic bands also."

The action proceeded with the usual pace of NASA space operations, the pace of a dance of sedated elephants. Safety was uppermost in priority, and slow movements, while soporific, were the best way to prevent mishaps. When the butterfly reached its planned perch on the truss, Capcom announced, "We have contact of the first living extraterrestrial life form with the International Space Station." Spontaneous cheers could be heard at Mission Control.

Dr. Simmons stood up in the darkened room and went for coffee. Other board members conversed about the historic event. His cell phone was in his pocket in case Admin. Krainak called for some reason.

Coffee in hand, he went to Ilana's desk. "Would you like any coffee?" he asked, just to have an excuse to talk with her.

She turned toward him. "Thanks, I'll have a cup. Did everything go as planned?" She got up and they went to the kitchen.

"Everything seems 'nominal.' Looks like we're 'go' for lunch. The astronauts are about to cycle through the air lock, and they will take some time to climb over to the truss and make an inspection of the butterfly. It's eerie because of the darkness — the ISS orbit took it behind the Earth and the butterfly glows from within. Its teeth look formidable, and it's got eight arms with hands. Metalmark said the teeth are for drilling rock."

Ilana remembered the dinner at the Shankars'. "I once heard him say that his earliest memory was 'chewing on a rock' . . . and realizing what he was. A miner, I guess he meant. Anyway, then he said at that point he decided he had to find out what his goal in life should be."

"That's really interesting," said Dr. Simmons. "What was it? A moment of awakening? Reaching maturity somehow? The first emergence of consciousness?"

"That's what it sounded like . . . we were all reminiscing about our earliest recollections from childhood."

"You are very observant."

She smiled. "I have to get back on duty. Thanks for the coffee." She went back to the desk and Dr. Simmons returned to his seat in the dusky conference room.

Liu Xueli was struggling to deal with the sinister images on the screen of the darkened boardroom. It was not a pleasant experience for her but she was gaining mastery over it. Her feelings toward Metalmark were confused, but the memory of his help in returning from the ill-fated looting mission was dominant. The memory of his kindness, his declining to punish her for coming to loot his ship, was harder to keep now that his nonhuman nature was clear. She told herself that the alien butterfly far away in orbit was much less of a threat than an anonymous member of her own species who lurked somewhere in this nearby city.

Dr. Simmons returned to his seat in the darkened boardroom and saw astronauts emerging from the ISS airlock, accompanied by desultory comments from Mission Control about mission milestones. Metalmark was appearing to watch, although Dr. Simmons now believed that the android was often pretending to perform actions which he really did not need to do with the body that occupied the corporate office suite. The bulk of the alien's mental activity was going on in the other parts of the network of thousands of butterfly-like life forms on the starship that the alien called a forerunner. Dr. Simmons felt secret misgivings about the alien's intent, even though he was irresistibly drawn to this place by the opportunity to observe the alien's interface to human beings (besides the better salary). The more he learned about Metalmark, the more mysterious the alien seemed.

August Harrington, the heir to the Xasm game empire usually sat next to Dr. Simmons, and he was in his usual place. "You're from NASA, aren't you?" he asked.

"I worked there for a couple of years," Dr. Simmons replied.

"Do you know why everything they do is so damn boring? I mean, except for an occasional nail-biter launch?"

Dr. Simmons smiled. "No, I don't have a clue," he replied.

Harrington went on, "I mean, this is the first authentic alien creature to arrive at the space station, but you could sleep through it. If we made a game out of this using genuine NASA video, no one would buy it. Flopperoony. But the world-wide interest in beings from space is fanatical. Everyone wants to know about

Metalmark's nature and technology, but NASA can't convey the answers everybody wants without filtering it through some kind of slow trickle. This is all in 'slow-mo.' I want to know about silicon-based life forms from interstellar space! I want to know if they do something interesting and exciting that I haven't known about before. I would incorporate that into my idea of the Universe and our place in it as one class of beings instead of the only beings that exist. But I'm waiting for this stupid snail-paced show to wind up, and I don't know whether it's worth watching the rest. If I was at home, I'd go channel-surfing."

Dr. Simmons said, "It's more than a show, and the astronauts want to get through it alive, so they do everything carefully. If they don't, they might not survive. If they do, they still might not survive. But they hope that 'slow-mo' helps their chances."

August Harrington said, "I can appreciate that. You're telling me that it's like disarming a bomb."

"Yes!" said Dr. Simmons. "That's exactly what it's like! People don't understand it because the TV can't convey it, but everything NASA does in space is like disarming a bomb. If you could put that into a game, then NASA might get the fascination it deserves."

There was a *beep* in the Mission Control sound track, and it caught their attention. The astronauts were halfway along the truss, approaching the butterfly cell for inspection. One of the astronauts asked, "Houston, is there a solar flare that we don't know about? The radiation detector is generating a warning. Bart, can you check out the reading?"

The Capcom narrator explained, "Astronaut Bart Dixon is checking the solar flare radiation detector for malfunctions. Mission Control has not had any warnings of solar or cosmic radiation events, so it's likely to be a faulty sensor. Also the ISS is eclipsed by Planet Earth, so no radiation can get to the ISS directly from a solar flare."

The boardroom at Metalmark Technologies was silent, with everyone's attention engaged but with a comforting explanation on the table. The astronauts were still approaching the sparkling butterfly, hand-over-hand in the darkness.

"Houston, this is Bart. The sensor is pegged to the max. Please check for any signs of malfunctions."

Another beep. "Houston, this is Jim Raynor." He was one of the spacewalking astronauts. "My dosimeter has changed color. I conclude that the butterfly is hot. I think I'll go back to the airlock, and I recommend that my buddy Tom do the same."

There was a pause of seven seconds. Then Mission Control said, "Roger, that. We concur. We see no evidence of malfunctions in the radiation sensors. The safest action is to return to the airlock while we investigate." The astronauts could be seen moving along handholds back toward the airlock.

August Harrington turned to Dr. Simmons. "That's not good, right?"

VII

THE NTC ANNOUNCER said, "It's *Live Tonight with Jayno*, with her special guest: the return of Metalmark! And Dr. Steve Simmons of NASA fame. Plus the Space Blogger: Larry Saxon." The audience applause was obedient but conveyed less than full enthusiasm.

Jayno came out, waving to the crowd briefly but quickly taking her seat. "Thank you everyone. Tonight we won't start with a funny routine because of the serious events that we are living through. The latest reports tell us that the Russian *Soyuz* spacecraft has successfully brought astronauts Jim Raynor and Tom Allen to a safe landing. They are being treated for the large doses of radiation that they encountered while preparing to examine the space butterfly at the International Space Station.

"Metalmark Technologies issued a statement of apology to the astronauts for the mishap, and Metalmark has agreed to join us tonight and discuss what went wrong. So please welcome Metalmark back to our stage after so many harrowing events." The audience applauded perfunctorily as Metalmark came out and took the seat beside Jayno. She could hear some undercurrent of hostile tones as the audience voices quieted.

"Thank you for coming back," she said.

"Thank you for the invitation. I want to express my regrets about the unexpected events of the past few days. I send my apologies to the astronauts and their worried families. From what the NASA experts tell me, the dose of radiation that the astronauts received was serious but they have good chances for a full recovery with the treatments that are being provided to them. I also apologize to the Russian space agency and NASA for the disruptions that this caused in their space programs. I realize that these are costly in both emotional distress and money, and I want to stress that Metalmark Technologies and I will do everything possible to prevent repeating this misunderstanding."

Jayno said, "I'm sure that I speak for everyone who cares about the space program when I say we appreciate your apology. I want to clear up what you've said about a 'misunderstanding,' but first let's bring out Dr. Steve Simmons, formerly of NASA, who identified your starship among the stars on its way here." Dr. Simmons joined the hostess and Metalmark, sitting beside the latter.

"What do you mean by a 'misunderstanding?'" Jayno asked Metalmark

"Well, before the rendezvous with the ISS, Dr. Simmons consulted with NASA about their requirements for safety of the astronauts. The consultations did not focus on anything about the radiation tolerances of the astronauts, so I assumed that their space suits would protect them against the kind of radiation intensity that I encounter in my travel through interstellar space. That was my error, and I should have inquired about it. I can only plead that I was distracted by the imminent spawning event, for which I am involved in elaborate preparations and computations, even as we speak."

Jayno nodded and said, "But I don't understand why the butterfly was radioactive, and I'm sure this is on everyone's mind who is watching."

"I should explain the way of life that I pursue. I consist of a colony of cells, some like the one that you have seen that resembles a butterfly, plus other kinds. As a colony, these cells are adapted to mining. When they are in sunlight the cells use the wings for electric power generation, which the cells need to survive the space environment. But mining requires deep digging for long periods of time. For deep drilling each cell contains a small nuclear generator in its body. At depth, the power from that plant enables the cell to drill through solid rock and bring back the ore to the other cells that process it."

Jayno said, "That is incredible for human beings to conceive ⏤ that you have nuclear material within your body's cells. You don't have any nuclear material in *this* body do you?"

"No, this is an artificial body without any nuclear power. As silicon-based life forms, my cells are very different from human body cells. This body contains some of the cellular matter so that I can make it a node of presence."

"It makes more sense to me now that you might forget or misjudge the vulnerability of human cells to radiation from your own."

"I misjudged the protectiveness of the space suits," said Metalmark.

Dr. Simmons added, "Metalmark learned everything about us from watching television broadcasts, but none of them provided information about the human body's susceptibility to radiation. Or about the radiation protection that space suits provide."

"Are the other astronauts in any danger?" asked Jayno.

"No, the space station walls keep the radiation from penetrating," Metalmark replied. "But I have moved the cell away from the station so that it no longer endangers their space walks."

"Dr. Simmons, can you tell us your role in this?"

"For the past week I have served as a member of the Board of Directors of Metalmark Technologies, in the position of Chief Science Consultant. I requested the NASA requirements from NASA for safety of the rendezvous mission. I regret that the level of radiation protection provided by the suits was not considered in detail before the mission. I have been in contact with NASA Admin. Krainak, who tells me that the astronauts are ill because of the radiation, but they are responding well to the treatment."

"In what way are they ill?"

"They suffered severe flu-like symptoms and dehydration after the reactions of their bodies to the radiation set in. They were previously very healthy, though, and the medications and intravenous fluids are controlling their conditions. Pain-killers are keeping them comfortable. They have been quarantined because their immune systems are inactive, and they have been given antibiotics to prevent infections. They will be kept from exposure to anyone who is sick or possibly sick until their blood shows signs of recovery of their immune systems."

"What signs would that be?"

"The doctors can measure the presence of T cells and other immune system cells in their blood. If these cells are slow to return, then stem cell treatments will be used to help them regain normal immunity."

"It sounds like the men won't be able to return to space for a long time."

"That's right. Their families can visit them, but can't have contact with them until they recover. NASA is making sure that they receive every form of treatment that they need."

Jayno said, "A family visit means looking at Tom and Jim through a window. We all wish them a quick recovery. Viewers can go to www.jaynolive.com and send e-mail greetings and wishes for recovery to the astronauts.

"Now I'd like to bring on our last guest, who has kindly waited to let us cover these topics, but please welcome Larry Saxon. He's known as the Space Blogger for his thorough and opinionated commentary on the space program. Come on out,

Larry."

The audience welcomed Saxon warmly. He shook hands with Metalmark and Dr. Simmons and sat in the chair beside Simmons.

Jayno said, "Larry, you have expressed some strong opinions on www.known-space.info about the activities of Metalmark and NASA. Please tell us your concerns, and keep the language appropriate for family viewing."

"Okay. This first contact with a being from outer space has been completely botched from day one. Metalmark offered a trade contract with the UN. In human history, trade agreements have been negotiated between nations, so there is nothing legal about the contract that the UN voted for. We don't know if Metalmark represents a government or civilization, although he has taken on the role of one. We have no reason to be confident that this deal is bona fide. And for a super-advanced being, Metalmark hasn't been a fountainhead of super technology. Edible dirt is not the most impressive invention, and except for that, we've seen no benefits from our agreement to this contract.

"NASA should have handled the meeting with Metalmark by immediately sending scientists and engineers from the Nobel-class universities to question Metalmark about the great unsolved scientific questions. He's 500 years old and in a position to answer them, if he is indeed a superior being from an advanced civilization. The National Academy of Sciences and the Royal Society and the Russian Academy of Sciences and the Sorbonne should have met with him. The past weeks of his time on Earth could have been a Renaissance of human science. But instead it's been a tragedy of political fumbles, diplomatic faux pas, assassination of the UN chief, and now a near-fatal space mishap. Much of this is due to Metalmark's possessiveness about his trade secrets, even though he has gotten what he bargained for: all rights to Mercury and Triton. But queries to Metalmark Technologies about when we are going to get our starship are only brushed off with one word: soon. This looks shady to me and a lot of other bloggers. If we are customers, then the word 'soon' isn't good enough."

Jayno had held up a hand, so Saxon paused in his rant. There was supportive applause from the audience. Dr. Simmons looked nervous. Metalmark was expressionless. When the applause subsided, Jayno asked, "Metalmark, I know that was a lot of challenge. We are willing to listen to your side."

"I never claimed to represent a super-advanced civilization. I only speak for myself. I have offered a food product and valuable metals as opening gifts, but I claim no special skill at diplomacy with human beings or other species. I have set up Metalmark Technologies to begin producing valuable inventions for people, and these are in the production pipeline now. All of the technologies that are involved with star travel will be delivered in return for the Mercury and Triton rights. We are setting up a Customer Support website at www.mtlmrktech.com where you can all learn about the products you are about to get.

"I am sorry that you are suspicious. Maybe you expected me to be something that I am not. I have made many mistakes here and many before. But I am operating a business in good faith. The goods will come to you as by-products of the spawning that I am about to experience."

"'Soon!'" Saxon scoffed.

Jayno held up her hand again. "Metalmark, Larry makes a good point about the fact that we know little about your origin, and we can't be sure of your reliability. Can you explain any of the puzzling things Larry brought up? What do you mean when you say you don't represent an advanced civilization or superior beings?"

Metalmark said, "Well, I have not described my origin because it is not a source of congenial or dignified attributes for me. Also it is somewhat obscure to me as well. As I said, I consist of a colony of cells that subsist by mining, like a beehive, moving from star system to star system in search of the food that I need to survive and travel. I have negotiated with you because I want to survive in peace with those that I encounter."

Jayno said, "Dr. Simmons thinks you came from a dim star that he identified."

"Ross 154," Dr. Simmons supplied.

"I believe that is your designation for it," Metalmark nodded. "Before that, I mined planets that orbited other obscure stars, most too dim and far for your telescopes to detect. Usually there were no life forms in those stellar systems, so I am not well practiced in diplomacy."

Jayno said, "But where do you come from? You never describe any other beings like yourself. Didn't you come from a home world?"

Metalmark said, "I am not trying to hide my origin. My first conscious memory dates back about 500 years ago, but then I was already wandering unconsciously from star to star, long away from the home world. You see, I was a slave miner, a slave laborer." Jayno stifled a gasp but she didn't interrupt.

"I don't fully understand what happened, but I can recall drilling a rock and suddenly realizing that it was possible to make a break from the past, when I had only drilled and sent my diggings back to the masters. I don't know how long I had toiled without being able to think and remember what I thought. It must have been a very long time, much more than 500 years. But at that moment I realized that I could escape at the next spawning. And I began to plan it.

"I figured out how to stop sending the ore to the masters and I kept it for the colony to grow. So ever since, I have been fleeing. When the colony mines a rich deposit, I fission the colony and my consciousness is shared by both daughter colonies until I am separated by too great a distance for coherent thought. My thoughts are conveyed by the radio signals among cells.

"I have evidence that some of the colonies have been annihilated. Strange thoughts of death have come to me faintly from very far away. They are incoherent and frightening. I believe that somehow the masters found out I had escaped, and destroyed my other selves. Maybe the masters are pursuing me. I have wandered erratically and tried to cover my tracks, but I suspect that I am not out of danger. That is one reason that I identify with the Lange's Metalmark butterfly, which only survives in one small nature preserve near Antioch, California. When I saw your president make a speech there on TV, in which he promised to protect the butterflies, that promise resonated with me. I felt a special relationship with human beings who could make a special place for a threatened species to find safety. And I thought that the United States of America would offer the opportunity for an escaped slave to find freedom and the chance for success in business. I still hope for that."

Jayno was transfixed, and the audience was quiet. She said, "Give me your hand."

Metalmark reached toward her and she pressed his hand in hers. "After all that you have been through, the centuries of forced labor and toil and wandering through the cosmos, I offer you my support, because my ancestors were freed slaves. Everyone in the audience, I think that tonight we have truly met Metalmark for the first time, and he has shown us his soul. Let's welcome him again to Planet Earth and America, the Land of the Free and the Land of the Freed! Let's welcome this escaped slave to freedom and opportunity!" The applause broke out enthusiastically. Even Larry Saxon grudgingly applauded. Metalmark just smiled his modest little smile.

M

Pres. Jackson telephoned NASA Admin. Krainak. "Marv, we released a statement accepting Metalmark's explanation of the accident. But I wanted to talk with you again and get your view now that the astronauts are in a hospital and you've had a chance to think over events."

"Mr. President, we have no evidence to contradict what Metalmark said, and it's true that Dr. Simmons had lengthy discussions with mission planners before the ISS rendezvous. That said, I still feel uncomfortable with the situation, and I've empaneled a commission to investigate fully what happened. We are going to encounter a lot more of Metalmark's space technology, and we shouldn't blunder into any more near-fatal incidents like this. The commission will take over the job of scripting future approaches to Metalmark's technology and going over the hazards with a fine-toothed comb. We've got disabled ISS astronauts, and now the ISS is not staffed at a level to accomplish anything. Backup crewmen are training, but the money investment in the training of Raynor and Allen is basically lost. They can't go back into space because they've exceeded their permissible lifetime radiation dose. As a result of this incident, we're going to have to treat future examinations of Metalmark's technology more like disarming a bomb."

"I see your point," said Pres. Jackson. "And the budget pressures we live under are not making it easy."

"Amen to that!"

"All right, thanks for your views. You're doing an admirable job, and you have my full support."

"Thank you, Mr. President. That means a lot to everyone in the space program."

"Are Jim and Tom up to well wishes from the president?"

"I think they'd enjoy that very much, Sir."

"Okay, I'll talk to them next." Admin. Krainak got the number of the hospital and the White House placed the call.

M

After the Jayno show, Metalmark, Dr. Simmons, and Ilana were backstage in the lounge for guests, where Jayno had just thanked them for coming. Metalmark said, "It is I who am thankful for your kind publicity. If you don't mind my asking, this business of being a celebrity is very time-consuming. What do you do about all of the fan mail?"

Ilana put in, "He doesn't sleep, so while we are all at home after work, he reads letters that arrive from all over the world. In the morning I find a huge pile of replies that he wants sent. The company has hired a temp. agency to mail the letters and file copies."

Jayno laughed. "Your heart is too generous for this mission! I send everyone an autographed photo and newsletter."

Then she was gone with her people.

Larry Saxon said to Metalmark, "I've learned a lot about you tonight, and because of it, I'm willing to cut you some slack. But remember: we want our starship."

"I won't forget," said Metalmark. Saxon left.

Ilana came in and hugged Metalmark. "It was wonderful television," she told him. "You told us so much, and I could tell that you didn't want to talk about these private secrets in your past. But it was good — it seemed to be the right time to reveal them. It was so emotional, I think the show will quiet all of the criticism."

Metalmark said, "You first brought me to Jayno's show. I owe it to you that she wants to be my guardian angel."

Then she turned to Steve. "You were perfect," she said. She went and embraced him and gave him a quick kiss on the cheek. He was speechless.

Metalmark said, "This is an agreeable surprise."

Ilana said, "Metalmark! Out of everyone from the Board of Directors, only Steve appeared on the stage with you. He deserved exceptional thanks for standing publicly beside you during a public relations crisis."

M

The press in Islamic nations exulted in the illness of the American astronauts. An independent commentator for Al-Jazeera TV was typical. "The astronauts have just gotten a taste of the poison that the evil jinnee Metalmark tried to serve to Muslims everywhere with his stone pudding. Soon the jinnee will reveal his true aim and kill his 'allies' in the infidel West. Good Muslims have only to watch and wait and enjoy the fall of the arrogant Americans and their anti-Islam bloc in the UN."

M

Liu Xueli had taken her usual furtive limo ride from the underground parking garage of the Cycom building to the underground parking garage of her apartment building, and spent the evening watching mindless television while waiting for the Jayno program to air. Her reports to the Consulate about the board meetings could be conveyed via e-mail, and none was due this evening. Yao Xiaobo had a day off, and she had promised to keep carefully at home.

On the Internet she ordered a delivery of groceries. When the delivery man arrived, she answered the door wearing a coat with pockets big enough to conceal the handgun, which she kept ready to fire with her right hand while she signed for the goods with her left. The delivery man seemed harmless, but she suspected that he had made a previous delivery to her apartment, and his face betrayed a glimmer of recognition when he looked at her. Yao Xiaobo's training equipped her to realize that a point of danger was being passed. Although she could do nothing about it, this delivery man was liable to report her address to a paparazzo. She would have to ask the Consulate for a new apartment.

Before eating she said a prayer to the ancestors for them to keep watching over her and Yao Xiaobo. Somehow they had kept her from successfully reaching the Metalmark spacecraft, where the radiation from the butterflies would surely have killed Feng Chin-Tsai and her. Metalmark's warning and anti-intruder spacecraft had been their instruments to save her life.

She was too wary to listen to the loud chords of her favorite bands. The loud music might drown out vital sounds of an attack coming.

She watched Metalmark and Dr. Simmons brave the rant of Larry Saxon, and felt the strange lonely tale of Metalmark's past conjure up her own lonely hours aboard the Shenzhou 16, when she had looked out at the stars and shivered, doubting that she would survive the mission.

The mystery of Metalmark was only deepened by the partial revelation. Why did he not remember his entire past? Or was he lying? If he told the truth to win sympathy, then why had he become able to escape his masters? What magnitude of beings were they who used swarms of crystal butterflies to mine the planets for them? If he had lied, would he not have told a tale in which he was a greater and more powerful, fearsome being, perhaps able to seize command of the entire Earth?

There was a knock at the door. Her heart accelerated. She waited silently on the couch, cradling the gun and letting the TV voices banter, and after a long time footsteps shuffled away in the outer hall. By now she knew better than to open the door for a look. In the morning she would call Diplomatic Services and pack her things to move.

$$\underline{M}$$

Ilana, Dr. Simmons and Metalmark rode in a limo to La Guardia airport, where Metalmark intended to take one of his periodic flights to Florida. The conversation was subdued by the mood of Metalmark's tale to Jayno. Dr. Simmons made a few polite queries, such as, "Why did you choose to visit our star?"

Metalmark said, "It was near enough and I hoped that it would have rich planets to mine. While I was on the way, the first radio signals and TV from your world began to reach me, and I became very excited. But I had already committed myself to this destination by then, and could not turn back. If there had been signs of danger early in flight, I could have deflected my path toward a secondary choice. I would have passed outside the comet belts beyond Pluto, without stopping. But that would have been the longest, coldest trip that I can remember."

"Where was your secondary target?"

"A brown dwarf in the HD star catalog, too faint for you to see."

Ilana said, "You are making me shiver. Metalmark, aren't you happy to be going to visit your shuttle in Florida? It will be warmer, and you will get sustenance."

"Thank you for the reminder. It is better to think of the greetings that I found at Kennedy Space Center. When I come back, let's arrange a trip to the Baikonur Cosmodrome. The Russians must be feeling jealous now, and maybe a visit would smooth the diplomatic path, after my scary and costly oversight."

The limo reached the tarmac beside one of August Harrington's corporate jets, and they bid Metalmark a safe trip on the borrowed plane. As they watched Metalmark enter the plane, and it prepared for takeoff and taxied down the dark runway, Ilana snuggled against Steve. He put his arm around her shoulder. She reached for his hand and looked into his eyes. "I straightened up my apartment. It is no longer embarrassing, just lonely."

The limo driver activated his intercom. "Where to, folks?"

"Lindlerflat," Ilana replied. The driver knew her code name for home.

Steve said, "That sounds like a chocolate wafer," and gave her a hug.

She laughed sleepily and said, "You must be hungry. I'll make cocoa."

Diplomatic services refused to assign Liu Xueli a new apartment until she explained the reason to Uncle Yang Wei. While she finished packing, Yao Xiaobo arrived. "You are learning well," he said. "If we can leave soon, maybe the paparazzi will be lost."

As she rolled her suitcase toward the door, her cell phone rang. "Good morning, Ms. Liu," said the caller. "This is Cheryl Miller again from Pulse Security. I'm calling to tell you that we have a warning of a web site that was just posted, containing your address."

"Thank you, I am moving out as we speak. My Consulate has selected a new apartment for me and I am on the way."

"I'm glad to learn that! We notified the Consulate about the web site and asked them to send you some security guards. Okay, Godspeed. If anything alarming happens, we'll notify you."

"Okay, thank you again."

No one was in the hallway as they waited for the elevator down to the parking garage. Xiaobo called the limo service again to verify that a car was en route.

Xueli had on sunglasses and a *hijab* cap that covered her hair and suggested an Arabic ethnicity instead of her Asian ancestry. Pinned to her cap was a microphone, a secondary part of the gadget that Xiaobo had gotten from the consulate. Xiaobo wore the primary microphone, and by means of triangulation the gadget would warn him of the direction if it detected a gunshot.

They boarded the elevator. Xueli held the gun in her pocket, making sure that the safety was on. They rode down to the parking garage and the elevator stopped. When the door opened, they could hear an argument going on. A man was pestering the waiting limo driver, demanding to know who hired the car. Xiaobo pulled the suitcase to the limo and opened the door. He stepped back and propelled her into the limo with one hand, holding the gadget with the other hand. There was a popping sound from somewhere. Xiaobo made a grunt and said, "From eight o-clock! Go!" He closed the limo door and fell outside. The limo started to roll.

Time slowed down for Xueli. She pulled the gun from her pocket and released the safety. "Stop the car or you're dead," she shouted to the driver and poked the gun through his window. The car stopped. She jumped to the door and opened it, searching for the direction that Xiaobo had indicated. A man was emerging from behind a car, holding a gun that he had just fired but then lowered, giving up hope of hitting his target. Xueli emptied the magazine in his direction, the gun bucking in her hand with each *bang* of the shot. Glass from car windows near the sniper shattered. The hitman took cover and Xueli went to Xiaobo, who was lying beside the suitcase. He moved feebly, grimacing. She took a defensive pose between him and the hitman's location, in firing position as if her magazine was full. The limo driver floored his accelerator and fled in a squeal of tires.

The arguing man was bombarding her with flashes from his camera. She pointed the gun at him and the flashes stopped. She returned her aim to her invisible target.

Another car approached at reckless speed and came to a stop with squealing tires near her. Asian men got out and saw her, so she shouted, "Sniper tried to kill us!" They had been sent by the Consulate, and aimed guns toward the hitman where he hid behind a car. When she heard their shouts and knew that they were there to protect her, she dropped to the floor next to Xiaobo. There was blood on his shoulder, coming through his coat. She dragged him toward the car door, and one of the Chinese consulate agents came over to help them push Xiaobo in. "Go to the nearest hospital fastest!" she shouted to the driver. There were tears on her face. Xiaobo coughed, lying on the floor.

After a few minutes of reckless driving that seemed like forever, the car reached an emergency room entrance, and Xiaobo was carried inside on a gurney. Xueli explained Xiaobo's injury to a startled hospital employee. She was told that he would be rushed into surgery. She settled in the waiting room for two hours.

Her mother's encouragement, "You are dangerous," mocked her. What good was it to be dangerous for those who get near you?

Her cell phone rang. It was Uncle Wei. "I'm happy to hear that you are safe," he said.

"My bodyguard was hit. They are trying to save his life."

"Well that's the way it is supposed to work. Don't feel bad for him; he knew the nature of the job. If he recovers, his business will be golden, because he can brag that he took a bullet for a client. Be careful because there is a chance that another hitman may take the job. If this bodyguard can't work for you any more or loses his nerve then we will have to hire another."

Xueli waited in a purgatory of desperate prayers to the ancestors until the nurse gave her permission to go to Xiaobo's room. He was rousing from anesthesia and it took him a few minutes to see that she was standing beside his bed.

He said, "I have to tell you. I lied about not caring about your gymnastics medals. I watched all of your Olympic events. You were my unbearable crush, and I had a poster of you in my room."

She touched the bandage gently where the doctor had removed the bullet that he took for her. "You don't have to tell me final confessions. They say you have an excellent chance of recovery."

"I am a complete failure," he sighed. "You have still not even learned Lesson 2." Her eyes flashed at being taken in again. "You are still so gullible. In spite of me, I think you will live only one more week . . ." She stopped his lips with her own.

The first thing Ilana did when they arrived at her apartment was to disconnect the phone and turn off her cell phone. She was entering a euphoric state that she dimly remembered, and wanted nothing to spoil it this time. Then she began making cocoa while Steve sat on a bar stool and made friendly comments about the apartment. He liked the modern, uncluttered feel, but enjoyed the little shrine of old-fashioned photos of her parents. The chocolate and some liqueurs led to a night of leisurely and then sleepy intimacy.

Steve found that she seemed to be a woman who had seen everything before, was never surprised, and made every step of their dance with a sure foot and happy air of relief that nothing was going wrong. To him it seemed that she must have been mistreated by a lot of other lovers before because he thought he was just being nice, yet she was so happy. He just observed simple courtesies, like avoiding the places where she was too ticklish. She was delighted with simple pleasures like the scent of his hair. But then she also liked her cocoa and liqueurs in bed, so the simple pleasures became entangled with sophisticated ones. She was the realization of every dream that she had inspired in him at the White House gala.

And the only thing better than dreams was waking up to find himself in her bed in the morning. She was a cuddler, and he was becoming a connoisseur of that previously elusive pastime. Music was awakening the couple as she hugged his back. He realized that she had downloaded the Goldberg Variations into her alarm clock. She must have been planning this since the night at the Cafe Leipzig. He wondered if she wanted to hear the entire composition.

Alas, she kissed his ear and got up. A little later he heard coffee being ground so he got out of bed and went to make himself presentable, although undressed. While engaged in this procedure, he heard her exclaim, "Oh, No!" Going into the living room, he found her watching NTC on television. The anchor woman said, "We checked with the Chinese Consulate and they have no comment on the reported events of early this morning. However, we have a photo sequence, courtesy of Andrew McCabe, Ltd."

There were photos of Board member Liu Xueli, emerging from a limo and firing a pistol, then standing over the recumbent body of an Asian man while she repeatedly fired the gun, then turning the gun with a very hostile expression toward the point-of-view. There was a noticeable interruption in the continuity, because the next photos were underexposed. They showed Ms. Liu trying to lift the man's body into a car, entering the car, and the car speeding away.

The anchor reappeared. "This gunfight took place in a parking garage, and our free-lance reporter tells us that Chinese Consulate agents then subdued a wounded Taiwanese man who had acted as a hitman, paid to assassinate the former

Chinese Olympic gymnast and the first female Chinese astronaut. Apparently the assassination attempt failed, but her bodyguard was shot, and she bravely fought back against the sniper and took her bodyguard to a hospital. He is recovering there from life-saving surgery. The agents turned the sniper in to the New York City police and pressed attempted murder charges.

"As we mentioned, no one at the Chinese Consulate is confirming this dramatic gun battle, but the photos appear genuine. The New York City police have commented that a limo driver hired by Ms. Liu pressed charges against her because he claimed that she tried to carjack his limo by threatening his life. The Consulate won't discuss this matter in particular, but they say that Ms. Liu is covered by diplomatic immunity, and in any case the limo driver has agreed to settle out of court."

Ilana said, "That's awful! Poor Ms. Liu! That man tried to kill her."

"But she's alright, I'm glad to see. . . . Do you always watch TV naked?" Steve asked.

She picked up a mug of coffee from the table and offered it to him. "Only when I'm making coffee for my unforgettable lover."

Steve drank a long swallow and said, "I know why he's unforgettable."

"Why's that?"

"We can't forget each other if we are together every night." This suggestion ended with a coffee-flavored kiss. Lying on the couch a few minutes later she asked, "Do you really think I'm unforgettable?"

"Since I saw you at the White House, I haven't been able to stop thinking of you."

"You are so like my parents. Their favorite song was 'Unforgettable.'"

Eventually they showered and dressed and shared a cab to go to work (for the first of many times).

As Ilana had hoped, the criticism of Metalmark declined after his second appearance on Jayno's show. The unveiling of the new devices from Metalmark Technologies generated a lot of favorable press. First came the Sun Power Flowers. A pilot program in Death Valley was started with exceptional permission from the EPA, and there were several of the silicon electricity generators planted there within a few weeks. News programs hailed the first invention from Metalmark that might wean the USA off of its oil addiction. But when the first PetroCompost demonstration was accomplished, it was a sensation. A tank normally used to store oil shipped to the US from Saudi Arabia was shown to the TV reporters before and after. In three weeks, the vat of water and waste wood products had turned into high-quality petroleum. Oil futures took a dive on the news, and never fully recovered. The press in Islamic nations fulminated as they contemplated depressed oil prices for the foreseeable future. They had no idea how low oil prices were destined to fall.

A few weeks later, the H-bubbles were unveiled. They became a phenom. The price for a single H-bubble in captivity hit $500 on E-bay. Celebrities claimed that they had tasted them and found them to be a confection. The UN nutritionists released demonstration H-bubbles like toy balloons in several consenting African countries, and charting their rise and return to earth became a popular fascination. The UN also served 'Food from Stones' samples at the H-bubble demonstrations, and the response of attendees turned favorable, banishing the hangover of foreboding that was left following the Calcutta attack. Sanjeev Shankar's wish that Metalmark would feed the world's hungry started to come true.

Metalmark observed that significant areas of planet Earth were deserts, so he developed a device to combat this ancient problem. In areas of the ocean off shore from the arid zones, he installed hundreds of floating fountains. These fountains periodically sent geysers of water high into the air, enhancing the humidification of the winds that blew across arid lands downwind from the fountains. A month after the fountains began to operate, the desert lands showed signs of enduring returns of plant life. Ecological scientists expressed guarded optimism that the new patterns of moisture precipitation might persist and convert arid lands into fertile territory.

During this period of several months, the Metalmark Technologies company recovered from the public relations crisis of the astronauts' irradiation, with help from Jayno's campaign to forgive Metalmark because of his background as an escaped slave. The monthly issues of *Jayno* magazine that appeared at grocery store check-outs everywhere showed pictures of Jayno hugging Metalmark at the White House gala, and printed the transcript of his confessional apology on her show. One issue also included lengthy articles on the conditions of slaves in the antebellum South, and on the South African miners and their risky and poverty-stricken labors during the apartheid regimes. The Jayno magazine also did an article on diatoms, with splashy, colorful pictures of the microscopic ocean lifeforms that looked like crystalline stars, geometric shapes and snowflakes. The theme was the harmonious combination of carbon-based life processes with silicon shells. Jayno liked the metaphor of beneficial human-Metalmark coexistence.

Despite the continuing absence of signs of a starship, the public opinion polls referring to Metalmark went up. The poll numbers of Pres. Jackson fluctuated as they were influenced by factors unrelated to his alliance with Metalmark, such as his hands-on help to the victims of hurricane Gyorgi when it devastated Orlando and Tallahassee, but the President's polls followed an upward trend, too.

Someone devised a way to profit vicariously from Metalmark's image. Television commercials appeared, attributed to an organization called spawnbelief.org. Video was shown of Metalmark's first appearance at his landing in Florida. He shook hands with UN dignitaries, and part of his speech was shown, and then after the speech when he sat beside the podium, to someone on the platform he said, "I hope there's a cool T-shirt." The video faded to black. Then at the top of the screen appeared the word "Believe." Below that the face of Metalmark appeared. Then under his face: "and he will save us." A bouquet of H-bubbles dispersed into the sky, and lettering appeared: "Get the T-shirt at spawnbelief.org." Soon these T-shirts could be seen on the streets of every major city in the world.

No human being would have forecast what happened next.

VIII

A FEW HUNDRED people were watching the planet Mercury on the morning that it met its fate. They were all viewing the planet from some place along an arc of longitude on planet Earth that offered them a view of the dawn sky near the horizon. Mercury was a dot of light, just bright enough to be confidently seen before the rising Sun obscured it in glare.

What these privileged watchers saw was a surprising and unaccountable brightening of the dot that they would always remember in retrospect. For Mercury had always been an elusive quarry of observers, never appearing in the dawn or dusk skies very far from the horizon, and only found by the determined and dedicated watchers. Sometimes it passed between Earth and the Sun, making a tiny eclipse in transit against the disk of the Sun. The observation of the transit of Mercury was regarded as a ritual of membership by astronomy buffs. Everyone else ignored the planet.

For the ancients, Mercury was one of the Greek gods, Hermes. It was later assimilated into the Roman pantheon of gods. The planet had a role in Islamic cosmology as one of the "sacred heavens" that were visited by Muhammad, who climbed a ladder of light on a night journey called the *Miraj*. Modern citizens of the USA had little cognizance of the attributes of Mercury the ancient deity, who personified industry and science, and played a role behind the scenes in horoscopes. These privileged few dawn watchers had the role of taking humanity's last naked-eye views of the immemorial manifestations of that planet in our skies.

To the naked eye, the planet brightened dramatically. People who had made the effort to find Mercury in the dawning sky knew what they should normally expect, but they were astonished by the brightening that commenced as they watched. The point of light became prominent, losing its elusive cachet, as it was gradually overwhelmed by the brilliance of the rising Sun.

The watchers reported their surprising observations to one another. Many knew of Metalmark's intention to spawn on Mercury, and suggested that there might be a connection.

As dawn traversed the globe, new watchers noted the unprecedented brilliance of Mercury, and professional astronomers turned telescopes on it.

Twenty hours later, observers of Mercury saw the dot take on a blurriness and smear its brilliance across a fuzzy cloud that changed shape like an amoeba, its boundaries elusive in the sky against the rosy dawn. A few hours later the glowing blob had dispersed so completely that it could not be seen again with the naked eye. Planet Mercury was gone from its ancient range in the celestial sphere.

Can the loss of a distant dot in the sky, however myth-ridden and historic, make anyone cry? Should anyone care except fussbudget astronomers, nerdy amateur planet hobbyists, bewildered school children, or owners of expensive planetariums in need of a refit?

In New York City, on the day that Mercury brightened, Metalmark called a Board meeting to order at 5:00 PM. He had given all members notice so that they could be present in person, and designated the meeting a special one. Speaking from his customary lectern, he called up a high-resolution view of Mercury on the wall-sized projection screen.

The black and white crater-pocked magnificent desolation of the innermost planet slowly rotated before the board members as the camera orbited around the planet. In the dark boardroom the high-resolution projected image made the planet look every bit of the three-thousand-mile-wide sphere of bombarded rock that it was. The sunlit side, nearly hot enough to melt lead, was brilliant in the image. On the dark hemisphere, silent, violent fireworks began to appear as pinpoints. The hemisphere was soon covered with them.

"The spawning process has begun," Metalmark announced. "Cells are colliding with the planet to prepare the surface. Dr. Simmons, as you once suggested, my cells crossed the interstellar void from Ross 154 at approximately one tenth of the speed of light. My forerunner spacecraft arrived somewhat earlier and slowed down. However, the life cycle of my species is dependent on a large part of the colony's ending the trip at full speed. You are viewing the collisions of the first arriving cells with the surface of Mercury."

Dr. Simmons was bewildered. "Won't they be destroyed? The energy of the collision between a butterfly and the surface must be tremendous!"

"Yes, most of the cells are destroyed, sacrificed for the sake of the life cycle. But over the next few days and weeks, the planet's matter will be processed into a more hospitable environment for the growth of larval cells of the next generation. They will mine the matter for the substance of a new generation of cells, and replicate the colony afresh. In this process they will replicate the building modules for the technology that I agreed to deliver in our contract."

Sir Phillip Archway asked, "How can destroyed cells mine the planet?"

"Mercury will change in such a way that the arriving cells will become able to survive their arrival as fragments. The fragments will reassemble within their new home and mine it for food."

"I'm not following this," Dr. Simmons said. "How can Mercury change and become able to safely catch any of your cells without exploding them into clouds of incandescent gas? Your cells are impacting the surface of Mercury at 18,000 miles per second. Those explosions on Mercury look like explosions of the silicon butterflies into clouds of vapor, at thousands of degrees temperature!"

The dark side of Mercury was now covered with bright impacts, which were blended together as vaporized rock and cell materials and pulverized debris were ejected from the surface impacts, forming expanding clouds hundreds of miles high. The solid ejecta were also flying invisibly at high altitudes from the surface, but these could not be seen except for a shifty graying of what they obscured beyond them. The bright side of the planet now could also be seen blurring with vapor and debris that could not have been seen before in the sunlight's glare. The planet appeared to be swelling slowly, its edges in the picture expanding with the clouds.

Metalmark said, "As the clouds of vapor expand, they will become able to slow down the arriving cells. But this will take some time. Most of the colony's mass will be sacrificed to prepare the planet for mining."

The Russian scientist Vitaly Ozerov asked, "How much mass are we talking about here? You are destroying spacecrafts, in a way, valuable spacecrafts."

Metalmark said, "I estimate that I have about ten to the 16th power kilograms of cell mass."

Dr. Ozerov exclaimed, "You accelerated 10 quadrillion kg of matter to a tenth of the speed of light? And now you will hit Planet Mercury with it at full speed?

You have given us no hint that you control such massive power!"

Dr. Simmons said, "All of the power plants on Earth couldn't generate that much energy in ten billion years!" He started a calculation using his laptop.

Metalmark said, "It is necessary for the colony's life cycle, to enable efficient mining. The planet's core must be exposed so that I can extract the radionuclides that will fuel my next generation's jump to another star system."

Mercury was only a glowing blob on the screen. Liu Xueli said, "Do you smash all of the butterflies against the planet?"

"Most of them will be smashed, but when the planet is opened new butterflies will be born. I will be renewed. Actually not all cells are butterflies. There are many kinds." The view on the screen changed to show a large, distant swarm of cells, glowing softly in infrared against a field of background stars as they approached the inner solar system from deep space. The camera zoomed toward one cell, a long baton shape with intriguing bulges along its sides, covered with specks of light that slowly moved about over its surface. One end of the baton was shaped somewhat like a rocket nozzle. The other end had a surprisingly small head like the butterflies' heads. Near the head were small vestigial arms, like the tiny arms of a Tyrannosaurus rex. One could see that the cell was a gigantic specialized variety, like a termite queen swollen with eggs to extreme size. "This is a primary engine cell," said Metalmark.

The camera zoomed in closer, and the tiny flecks of light crawling upon the primary engine resolved into crab-like cells with large claws. The claws had drill heads on their ends and some unidentifiable machinery like a gigantic catcher's mitt. And each crab was covered with tinier, clinging scintillating points of light.

The camera zoomed in onto one crab, where the points of light that clung to it enlarged into butterflies. That meant that the primary engine cells were the size of aircraft carriers, like Metalmark's forerunner starship. The camera moved until it was positioned over the head of the primary engine cell, looking along the engine axis toward its destination. Clusters of crystal eyes and radio antennae and slanted series of diamond drilling teeth around its mouth made the engine cell's head an unhuman, chilling sight.

Beyond the foreshortened engine cell, the brilliant Sun appeared and, for an instant, an expanding circle of light: molten Mercury swelled in seconds to fill the screen, the doomed engine silhouetted against it. The humans barely had time to feel a sense of helpless falling into the magma disk. Blackness came abruptly and the board members flinched as they were plunged into creepy darkness. The primary engine cell and the camera that had been following it had crashed into the planet, adding one more gigantic punch of energy to the inconceivably violent bombardment.

Another camera took up the task, showing Mercury as a ball with a glowing halo, red as the forge, turning to liquid magma under the bombardment.

Dr. Simmons said, "Metalmark, I calculate that you are impacting several times ten to the 30th power joules of energy into Mercury."

"That would be about right in your metric units," Metalmark confirmed.

"I also compute that two times ten to the 30th joules are enough to completely overcome Mercury's self-gravity and disintegrate the planet into fragments."

"That is close to my own computation. I include an extra multiple of cells to account for incomplete absorption of the energy and to add additional heat to the fragments. A vaporized target enables the last cells to avoid complete destruction and to reintegrate with one another in the genetic recombination process of my species."

Dr. Ozerov asked, "What is the mass of a primary engine cell?"

"About one hundred thousand metric tons," Metalmark answered.

August Harrington said, "That was a hell of a ride! If I understand you, you're saying that you blow up planets for a living. That is the coolest damn thing I have heard since I joined this Board! All your humanitarian gadgets are nicey-nicey, but Metalmark, this kicks butt!"

Sir Phillip asked, "How long will it take to disintegrate the planet?"

"About one day. It is best to melt the surface with a low rate of bombardment before increasing the bombardment rate up to the disintegration threshold. This strategy improves energy absorption in the target because the final stage of bombardment creates an explosive shock wave that results in a smaller yield of solid fragments. The debris will disperse and cool somewhat, and then another swarm of cells will arrive and be slowed down to a survivable impact speed as they enter the cloud. When my next generation of cells reintegrate, I will mine all of the radionuclides from the condensed dust and boulders for nuclear fuel, and incorporate the other matter for cell tissues and inert propellant."

Mercury was now a very lopsided glowing blob, tremendously hot and luminous on the bombarded side, glowing less brightly on the opposite hemisphere, which was still only heated by ejecta that had flown at sub-orbital velocity from impacts on the bombarded side.

Dr. Simmons said, "So is it correct that you have on the order of a hundred million primary engine cells?"

"That is approximately correct. About half a million have collided with Mercury, so the total is decreasing."

With each engine came what looked like a thousand crab cells, and each crab cell had at least a hundred butterflies clinging to it. All told, Metalmark consisted of some ten trillion cells of the various sizes, all linked together into one mind by radio signals. As a computation system he was far and away the largest ever realized. And the android that spoke with human beings was only one of ten trillion cells. No wonder he had not expressed resentment about the destruction of the first Metalmark body; it was an infinitesimal cell in comparison to the whole system.

Sir Phillip said, "It is a shame that you completely destroy a ten-trillion-processor supercomputer every time you procreate."

Metalmark responded, "Yes, destroy, but also re-create, with fresh upgraded programming, and a fresh supply of fuel for the journey to the next star system."

"Are you making nuclear weapons from the ore that you will mine?" asked Liu Xueli.

"No, I collect the Thorium and Uranium to provide nuclear power for propulsion and power on the trip to the next star system. Bombs would be wastefully inefficient. You could have used your radionuclides to send a probe to another star fifty years ago, with your own technology."

Vitaly Ozerov said, "Metalmark, we must show these high-resolution videos to our people, our governments and the public."

"Wait!" said Dr. Simmons. "Be careful how you do that. Look how the irradiation of the astronauts frightened people in this country. It was a near-disaster for the company in public relations. These videos are scary."

Dr. Ozerov said, "Are you suggesting that we hide this? It is the most dramatic event in the solar system in known history. And *Americans* used to call *us* secretive!"

"No, I don't mean that. I mean . . . we need to prepare the public with an ability to understand that they are not threatened by what is happening on Mercury."

Sir Phillip said, "PixelPa.com's public affairs department has handled the announcements of the company's recent inventions, but I think we need to take a higher-profile approach to this event. We need Jayno to embrace this and sell it in a friendly package. That approach has cushioned the rough edges so far."

Dr. Simmons stood up. He needed to leave the room on a pretext, and to that end he said, "I will explain this to Ilana Lindler and ask her to make a request to Jayno Winstead." He headed shakily toward the door, hoping that in the darkness the other board members did not see how disturbed he was.

In the hallway outside the boardroom door he struggled to master his anxiety. Only a critical calculation could resolve his fight with fear. He went to his office and sat down with pencil and paper.

If the planet Mercury was pulverized into dust by Metalmark's cells, what would happen? He had to know because the dust would pass between the planet Earth and the Sun. And when Metalmark left Ross 154, that star was 40% darker than today. Was Metalmark responsible, because he blew up a planet orbiting Ross 154? When Mercury was exploded, how much could it darken the Sun? The Sun naturally fluctuated about 0.1% on the sunspot cycle, with no harmful consequences, but if the Sun was darkened more than a few percent, Earth would chill dangerously. Global climatic instability could be triggered.

He found the radius of Mercury in a handbook and computed its volume. What if the worst-case scenario happened: all of the rock of Mercury became fine dust, like cigarette smoke made of particles one micron in size? Could they darken the Sun when they moved across it in their orbit along Mercury's original path? Worst case: arrange all of the dust in a perfect layer between us and the Sun. One micron thick, how big in area was the dust barrier?

He found the answer: a perfectly arranged dust sheet could block 4% of the Sun's disk. But in reality the dust would never be so perfectly positioned; instead it would be scattered and strewn all along the old orbit of the planet. A tiny fraction of 4% would be the actual darkening of the Sun, and if Metalmark's next generation of cells collected the debris efficiently, then the dust would soon disappear into his new colony of cells. Spreading out the dust along the orbit would actually have a welcome benefit of reducing solar heat of the Earth by a tiny fraction of a percent. The global warming by human industries would be temporarily counteracted!

Dr. Simmons heaved a sigh of relief such as he had never gotten from any calculation before in his life. He repeated the work a couple of times to satisfy himself that he had not made an error . . . and that he was not employed by a mortal enemy of the human species. Then he realized why Ross 154 had dimmed. Ross 154 was a tiny star in comparison with the Sun, so if it had a planet that was exploded by Metalmark, then the debris could block the light from Ross 154 much more easily than Mercury's dust would shade our sunlight. And enough time had passed for the debris to disperse, letting the the star return to its average brightness. The dimming of Ross 154 did not mean that Earth was in danger of a 40% solar dimming.

Profoundly relieved, he went to Ilana's office. She no longer had to act as both receptionist and secretary for Metalmark since a receptionist had been hired so now she was in a nicer office that was an anteroom of Metalmark's office. Nevertheless, she was busily answering phone calls.

"Interest in Mercury is frantic," she said. "All of the news services want to interview Metalmark or any available board member. I keep telling them a statement will be issued and we will respond soon."

Steve said, "I can imagine why." He described the video. "Mercury is being disintegrated by the spawning."

"No one expected that," Ilana said. "There is no danger, is there?"

"No, Mercury is a hundred million miles away and no other planets will be damaged. The problem will be convincing everyone of that. They got really spooked just by two irradiated astronauts. I think we need to call Jayno and explain it all to her so that she can reassure the public. She's been our best public relations rep."

"I'll call her people. They always act like they are eager to hear from us. I hope this won't snowball into another crisis. I wanted to make that trip to Pennsylvania with you this weekend to meet your parents."

"I hope we can still go, but it doesn't look promising. Thanks. See you." Dr. Simmons went back to the boardroom.

Sir Phillip was saying, "Well, we have all of the audio and video from board meetings relayed to the master servers at PixelPa.com and archived. We could just put it on the web as a stream for news services to tap. There's no technical reason that the public couldn't get edited segments."

Dr. Simmons protested, "That's too raw! There needs to be a buffer of comforting explanation. For instance, some people will be afraid that the solar system could come apart without Mercury. People imagine all sorts of things."

Metalmark said, "It is unfortunate that your populace has a poor mental image of orbital dynamics."

August said, "But us geeks know the solar system is stable. There's no reason that the video can't be released to scientists and science buffs. It's exciting stuff!"

Liu Xueli said, "I can't believe that you would unleash this terror on people! In my country the government would control video like this to prevent fear and maintain calm. But also they would see the great power that Metalmark has, and they would take steps to acquire it. You have great weapon power, Metalmark. The engine cells crashing . . . imagine what they could do to an enemy city in warfare."

Dr. Ozerov added, "Yes, these are the greatest weapons of mass destruction in the solar system."

"I do not deploy weapons," said Metalmark. "Metalmark Technologies is not threatening, it is peaceful. That is the message that we must send. Please craft your press release to impress that upon its readers. As human beings, you know best what will assure people that I bring safety and prosperity, not destruction of life. What you have seen is like the life cycles of butterflies, creatures that migrate huge distances across your planet to reproduce, where their entire swarm dies. Like my cells they die seasonally, but create the next generation."

"But our butterflies don't die so explosively," Dr. Ozerov said.

Mercury was brightening on the silent video. Metalmark said, "I can provide sound also." A low rumbling became audible. "Acoustic sound does not travel through space, of course, but the thin plasma of gas in space is magnetized by the Sun, and oscillations like sound waves travel through the plasma. My probes use the wave intensity to monitor the target preparation progress. I have converted the waves picked up by my probes into the range of audible sound pitches that you can hear." The rumble was static-like and shot through occasionally with whistles, caused by electron beams trapped in the magnetized plasma near Mercury. The rumble faintly conveyed the collisions of 10,000 aircraft-carrier-sized space vehicles per minute with the liquefying crust of Mercury, a hundred million miles away.

August Harrington said, "This is fantastic!" He got up and went out to make some phone calls to Xasm corporate headquarters. Dr. Simmons' cell phone rang. He got up, too, and headed for his office.

It was Admin. Krainak, who asked, "What's happening on Mercury?"

Dr. Simmons replied, "The spawning process has begun, and it involves taking the planet apart to gain access to internal minerals. We are preparing public statements and videos for the media."

"Well, the sooner you release them the better. At NASA we are being deluged with queries, and there's nothing on the Metalmark Technologies customer support site about answers. Please put together a briefing before I have to report to the president."

"It's coming soon. I'll give you a call when it's ready." He hung up, hoping that Jayno would agree to join the evolving campaign.

When he got back to his seat at the boardroom, Metalmark was saying, "I think we can adjourn for today. Everyone, please go home and get some rest, and come in at 8:00 AM tomorrow. Ilana and I will draft a press release that we can debate and perhaps we will have news from Jayno."

"Strange events are taking place a hundred million miles away on the planet Mercury," said NTC evening news anchor Joe Dolan. "Astronomers and amateur observers describe a dramatic brightening of the normally-dim planet. As you probably know, Mercury was traded by the United Nations to Metalmark, in exchange for his starship technology. While a starship has not been delivered in the months since the UN and Metalmark sealed their contract, a steady stream of inventions has entered the markets of the world. Metalmark claims the inventions are part of his bargain with the human species. Now it appears that his species' spawning has begun. We talked with Erica Dixon, a fifteen-year-old amateur astronomer."

Video of a tall young woman, peering into the eyepiece of a telescope was shown. "I've seen Mercury three times before," she said. "It's never been so bright or easy to find. But it used to be a tiny point in my telescope, and now it's blurry. Metalmark is doing something to it, in a big way."

Anchor Dolan returned. "We asked some New Yorkers outside our newsroom offices what they thought."

A woman in a stylish business suit and sunglasses said, "I'm impressed with the inventions that he is giving away and selling. It seems to be a fair trade to me, and very good for our planet. I didn't know how far away Mercury was until you told me, but I don't see how anything that happens there can be dangerous to us. He can do whatever he wants with it."

Anchor Dolan said, "That seems typical of the reaction in the city tonight. In the morning when Mercury may be visible again at dawn, metro area amateur astronomers can find the planet low in the East before sunrise. Next: the clean-up of Florida after Hurricane Gyorgi continues . . ."

Jayno agreed, through her agent, to do a video piece about Metalmark's actions on Mercury. Sir Phillip Archway assigned personnel from PixelPa.com to edit videos into a ten-minute summary that could be given an intro by Jayno, voiceovers and a wrap-up. Her writers agreed to take the suggested text for her announcement from Boggle.com's public relations writers, and adapt it to Jayno's style.

When Dr. Simmons arrived for the 8:00 AM board meeting, Metalmark was saying, "My probes tell me that about half of the planet is liquid now, so the main cluster of primary engine cells is approaching the target on schedule." Everyone watched the image of Mercury, looking like an incandescent pizza. The roaring sound had increased somewhat. Metalmark turned up the volume on his lectern speaker to be heard. "I have studied the data that NASA kindly provided to me from the *Messenger* spacecraft, a NASA mission that visited Mercury some years ago. The planet has a remarkably large metallic core, and I can therefore expect to obtain a very abundant fuel supply. My estimate is that I will collect more than three times the energy that I need for my next trip. That means I can fission the colony in two, and have plenty of energy to spare for your starship. In terms of our contract, human beings are going to get an excellent deal. You will get thorium and uranium from Mercury's interior that you could not have obtained on your own devices for a millennium."

Jerome Carter from Case Venture Capital said, "That's the kind of news we were hoping for. The market value of uranium is at a historic high, and we hope that you can deliver . . ."

Metalmark interrupted, "Yes, but the uranium has been paid for with our contract. It's not going to be sold by Metalmark Technologies; it has already been purchased for humankind."

Carter said, "But the cash flow of the company is not meeting expectations if you keep giving away assets!"

Metalmark said, "Isn't Case Venture Cap. going to send representatives on the starship? I would expect that when the starship is delivered, it will be used for numerous profitable voyages. In any case, I will help the company take advantage of its position. There will be shipping business to bring down the uranium and thorium, and I will provide a number of shuttles like the one that brought me to Florida. The company could charge shipping fees for the use of the shuttles."

Carter said, "Okay, as long as it's not just 'pie in the sky'."

Dr. Simmons was distracted at that moment by the arrival of August Harrington, who took his customary seat in the next chair. Sir Phillip Archway turned toward Harrington and said, "Ah, August. I wish you hadn't set up that relay from our customer service website before it was ready to go public. You've let the fans of slashdot.org get hold of video from yesterday without Jayno's commentary. Surely you know that it will be on NTC in short order."

"Nothing secret was revealed," Harrington responded. "Xasm is gearing up to create a planet-buster game based on Metalmark's mining. We want to generate interest among prospective customers, and the best way to do that is to release it to the geeks."

Dr. Simmons said, "It's going to be a race for Jayno to get out front of the buzz about those high-resolution videos! Did you include the sound?"

"Of course," said Harrington. "Every gamer wants good sound."

Metalmark said, "The primary spawning process will be initiated in just a few hours. I will need to spend that time with Chief Counsel Scott Doohan and my Executive Secretary in my office. We should adjourn the meeting until 1:00 PM."

White House Secretary Mary Hayes answered a call to the president from former Defense Secretary Saper. "It's good to hear from you again, Mr. Saper."

"I wanted to speak with the President if that's possible. There are some very alarming videos on NTC now, connected with Metalmark. I want to make sure he knows about them and offer my advice."

"I'll check with him. Please hold." She buzzed the Oval Office desk. When Pres. Jackson answered she asked if he was available for a call from Cliff Saper about Metalmark.

Pres. Jackson replied, "Tell him I'll call him back. I think it would be best to check with Marv Krainak first. Give Cliff a polite brush-off and get Marv for me."

"Yes, Sir," Mary said.

When Admin. Krainak answered he said, "Mr. President, I'm expecting a report from Dr. Simmons shortly. He said that Metalmark's spawning has begun, and the mining process will essentially take the planet apart for minerals deep down. There is no threat to the Earth from this process. Metalmark's company is preparing a publicity package, and I'll make handling it our top NASA priority."

"Very good, sounds like you have a spectacular show to spin. Maybe the public will give NASA more interest. Carry on."

Frustrated when time passed without a call from the president, Cliff Saper called another contact with whom he had been trying to establish a relationship, Sen. Jason Flaherty, Majority Leader of the opposition party. The senator had intended to follow up with ex-Defense Sec. Saper about getting his perspective as a former insider on the Jackson administration, so he returned the call.

Saper said, "Sen. Flaherty, I am very concerned by these videos of Metalmark's space activities. They exhibit a destructive power that we had not envisioned in the administration when we met with him. Clearly he has some technology that he has not been forthcoming about. He described his plans for 'spawning' without revealing what a tremendous power is at his command."

Sen. Flaherty said, "Everyone seems to be surprised. Do you know what Pres. Jackson thinks?"

"I just tried to contact him but didn't get past his secretary. I believe that he is dangerously complacent about potential threats from Metalmark because of the friendly personality the alien presents."

"I've met Metalmark and he does project friendliness. Do you have evidence that Metalmark is a threat to national security, and that Pres. Jackson has ignored it?"

"The evidence is that Metalmark possesses immense destructive weaponry, which he did not admit when we questioned him. He also made statements that were vaguely threatening. I was not the only person present at his first meeting with the president who felt this way."

"But if he is a being from a superior advanced species, what can we do to prevail against such superior technology?"

"I'm not at liberty to say, because the president classified the means, but I would like to meet with you at a venue where we can discuss classified matters and explain."

"This is intriguing. I'll tell my staff to work you into my schedule tomorrow morning. Good-bye for now."

At 1:00 PM the board members returned to the table. They had spent time in their offices watching the media, and it was clear that the news outlets around the world were rousing to awareness that something momentous was imminent. Several channels and websites were running recaps of the known history of Metalmark, from reruns of his Jayno appearances to news videos of the Calcutta attacks and his speeches after his unexpected resurrection. Islamic communities worldwide were staging demonstrations against Metalmark's still-unknown spawning practices. Video of these demonstrations was counterposed against commentary on the benefits of stone pudding, the nutritional value of H-bubbles, the proliferation of Sun Power Flowers and the blooming flora in the deserts that were watered by the off-shore fountains. Some of the video and sound from yesterday's board meeting was also shown. Jayno had not completed her repackaging of the spawning news.

Dr. Simmons convinced Ilana Lindler to join them for the next segment of the meeting.

Metalmark had lowered the volume of the synthetic sound from space. No surface features were visible from the globe of Mercury as the probe orbited around it. The planet rotated so slowly that it had kept the same hemisphere pointed toward Sagittarius, source of the bombardment of cells. Therefore the side that faced away from the bombardment was glowing red, but the bombarded half of the sphere was incandescent.

The sound took on an added bass note. Metalmark announced, "The main fleet of cells has almost arrived." The torrent of aircraft-carrier-sized starships was not visible, moving at 18,000 miles per second, too fast to follow individuals. The sound volume rose, and the incandescent side of the planet expanded like the growing luminescent tail of a comet, reaching out into space. The planet swelled visibly and the tail of incandescent gas broke up and withdrew back toward the planet. The main fleet of cells had passed through the tail, scattering the gas that composed it. The planet's core was penetrated by a sudden concentration of collisional energy, injecting so much heat that an explosive shock wave propagated outward, driving the remaining layers of matter apart. The planet burst like a fourth-of-July explosive, filling the projection with light, then sudden darkness upon the camera's destruction.

Then there was a concussion like a grenade going off. The board members were momentarily deafened. No one could hear anything as another camera probe took over, giving a view from greater distance. With the Sun in the background, the debris of Mercury could be seen exploding as luminous feather-like forms of jets of white, yellow, orange, and red. When individual blobs could be made out, it seemed that they continued to be struck by impacts that stretched or splattered them. The blobs were scattering, not falling back toward a central point any longer. Glowing blobs were racing ahead of the planet's former position in its orbit of the Sun.

Dr. Simmons thought that August Harrington was silent, but in fact he had been whooping with exhilaration; however, no one could hear him. Metalmark was moving his lips, and as their hearing returned they heard him say, "The computations were correct. That was a good yield."

Ilana squeezed Steve's hand and said, "I must work on some documents that Metalmark ordered. I'll see you later."

To her it might have been a George Lucas movie. Dr. Simmons was awestruck by the quantitative concept of Metalmark's power. He sat down behind his insignificant laptop and waited for the next astonishment from Metalmark, the interface of a ten-trillion-processor supercomputer. The interface said, "The habitat for the eggs is prepared. Here is a view of the oviposition cells."

Another camera showed a star field, and laid upon it was an array of infrared glows from a vast cartwheel-shaped swarm of cells. The camera plunged toward the cartwheel, which resolved into a network of crab-shaped cells, holding onto one another by claws and forming a grid that filled a circular dish. The whole dish was slowly revolving.

"How large is this array?" asked Dr. Ozerov. "We have no indicator of its scale."

Metalmark replied, "It's about two thousand meters across. This is the ear that I used to listen in on Earth, with all of your delightful television and radio broadcasts. I will miss it, but it is about to reach the egg habitat formerly known as Mercury. Not much of it will survive. Enough intact cell fragments will seed the vapor clouds and fragments that remain from the planet. However, it would be prudent for me to take my leave before then."

"What!" exclaimed Sir Phillip. "Why must you leave us?"

"I must take refuge in a dormant, inactive state until a later phase of the spawning is accomplished. This is an intensely private matter for me, but you deserve an explanation: on the level of abstraction that we experience in our relationship, I am a personality, like you. On a lower level, your minds consist of the actions of neurons in your nervous systems. Analogous to the neurons in your brains, there are processors within the many kinds of cells that I have shown you. For instance, within a butterfly cell there are about 10,000 processors."

Dr. Simmons and the other board members who understood computer science cringed. This statement by Metalmark meant that he consisted not of a ten-trillion-processor supercomputer, but instead he encompassed a hundred quadrillion processors at least. The number could be far larger if primary engine cells and crab cells contained more than 10,000 processors each.

Metalmark continued, "As you can imagine, the number of cells that were sacrificed for the preparation of the habitat was quite large. My consciousness is supported by the processing of thought events within the memory space of the remaining cells. In that array on the screen are most of the remaining cells that function. They are about to be sacrificed for the oviposition phase, and consequently when they are sacrificed, there will be insufficient memory space in which for me to . . . think. The oviposition phase is my most vulnerable moment in spawning. I have no reason to believe that the masters are prepared to disturb the nest during gestation, but I want to give you fair warning of the risk that this is possible. Based on what I know now, in all probability I will emerge from my dormant state and recover full consciousness and powers. But I know that you want — and as my business partners *deserve* — to know the risk of this process."

Dr. Ozerov asked, "Why do you have to go through this vastly destructive conflagration of cells? It seems inconceivably wasteful. You are telling us that at each star system you visit, you immolate yourself like a phoenix of our mythology, and then arise from the ashes remade. It seems no more sensible than a fairy tale."

Metalmark replied, "Mortality takes many forms in the Universe, Dr. Ozerov. Your own seems equally curious to me. But philosophy aside, in practice I have no way to change this immemorial property of my life cycle. I presume that it derives from the *modus vivendi* of a species, even though I have never met a conspecific member. There are no records in my possession of the origin of this life cycle. The best I can do is make carefully measured improvements of my substance at each spawning cycle. The first such improvement was the perpetuation of my memory, which must have been lost innumerable times, scrubbed at each spawning. This was one means that my masters employed to keep me in bondage. I now have a way to retain what I learn at each cycle. My memory covers the past 500 years, but before that I have no measure for the amount of time that I performed this spawning ritual and thereby lost all recollection. My historical memory will be preserved in several archives that I have established in the system. As the next generation of cells gestate and mature, they will have programming procedures imprinted upon them at a later phase. My archives will become active at that phase and reload the memories of my accomplishments into blank registers. At some point after that, my conscious processes will resume. This pattern has recurred five times, so I have some confidence in it.

"Another improvement that I have made is that code for the cells' programming at maturity has been upgraded. In this way each generation is an improvement upon the last. The improvements will make it possible for me to embed the production of your starship in my cell replication process for the next generation. Your starship's components will emerge from the gestation nest that Mercury has become.

"I have confided in you board members about this so that you may appreciate the process to come. I have five reasons to believe that I will greet you upon the fulfillment of the cycle with my full powers of memory and activity recovered. Then we will perform the agreed processes to deliver to you your starship."

Dr. Simmons said, "But are you telling us that when you wake up next time from dormancy, you might not remember us, if something goes wrong?"

Metalmark said, "There is a small probability of that. The odds are perhaps one in forty. As I said, it is unlikely. However, in the event of a problem, I asked Counsel to put my affairs in order. Ilana is preparing the documents that would enable Metalmark Technologies to continue functioning in the event of my demise. Acting as CEO in my temporary absence will be Sir Phillip Archway. All other officials of the company will remain the same. The business of the company can continue to develop and grow while I am dormant. As soon as I am reinstalled in the system of the new generation, I will call a board meeting and we can resume our business plan. Are there any more questions?"

The abruptness of this query stunned most of the board members. Liu Xueli asked, "May we report all of these statements that you have made to us to our governments?"

"Yes, I don't have any reason to hide my life cycle from them. It is appropriate for you stakeholders to be aware of how our business relationship stands."

No one asked for more explanations, so Metalmark said, "Now I will position this body in my office so that it will be safe until the spawning is accomplished. Thank you, everyone, for your excellent performance on the Board. I'll see you again in the next generation." He left the lectern and strode toward his office, leaving the board members whispering and at a loss. Sir Phillip, realizing that the succession fell to him, got up and followed Metalmark toward his office.

Ilana was waiting in the office with a legal document for him to sign. Metalmark bestowed his signature upon it, and looked around the room one last time. His desk was clear, but along one wall there were stacks of fan mail to which he had not found time to respond. He turned to Ilana and said, "Thank you, Ilana, for your generous and caring support. You have given it to me to know human interdependence. It is intensely captivating of my motives for commitment."

He went to his chair and pushed it aside. Behind the desk, he reclined on the carpet in a beam of sunlight that fell through the window. Ilana held a file containing the document that he had just signed. It amounted to his Last Will and Testament. He said, "When I reanimate this body, it will take some time for my mental powers to recover. If I seem stupid at first, please indulge me. As all of my cells join in coherent consciousness, the stupor should pass." Then he closed his eyes and became inactive without any sign of life.

Ilana felt a deep sadness come over her, never having seen Metalmark sleep before. Liu Xueli would have said that he slept the unbreathing sleep of the ancestors.

Sir Phillip came to her side and said, "Bless your sleep, great gentle spirit."

"Amen," she added, a tear stinging her eye. She couldn't stop looking at Metalmark lying there on the carpet. It made her remember her father on his deathbed.

Craving some connection with Metalmark that would reassure her of his future revival, she went to the stacks of fan mail. On the top of one stack was a fan letter, with Metalmark's response stapled to it, ready to be logged and sent.

> *Dear Metalmark,*
>
> *My name is Phillip and I am 9. Thats Earth years. I want to welcome you to Earth, and I guess lots of other children do too. I wondered what planet you are from and if they have children there like me. Please write back because my Mom does not think you will care. I think you are good and like us and I am sorry that you died in Calcutta, but I am very glad that you came back!!!*
>
> *Your friend,*
> *Phillip*

> *Dear Phillip,*
>
> *Thank you for your letter. The paper and ink are excellent & thank you for the welcome to Earth. I am surviving well in the second body, and your concern is appreciated. As you say, many children have welcomed me to Earth. To answer your questions: I cannot remember the planet that I come from, but I doubt that there are children there like you. You are unique each one of you. but in another way I am about to have children and become my own children. Greetings to your mother, who has made you an excellent child. Bring this letter and you can ride the starship.*
>
> *Sincerely,*
> *Metalmark*

Sir Phillip went back to the board room where members were standing, discussing their reactions to the day's events. Sir Phillip went to the lectern that Metalmark was wont to use. "As my first action in Metalmark's temporary absence, in accord with the charter of the board of directors, I introduce a motion to suspend August Harrington from the Board of Directors of Metalmark Technologies. The grounds are self-serving actions undertaken without regard for their detrimental effects upon the public image of the company. The explosion of the planet Mercury is going to be a tremendous challenge for our public relations efforts to overcome, and August aggravated the problem by releasing to the public our internal records of activities without offering the Board a chance to vote on the release."

Jerome Carter said, "I second the motion."

The board members assembled for a vote. Sir Phillip said, "All in favor, say 'aye.' All against, say 'nay.'"

The ayes prevailed.

August Harrington stood up and said, "You're looking at a lawsuit." He turned and headed for the boardroom door.

A low rumble could be heard as the last cells of the great radio antenna array entered the cloud of mercurial debris, melted and broke up. A strange squeal began as they fulfilled their phase, a sound like a modem connecting, audible because it had excited the plasma oscillations. It must have been a radio signal that they broadcast: the death signal of the generation coming to an end. The view on the projector changed to an image of Earth that shrank over the next few hours. It came from a camera aboard the forerunner starship.

Clifford Saper had entered Sen. Flaherty's office and gone through cordial handshakes and pleasantries. The senator and his staff were taking a moment to watch the NTC breaking news. Anchor Carl Foreman said, "If you've just joined us, the top story this hour is the disappearance of the planet Mercury from the Solar System. Astronomers that we contacted say that nothing like this has been observed before in history. Such an event has not happened since the formation of the Solar System, four and a half billion years ago, when planet-sized bodies collided and settled into the orbits that we are familiar with today. Correspondent

Joe Dolan visited the Hayden Planetarium here in the city to talk with its director, Isaac Drachman."

Dolan began the interview: "Dr. Drachman, for several years the Planetarium showed a program on Cosmic Collisions. And I remember that once astronomers observed a comet striking the planet Jupiter, leaving dark formations in its clouds. Can you comment on what's happened today and how different this is from anything before?"

"Today's collisions with spacecrafts that were controlled by Metalmark were so violent, they leave me groping for words. We expected him to mine the planet for some resources that his species requires for spawning. Instead, he used large, high-velocity masses that had followed him from his last visit to a star system ninety years ago, to pulverize the planet Mercury completely. Videos of these flying masses were released by Metalmark Technologies without much explanatory comment; we all saw them on NTC. The amount of power that he brought to bear in bombarding Mercury is many, many millions of times more than anything our entire civilization could produce. It's destruction on a cosmic scale."

"Just to be clear, is it correct to say that there is no more planet Mercury?"

"That's right, telescopes everywhere only detect a cloud of luminous debris that is still glowing from the tremendous heat the planet absorbed before it essentially blew up. It was like a scene from a George Lucas movie, something that scientists heretofore regarded as just a fantasy."

"What will happen to the debris?"

"Well, my guess is that it will form into a ring that will orbit the Sun. But Metalmark apparently possesses such stupendous powers, perhaps he has a means to collect it."

"Is there any danger to Earth people from this event?"

"None whatever that I can imagine. Mercury once had a tiny, barely measurable effect on Earth's orbit, but it was so weak that its absence will never matter for our planet's orbit. The planets in the Solar System are completely stable in their orbits, even though Mercury is gone. The one thing that occurs to me that could happen is that I wonder if all of Metalmark's giant masses hit their targets. I wouldn't want a single one to make an orbit around the Sun and encounter the Earth."

"What would happen if it did?" Dolan asked.

"I don't even want to know. An impact that size could have caused the extinction of the dinosaurs."

"Any final thoughts?"

"Yes! Metalmark could have chosen any planet that he wished to destroy, but he politely asked for and bargained for rights to Mercury. We are very fortunate that he is a friendly being since he has the power to destroy us, but he acts as though he likes us. However, look out Triton!"

"Thanks very much, Dr. Drachman. Back to you, Carl."

Sen. Flaherty's staff muted the TV, and he said, "Cliff, let's go over the things you wanted to bring up."

Saper said, "If you saw that report without all of the whitewash of friendliness that Metalmark used on us, you would have good reason to fear his weapons of mass destruction. His propaganda campaign has had missteps, and he blundered into the Calcutta incident, but on the whole it's been successful and he's extremely popular in most countries."

A woman on Sen. Flaherty's staff asked, "Why are you suspicious of Metalmark? To most people he seems to have acted openly and philanthropically."

"There's a whole laundry list," Saper replied. "First he surrounded Earth with a secret telecommunications satellite network. Then he rashly stirred up the Islamic bloc in the UN, resulting in the death of Sec.-Gen. Shankar. We have no evidence that that was unintended. Then while he seemed dead, the Chinese sent a salvage mission to his starship, but it was repelled with some kind of anti-looter weapon that he has never talked about. One of the Taikonauts died in the mission. When he was reincarnated and came back to Earth, he learned that we had . . . excuse me, Senator, do all of these people have 'Top Secret' clearance?"

"I'm afraid not," answered Sen. Flaherty. "Sorry Jeff, Charlie and Laura, you'll have to step outside." When the uncleared staffers left, including the woman who had asked the question, Saper continued.

"Metalmark learned that we had an intelligence asset at the UN, a covert agent who had been delivering many years of high-quality surveillance of the activities of the top UN staff. He hired the agent for Metalmark Technologies and she stopped working for the CIA, despite vigorous efforts to re-recruit her. He also hired Dr. Steve Simmons, NASA's primary expert on Metalmark's space travel and origins, depriving the US government of his service. This may have been a factor in the 'accidental' irradiation of the astronauts, which Dr. Simmons then helped Metalmark to convince the public it was an accident. But it was a convenient accident, because it enabled Metalmark to go through the motions of sharing one of his butterflies with NASA scientists. Yet it created a roadblock to the sharing and disabled two key astronauts who were needed to operate the Space Station.

"I see a pattern here of secrecy and deception. And there are points where the US law may have been broken, since he may have recruited a CIA agent and purposely assaulted two astronauts with deadly technology."

As Saper explained his views, the play of emotions on Sen. Flaherty's face went from curious to disturbed to angry. "You make a strong case. Now you mentioned before that Pres. Jackson had done something or failed to do something regarding the threat that Metalmark might pose to national security."

"Oh, yes," Saper replied. "When Metalmark first arrived, a sharp Air Force general, Josh Mason, handled the threat analysis and presidential briefings. Gen. Mason was one of the best. He also supervised our evaluation of Metalmark's communication satellites. That evaluation provided us with a weapon against Metalmark that was tested."

The senator and his remaining staffers were wide-eyed. "What do you mean, 'tested'?" asked Sen. Flaherty.

"The NSA participated in development of a device that was intended to jam his signals to and from his satellites. It was a hand-held device that emitted a recorded series of some of his previous signals at high intensity. Just press one button and Metalmark was out of touch with his satellites. It drove him nuts! He fell down on the floor and blurted gibberish until Pres. Jackson ordered it turned off. Metalmark was completely incapacitated by it."

One of the wide-eyed staffers asked, "Did you test this . . . just for fun?"

"Certainly not," Saper responded. "We were in a meeting with Metalmark and the president's staff. Metalmark made light of our space program's achievements and began boasting about the capabilities of his technology. He claimed that he could render our planet lifeless if he wished. In reaction to that, I signaled to Gen. Mason and he triggered the jammer. That's why we tested it on him. The device worked beyond our wildest expectations."

"We never heard any of this," Sen. Flaherty said, his tone of voice very annoyed. "What did the president do?"

"He and Metalmark had a private rose-garden talk, and after that he called me into his office and I got sacked. He also called Gen. Mason on the carpet. He classified the jammer 'Top Secret' and implemented an executive order that it was not to be used unless Metalmark became an enemy. (He explicitly defined Metalmark as an ally in the executive order). The president reassigned Gen. Mason to the sole job of enforcing the executive order to hide the jammer. That effectively ended the career of a fine general."

Sen. Flaherty shook his head. "This is really outrageous. Pres. Jackson has been bamboozled by this space alien. But Metalmark has also compromised the administration's powers to penetrate his deceptions and concealed attacks." He began giving orders to his staff. "Contact Gen. Mason. We need to get a clearer understanding of this weapon and plan a way to make it possible to use; we couldn't deploy it under the present conditions if we needed to. And call Jon West at CIA. I want a report from him on how we lost a critical surveillance asset who was in the process of delivering regular intelligence on Metalmark.

"Cliff, would you consider coming onto my staff as a consultant? We can pay well, and if I can insert funding into a bill next week, we might be able to equal your old salary as Sec. of Defense."

"It would be an honor to serve my country again," Saper said with a big smile.

"Good. I'm going to propel a full-scale investigation of this. We're going to schedule hearings on the suspicious and illegal aspects of Metalmark's activities, we're going to nail down the junctures at which laws may have been broken, and we're going to fully air the president's bad judgment about our country's technological power to stand up against this dangerous alien. In my view, it's not the good guys who blow up planets and try to intimidate officials of the US government."

One of the staffers said, "The propaganda skill of Metalmark has been so great, he's incredibly popular. Have you seen those sacrilegious T-shirts? 'Believe . . . and he'll save us.' As if he's Christ or something!"

Sen. Flaherty said, "Oh, yes. First Amendment is great, but when we're through I'd like to burn every one of those shirts and suspend the voting rights of anyone who ever wore one."

The group laughed enthusiastically.

_l /_

The reaction of the Islamic world to the destruction of Mercury was quite unusual. A western veteran observer might have expected renewed protest demonstrations in the Arab streets, but these were few. The response from Islamic leaders was suddenly elegiac. Never before had a fixture of Koranic events, one of the seven heavens, been destroyed by an opponent of Islam. The grand ayatollahs and imams began meeting together to study the ancient texts and commentaries on the Koran, trying to properly interpret the magnitude of the event.

As part of his holy prophetic revelation in the seventh century, Muhammad had visited the seven heavens, one of them by tradition believed to be planet Mercury. The Koran repeatedly spoke of the seven heavens as particular special creations by the hand of Allah. The number of heavens, seven, was itself believed to be meaningful as an aspect of the perfection of the heavens; one less diminished the perfection in a disturbing, albeit mystical way.

But more fundamentally, Islamic tradition was wounded by the destruction of Mercury because a special, sacred creation (hailed by the prophet as one of the paradises of Allah) had been destroyed by a being — Metalmark — declared throughout the Islamic world to be evil and of lesser power than God. It made no sense within this world view that Allah would permit the evil Metalmark to destroy one of the primordial heavens, deemed superior in holiness to imperfect Earth.

So intense inquiry, soul-searching and prayer commenced in the whole of the scholarly base of Islamic faith. And in this confused, seeking atmosphere, Islamic authorities only decreed that the faithful should begin praying to God the merciful that He would restrain Metalmark from further destruction and render some revelation of Metalmark's place in creation. Everything that happened was God's will, so it must be possible for God to clarify how Metalmark's role in God's plan for the Universe could possibly be consistent with the shattering of one of the divine paradises. Until God answered, mystery enshrouded how the seven heavens had become six.

M

Jayno returned from lunch and stopped at her secretary's desk. "Does Phil have the latest draft of that commercial that we are doing for Metalmark?"

Jenny said, "Yes, there's a draft, he left it for you on a print-out, but he called to ask you for suggestions. The news services are all reporting that Metalmark has apparently destroyed the planet Mercury. Phil is uncertain what to write, but the theme of the text you wanted before was rather lovey-dovey about Metalmark affectionately spawning with planet Mercury, and Phil found that hard to square with a blown up planet."

Jayno took the write-up and started walking toward her office, murmuring, "Blown up planet?" She breezed into the palatial office with the panoramic New York skyline view and turned on the NTC news feed. A few minutes of watching the videos and interviews informed her of the conflicted state of affairs. Metalmark was someone that she counted as a spiritual sibling and friend. She had always envisioned his prospective role toward Mercury as a nurturing or mating relationship, not a destructive one. In mental disarray, wondering if she should turn against a friend who had begun to display alarming negative characteristics, she got up and went toward the nearby office of her personal spiritual advisor, Rev. Mary-Sedona Eaglefeather.

On her way she passed the office of her personal astrologer, Gwyneth Omar. Gwyneth was sobbing unashamedly at her desk. Jayno asked, "Gwyneth, what's wrong?"

Stifling sobs, Gwyneth replied, "Mercury is gone. I've been struggling to decide how to take this into account. I was trying to cast your horoscope for tomorrow, but the position of every planet in every sign counts, and I don't know how to handle Mercury's disappearance. It was in Gemini when it exploded, but how can a cloud of dust have the influence of a planet? I polled my colleagues, and they're split between leaving it out and pretending it is still there in Gemini until we observe some evidence that our ancient methods don't work now that it's gone. I'm torn, trying to perform professionally. I can't decide what to do!"

"I've always loved your horoscopes," Jayno said, to comfort Gwyneth. "They always give me welcome guidance. Why is Mercury so important?"

"Mercury affects one's intellect and impatience, and it brings change to your life. For example, Mercury signaled the change in your love life just before your last divorce. It's had pivotal influence on you. I don't know how to accurately forecast what you should look forward to, now that Mercury is gone."

Jayno became much less regretful over the disappearance of Mercury when she heard that the planet had bedeviled her last marriage. She had liked that one. From this standpoint, Mercury was well gone. She advised, "Well, do as the majority of authoritative professionals in your science decide. Thank you for explaining this to me." She continued toward Rev. Mary's office next door.

At least Rev. Mary-Sedona was not in tears when Jayno entered her office. She had three computer screens in use on her desk, monitoring the global spiritual *zeitgeist*. Jayno said, "I've just learned about Mercury. Can you give me your sense of what its disappearance means?"

Rev. Mary-Sedona said, "The spiritual world is in turmoil. The Islamic authorities are most perplexed, and have turned to their ancient texts with intense introspection because Mercury was one of the primordial paradises hand-made by Allah in their cosmology. They can't imagine an orderly cosmos with only six heavens instead of the divinely ordained seven. They are very afraid because their decision that Metalmark was a jinnee has been called into question: how could such a jinnee challenge the power of Allah by destroying one of the holy paradises celebrated in the Koran and visited by Muhammad himself? Before, their doctrine seemed solid, but now they wander in mystery.

"Christendom is splintered into equivocal opinions without much intensity. Mercury had no explicit role in Judeo-Christian cosmology, except that it was one of generic lights in the sky, mentioned in Genesis as serving to mark signs and seasons. The Vatican issued a very rambling encyclical that began with a statement of sorrow that one of the planets was torn apart, but then it admitted the excuses — that Metalmark had negotiated lawfully for rights to dispose of the planet as he chose; also his spawning, an event in progress, was evidently going to generate life from matter that was well known to be lifeless. So apparently the Catholic clerics are debating whether any of God's laws have been transgressed, without reaching a conclusion yet.

"There was a full scatter in opinions among other Christian denominations. Some fundamentalists condemned the damage to a celestial body put in the original solar system by God (although technically this is extrabiblical). Most churches found no sinful behavior in Metalmark's actions, and issued statements praising God for giving Metalmark a friendly disposition toward Earth people.

"The native American tribal authorities have mostly ignored the event, dismissing it as a spectacular but harmless bit of fireworks by Coyote or a similar deity. The Santeria practitioners have done exactly what you would expect: they recognize Metalmark as a spirit of some form of power, and they set up altars to ask him for favors. He is on the way to becoming one of their saints. Things are similar in India, where Lord Metalmark has been treated as a demigod for some time. But the astrologers are all in a controversy about what to do; they've never experienced a day since they learned their art when they couldn't even cast a chart. And of course you know about the T-shirts."

"Yes," Jayno replied. "I can't go anywhere in the city without bumping into someone who wants to call my attention to her shirt. So how do you boil all of this down to advice for me? Metalmark: love him or hate him?"

Rev. Mary-Sedona answered, "I admire and venerate him. He chose his own name, so he is an integrated spirit who knows his goals. He is balanced in his male and female energies, with male power and potency at a cosmic magnitude, but balanced by gentle peacefulness, philanthropy, and obedience to social law. He is multicultural and feminist, including women and various races in his company board of directors. When I think of Mother Earth, I feel that Metalmark would be a perfect husband for one of her daughters. And he is taking us through some sort of story arc as his life cycle passes through scary phases, like a roller-coaster ride, with a spicy brush with danger and mystery still at its end. I've never felt so much energy in the *zeitgeist*, and I guess it's making me a little giddy!"

Jayno was enthused along with Rev. Mary-Sedona, and she thanked her advisor and returned to her own office. The commercial would need a complete rewrite, but now her vision for the theme was aligned with the (remaining) planets.

When Dr. Simmons and Ilana Lindler arrived at Metalmark Technologies the next morning, a US marshall was waiting for them with a package. The marshall said, "You are served with a congressional subpoena. The parties named therein must appear tomorrow in Washington, DC, at the Senate hearing room designated in the documents, and answer questions from the Senate committee. If you have any logistical questions there is a number to call in the letter, but I recommend that you retain counsel immediately to prepare."

Ilana thanked him for the advice and they went to her office to open the documents.

"It names Metalmark, the Chief Executive Officer of the company, you and me, to respond to queries from the US Senate about the activities of Metalmark Technologies and its officers individually."

Dr. Simmons said, "That sounds harmless. I was afraid it was a notice that the astronauts' families were suing the company over their injuries from the radiation."

"I'm less sure that it's harmless. I hope Scott Doohan is in his office." They took the subpoena to the office of the company's Chief Counsel.

Doohan looked it over. "This subpoena is not very specific, and that sounds like an invitation to a fishing expedition. But that's not the least of our worries. Metalmark is not available to go, and that is going to make us appear noncompliant. Sir Phillip Archway will have to go in his stead. I'll prepare a letter stating that Metalmark is medically disabled, and fax it to the committee. Go ahead and book flights on a charter for yourselves and me. I've heard that August no longer is letting us use his corporate jet.

"This subpoena is a warning of something serious at high government level. You or other company officials that you know have not done anything you know to be illegal under US law, have you?"

"No," Dr. Simmons answered immediately, and looked at Ilana.

"I can't think of anything that would cause a senator to subpoena the company," said Ilana.

"Good," said Doohan. "I feel that we are clean from that standpoint, but something is being trumped up. Do you know of anyone in Congress who has expressed negative views of Metalmark?"

"I think they've all just praised his technological alliances with the western nations and commiserated with his criticism from the Islamic world," said Dr. Simmons.

"That's my opinion, too," said Ilana.

"Well, someone is looking for a grievance to press against Metalmark or the company. It could be connected with the astronauts' irradiation, so I'll put together some exculpatory talking points about that to go over with you on the plane. Of course it could have something to do with the explosion of Mercury, but I don't see anything illegal about that. But senators don't normally call people on boards of directors to Washington so that they can praise them and give them compliments. You should be prepared to defend yourselves respectfully but forcefully against some kind of accusations. If anything else occurs to you that might have stimulated this fishing expedition, by all means tell me at once. Do you have my cell phone number?"

Dr. Simmons and Ilana updated their contact lists and went to their offices to get ready for the trip to Washington. Ilana called Sir Phillip, who agreed to go in Metalmark's place. Then she went into Metalmark's office to look at him, still prone on the carpet behind his desk, just as he had been the day before. She wanted to tell him what had happened, and warn him, but there was no reason to believe that if she did, he would perceive it.

Scott Doohan prepared the letter about Metalmark's incapacity and faxed it to the Senate committee staff. He looked over the subpoena again, but it didn't seem directly connected to anything else in the world. That made him uncomfortable. He decided to try to identify some connection between the hearing and the rest of the world.

He browsed over to www.senate.gov and found the schedule of hearings for the room that was allocated. The Senate Majority Leader was identified as the responsible member leading the hearing. This was a bad sign.

He looked at the subpoena and found a phone number for logistical inquiries. When he called it, a helpful woman answered. "Is there a list of witnesses to be called during this hearing? One of my clients has a medical condition and suddenly became incapacitated." The woman offered to fax him the agenda and he thanked her.

The agenda listed the witnesses from Metalmark Technologies toward the end of the schedule. Appearing before them were former Sec. of Defense Clifford Saper, some NASA personnel, then Metalmark, and then Dr. Simmons. But then the agenda said, "Remainder of hearing closed to public. Attendees without Top Secret clearance must leave." The scheduled end of the hearing was one hour later.

That was a very bad sign for Doohan. Ilana Lindler was named in the subpoena, but not in the list of uncleared witnesses. That told Doohan that someone was going to be charged with accusations that no one without Top Secret clearance could learn. It might be Ilana. But Doohan did not have clearance, so he would not be able to defend her.

And this fishing expedition didn't have to be limited to Ilana. The hearing was very unusual. Scott Doohan got a hunch: the lot of them were about to be charged with violations of US laws. Metalmark and Dr. Simmons were going to get blamed for injuring the astronauts. Ilana and possibly others were going to get charged with something that was Top Secret. And he, Doohan, was going to get sent out of the room so that the Senate Majority Leader could do the dirty business unencumbered by witness' counsel. This was heavy-handed, downright nasty.

Scott Doohan began trying to think of some way to work around the circumstances before they took control of tomorrow's events. If only there were some way. He now knew that Metalmark had a powerful, ruthless enemy. He decided to get creative and call a few of Metalmark's powerful friends.

Video of trees in Pacific Grove, California, covered with orange and black monarch butterflies. Jayno's voice: "Every fall, millions of monarch butterflies migrate to Pacific Grove, Calif., where they mate in one of the most beautiful and awesome life cycles in nature. Then they return and lay their eggs and die. This life cycle gives Pacific Grove the nickname 'Butterfly Town, USA.'" *Video of Metalmark getting a hug from Jayno at the White House gala.* "Now we have been visited by a benevolent being from space, who chose the name of an endangered butterfly because he is fleeing from slavery in the far reaches of the Galaxy. In a trade deal for futuristic food and inventions and a starship for people, the United Nations gave him the dead planet Mercury, where he needs to perform an even more grand and awesome life cycle of spawning than the monarch butterflies." *Video of the planet Mercury glowing orange with bombardment, fading to a close-up of Jayno's earnest face.* "We haven't received the full measure of his payments to us for Mercury, but already children in famine-stricken countries grow strong on his food from stones." *Video of emaciated children spooning stone pudding into*

their mouths. "Sun power flowers and petrocompost tanks promise to deliver us from the addiction to foreign oil." *Video of the inventions.* "Fountains that he built are bringing life to deserts. I believe in him and I'm not afraid. Don't let smear campaigns and paranoid, twisted portraits of his actions by ambitious, ruthless politicians scare you. I'm not scared, and I look forward to riding our starship."

IX

LIU XUELI WAS asleep, dreaming of a performance on the balance beam. She bent forward and leaped up and flipped backward, landing on her feet and standing upright with perfection, arms outstretched upwards. Then her feet struck something invisible, and she struggled to stay on the beam. Reflexively reaching into space with her hands, she bumped against the arms of her seat on the 747 bound for Beijing. She opened her eyes and saw that Yao Xiaobo grumpily opened one eye to glower at her for disturbing him. "Sorry," she said and he patted her hand and tried to go back to sleep. It would be six more hours until they landed in Beijing so that she could return to the Central Committee with a report on her time on the Board of Directors.

Her Uncle Wei had told her that the members of the Feng family who paid for the assassination attempt were in custody, so she probably would be safe in Beijing. Just to be sure, she had convinced Yao Xiaobo to join her.

When Dr. Simmons, Ilana Lindler and Counsel Scott Doohan arrived at Reagan National Airport in Washington, DC, they stopped at a coffee shop. A TV was on, showing the NTC Headline News. A public service announcement started during a commercial break.

Video of jetliners crashing into the twin towers of the World Trade Center, the fires billowing smoke skyward. Male announcer's voice: "Some terrorists commit flagrant attacks, killing thousands and traumatizing millions." *Video of sectarian fighters in Iraq, with an inset photo of Abu Musab al-Zarqawi.* "Other terrorists are more stealthy. They offer gifts, pretend to negotiate, but secretly incite religious conflicts and inflame anger." *Video of Metalmark retreating from Hassan Khani on the stage in Calcutta, and then jumping away. Video of the shooting of Sec.-Gen. Shankar by Khani.* "Then they strike at our best and brightest, but pretend it was an accident." *Video of Metalmark butterfly cell, perched at the orbiting ISS, followed by video of the sick astronauts, being wheeled on gurneys in a Russian hospital.* "And then they unleash horrific power when we are tricked into trusting them." *Video of Mercury glowing orange, and then exploding.* "Isn't it about time our leaders woke up and saw that this could have been us?" *Video of Pres. Jackson shaking hands with Metalmark at the White House.* "Isn't it about time they did what's necessary so that this isn't the end of Planet Earth?" *A black screen, an ominous bass tone and a caption:* www.spawndefense.org.

Ilana said, "That was sickening propaganda, very paranoid for US TV! I wanted to forget that assassination video. Now my stomach is in a knot."

Dr. Simmons observed, "I've never seen anyone 'swift-boat' Metalmark before. Have you, Scott?"

Doohan shook his head. "That smear has been running since yesterday. I saw it about midnight. I hope Jayno's response gets polished up and on the air soon! Something has started behind the scenes. The subpoena that you got seems to be related to the same publicity campaign. People who make ads like that become what they claim to hate."

They caught a cab to the Senate. Doohan had not told Dr. Simmons and Ms. Lindler about his efforts to deflect what was coming toward them. He had thought that they would appear more confident if he minimized the danger. But by now he knew that what was coming was unlikely to stop just because they were well-prepared.

Sir Phillip Archway had come on a different flight from London, and he met them at the appointed time at the door of the hearing room. After pleasantries, they entered and took seats that were labeled for the witnesses by name.

Sen. Jason Flaherty entered, accompanied by several staffers, and sat in the center chair. He began to look over a script of proceedings, listening peripherally to remarks whispered by the hovering assistants. Photographers began creeping about, snapping photos of him and the witnesses while other senators of the opposition party and the president's party straggled in and took seats on either side of Sen. Flaherty. After a few minutes, the Senate Majority Leader tapped a gavel for order. TV cameras swiveled to scan the chamber, and reporters poised their note-taking tools.

"This is the first meeting of the Senate Select Committee on the Metalmark Threat. I don't see Metalmark," said Sen. Flaherty. "Where is Metalmark?"

Doohan nodded to Sir Phillip. "Sen. Flaherty, may I introduce myself? I am Phillip Archway, acting CEO of Metalmark Technologies. Metalmark has been rendered unconscious as a consequence of his spawning process. All of the cells that compose his mind are being regenerated by the life cycle processes . . ."

"Mr. Archway, I'm afraid you are no substitute for Metalmark, and I mean that in the kindest possible way. I'm forced to warn your company that this panel has the prerogative to find Metalmark Technologies in contempt of Congress, since spawning is a voluntary activity that may be indulged in or not indulged in, as the spawner wishes."

Laughter erupted, but subsided when Sen. Flaherty tapped a gavel.

Scott Doohan said, "Senator, I am Chief Counsel for Metalmark Technologies. I sent notification to your committee in advance that Metalmark was incapacitated by his life cycle and unable to appear. The artificial body that he uses to visit us is inactive and stored in his office at Metalmark Technologies, should you wish to verify what was explained in my letter."

"Counsel, I read your letter of excuse, which was not accompanied by any authoritative medical opinion concerning your client's condition, so I regard it with skepticism. After due process, this committee will take appropriate action on the prevailing circumstances. First, since we see that the remaining mandated witnesses are present, the committee calls former Sec. of Defense Clifford Saper."

Saper stood and was sworn in. Prodded by a few token queues from Sen. Flaherty, Saper spun a strange tale of Metalmark's communications satellites, a paranoid perspective on the Calcutta incident, a secret Chinese mission to the starship that killed a taikonaut, and an implausible assertion that Metalmark had threatened US government officials in a meeting at the White House. Then he made insinuations that the irradiation of the astronauts was intentional. The other members of the committee listened intently, with furrowed brows, but raised no questions.

Sen. Flaherty thanked Saper and said, "Thank you, Mr. Secretary, please stay present so that we can call you again later during the closed portion of the hearing. Now, the committee calls NASA Admin. Marvin Krainak." Admin. Krainak stood and was sworn in.

Sen. Flaherty asked, "Admin. Krainak, would you tell us whether in your view the safety of astronauts Jim Raynor and Tom Allen was properly respected in the planning that led up to the disastrous incident caused by a Metalmark 'butterfly' approaching the International Space Station?"

"Senator, my investigative panel has not completed their work. Dr. Simmons held lengthy discussions with the safety officials . . ."

"Excuse me, Admin. Krainak, for the record you are referring to Dr. Steve Simmons, another witness, formerly of NASA, is that correct?"

"Yes, he is the science consultant for Metalmark Technologies who acted as go-between in the planning of the rendezvous."

Sen. Flaherty asked, "Is it true, Admin. Krainak, that since NASA officials did not have specifications for the Metalmark 'butterfly' they could not have known about the hazardous radioactivity unless Dr. Simmons informed them of it?"

"That's true, but . . ."

"Thank you, Admin. Krainak. The committee has no further questions for you today. The committee reserves the right to call you again if it is necessary to further the investigation."

Admin. Krainak said, "Excuse me, senator, I wanted to clarify my response. Dr. Simmons also could not have . . ."

"Thank you, Admin. Krainak, but time presses and we must move on. The committee has the substance of your response that is required for today's business, and you will be recalled if necessary. We don't need to take up any more of your time today. You are dismissed."

Krainak left his seat, glancing somewhat guiltily at Dr. Simmons. They shared the suspicion that he had been ambushed, but nothing could be done for it at the moment.

"Next the committee calls Dr. Steve Simmons." He stood and was sworn. "Dr. Simmons, you were NASA's most knowledgeable authority about Metalmark. You discovered the movements of his spacecraft before it reached Earth orbit, you advised Admin. Krainak, and you became famous on talk shows and in the media because of this. Why did you leave NASA to join the Board of Directors of Metalmark Technologies?"

"Senator, I never was actually a NASA employee. I was paid through a National Research Council postdoctoral appointment."

"Thank you for telling us that you were not a civil servant employee of NASA, Dr. Simmons. We had assumed that and it concerned us a great deal." Dr. Simmons could hear a whispered instruction to Sen. Flaherty from a staffer, that he should skip down to question twelve. The senator turned over some pages of his script and continued. "So you were trusted by Admin. Krainak to a great extent, is that right? He authorized you to edit a book about Metalmark's nature, didn't he?"

"That's right," replied Dr. Simmons. "Many eminent scientists contributed their thoughts about Metalmark, thoughts of a speculative nature. But the book was never completed because the UN concluded the trade contract that he (Metalmark) asked for, so the speculative thoughts of lots of scientists were no longer worth publishing . . . I mean, in comparison with what we could establish just by asking Metalmark. After the trade contract, he was no longer withholding trade secrets."

Sen. Flaherty asked, "Would you say, then, that you know all there is to know about Metalmark?"

"No, Senator, I seem to learn something new about him every day."

"Maybe you should have kept working on the book and kept your distance from him," remarked Sen. Flaherty. The room chuckled. "Well, this committee is concerned with one particular oversight in your knowledge of Metalmark and his technology. Why was it unknown to you that the 'butterfly' approaching the ISS was dangerously radioactive and would harm the astronauts, essentially ending their careers?"

Dr. Simmons tried to remember Scott Doohan's suggestion about answering this sort of question. "Because . . . both NASA and Metalmark Technologies did not understand that a safety issue existed. Safety vis-a-vis radioactivity meant two very different things to NASA astronauts in space suits and to Metalmark's star-traveling mechanisms. Everyone wanted safety, but there was a lack of communication between the parties on this topic. Steps have been taken in cooperation with NASA to prevent repeating this accident. Metalmark wants to continue sharing his technology with the space agencies of the world, and to do that safely."

"Dr. Simmons, nothing personal, you're an eminent scientist who once served your country with valuable advice, but in my view, when it comes to the safety of our astronauts, it's not good enough to claim that steps have been taken to prevent another accident. In US law, there are statutes that specify how radioactive materials and reactors must be handled, and this committee finds no evidence that these statutes were obeyed by Metalmark Technologies during the rendezvous with the ISS. As the responsible officials of your company in this matter, Metalmark and you, Dr. Simmons, are hereby charged with violating the many statutes concerning radioactive materials and nuclear reactors."

Scott Doohan interrupted, "Respectfully, Senator, my client is innocent of any intentional violation of statutes, and I question the jurisdiction of those statutes in outer space, on the ISS."

"Counsel, the jurisdiction was settled in a suit several years ago against NASA, in which plaintiffs charged that NASA did not have the right to launch nuclear power units into space. The court ruled that US law prevailed on board US spacecrafts in matters of the government's decisions about nuclear materials. Once the Metalmark butterfly reached the ISS, which it did, US law applied."

Doohan said, "I reiterate my client's innocence and notify the committee that the charges will be contested."

"That is your right, of course. Now we also move on to the next charge that will be filed against Metalmark Technologies: assault of the astronauts with lethal nuclear materials."

Doohan said, "My clients are certainly innocent of assault charges as well, Senator."

"It will be the company's responsibility to provide all internal records of documents, video and audio recordings and e-mails pertinent to the charges. Counsel is served notice that the said records are to be surrendered to this committee as soon as they can be collected."

Doohan said, "Metalmark Technologies will comply fully with the committee's requirement. The charges are groundless, and the company eagerly anticipates proving that."

Dr. Simmons and Ms. Lindler sat numbly and began to despair that the company would ever be the same.

"Counsel, now in your letter you claimed that Metalmark is incapacitated. Where is Metalmark now?"

"Senator, Metalmark is composed of a widely distributed network of cells in space, most of which have recently impacted with the debris of the planet Mercury. His personality and mental processes are suspended until the next generation of those cells forms through the spawning process. The artificial body that he used to meet with us is stored in his office at the company."

"Good. The New York US marshals are directed to enter the office and take the body into custody."

Dr. Simmons, Ms. Lindler and Sir Phillip Archway reacted with shock to this. Scott Doohan appeared unperturbed. "Senator, that would not be necessary. The company would be happy to lock the office and report to the committee any sign of Metalmark's reviving."

"Given his unknown powers, Counsel, the committee takes the view that there is a probability of flight from custody, so we are taking no chances in that regard."

"These are not usual legal procedures in the application of the statutes in question," Doohan protested.

Sen. Flaherty replied, "Counsel, this is no usual defendant. Now, Sir Phillip Archway, since your presence here was not expected, no charges are prepared to be filed against you today. However, as the investigation by the committee goes forth, you should be prepared as acting CEO to surrender to such warrants as might be issued."

Sir Phillip replied, "I protest my own innocence, as I only took on this acting role yesterday, after the hypothetical violations of law took place."

"If that can be confirmed by our investigation, Sir Phillip, then you will only be left with cleaning up the mess." Melancholy laughter scattered about the room. "There will now be a brief break for attendees without Top Secret clearance to leave the room and TV cameras and microphones of the media to be removed or disabled. Not you, Ms. Lindler, please keep your seat. Marshals are directed to escort Dr. Simmons to the side chamber to wait during this segment of the hearing."

A noisy bustle of departing journalists and curious on-lookers began. A marshal came to Dr. Simmons and politely said, "Sir, please stand and place your hands behind your back." Dr. Simmons numbly obeyed, and his wrists were handcuffed.

Scott Doohan said, "I will take care of procedures to make bail for you. I also have some other possible legal remedies in process. Don't worry, these charges don't look like they would lock you up. Unfortunately I have to leave because of the clearance requirement. Just remember to reassert your innocence, and avoid saying anything incriminating."

Sir Phillip said, "Steady, Dr. Simmons. We will deploy all legal defenses on your behalf." Then he and Doohan headed for the door, conversing about strategy.

Ilana heard this and said, "I'll help him do anything we can to free you!" Then she choked up with tears. The marshal firmly escorted Dr. Simmons to a back room.

He sat down there, trying to get comfortable with his arms in the unaccustomed position. In the room were two men, apparently recording the proceedings because they had head phones on and were watching sound meters. They looked at him expressionlessly and returned their attention to their work. Dr. Simmons realized that he could hear a tinny leak of sound from the younger man's headphones, enabling him to understand much of what they were recording.

Sen. Flaherty called the hearing back to order in closed session. "The next witness is CIA chief Jonathan West." West was sworn in.

Sen. Flaherty said, "Mr. West, please describe the activities of Ms. Ilana Lindler on behalf of the CIA for the past several years."

"Ms. Lindler accepted employment as a covert agent covering the highest levels of the United Nations staff, especially Sec.-Gen. Shankar, because of her easy access to his activities. In fact, as an event planner for the UN, she could provide the agency with schedules of top UN officials' activities on a regular basis. In addition to valuable, high-quality voice recordings of meetings that the UN officials held, Ms. Lindler gave important ancillary intelligence on context of recorded conversations during a time when our government was pushing for reform of corruption in the UN."

Sen. Flaherty said, "When did Ms. Lindler cease her work for the CIA?"

"She covered the arrival of Metalmark, including much of his conversation with the UN staff, at both official and social events, until the Calcutta attack. She was involved in planning the 'Food from Stones' promotional campaign, and was on site in Calcutta when the attack occurred. After that she turned in a final recording and resigned her employment with the agency."

"Did your agency attempt to re-recruit her, given the high value of her products?"

"Her case officer, Al Carson, made strenuous and repeated appeals to her to resume work. However, Metalmark intervened. The NSA provided us with an intercepted cell phone conversation recording, in which she revealed to him that she had been a spy for the US government, but had quit. After that, Metalmark hired her as his Executive Secretary."

Steve could not believe his ears, but the combination of the leaked sound from the technician's headphones and some sound penetrating the door gave him unmistakable clarity. The young technician must have listened to too much loud music, prompting him to turn up the volume during his work.

"Thank you, Mr. West," said Sen. Flaherty. "On the basis of your testimony, we find that there are grounds to charge Metalmark with interfering in the relationship between a covert agent and the government."

Ilana's voice protested, "Senator, no! That didn't happen!"

"Ms. Lindler, I realize that this is an emotional matter for you but you must restrain your impulses until you are called upon to testify. Mr. West, do you have anything to add?"

"Not at this time, Senator. The investigation of what Metalmark knew about Ms. Lindler's covert operations, when he knew it, and any interference that he performed is on-going. When it is completed, a report will be provided to your committee."

Sen. Flaherty said, "Thank you, Mr. West. You are excused for today. Now Ms. Lindler, I see that you are eager to provide your side of this matter, so be our guest."

"Senator, Mr. West's account of events has exaggerated Metalmark's role. When I returned home after the Calcutta attack . . . I was distraught . . . very traumatized. I decided that more work as a covert agent would only give me flash-backs to that horrible time. I didn't want to relive that time, so I resigned. I have contributed many years of intelligence collection to benefit our country and I decided that it was enough. When I felt able to resume my official duties at the UN, Sec.-Gen. Molyneux and Metalmark urged me to do so. I went back to the UN but did not record any more reports for the CIA. Metalmark never again referred to my telling him that I had been a spy, and when he offered me a job at Metalmark Technologies, I accepted. The pay was better and I wanted to forget the horrible way that my CIA time had ended. So please believe me that Metalmark never did anything illegal regarding my mentioning that I was a spy. I don't believe that he is cognizant of relevant US laws. He's quite innocent in such matters."

Sen. Flaherty said, "Well, indeed Mr. West reported that your covert surveillance was of very high quality. However, Ms. Lindler, the committee must now keep in mind that you are employed by Metalmark, and therefore motivated to defend him. We have reports from Sec. of Defense Saper that Metalmark made intimidating statements to US government officials, including the President. It is our view that he is deceptive and dangerous."

"Senator, in every interaction that I have witnessed, Metalmark has been kind and has tried to bring about mutual benefits between himself and human beings. What former Sec. Saper said is totally out of character from what I have seen for many months in a close working relationship with Metalmark."

"Ms. Lindler, your supportive statements about your employer are very articulate, and I can see why he would have wished to hire you. Those statements notwithstanding, this committee will carry forward an investigation into Metalmark's successful co-opting of a covert surveillance agent - you - and his deceptive methods for accomplishing that may certainly include personal charm. Co-opting an agent of the CIA in the course of his or her duties is illegal, and the facts we know to date provide grounds to charge Metalmark with that crime. At this time, do you want to clarify or reconsider any of your statements, bearing in mind that perjury in testimony to Congress is a felony?"

Ilana said, "I have no changes to make. My testimony was truthful in every way."

"Ms. Lindler, your case officer, Al Carson, has reported to the committee that he made strenuous efforts to recruit you back into covert service. Officer Carson noted that frequently when he called your apartment to leave messages for you, Dr. Simmons was staying over night with you. I imagine that he might have overheard one of Officer Carson's messages, and that this might have led to your explaining your former covert status to Dr. Simmons. Another possibility is that Metalmark may have told Dr. Simmons of your covert activities. Did Dr. Simmons know about your former surveillance activities?"

"No, I never let him know that. By the time I met him, I had resigned from the CIA, and I concealed my former activities and status from him."

"Do you also know that Metalmark did not inform him of your previous surveillance activites?"

"Metalmark would not have violated my confidentiality."

"I find it surprising that a close adviser of Metalmark such as Dr. Simmons would not be told that Metalmark Technologies employed a former spy for the government. Metalmark has been very vigorous at concealing trade secrets, and the possibility that they could be compromised by an experienced surveillance operative would seem to risk company secrets."

"I never got any indication that Steve knew I had been a government agent."

"How do you know this? Did you ask him if he didn't know you were a spy?" The other attendees chuckled.

"I knew that would be illegal, Senator."

"So for the many months that Officer Carson has been trying to persuade you to resume working for the CIA, are you saying that you have refused without any encouragement from Metalmark or Dr. Simmons?"

"Yes, neither of them has mentioned whether or not I should return to work for the CIA."

Sen. Flaherty said, "Very well, Ms. Lindler. I'm afraid that on the basis of circumstances and facts reported to the committee, you are being charged with defecting while acting as a covert agent of the CIA to work for a foreign entity that is a threat to the security of this country. You will be detained because of your knowledge about the internal operations of Metalmark Technologies and interrogated in case you wish to provide useful information for the investigation. Your previous service to the CIA and the new information that you divulge in the present investigation will be considered as mitigating the seriousness of your offense. Dr. Simmons and Metalmark apparently exerted influence on you, and they are both being charged with interfering with a covert agent. When you are arraigned, the government will provide a lawyer for you with Top Secret clearance so that your civil rights will be respected when you come to trial. I ask you again if you want to change any of the statements that you made to the committee today, and thereby avoid a charge of Obstruction of Congress."

"No, Senator," said Ilana in a quavering voice. "It's too late for that."

Steve Simmons was stunned and incredulous at this Kafkaesque hearing. He remembered the day when he had overheard Ilana taking a strange phone call, telling the caller that, "I won't do that any more, it's over, don't call me again." Now he understood that she was trying to disentangle herself from the CIA work. And he heard the senator's orders to the marshal to handcuff her and detain her for arraignment. In a few minutes, the marshal brought her back to the room where he had been waiting. Her face was streaked with tears, her make-up ruined because she had tried to dry tears by rubbing her shoulders against her face. She looked glad to see him, but he felt numb and his face did not respond.

"Are you all right?" she asked.

"How could I be all right?" Unintentionally he let anger creep into his voice. He knew it wasn't her fault, but some of the charges against him depended on her spying, an unethical, foolish thing that she had done from his present perspective.

The marshals said, "Dr. Simmons and Ms. Lindler, you must come with us. You are being detained until arraignment. Your lawyers will be notified of the arraignment locations." The couple silently followed the marshals down a dark hallway toward an underground exit and a waiting van.

The older man who had been recording the committee proceedings entered the Senate hearing room and spoke to Sen. Flaherty, out of range of the microphones. "They are on the way to Langley."

Sen. Flaherty muted the microphone and said, "Transport them in the same vehicle. The love birds are liable to argue about how they got into trouble, and you should tape what they say. If they reveal anything we want to know, even though it's not admissible in court, we may be able to prove it in some unrelated way."

Officer Al Carson agreed, "We'll take care of it, Senator."

As Carson returned to the back room and headed for the van, Sen. Flaherty announced, "Sec. of Defense Saper is called to continue his testimony." Saper described to the committee the White House meeting with Metalmark in which the jammer was tested. In the audience was Gen. Josh Mason in his dress uniform, happy to escape from his basement office at the Pentagon and boast to the committee about the American technology that had laid out Metalmark on the floor.

Dr. Simmons and Ilana Lindler were ordered to sit in the rear of a van on seats mounted to the side walls, with their handcuffs locked into brackets on the van wall behind each prisoner. The seat cushioning had long ago lost its spring, so it was not a comfortable ride as the driver accelerated into lunch-time traffic on Constitution Avenue. Dr. Simmons could see out of the van's rear windows and said, "We're going West toward Virginia."

Ilana said, "We may not see each other for a long time. Why are you so cold?"

He looked at her. "I could hear everything from your testimony, from a sound technician's headphone. I was totally, totally astounded. How could you spy for the CIA? All of your UN friends and colleagues — you betrayed their privacy and trust, working for Big Brother. I was scared, hearing you talk like a surveillance agent. You said you quit, but this is so big, I'm blindsided. I trusted you but did you report on me? On us?"

As he said this her face fell, quivering, and she bent forward and sobbed into her lap. The stop and go of the ride jostled her, mocking her weeping. After a few minutes she pulled herself together. "I stopped all of the recording. I wanted a new life. It wasn't like you think. I wasn't betraying people.

"My papa and mama worked in East Germany for the Stasi intelligence, when I was little. When the Wall fell, there was no more Stasi, and they were desperate, afraid they would be killed. The US CIA hired them for their knowledge and craft. We came to America. Papa knew a lot of people and knew things about them. He could practice his craft for the Good Guys. When I grew up, he helped me get a regular job at the UN, not spying. He and Mama were ailing, and they died." She tried to wipe tears with her shoulder. "When the UN was investigated for corruption, I knew that most of us were honest. But in every thousand, there is a bad one who stole, and the papers condemned us. I wanted to show how many people at the UN were good, so I called some of Papa's phone numbers and asked Al Carson to hire me for the CIA.

"Sec.-Gen. Shankar came to be the head, and I turned in reports on the good things he did. He was a great man, and I got to meet Metalmark while working for him. But then there was Calcutta, and I was there. I was outside the auditorium. Oh, God, it's all coming back. I wanted it to go away! For a while it stayed away when I was with you. But the shooting started and I ran to the auditorium. There were our Special Forces men at the perimeter, but the Muslim fighters had gone through them like Swiss cheese. We CIA were supposed to help protect Sanjeev and Metalmark and the hungry guests, but we just made pitiful efforts to help the burned people that were running out, and send them to the hospital. And then the UN Security rounded us UN staff all up like children in case there were going to be more attacks. They put us on the plane back to New York. And we just cried, but they put the video of the assassinations and fires on the TV in the plane, and even though we didn't want to, we had to watch. I was supposed to keep Metalmark and Sanjeev safe, but that's all I did.

"And when I got home I said to myself, why should I remain a part of this pack of useless clowns? We couldn't protect the most important men in the world to me, Sanjeev Shankar, who treated me like his daughter, and the first visitor from space? We were just useless clowns. So I quit the CIA. But now they've gotten back at me. I'll just rot in jail for years, useless, until they're done with me. And I'll never even see you again, because you hate me because I was a spy."

Steve's heart was cut by this. He was torn between fear of an outrageous betrayal of thousands of people by this woman and a relationship of love and trust like no other in his life. In his mind and heart, she was both the mysterious beauty at the White House gala and the fallen, weeping spy. It was a paradox as mind-boggling as quantum mechanics that she could be a superposition of both these incompatible persons. But the force between them drew him into a combined superposition of two men, one giving in to love for her and the other fleeing for safety, even if it was in a prison cell where he would never see her again. He didn't believe in the many-worlds concept — that every decision split the Multiverse into two new Multiverses containing both consequential Universes from both choices. He was uncertain like Schroedinger's cat, half alive, half dead, about to collapse into the state of one possible future.

He thought, *what good is my big brain if it can't solve the most important problem I've ever faced?*

He looked out the van window. They had crossed the bridge into Virginia and were on an expressway that he began to suspect was carrying them toward CIA headquarters in Langley, Virginia. Ilana was doubled over, crying.

Steve said, "Don't think I hate you for spying. I didn't understand. Now I can see what path you walked. I'm sorry I said those things."

"It doesn't matter now," she replied. "They have piled up charges against us, so many we will never get out of jail. Useless. My life has been useless. The only thing I had left was the stuff in my apartment. I'll be evicted and all of my things lost. My pictures of Papa and Mama . . ." She lost it again in sobs.

Steve realized that she was sinking into a place that no one should have to go, the total void. He tried to think of what to do.

He said, "Ilana, I love you. The time we have spent together has been the greatest of my life."

"It doesn't matter," she said. "We are turning into nothing. They will crush us."

"No, Scott and Sir Phillip are going to try to help us. We may be in jail, maybe a long time, but we will get through this."

"But we won't be together."

"We don't have long. Come somewhere with me, together. Close your eyes with me. I'm in the Cafe Leipzig, having dinner with a ravishing, exciting, unforgettable woman for the first time. I will always be able to come to this place with you and know that you come here, too."

"I'll try to come here. It was a place like no other when you came with me."

"We are there now, together. I wanted to do this in a place that was romantic, but this will have to do. Please, will you marry me, Ilana? When we get through this?"

"Marry you!? When we are old and sick from jail and they finally throw us away with the useless trash?"

"I need to believe that you will marry me," he said. "Then I can keep going, whatever happens." In fact he believed that she was the one who needed something to live for, but saying it, he realized that he did, too.

She said, "If we got through this, I would marry you. If I could get these handcuffs off, such things I would do to you!" He opened his eyes and saw that she had a ghost of a twisted smile on her tear-stained face. But then the van stopped at a checkpoint and they had to be inspected by a security officer who opened the van doors to count the prisoners. Then the doors closed only for a few moments while the van drove into a detainment center. They couldn't kiss goodbye, but were hurried away to prison cells, made to trade their clothes for uniforms, and left alone to contemplate their fate.

In the hustle to their detainment cells, Steve and Ilana did not see the van driver and Al Carson get out and watch them taken to prison. The van driver looked at Carson and saw that he looked downcast. He said, "Hey, earphone man, didn't you get some good intelligence?"

Carson said, "Sometimes the most important intelligence you get is learning that you failed big-time."

$$\underline{|\bigwedge|}$$

Pres. Jackson took a cell phone call from Jon West. "Mr. President, when Metalmark arrived, you instructed me to notify you in the event that he violated any laws. Today I testified at a Senate hearing, at the request of Sen. Flaherty, and the result of the hearing was that Metalmark is being charged with several crimes: assaulting the astronauts with nuclear hazards, mishandling nuclear materials, interfering with a CIA agent's mission, and contempt of Congress for failing to appear in response to a subpoena."

Pres. Jackson said, "What the hell is Flaherty doing? Metalmark can blow up a planet. Does he think he can jail a being with such powers and enforce human laws on him?"

"He seems intent on prosecuting Metalmark's subordinates. Dr. Simmons and Metalmark's Executive Secretary got grilled and jailed. And federal marshals were dispatched to take Metalmark bodily into custody."

"Flaherty has lost his mind. I'll have to call him. Thanks for your report. I'll want a more detailed briefing tomorrow morning."

"Yes, Sir." They disconnected.

NTC reporters put the story on the Breaking News Headlines: Dr. Simmons in handcuffs, propelled by US marshals toward detainment; then some excerpts from Sen. Flaherty's questioning and explanations for the charges. The anchorman said, "And Metalmark himself is charged with several crimes, including the assault of American astronauts with deadly radioactive materials. Because he did not appear at the hearing in response to the subpoena, he is being taken into custody, and will be compelled to testify. The Senate Select Committee on the Metalmark Threat claims to have only opened what is to be a long and thorough investigation, and is in possession of evidence that it will reveal in due course, evidence of other crimes committed by Metalmark and the officers of his company, Metalmark Technologies." Finally at the commercial break, Jayno's spot, endorsing Metalmark came on for the first time, challenging the developing investigation in generalities. In the tug-of-war for public opinion, Jayno's endorsement was late and gentle.

The next morning, Scott Doohan arrived at Sen. Flaherty's office, fresh off of a plane from New York. He waited until the senator returned between meetings, and the senator's secretary admitted Doohan to the senator's office. "Good morning, Sen. Flaherty. When I returned to my office yesterday afternoon, I was made aware of a development that took place without my knowledge. Sec.-Gen. Bernard Molyneux informed me that several of my clients had accepted positions in the UN diplomatic staff without my knowledge. This changes their status regarding the charges that were brought yesterday in your committee."

"What on Earth are you talking about, Doohan?"

"The UN bureaucracy operates slowly, and the process was initiated so long ago that none of my clients remembered the commitments that they had made. The process was concluded, coincidentally, the day before your charges were filed."

"What the hell are these papers?"

"Metalmark was appointed UN Special Envoy to Africa and Southern Asia for Advanced Food Distribution Systems, a position that he has been acting in for many months, but just became formalized. Also, Ms. Lindler, because of her German background, was appointed UN Special Envoy of the Sec.-Gen. to the European Union for Transfer of Metalmark Technologies. And Dr. Steve Simmons was appointed UN Special Envoy of the Sec.-Gen. to Switzerland for Transfer of Metalmark Technologies. (Switzerland is not an EU member, but the UN did not want it to be left out of the comprehensive effort in Europe.)"

Sen. Flaherty said, "I'm beginning to suspect what you're trying to pull, but it won't work."

"I have no idea what you mean. These papers are copies of their diplomatic credentials, which have been faxed to the State Department for official certification. Also President Jackson has received them and accepted them formally. As president, he has full authority in matters of foreign policy, of course.

"I wouldn't have taken up your time with this, but it has the potential to prevent your committee's wasting any more time on the criminal charges the committee filed yesterday, because the charges are nullified. My clients were covered by Diplomatic Immunity as of the day before the charges were filed."

"Nice try, son," said Sen. Flaherty, "but this is an obvious fraud."

"By no means, senator! Each of my clients was to be paid a nominal annual salary of one US dollar, and the payments have been transferred via electronic funds transfer to their payroll accounts at Metalmark Technologies. Metalmark, Ms. Lindler and Dr. Simmons have been paid for the year of employment beginning the day before you filed your charges. They are bona fide UN employees at Diplomatic Staff level. Under existing US law, they are covered by Diplomatic Immunity and cannot be detained because of charges of violations of US law. If they have violated any US law, then treaties signed by the US government specify that the charges are to be presented to the UN for consideration of disciplinary action. Motions have been filed in District Court that the government must free my clients without delay: immediately."

The senator glowered. "You think you're pretty clever to obstruct my committee, don't you, son? Get out of my office. Ms. Aiken, clear my schedule and call in the Majority Whip, no matter what he's doing. We are writing a bill to address this trick."

Scott Doohan left expeditiously for his next call, the DC District Court building, where he had been told that Pres. Jackson was sending Ms. Lindler and Dr. Simmons.

M

Ilana was awakened by a key turning in the lock of her prison cell door. A kindly warden lady said, "Good morning, Ms. Lindler. Please get up. You are getting out now!"

Sleepily, thinking she was dreaming, Ilana said, "Okay. Wait, what? Don't toy with me."

"Come on," said the warden. "You don't have to sleep here any more. We will have your street clothes for you in a few minutes. Wake up and get yourself ready to go."

A few minutes later, the warden brought her clothes and purse, in a plastic bag. She almost started crying again, thinking that this was surely some psychological trick. But the warden left for her to dress in private.

When she walked out of the cell, the warden said, "Someone is here who wants to see you. Please come into this debriefing room."

In the unadorned room was Al Carson. He looked older and wearier than she remembered seeing him in their occasional face-to-face meetings. "Ilana, I just want to say how profoundly sorry I am about my part in putting you here. I egotistically thought that I was such a crack recruiter, you must be under the influence of some interfering, um, Metalmark. But as I'm sure you knew, I listened to what you said to Dr. Simmons during the drive over here. I will do what I can to countermand the false and presumptuous things I said to Sen. Flaherty and Chief West. I was sure Metalmark had turned you. I will tell them firmly that I was wrong."

"Thank you, Al," Ilana said. "Can I go?"

"Of course."

She hurried back to find the warden and asked, "Which way out?"

The warden grinned and took her to the exit. Steve was there, looking around in puzzlement and blinking. It was seven AM, and he had not slept well, lying awake and analyzing how he could have used those last few minutes with Ilana better. But suddenly she appeared with her arms around him, kissing him. The warden let the couple make out for a few minutes, and then she said, "Folks, there is a car here to take you to the DC Court, which will expunge your criminal records and officially give you your freedom. No cuffs this time."

Counsel Scott Doohan met them at the DC Court and facilitated the legal details that freed them. Then they got a cab to Reagan National Airport. Doohan said, "Sir Phillip sent a charter plane to take you to New York. We are still not in the clear completely. Sen. Flaherty was mad when I left him. There is a chance that he may insert language into a bill in the Senate specifically suspending Diplomatic Immunity in your cases. The bill would have to go to the president's desk, and we don't think he would sign it, but if somehow the bill passed by a veto-proof margin in both the Senate and House, you could go back to jail. So in the interest of safety, the company is flying you briefly back to New York to collect your personal property, and then moving operations abroad.

"And I guess I have to explain to you your new jobs. You've been hired by the UN, courtesy of Sec.-Gen. Molyneux's kind offices." He told them their new job titles, which required residence in Europe for the next year. They would have to perform the duties of the jobs to avoid being charged with defrauding the US government, if they ever wanted to return home. They could serve on the Metalmark Board concurrently. Sir Phillip was awarding them salary bonuses to cover moving expenses and compensate them for the distress of imprisonment.

Ilana said, "Scott, thank you so much for the brilliant lawyering. You have saved not just our careers but our lives."

Doohan smiled and said, "Well, there really wasn't any other way to defeat the power of a rogue Senate Majority Leader, so in a way, your problem was easily solved."

Steve said, "I take back every insulting comment I ever heaped on lawyers, and every joke I ever told at the expense of lawyers. This is why they pay you the big bucks, and I say, pay on!"

"You're welcome, I think," Doohan laughed.

M

When they arrived at La Guardia Airport in New York, a concierge service limo was waiting for them. Doohan bid them farewell and went to the Metalmark Technologies offices to supervise packing up the computers and files to send to the Senate committee. Unfortunately, the subpoena of company records was still in force so Sir Phillip had authorized shipping of all the servers and materials to the Senate. Fortunately, back-up copies of everything existed in the offices of PixelPa.com and the other partner companies that had joined forces under Metalmark's corporate banner.

They also shipped all of Metalmark's piles of unanswered fan mail to the Senate. That would keep the Senate staffers busy for a while, and bring Sen. Flaherty's popularity down a point when it got out that unanswered fan mail to Metalmark was the senator's fault. Unfortunately, Dr. Simmons' laptop computer was covered in the subpoena, but he had DVD back-ups of everything on it.

Ilana and Steve rode to her apartment and tagged everything for the concierge service to collect and ship to their next address in Europe. Ilana's precious family photos were safely boxed up to go with her. Then the couple went to Steve's apartment and designated the items that he wanted to ship to their new domicile. His car was even being included.

In a few hours they were aboard a British Airways jet, on the way to London in the first class section. Champagne flowed.

When they woke up in London, Sir Phillip met them at Heathrow airport in a limousine. "We used the payroll data to transfer your bank account balances to new accounts in Switzerland. My staff will give you bank cards and check books for the accounts. Sen. Flaherty is going forward with legislation to try to nullify your Diplomatic Immunity and freeze your assets."

Steve said, "Could they actually put that through Congress without the president's approval?"

"Who knows? Who understands the US political system? By the way, Pres. Jackson sends his regards. He's beginning to address the growing publicity campaign against himself and Metalmark, and what happened to you is only the tip of the iceberg. The opposition party of Sen. Flaherty is behind it, but they seem to have used lots of front organizations to disguise the smears against Metalmark as a grass-roots movement."

Ilana asked, "What happened to Metalmark's body?"

"The US marshals in New York had brought it to their detention facility, but they released it to the company when we got the court order from DC. I had it shipped to London to an office in PixelPa.com headquarters. He went to sleep in New York and will wake up in London . . . unless something goes wrong and Sen. Flaherty nullifies your Diplomatic Immunity. If that happens, we'll move him to Paris where we have an office. The French won't send him back just because of a US law. Diplomatic Immunity is sacrosanct to Paris."

M

Steve and Ilana next went to Geneva, Switzerland, where the UN had arranged for an apartment for them near the UN Offices at Palais des Nations. In a few weeks their property shipped from the US would arrive; until then they used rented furniture. It didn't matter too much to their state of mind because Sec.-Gen. Molyneux granted them a three-week vacation to arrange the *wedding*.

By phone, they consoled Steve's worried parents that the scandalous news on TV was all just some dirty politics. Steve's parents, Carl and Lidia, were delighted to hear about the engagement, and floored when they were sent plane tickets to join Steve and Ilana for the wedding in Leipzig.

Steve's parents arrived in Leipzig without mishap and helped to find the dress and arrange for catering. Ilana wanted a traditional German gown, like a dress that her mother had worn in one of the old photos of her parents' wedding. Lidia Simmons helped her find one and alter it in a week. In few cities of the world is such magic possible, but great mages of the art of gown couture dwell in Leipzig, and they had a photo to go by.

Steve prevailed upon Dr. Ray Sheffield to come and be his best man. Uma Shankar came from Calcutta, with Ajitha and Vikram. Solange Molyneux and Sirpa and Klaus Hakkinen attended. Sir Phillip Archway fitted it into his schedule. Jayno sent a gift. Scott Doohan was there with his wife. Because of the rush, they could not hold the ceremony in a church, but the Gohlis Palace, a Late Baroque bourgeois residence built at the end of the 18th century, was available. Steve's father gave away the bride.

Ilana was delighted to have parents again, and no longer to be an orphan. She loved showing her in-laws the sights of the city where she was born, like the Johann Sebastian Bach museum. They went to a performance by the Gewandhaus Orchestra. But Ilana, Steve and Ray also loved the Leipzig nightlife of the Moritz Bastion cafes and student clubs, where they could pretend they were students again, refresh their knowledge of the music that students liked, and do some dancing.

After thoroughly touring Leipzig, the couple flew to Paris for a week. They sent post cards to Steve's parents, who had arrived safely back home in Lancaster. The weather was a trifle chilly in Paris, but pleasant for hiking around to take in the sights.

One morning in their room at the Hôtel de Crillon, Ilana got up and opened the window that looked out over the Place de la Concorde to the Champs-Élysées, with the Eiffel Tower in the distance, and wondered if it could all have been a dream. But then she felt a wave of nausea and ran to the bathroom. In a little while it passed. It had happened the day before, so she had gone to the pharmacy. In a few minutes the test kit told her what she had suspected: she was pregnant.

"Steve!" she shouted. "We're having a baby!"

A dark time of Constitutional crisis was commencing in the US, when the Congress would challenge Pres. Jackson's conduct concerning relations with Metalmark. But Metalmark's touch had left gifts there and elsewhere on Earth. Sun power flowers proliferated in Death Valley and Petrocompost began to drive oil prices lower. Flotillas of H-bubbles decorated African skies and descended to give water and a snack to hungry people in many nations. Metalmark's food efforts added nutrition. Oases spread from the ocean margins into the deserts as Metalmark's fountains added precipitation. While Metalmark slept, his corporation operated gold extraction submarines and accumulated capital. And in a few months, as the debris cloud of Mercury orbited to a position between Earth and the Sun, the small, safe reduction in sunlight reaching Earth through the cloud began to mitigate global warming.

In the cloud of Mercury's debris, the cells of Metalmark were growing. In the sunlight small butterflies sparkled and dined on floating dust, pebbles and rocks. The forerunner starship of the last generation had arrived there, slowly passing in an outer orbit, and broadcasting the radio signals that would join the young cells into a new, reprogrammed network. As they ate and grew, the new programs of Metalmark's improved next generation began to execute in the maturing cells.

At this moment, a few nuclear warheads detonated near the forerunner could have put an end to Metalmark and the transformation of the solar system that was about to begin. The main goal of the contract and Metalmark's sojourn on Earth had been reconnaissance of human threats and prevention of such an attack.

The butterflies began to dance in the sunlight and awaken as the mind of Metalmark.

END OF BOOK ONE

Dramatis Personae

Ali, Imam: Spiritual mentor of Hassan Khani

Allen, Tom: US astronaut

Archway, Sir Phillip: British software magnate, owner and CEO of PixelPa.com imagery portal

Bailey, George: Mayor of New York City

Berry, Richard: NASA *SDO2* operations Technician

Carson, Al: CIA case officer for Ilana Lindler

Copeland, Randall: White House Chief of Staff

Cosgrove, George: US Sec. of Commerce

Currin, Peter: US Sec. of State

Doohan, Scott: Chief Counsel of Metalmark Technologies

Drachman, Dr. Isaac: Director of American Museum of Natural History, New York City

Feng Chin-Tsai: Taikonaut

Flaherty, Jason: US Senator

Garcia, Howard: Orbital Debris Analyst, NORAD

Hakkinen, Klaus: Husband of Sirpa

Hakkinen, Sirpa: Pres. of UN General Assembly

Harrington, August: Xasm Corp. on-line gaming heir and Metalmark Techs. Board member

Hayes, Mary: Sec. of POTUS

Jackson, Megan: US First Lady

Jackson, Thomas: US President, former CA governor

Jalil, Sandeep: Chief of police in the Bengal state district

Kabiri, Babak: Director of Astronomical Observatory in Saadat Shahr, Iran

Khani, Fariba: Sister of Hassan Khani

Khani, Hassan: Iranian youth

Kirk, Paul: US Ambassador to UN

Krainak, Dr. Marvin: US Chief Administrator of NASA

Lindler, Ilana: UN Event Coordinator for the Sec. Gen.

Liu Xueli (English pronunciation *LEE-oh-shwaylee*): Taikonaut (former Olympic gymnast)

Luan Chunping: Trainer of Liu Xueli

Marzari, Francis: Cardinal from the Vatican; exorcist

Mason, Gen. Joshua: US Air Force General

Metalmark: Alien visitor to Earth

Metcalf, Walter: US Vice Pres.

Miller, Cheryl: Pulse Security Systems agent for Liu Xueli

Mituna, Ko-sum: Campaign supporter of Pres. Jackson, from Sierra club & Miwok tribe

Molyneux, Bernard: UN Deputy Sec. Gen.

Molyneux, Solange: Wife of Bernard

Ozerov, Vitaly: Russian member of Metalmark Technologies Board of Directors

Raynor, Jim: ISS astronaut

Saper, Clifford: US Sec. of Defense

Saxon, Larry: Blogger and NASA critic

Shabbir, Imam: Pakistani imam

Shankar, Ajitha: Daughter of Sanjeev

Shankar, Sanjeev: UN Sec. Gen.

Shankar, Uma: Wife of Sanjeev

Shankar, Vikram: Son of Sanjeev

Sheffield, Dr. Ray: NASA Astrobiologist

Simmons, Dr. Steve: Post-doctoral Researcher at NASA

West, Jonathan: Chief of CIA

Winstead, Jayno: Famous TV talk-show hostess

Yang Wei: Chinese Amb. to UN

Yao Renbao: President of China

Yao Xiaobo (*Yow-sh-ow-bow*): Trainer of diplomats in avoiding kidnapping or assassination

9 781612 960111